Ruth

Stephen W Follows

Stephen W Follows

Published July 2010 by Stephen W Follows

Copyright © Stephen W Follows 2010

All rights reserved. No part of this story may be reproduced, stored in or introduced into a retrieval system, or transmitted in any form or by any means (Electronic. Mechanical, photocopying, recording or otherwise), without the prior written permission of the author.

Authors note

Although some actual locations and titles are used, this is a work of fiction.
Any resemblance to actual events, organisations, or persons, living or dead, is entirely coincidental.

ISBN 978-0-9566 109-0-4

Published by Stephen W Follows
Jericho Road
Newark
NG24 3GT

Printed by CPI Antony Rowe
Bumpers Farm, Chippenham

Cover design by Aimee Fry

Stephenwfollows.co.uk

Acknowledgement

My everlasting thanks to Stephanie Hale and Leigh Ferrani; for being my light at the end of a long tunnel.

1

Just after 11 p.m; in a quiet street, on a still night, two kilometres from the centre of Munich, a dirty, grey van stopped at the roadside in a poorly lit area between two Cypress trees. In the back of the specially adapted vehicle, a man sat in his wheelchair, facing the rear, looking around him for signs of movement from pedestrians or vehicles. There was neither. He turned out the interior light and rubbed both hands across his bald head as he took a deep breath. His blue, calculating eyes were almost covered by his white, unkempt eyebrows. He rolled up his right hand sleeve and slowly rubbed his left hand over the thick hairs on his forearm that covered a tattoo of a lion.

The driver of the vehicle went around to the rear doors and opened them. Moving very slowly and quietly, he reached into a shallow container and pulled out a rifle. From another container he took out a small magazine with three 9mm rounds in it and clipped it onto the rifle in one professional movement. He handed the rifle up to the big man in the wheelchair, closed the rear doors, and returned to his driver's seat.

The wheelchair moved slightly as the big man kept a finger on a button until the rear window was lowered by 15 centimetres. He carefully folded a small cloth and placed it on the top of the lowered window. The barrel of the rifle settled easily on the folded cloth as he adjusted the sights. He focused on a doorway, some one hundred metres away, and the old stone steps leading to it.

Marcus Hanson had enjoyed himself. The Bier Platz had once again, provided good food and good entertainment. One of his colleagues in the Canadian Secret Service had joined him to dine at his favourite tavern and they had swapped stories and reminisced about the good, and not so good, assignments they had worked on. They had both been in Munich for a year; the CSS had had an office there for some time and they had worked closely with other governments and police forces in their tenacious work against international crime.

But tonight had been a time for enjoyment; it was Marcus's thirty fifth birthday. Both men had eaten well and drunk heartily. Some local girls had flirted with the handsome Marcus Hanson, but he valued his relationship with his partner, who was working that night on the other side of the city. She too was a CSS employee and they cared for each other unquestionably.

As he walked the short distance home, he wanted to start whistling; but his training and intrinsic discipline got the better of him. He turned the corner and walked towards the large stone steps that led to his apartment.

He paused halfway up the steps to search for his door key.

The first bullet hit him in the ear. It went through his head and splattered out of the other side as the force threw him back onto the concrete balustrade. The second bullet hit him in the chest. He died three seconds later. His blood and the grey matter from his brain started to flow down the stone steps until it came to rest on the pavement. Some of it gathered around the base of one of the cypress trees that lined the street.

Tom Delaney, Managing Director of TOLA - The Overseas Liaison Agency - was walking towards the dead body fifty minutes later. He had seen it all before. The flashing lights, the cordon, the white sheets surrounding the 'death' area and the pathologist stooped over the body.

But this was different. The victim was a CSS agent and Tom Delaney knew him.

The pathologist looked up at Delaney and removed his gloves before he spoke. 'Well, I can promise you this, he never felt a thing.'

'So I see; high velocity?'

'Oh definitely, I'd say nine millimetre, one through the head, the second right in the heart, probably from long range, with a night scope, but wherever it came from, it was fired by a professional; a good professional.'

'Why long range?' Delaney asked.

'Any closer and it would have taken his head off. Do you know him?'

Delaney acknowledged. 'He was CSS, Canadian Secret Service.' He looked around him to see that the area was surrounded by buildings of different heights and parked cars next to old well grown trees. The bullet could have come from anywhere and the perpetrator, and his spent cartridges, would be long gone by now.

He spotted a woman walking towards him. It was Sally Curtis, the dead man's CSS partner and girlfriend. They had worked together long enough to know each other's cases and had been lovers for a year. He didn't stop her. She too, was CSS and had seen it all before. She moved close to what was left of Hanson's body and stood looking for a while, motionless. Then she dropped to her knees burying her head into what was left of his chest. After a couple of minutes, she turned to Delaney; Hanson's blood in her hair. He held her by the arm and walked her away from the area as she held her head in her hands. 'Who told you?' he asked.

'The police phoned me to say you had been informed; they know we work together sometimes.' She took off her spectacles and wiped the tears from her eyes.

'None of his current jobs were category A, Tom,' she said. 'What the hell has gone wrong?'

'I don't know, Sally, I'm sorry,' he replied.

'You and your people were supposed to be looking out for both of us. That was the deal; seven days a week, twenty four hours a day. That was the deal! Oh Jesus!' She held one hand to her head and wiped her eyes with the sleeve of her jacket.

'I know what the deal was, Sally. I'm so sorry. We had you both down as working on a category C case, as you say, not a category A, and we only shadow for 24 hours on category A's; unless we're told otherwise.'

'Well something's not right, for crying out loud! Anyone making a hit like this doesn't do it unless it's serious.'

'I know I know; come on, let's get you away from here; and me. We'll start by going through some of Marcus's more recent jobs.'

Delaney led her to his car and they drove back to his Munich office. Curtis didn't speak at all during the journey. She stared out of the side window with a look of contempt. No one out there understands what goes on, she thought. No one knows the danger and the grief we have to go through.

They arrived at the office at 1am. As they got closer to the light of the building, he could see she had been crying more. He watched her for a while, considering how she would handle this. Her strong will and tenacity were well recorded. His years of experience told him that this one was going to get personal; and onerous.

2

In block G of the second Victorian radial building at HMP Manchester, Alan Farrah was sitting in his cell, reading a book about medieval weaponry. The subject fascinated him. As he read, he remembered being a young child and how his father would hang paintings of famous battles and artillery guns around the walls of their old terraced house in Southampton.

His father had been good to him and his younger brother; most of the time. Like most of the kids on the estate, they got into trouble now and again and their father would reach for the leather belt he kept in a kitchen drawer. One day, when their mother had found out that they had stolen some three penny pieces from her savings jar, the brothers had been locked in the outside shed all night. They were dragged out the following morning and were made to sit in front of their parents while their father told them of the importance of money and how bad it was to steal.

It was on that day, when he was 13 years old, that Alan Farrah promised himself that he would be very rich one day; and nothing would prevent that happening.

He put the book face down on the table as he yawned and rose from his seat and rubbed his backside. 'Bloody chair,' he said to himself, 'I'll break the bastard thing in half when I leave.'

Standing in front of the mirror, he exercised his neck and shoulder muscles. He held out his arms in front of him and twisted them from side to side, pausing for a moment to rub a hand over the lion tattoo on his right forearm. He never combed his short grey hair, preferring to sweep his hands through it after covering his head in cold water. He moved his face closer to the mirror and scratched the three day old stubble on his chin. He was not a handsome man and he knew it; but he was rich and that was all that mattered to him. Looking into his own shallow, grey eyes, he spoke to himself again. 'Not long now mate. Not long now.'

A knock on the door was followed by the voice of Prison Officer Simpson. 'Put your shirt on Farrah, and come with me. The Governor says you can take a phone call in the meeting room. It's your cousin; something about your uncle.'

'What's the matter, Mr. Simpson,' Farrah said with a smirk on his face. 'Are you jealous of my finely tuned body?'

'Working out in a gym everyday might make you stronger, Farrah; but not tougher. Move yourself.'

Farrah reached for an old shirt and walked towards the door. He strolled slowly down the corridor, Simpson following, ten feet behind. The meeting room was small and white, without windows. The telephone handset was hanging down from its wall bracket and Farrah raised it to his ear as Simpson sat down near the door.

'Hello?'

The voice on the other end of the line was low and laboured. 'Hello, Alan it is your cousin, Bill; it's about Uncle Stanley.'

'I heard he was on the critical list; how is he?'

'He passed away, last night, suddenly.'

'Oh, I'm sorry. When is the funeral?'

'Soon, I'll let you know. Other people are taking care of the arrangements; I have to go to Cologne to visit Cousin Heidi.'

'Okay, well take care. And thank you for letting me know.'

Farrah put the handset down and turned to face Simpson. 'Thank you, officer, kindly escort me back to my room now.'

Simpson curled his mouth down and tutted. 'Funny bastard; come on then.'

The two men made their way back to Farrah's cell. Simpson left the door open and reminded Farrah that it was almost time for breakfast. Farrah said he wouldn't be having breakfast, picked up his book and continued his reading. After a few pages, he hesitated, thinking of the telephone conversation he had just had. Where would I be without my cousin Bill, he thought to himself, as he looked up at the calendar on the wall, he is always so efficient.

3

The morning flight from Munich to London had been a quiet one. Sally Curtis didn't say much and spent a lot of the one and a half hours looking out of the window, declining the hospitality food, but not the offer of a drink. Tom Delaney glanced at her and then at his watch as she ordered a glass of wine. She noticed and looked back at him for a while before saying, 'What?'

'Sorry,' he said, 'you go ahead.'

'I will; and let's just remember which one of us is the customer here, okay?'

Delaney nodded politely. She was right, he thought. And perhaps he needed to be reminded of that more often. She and all of the others *were* good customers and good payers too. He thought of the amount on the last cheque he had received and how far away it was from the police training college wage slip.

When he had time to think of his life – which was not often – he usually considered himself to be relatively lucky. He had not been good at school and the headmaster of the comprehensive secondary had often reminded him of how good his elder brother was at everything whilst bringing his cane down onto the palms of Delaney's hands. 'Now, go and get on with things young man, and try to emulate your brother.'

He didn't. After being sacked from a motor vehicle apprenticeship, he joined the army and began to enjoy life, at last. His regiment was based at an old Luftwaffe camp near Paderborn in Germany and the training and exercises took them to places all over the world. Guarding the East West German border in the seventies was always a talking point at dinner engagements; friends joking that he still had the *Ipcress Files* under his bed or; had he ever been to a *Funeral in Berlin*. Two tours of Northern Ireland in 1972 and 1975 also helped his edification and he had developed a good sense of propriety by the time he left the army to join the police.

His calm phlegmatic manner gave him an edge over other recruits during the training programme; keeping a mild, level-headed disposition enabled him to think properly while others around him panicked. He was soon spotted as someone who could diffuse hostile, or potentially hostile, situations and make good decisions. One of his senior commanders was later to nick name him, his 'problem solver.'

He was soon elevated to a senior rank, dealing with organised crime, and working closely with overseas agencies in Britain and abroad. But the Home and Foreign Offices had a problem. There was only so much they could do 'by the book'. Delaney offered to set up some kind of overseas unit, but was reminded by a superior that his methods were 'very successful but not strictly legal and it *really was* stretching the rules'. So it was, that TOLA – The Overseas Liaison Agency – was created. A private company; registered as an 'international provider of diplomatic and mediating services'. It would be run as a business by Managing Director Tom Delaney and a staff of five. They would receive instruction from various government departments and carry out their duties, for which they would be paid.

The risks for TOLA were high – carrying out risky clandestine work - but the rewards were good; the government had to pay them the going rate for diplomatic services. Since its inception three years earlier, TOLA had many successes under its belt and Delaney, now well into his fifties, was still keen, still fit enough (given the odd bit of delegation) and still artful enough to be needed.

'More coffee, sir?' The stewardess brought him out of his subconscious thinking.

'Yes, thank you.'

She replenished his cup as Curtis, sitting next to him, passed her empty miniature wine bottle to her. 'Would you like another, madam?' the stewardess asked.

'No, thank you.' She looked at the stewardess and then at Delaney with an expression that was bordering on sarcastic. 'I'll wait until I get in the terminal and have a whole bottle.'

Delaney stayed quiet.

The plane landed at Heathrow on time and they made their way to the taxi rank. As they settled in the taxi, Delaney gave the driver his instructions then looked at Curtis. He was about to ask her how she was doing when she held up a hand to stop him. Her phone was ringing with one of the personal ring tones. She recognised the tone immediately, although the calls didn't come in too often. 'Hey Dad, how are you?'

'Fine, just fine; are you okay to talk?'

'Yeah, go ahead.'

'Just thought I'd say hi and see how you are. We haven't spoken for a while.'

'I know, Dad, I'm sorry; I should call you more often.'

'Well, I guess we both could try harder on that score. Still in London?'

'Mm, just arrived back from Munich actually.'

'Oh okay, job still going okay?'

'Yeah, I guess. Do you remember Marcus? You met him once when he came home with me a couple of years ago.'

'Sure I do. What's up? You sound a bit down.'

'He was killed last night.'

'Ah Jesus, Sally; you mean killed by someone you guys are after?'

'Probably.'

'Hey, you should some time off.'

'I'm okay, Dad. How are things in Thunder Bay?'

'Pretty much the same; the Robinsons and the Langs have been asking how you are again. Bob Robinson lost his job last month, so he's decided to retire early. His son, Ben, has just been promoted by the way; to Sergeant.'

The conversation went on for ten minutes; her father telling her about the usual things that she found mundane and she trying to dodge questions about her work and when would she visit home again. She finished the call with a promise that she would see him soon.

Thunder Bay, Ontario seemed a long way away to her right now. She had been born in Toronto in 1975. It was her father who had brought her up since the age of four, when for some reason, her mother left them to live with another man in Calgary. Having no brothers or sisters, the bond between her and her father was always close. He would take her to sports events and rodeos and it was the special parades by the Royal Canadian Mounted Police that first gave her the ambition to join them. Her thoughts started to wander and she dozed as the taxi made its way to Leicester Square.

Second-in-command at The Overseas Liaison Agency was Iowerth 'Taffy' Burton and he was waiting for Delaney as he brought Sally Curtis into their office near Leicester square in London. Two other employees; Brandon Jones and Ben Wyatt, were also waiting for them.

'Sally,' said Taffy, 'I don't know what to say, so I won't say anything.'

'Thanks, Taffy, anything said now probably wouldn't mean much to me anyway,' she said.

They sat down around Delaney's desk. Wyatt fetched them some coffees. Curtis spoke first. 'Tom, sorry if I blamed you back in Munich; it was the shock of it all. I just...'

'Forget it,' Delaney interrupted, 'you had reason. Are you sure you want to get on with this straight away, Taffy can take you home if you would rather...'

'No, Tom, let's get on with it. Marcus is gone. We're all hardened enough to handle it so let's get on with it. But I'm telling you all now, regardless of whether or not I have your help and regardless of whether or not things are allowed by my people back in Toronto, I'm going to find out who killed Marcus, and why; and they will be brought to justice. Or I'll kill them.'

Delaney looked at her with admiration. She was, he thought, as someone had once told him, a tough old bird for her young years. The flawless fair skin and the Jaeger spectacles hid the hardness of her character. He watched as she took off her jacket and sat down, wearing the usual jeans and shirt and 'sensible' shoes; her slim 5'4" figure settling easily in between the large arms of the old leather chair. He realised then that she was looking at him waiting for some form of response. He stayed leaning back in his chair as he spoke to her, not wanting to give a loud or strong answer and add more fuel to the aggravated fire.

'Okay,' he said calmly. 'But it shouldn't come to that. You know all of us will do our best for you; and for Marcus.'

'Yes I know, Tom. Marcus and I were so good together you see. I can't forget this; or let the perpetrators forget it.'

Taffy Burton walked forward and knelt at the side of her chair. He put his hand on hers and squeezed it mildly. 'This matter will be settled and the people brought to book,' he said. 'We're good at what we do you know, Sally.'

She looked at him and at the others. 'So am I,' she said, in a tearful but strong voice as she got up to walk out. She paused at the door and turned to face Delaney.

'I'll be back in tomorrow, Tom, to start looking into things with you, okay?'

'Sure,' Delaney replied. 'Be careful.'

Brandon Jones got up from his chair and called after her. 'Let me take you home, Sally, you shouldn't drive, it's been a bad night for you,' he said.

'I'm fine,' she replied without turning around.

Jones looked at Delaney who shook his head as an instruction not to pursue the issue.

Wyatt returned to the room with five coffees on a tray. He looked around and put the tray on Delaney's desk. 'Has she gone home?' he asked.

'Yes,' said Delaney. 'We'll go through a few ideas now, and then you guys can go and do a bit of fishing around before tomorrow.'

The four men settled into their chairs and started to go through what they knew. Marcus Hanson had been working for the Canadian Secret Service on some standard category C cases for the last few months and it was difficult to see how any of these cases could have warranted someone wanting him dead. There had been the left wing terrorists from Spain who had tried to kill a prominent Canadian diplomat while he was visiting Scotland, two cases of dealing with the Animal Liberation Forum who had links in Canada, two escort jobs for the Canadian UN representative and a more serious category B case involving gold and heroin smuggling which was passed onto Interpol some two months earlier.

After an hour discussing possibilities that did not seem to lead anywhere, Delaney called it a day. 'Let's leave it for now,' he said. 'We'll all think clearer on fresh minds after a bit of sleep. For the rest of the day, find out what you can will you about anyone Hanson was working with and then be back here at 9 a.m. tomorrow please.'

As he drove towards his home in Highgate, Delaney was thinking deeply about his life and his work. Both had been interesting, and the work had also been perilous at times. But today, Marcus Hanson was on his mind. Hanson was a senior agent with the Canadian Secret Service and this was the first time an agent he was working with had been killed. His usually calm feathers had certainly been ruffled this time.

As he opened the front door to his home, he saw that his partner Angela had not retired for the night. She put down her book as he approached her and kissed him. Angela was a quiet, easy going lady whose exercise regime kept her looking more like 34 than her 44. Her full dark brown hair was very attractive and the dark Mediterranean looks she had inherited from her father, went well with her dark eyes and full lips. She had always been a good listener and had always appreciated the fact that Delaney could not talk about every case he handled.

They had met just six months earlier. Delaney was allowed to use civilian secretaries based at the nearest police station whenever he needed more help with admin work and Angela had just secured a secretarial position there. When she had accepted his offer of dinner one evening, they both got on well together and after a few weeks she invited him back to her place. Their individual traits and maturity complimented each other and when they made love it would be passionate and intense. A few weeks later when Angela had had problems with her landlord, Delaney invited her to stay with him and they had got on well ever since.

Within half an hour, Delaney had finished a red wine and they had both retired to bed. As Angela dozed, Delaney struggled to settle his mind and the pictures he kept seeing were alternating between Sally Curtis and the body of Marcus Hanson on those stone steps.

The following morning, Ben Wyatt was the first one back in the office. At least he thought he was. Maggie Phelps was standing in the doorway with a cup of coffee. Maggie had worked for TOLA for two years. She had her own little room where she took care of filing and report writing and kept in touch with people when necessary. She hardly spoke and went about her work quietly and inconspicuously. 'Thanks Maggie,' said Ben, 'what a trooper you are.'

Wyatt was the undisciplined member of TOLA. Delaney had said that every team needs an undisciplined member when rule books were not always followed. When Delaney had interviewed him for the position, Wyatt had not come across well. Delaney had almost terminated the interview at the outset when Wyatt turned up in jeans and a sweatshirt with about three day's stubble covering his chin. 'Sorry guv; just got off a very long stake-out in Plymouth. We got the bastards though.' Wyatt rambled on a little too much and Delaney almost shut out the voice as he began to read Wyatt's CV. – Organised Crime Squad, Close Quarter Battle; top marks, Weapons and Tactics; first in class, Multi-skilled adaptability; second in class, Defensive driving; top marks, punctuality; sometimes on time.

When Delaney had asked him why he wanted to join TOLA, Wyatt ran his hands through his thin brown hair, leaned back and said, 'I just hate the bad guys guv, and maybe being part of your outfit will give me job satisfaction.'

Delaney had sent him the formal job offer the following day.

Sally Curtis arrived back in Delaney's office soon after Wyatt. Her boss in Toronto, Head of the Canadian Secret Service, Pierre Bouton, had given her permission to stay in London and spend as long as she wanted to on trying to track down Hanson's killers. Delaney, Burton and Jones arrived just as the coffee pot was boiling again. Delaney explained to Curtis what he had discussed with the others the day before. No one had fresh ideas.

Brandon Jones was pacing up and down in his expensive suit and his silk tie. If Wyatt was the undisciplined member of TOLA, Jones was the *disciplined* one. Formerly a Captain in the 1st Regiment, Royal Horse Artillery, he had come to Delaney after just two years in MI5. He spoke well, with a knowledgeable tone. His Barker shoes always immaculate, his black hair always neat, he was certainly a cut above Burton and Wyatt when it came to protocol and professionalism. He paused for a while at the window.

'Much happening out there mate?' Asked Wyatt.

'Oh the usual; thousands of people going about their business, one in four of them probably guilty of something.'

'How's that lad of yours by the way? Has he joined the old man's regiment yet?

'Give him chance; he's only ten.'

Delaney cut in. 'If you two are going to talk about something, can you make it pertinent to the case please.'

There was moment's silence. Curtis looked at Delaney and sighed. 'Do you all want to leave it to me, so I can try to sort it out off the record?'

'No we don't.' Delaney replied quickly. 'Okay, we may not be able to spend hours and hours on this anymore, what with the all the other cases we've got coming up, but we can still help when we have the time and I don't want you thinking you can't call on us if you need to. And I don't want you taking chances or risks on your own if you do get any ideas. Is that understood?'

Curtis started to smile, 'Okay Tom Okay, it was only a question.'

'Anyway,' Burton joined in, 'we've sort of got used to you bothering us now!'

'Yeah, yeah.' she retorted.

Taffy Burton had been with Delaney since day one of TOLA, after nine years working for Special Branch in London. He still had his Cardiff accent. His short, monosyllabic answers suited Delaney's usual style of questioning down to the ground and they had always got on well, while maintaining the discipline between boss and employee. His clothes never really suited him. The cheap suits and the dirty shoes were something that Delaney had got used to over time; although in the early days he had often dropped a hint. Burton's ruddy face and unkempt hair gave him a kind of likeable look and the scarred nose – courtesy of a gang of youths in Swansea – gave him the 'experienced' look that so many of the younger officers lacked. He settled his big frame down in the chair next to Curtis.

Burton, Jones and Wyatt swapped a few ideas about the rationale behind Hanson's killing as Delaney and Curtis listened. Some of Jones' and Wyatt's informants had offered some suggestions the afternoon before, but few were plausible. After a few moments silence, something crossed Delaney's mind. 'What about that heroin case that had links in Chicago and Toronto? The Farrah brothers did get put away didn't they?' he asked.

'Yep,' Burton replied, 'in 2008 for 18 years.'

Curtis filled in some details. 'They were convicted of smuggling it on three counts. Marcus was the one who put them away, but no one ever found the ninety million dollars they had made from it. There were some rumours about a top man in the CIA being involved but nothing was ever proven. They had people in Chicago, Toronto, London, Cologne and Nairobi working for them. Altogether 14 were put away; it was one of Marcus's most successful jobs.'

'Who's the CIA man?' Delaney asked.

'Charles Jerome.'

'Charles Jerome?'

'Yeah, know him?'

'Yes I do,' said Delaney. 'He was in charge of the Bannister case here in London in '99. The yanks pulled him out just before it got messy and I think he's some sort of Committee man now.'

'Spot on,' replied Curtis. 'He's in charge of the Eastern States Drugs Committee, based in Chicago; highly respected.'

Taffy Burton joined in as he leaned forward in his chair. 'Wasn't he suspected at some point of being involved with the Farrah's; for the wrong reasons if you see what I mean?'

'Yes, but again, nothing was ever proven and I guess it was all forgotten about,' said Curtis.

Delaney looked at Burton. 'Mm, right, Taffy, start looking at the records for that case will you? Go backwards from the convictions and see what Marcus had, how many statements, how many undercover helpers and how much it affected the drugs traffic immediately after the Farrah brothers were put away.'

'On it, sir,' Burton replied in his usual monosyllabic way. He got up and left the room.

Curtis looked at Delaney for some sort of clue as to what was on his mind. 'Well? What are you thinking?'

'Nothing specific; but always worthwhile looking back at these cases sometimes; especially with a fresh pair of eyes. Are you sure Marcus had put the case behind him? I mean, sometimes we get personal and if Marcus was hoping to get them a life sentence *and* get the money back, he could have been continuing his crusade on the quiet, against orders.'

Curtis looked surprised. She had never thought of that one. But surely Marcus would have told her. They always confided in each other, even on cases where they shouldn't have done. She stood and walked around for a while before sitting again to look at Delaney. 'Jesus Tom, do you think it's possible?'

'I don't know. It is possible, but is it probable? My guess is that Marcus was getting too close to someone high up. Whoever that was, they wanted him taken out. And we could be next if they know we're picking up the baton. Anyway, if he never mentioned it to you, it was either not happening or if it was, he was in deep and didn't want you to know in case you became exposed to danger too. Let's see what Taffy finds out first.'

On cue, Burton re-entered the room. Jokingly, Delaney said, 'what kept you?'

'Ha, well,' said Burton. 'I've just been thinking of something so I thought I would nip back and ask Sally while she was here.'

He went over to the window and stood with his back to it, before turning to Curtis.

'How about this, Sally? Marcus got involved with the Farrah brothers because of their links with Toronto; CSS territory, right?'

'Right,' she replied.

'So why was it that Marcus brought them to book for MI6, not the CSS?'

Curtis shook her head and shrugged her shoulders as she looked at both of them.

Delaney could see something was niggling Burton. 'Well Taffy, that's another question for you to answer then isn't it?'

'Mm, guess so, sir. Well we ca...'

The explosion tore through the window towards them all but Burton took the worst of it, being the nearest. He was thrown in the air and onto the floor, smithereens of glass piercing his back. Delaney and his chair were blown against the wall by the force of the blast. Curtis was hurled towards the door and just managed to hold her head before slamming into the brass handle. The whole room became a miniature hurricane as the shock wave threw furniture and ornaments against the walls. Jones and Wyatt who were in the far corner away from the window were knocked back by the shock wave. They were the first to get to their feet. Wyatt moved Curtis's unconscious body to one side and stayed with her. Jones went to where Burton was lying, he was still alive but his back was covered in blood where the numerous pieces of glass had penetrated. He then turned to Delaney who was moving. 'Sir, can you hear me?'

'Yes I can hear you, I'm alright, get those two out of here, we need a chopper in the air now! Get Arthur, go on I'm okay!'

Jones was an experienced operator and he knew what to do. 'Right sir; let me get you through to another office so you can use the red phone in there.'

Jones called to one of his colleagues to scramble a helicopter, authorisation to be confirmed. He got Delaney through to the next office and onto the phone.

'Arthur, it's Tom Delaney, get a chopper up now, they need to be looking around the south east of the building, a van, or lorry, something mobile, this missile or whatever it was couldn't have come from a building. It would be too traceable.'

The voice of Arthur Pope, Head of Airborne Division, answered in the usual concise way. 'Will do, Tom, there's one already up a few miles away.'

Jones rushed back to where Burton was lying, unconscious. He left him face down because of the glass in his back and lifted his head to one side slightly. Blood was pouring from a cut to his neck. Jones pressed a hand onto the bleed and felt Burton's pulse with the other. It was strong enough. Wyatt lifted Curtis up to rest her against the wall. She was conscious by then and he told her to stay still. He moved her hand up to her ear which was bleeding after hitting the door handle and told her to keep it there. She grimaced but looked at him with acknowledgement. Jones turned to look at Wyatt as he held Burton's neck. 'Can you check the boss again, Ben, I need to keep this pressure on here.'

Wyatt didn't need to check. Delaney walked back into the room holding his ear.

'You okay sir?' asked Wyatt.

'Yes I am, bloody glass nearly took my ear off.'

He looked at Burton lying helplessly, blood covering the floor underneath him. He took his jacket off and threw it at Jones. 'Use that Brandon, keep pressing hard.'

A silence followed. That kind of silence that lasted for a few seconds but seemed to go on for minutes. Curtis looked across the room at Burton on the floor; Delaney was looking at Jones and Wyatt. 'Keep your positions everyone, some good help is on the way.'

The paramedics arrived and went about their business. They went straight over to where Jones and Burton were. One of them took over from Jones keeping the pressure on while the other helped Jones get Burton on a stretcher, laid on his stomach so as not to push the glass further into his back.. Delaney watched them take Burton from the room. 'What do think?' he asked.

One of the paramedics on his way out, called back, 'He's bad sir, but we'll look after him.'

Another team of paramedics arrived and Delaney pointed to Curtis. 'See to her, we're okay.'

'Will do, but you two need to get to hospital as well to get checked over.'

'We will, we will, just see she is okay.'

'I'm alright,' said Curtis in a quiet voice. 'I'm just concussed.'

'Perhaps, which is why we're taking you to hospital,' said the paramedic.

When they had left, Delaney looked around his office. The window was completely blown out, the desk and chairs upside down, the glass cabinet smashed. Blood from Burton's back and neck was all over the floor. He knew that if Burton survived, they would all be very lucky to be alive. - Two years earlier, at a meeting in Paris, a similar device had been used and all seven people in the room had died. The windows in the building were the latest bomb proof specification and whoever did this must have used a weapon that was so powerful it might have taken out a few more offices as well, but it seemed it hit the building just to the side of the window. It was clearly aimed directly at the window and at him. A small personnel missile, he thought, or a rifle propelled grenade.

'This is serious, guv, to say the least,' said Wyatt.
'Yes it is, Ben; this one is going to get nasty.'

4

Twenty four hours later, Delaney was chairing a meeting with Jones and Wyatt and two more part time officers that he had 'borrowed' from the home office. He had told them all that he wanted them to gather as much information as they could. As he looked around the table, he noticed a few blank looks.

'Well?' What have we got gentlemen?' he asked.

Jones spoke first. 'Well so far, we have this. It was a Trakqvist rifle propelled grenade; low velocity, possibly launched from a large snipers rifle, three pound shell, low explosive; designed for maximum close proximity damage to property and people without spreading the explosion. The angle was about 20 degrees and the hole it left in the side of the building probably means it was fired from about 200 metres away, which puts the launch site on Smith Row, part of the old disused warehouse complex over there by the canal. The chopper didn't see anything, sir. We have people out there now, still looking.'

'What about the grenade, Trakqvist you say; where do they come from?'

'No known sources in the UK. The last ones we were told about were sold to a separatist party in Spain in 2005 but the chances are that this one was already in the country and had been for some time. Trakqvist manufactured them from 1998 to 2005.'

'Anything else?'

'No, sir, well not from me anyway,' replied Jones as he looked around the table in quiet hope. Blank faces stared back at Delaney.

'Great,' said Delaney, in his quiet but angry voice as he looked at each of them in turn. 'Highly paid operators with global terrorism information at their fingertips, helicopters, special branch, informants, undercover experts, and all I get is one answer from one man. Great; get out, all of you; and try to come back with something useful.'

They started to get up and move away. If Delaney said get out, that's what you did.

'Not you, Brandon, stay here please.'

Jones sat back down. As the last man exited the room, Delaney stood up and got his coat. 'Right, for the next few weeks I want you working with me. Get your coat; you can start by driving me to the hospital to see Taffy.'

Brandon Jones knew when to nod and just say, 'sir.'

For some reason, Delaney found himself counting the tubes sticking out of Taffy Burton's body as he lay in intensive care. There were nine.

A young looking doctor introduced himself as Dr Shungi and stood next to Jones on the opposite side of the bed to where Delaney was standing.

'No response then' Delaney said, looking at Mr Shungi. 'Will he be able to hear anything?'

'No, not yet, but he is stable and should come through this okay.'

'Good. I may send someone down to sit with him'.

Mr Shungi shrugged his shoulders in a relaxed manner. 'Okay,' he said, 'but the lady said she would stay for a while anyway.'

'What lady?'

'She has just gone for a coffee I believe. She was brought in with Mr Burton but was discharged a while ago.'

The doctor paused briefly as a woman walked towards them.

'Ah here she is now,' the doctor continued as he gestured towards the woman. It was Sally Curtis. She moved close to Delaney and put her hand on his shoulder.

'Hi, Tom, has Mr Shungi explained that Taffy will probably be okay?'

Delaney smiled at her and nodded. 'Yes. Yes he has. What about you?'

'I'm fine; a few cuts and bruises and an enormous headache, but they've checked everything and I'll live.'

Not wishing to sound rude and butt in, but thinking about his heavy work load, the doctor said quietly, 'Well, I'll leave you to it if I may. As I say, I am sure your colleague will recover, but it may be some time'.

'Yes, thank you'. Delaney acknowledged.

Curtis sat down on the bed next to Burton. 'You two leave the visiting bit to me. I'm sure you have plenty of things to be looking at. Any developments?'

'No, frankly,' Delaney answered. 'But I'm still waiting for some information'.

Curtis pulled her lips together and sighed. 'Well I'm sure you're all doing your best.'

'Yes we are, Sally,' said Delaney as he looked at Jones. 'Come on then, Brandon; let's get on with it.'

As they started to move towards the door, Curtis spoke again. 'Remember what I said, Tom, about getting Marcus's killer; and this happening to poor old Taffy here has made me even more determined'.

Delaney didn't look at her but nodded in acknowledgement as he left.

5

The Harris building in Chicago was built in 1994 and was named after its architect. There were 24 storeys housing various businesses and organisations. Some of these organisations were working there under another name and on the 10th floor, behind the guise of 'Looking Forward Computer Company' was the Eastern States Drugs Committee of the CIA. Charles Jerome had been in charge for five years since its conception.

He was a tall, heavy man. The years had taken away his hair and lack of exercise made him look like he had enjoyed the good life for too long. His fifty first birthday had been the day before and he could tell that he had had a little too much wine as he picked up the phone to make his first call of the day.

'Well I guess you know why I'm calling?'

The voice at the other end sounded worried but calm. 'I guess so, but I thought you might have phoned before now.'

'Maybe I should have done,' said Jerome. 'So, tell me, it was you who ordered the hit on Hanson, right?'

'It was me. Via a third party; someone just happened to available in Munich.'

'Was that necessary? The guy hadn't been involved for six months, he was on another case.'

'Yes but he had started to trace back to our case and was doing a bit of leg work for himself. He was taking it personally. I couldn't take any chances. And he was being helped by his CSS girlfriend; she might have to be next.'

'Your choice. Just make sure you keep everything clean,' said Jerome.

The person on the other end of the line sounded too calm for the situation. 'Don't worry, you'll get your 45 million, and long before the Farrah brothers are released. We just need to leave things say, another 12 months while things are still being forgotten about.'

'You're damn right I'll get my money, but just be careful. Forty five million each is a lot of money and I don't want it to get messy.'

'It's already messy, but we can handle it.'

'Good, and what the hell was that rocket attack on the Brits all about? Don't tell me that was your doing as well,' asked Jerome.

'Let's just say an over enthusiastic hit man; crazy bastard, but he's good. Probably the most expensive in Europe.'

'Okay, but this about getting rid of a few people, not frigging Apocalypse Now. How many enemies do you want for crying out loud?'

'It's alright; things will get quieter now, trust me, we'll be fine.'

'Right, well, keep me informed and be careful for Christ's sake.'

'Hey Charles, relax. We have the money locked safely away and the other bad guys are in prison.'

'Mm, okay, but just cool it for a while, yeah?'

'Sure, bye for now.'

Jerome put the phone down, took out his handkerchief and wiped his brow. There was a knock on the door and his PA walked in. 'You wanted a reminder Mr

Jerome; your meeting today with the police chief? It's at eleven.'

'Cancel it, I'm going back home, I don't feel too good.'

6

Curtis stayed with Burton at the hospital for a few more hours before making her way home. She parked her car in the only remaining place just down from the Georgian house in Muswell Hill where she was living. It was a bright but cold afternoon and she held her Rockport jacket closely around her as she walked to the house. The stone steps leading up to the front door reminded her of the steps in Munich where Marcus had died. Instinctively, she looked to her left and then to her right, wondering if she would be the next target.

As she climbed the steps, she noticed that her front window was acting as a mirror in the bright light and she could see a man looking in her direction from behind a small fence across the road. She did not turn around and opened her door to go inside. Once inside she ran upstairs and grabbed her surveillance camera from beneath her bed and slowly moved the curtain just enough to get the lens through and point it towards where the man was standing. She looked through the lens. He was gone. She opened the curtains fully and had a good look down the street in both directions and across to the fence. Nothing. There *had* been a man there. She was sure of it. What was he looking for? He may have been looking at someone, or something else, she thought, maybe nothing to do with her or her home. Perhaps; but she was not confident in dismissing the situation altogether. Something was getting to her. She thought of phoning Delaney for a few minutes but decided not to. It could have been just a nosey parker or someone looking around at properties. She decided she must not get paranoid.

At that moment she realised that her dog Rocky was standing by her and she had completely forgotten about him. The three year old German shepherd was only half wagging his tail as if to say, hey, don't you want to say hello to me today?

'Sorry boy! Hey, come on, let's get you something to eat and get out for a walk.'

Rocky had been a good companion to her since she took him from a friend in Luton who had emigrated to South Africa. He had been earmarked as a police dog but the canine review board had concluded, 'not quite up to it.' A neighbour, Mrs Henshaw, looked out for the dog when Curtis was away and he was popular with the neighbours and the children who would accompany him and Mrs Henshaw on walks.

Curtis walked him along the street to the gap in the fence where she had seen the man. It led to the open field where everyone seemed to stroll with their dogs, and mothers would walk out with their babies in pushchairs to enjoy the play area.

'Excuse me,' said a woman's voice behind her. Curtis turned to see another woman walking towards her holding out a small red purse in her hand. She was in her forties, slim and well dressed with black hair in a pony tail.

'You didn't drop this did you?' said the woman. 'It was back there near the bench.'

'No, it's not mine,' Curtis replied.

'Oh, sorry, I'll take it to the police station then, I'll be passing there this afternoon. What a handsome looking dog, how old is he?

'Oh only three, he looks older than he is,' said Curtis, not really wanting to stop and talk. But the other woman seemed to latch onto her somehow and they walked along together for a while discussing the weather, the lack of rubbish bins, dogs, children and families. The woman started to moan about her part time job and asked Curtis what she did for a living. Curtis told her she was a secretary and luckily the woman did not pursue any details. Then suddenly Curtis stopped in her tracks. A man had just walked quickly past them. His height, hair, build, gate and even his jacket were exactly like those of Marcus Hanson. 'Marcus!'

The man slowed down and turned. His face was weathered, his eyes small. 'Sorry,' said Curtis, 'I thought...' The man continued on his way. The woman asked her if she was alright. Curtis nodded and bid her farewell as she reached for her handkerchief.

Back at home, Rocky got his 'after walk treat' and she threw off her muddy shoes. Her coat smelled of the outdoors and she rested it across the chair next to the radiator. She removed her shoulder holster and put the Browning 9mm under the cushion on the sofa as she always did. She sat back and her thoughts were drawn again to her days in the Mounties.

She had done well in the RCMP. Working as a constable in Toronto, she soon got to know right from wrong and her 'solve and arrest' record was exemplary. Her father had served in the Canadian Army and she was determined to do well so he would proud of her. After just two years, having achieved the rank of Staff Sergeant, she was offered the rank of Inspector working for the Border Control Services. Three years later, she applied for the

Criminal Intelligence Unit and was offered a position as a Field Operative.

Then in 2002 she came top out of a class 24 in the Canadian Secret Service application process and she had been a successful CSS agent ever since. She became known as a no-nonsense agent; getting involved with organised crime operations and undercover work. There had been many a close call and she had lost some good friends along the way, but all that just reinforced her stalwart character. Colleagues found it hard to grasp sometimes, because her pleasant looks and quietness did not seem to go with her brawn.

Marcus Hanson had joined the CSS at about the same time and they had always got on well together. At times their relationship had been tenuous and their love making not as much at ease as perhaps it should have been. But they cared for each other, professionally as well as privately and Marcus's death would certainly leave her with an empty space for quite a while. Her mind went back to the sight of him lying on the steps in Munich; the blood dripping down the grey stone beneath him.

The ringing of the phone brought her out of her deep thinking. It was her boss in Toronto, Pierre Bouton, Head of the Canadian Secret Service. 'Sally? So how are things?'

'Not too bad, sir, thank you.'

'Good, are you having any luck in finding who was behind Marcus's killing?'

'Well we have a few ideas, sir, but nothing definite.'

'We? Who's we?'

'The Overseas Liaison Agency; that private firm employed by the Home Office. They're doing a good job.'

'Maybe not good enough; Marcus is dead.'

'That's unfair.'

Bouton did not respond so she took the opportunity to ask a question as something came to her. 'Actually, sir, do you know anything about the Farrah brother's case? Remember Marcus got them put away? Heroin and people trafficking?'

'Sure I remember,' replied Bouton casually. 'But they're inside and the whole thing is forgotten about now isn't it?'

'Yes they are inside, one in Manchester and one in Nottingham, I just wondered if you knew of anything else going on that's related to it.'

'Hell no, I'd start to look at other avenues if I were you. Anyway, as long as you're okay, give Delaney my thanks when you see him.'

'Yes I will, sir, are you're sure you don't want me back in Toronto to pick up on a new case?'

'No, Sally, you're okay, stay a while longer and we'll talk again next week.'

'Okay, sir, bye for now.'

She spent a few hours going through some of Marcus Hanson's old papers and thinking about other possible reasons for someone wanting him dead, before she fell asleep on the sofa, Rocky at her side.

The following day was a warm and sunny one. Tom Delaney had decided to take a few days leave and spend some time in the garden and with his partner Angela. The day grew hotter as they made their way out into Kent to find a nice pub and enjoy lunch.

The Wheatsheaf stood back away from the main road in Tunbridge and it was here they decided to stop and take a walk along the riverside before lunch. The hot weather always made Angela feel more sexual than usual and she jested with Delaney about making love in the bushes. He would have been more than keen himself usually but she could tell he had something on his mind other than the normal things he would usually think about or discuss.

They sat down on an old log near a clearing. She looked at him as he was looking at his hands. 'You need a haircut, my lovely silver-haired man.'

'Mm, I know.'

'Something heavy happening at the moment?' she said.

'Err, depends what you mean by heavy really. I'm just not comfortable with something.'

'Another top secret thing eh?'

'No not really. Remember that killing? Marcus Hanson?'

'Yeah, the boys from our station were the first to hear about it weren't they?'

'Yes, I wouldn't be surprised if it was you who translated the report for them,' said Delaney. 'You probably know as much as I do.'

'No I think it was Julie, the other secretary,' she said.

'Well anyway, I want to find out who did it and why, and right now it's not easy.'

'His girlfriend works over here as well doesn't she?' asked Angela.

'Yes. She's the main reason I want to get to the bottom of it.'

'Anything I can do?'

'No no, anyway come on, let's eat.'

They walked back to the pub and enjoyed a nicely prepared lunch before making their way back home. On the way towards London, the car phone rang. Delaney pressed the hands-free button. 'Tom speaking.'

'Tom, it's Mike Herbert.'

'Well, well, hello, Mike, how are you?'

'Fine, just fine thanks. Listen next time you're passing my office, will you pop in and see me? I've something you may find interesting, and I think it relates to a case you're working on with that Canadian girl.'

'Okay will do thanks, Mike. Perhaps we could catch up over a pint.'

'Just what I was thinking, see you soon.'

Herbert ended the call. Angela glanced at Delaney for an explanation. 'Mike Herbert? Where do I know that name from?'

'Head of MI6, no less. A good sort. If he says he has something useful, he means it. I'll call in and see him tomorrow sometime.'

Delaney spent some time in the garden and left Angela to continue work on her Open University degree in business studies which she was half way through.

The knock at the door took Angela by surprise and she opened it to find Brandon Jones standing there.

'Hello there, come in,' she said, 'Tom's in the garden, go through.'

Jones made his way towards the garden as he acknowledged Angela's welcome. 'Thanks, sorry to trouble you, are you having a few days off as well?' he said.

'Just a couple,' she replied.

Delaney had heard the arrival and had started to walk towards the back door. Jones looked apprehensive as he approached his Commander. 'Sorry to bother you sir, I would have phoned, but I thought you might want to hear this direct from me.'

'Don't worry about it, Brandon, I'm sure you wouldn't be here unless it was important.'

'No, sir.'

They stood together on the patio and Angela brought some beers out for them.

'There you go you two, and don't keep him too long, Brandon, he's on leave.'

Delaney took a welcoming drink of his beer as he put his trowel down on the table. 'Well, what have you got for me young man?'

Jones turned to see that the patio door was open and that Angela was working at her desk just inside. He looked at Delaney. 'Do you mind if I...' he said, as he gestured as though he wanted to close the door.

'Oh for god's sake get on with it man.' said Delaney. 'She's probably written more reports than you've read.'

'Of course, sir, right. Well I spoke to someone in MI5 yesterday and it seems that the Farrah brothers were put away but the money has still not been accounted for.'

'I thought we already knew that.'

'We did, sir, but hang on. Hanson had some papers in his flat here in London, which I've been going through and one of them was this.'

Jones took a folded letter from his jacket pocket and handed it to Delaney. The Commander opened it and noticed the good quality of the paper as he read —

Junger Commercial Bank
11 Trest Strauss
Geneva
34tp
January 3rd 2009

>Sir,
>Further to my letter dated December 17th 2008, I can confirm that your deposit is now registered in our Special Reserve Section and is available for your inspection and/or withdrawal as you would wish.
>Your PIC – Personal Identification Code - is in a separate information pack and will be forwarded to your Box Number in Paris as requested.
>Please contact me if I can be of any further help.
>
>Yours truly,
>
>Heini Maddersun
>Securities Section

Jones waited until he could see that Delaney's eyes were at the end of the letter.

'See the date, January 09, and the Farrahs were put away in September 08.'

Delaney looked up and breathed heavily. 'Funny, the letter doesn't state the addressee. It doesn't explain why it was in Marcus's apartment either. Right, well done Brandon, you'd better get onto Stephen in Paris and find out who owns that box.'

'Already have, sir, but the Gendarmerie want your code before they'll let Stephen get access to the information.'

'Okay, come on; take me back to the office.'

Delaney apologised to Angela and 50 minutes later he was back in his office on the phone to Paris.

Stephen Landers was what Delaney called his 'European' member of TOLA. Educated at Harrow and Cambridge, this well spoken son of a Chief Constable had had the sort of career many men would envy. After a short Royal Air Force career, he had worked in Paris for five years for Interpol prior to joining Delaney. His contacts with the Paris police, Interpol and the Gendarmerie were indispensable. His handsome, well groomed looks and his smart but casual attire - he never wore a tie - were complimented by the fact that he could speak French, Spanish and Italian.

'Stephen, how are you?'

'Yes, Tom, I'm good. Are you phoning to follow up on Brandon's call earlier?'

'Yeah, he tells me you need my code.'

'Yes please, you can punch in the numbers on your red phone, that should do it.'

'Hang on.'

Delaney asked Jones to leave the room and picked up the red phone. He dialled a number and after a while punched in his eight digit code. When the phone made the appropriate bleep he put the receiver back down and spoke again to Landers on the other line. 'Get it?'

'Hang on,' said Landers. 'It can take a while......right here we are, yep, it's got it. Your code has gone through to the Gendy. Now, you want to know about the owner of a box in Paris; well do you know how many boxes there are in Paris?'

'Surprise me,' sighed Delaney.

'Seven thousand.'

'Okay, seven thousand, but you know something don't you Stephen or you wouldn't have told Jones you needed my authorisation before giving out the information.'

'Quick as ever you old goat; I mean, sir. Well get this; all new boxes in Paris have to be registered with the Gendarmerie. It's a secure database, but our links with the Gendy mean we can access it. It's part of the inter-active information procedures they started after the Madrid train bombings. I looked at all new boxes registered between September 08 and January 09 and one name does stick out.'

'Right, and who might that be?' asked Delaney.

'Toobun.'

'Toobun?'

'Yep, Toobun.' Landers confirmed.

'So your idea being?'

'Well, Toobun; it's just not a name you would recognise from any country is it? Could be Flemish or something like that I suppose, maybe even middle-eastern.'

'Okay, so you don't know who he, or she, is. What's in the box?'

'Couldn't get that information from them,' said Landers. 'You need permission from the Gendy and they need authority from Interpol. Need I say more?'

Delaney paused for a while before responding. 'So you're telling me I need to get permission from my end to instruct the head of the Gendarmerie to get access to the information.'

'That's exactly what I mean. I'll leave it with you.'
'Okay thanks, Stephen.'

The Gendarmerie, Interpol or MI6 were not a problem for Delaney. He had dealt with their top men on many an occasion and he knew who to speak to; and if necessary, how to get through to the Foreign Secretary. Two days later, he had permission and authority.

7

'That makes it a bit more interesting, sir.' Brandon Jones was sitting with Delaney in the office going through the information they had received from Paris, after Delaney had obtained authority.

Delaney nodded slowly. 'Mm, it'll be interesting to see what Sally makes of it as well.'

Maggie Phelps brought in some coffees and laid out a few biscuits on a small ornate plate. 'You're spoiling me Maggie,' said Delaney.

'If you say so, Tom; but you're not going to leave them are you?'

'No, I suppose not, thank you.'

'I've finished that Munich report by the way if you want to see it, and the Home Secretary has left a message; something about Paris?'

'Okay, thanks, I'll phone him.'

Maggie left the room and Jones frowned at Delaney. 'Paris, sir; are you sure you want to phone him?'

'No. And I'm not going to.' Delaney had spoken to some very senior people to get the necessary authority for the Gendarmerie. He knew the Home Secretary would want to know why he wasn't informed.

'Shall I get Sally in here, sir?' asked Jones, 'her input could be useful.'

'Yes, I'll phone her.'

Delaney waited until he had enjoyed a plain chocolate biscuit before dialling.

'Sally, it's Tom, can you come down to the office today?'

'Sure, I've just got to do something for the Toronto office, could be with you about eleven?'

'Okay thanks, see you soon.'

Curtis had received a phone call from an assistant to the head of the CSS asking her to check up on an address of an informant they had been looking for and who had mysteriously disappeared a few weeks ago. Her dog Rocky was sitting by the front door in anticipation so she took him for a short walk, fed him and left him to sleep again before setting off. The address was almost en-route to Delaney's office so she made her way there guessing she could deal with the informant – or not – and still be at the office by eleven.

The house was an old terraced property with a small front garden and overgrown weeds. The front door looked old and poorly maintained, but had been used recently, she thought. The handle was clean but weathered and the ground was not dirty or overgrown. She knocked once and rang the bell. After a minute she knocked again. Then she noticed that the sliding sash window was slightly open and the breeze was making the lace curtain move around. She tried another knock and rang the bell once more, but there was no response.

The path leading down between the row of houses was damp and unused, but she could access it quite easily and decided to take a look around the back. Again there was no sign of life. She had been given permission to enter the premises if the need arose but it was clear to her that the informant was not at home.

Then she noticed the back door was open slightly. Almost shut, but not quite; about a half inch gap. Her training and experiences over the years had made her cautious and she decided not to go in via that route. She went back to the front window, pushed it upwards to open it further and carefully climbed in.

'Hello? Mr Bradshaw, are you in?'

No sounds were heard so she made her way through to the hallway. 'Mr Bradshaw?' Hello? It's Sally Curtis from the Bakery.' This was the word used to identify CSS personnel to informants.

There was no one there. A few days worth of letters had piled up by the front door. A tabby cat looked up at her from beside an empty cat dish. She went through to the kitchen.

At that moment she froze. The back door had a wire attached to its handle that went across to a small box which was placed on the kitchen worktop. She moved slowly towards the box and froze again. She could clearly see that the wire was attached to some type of timing device, and strapped to the inside of the open top box was just one stick of high explosive. A heat came to her face. Then the heat changed to a sweat. Behind her, she heard the tabby cat miaow. 'Stay there little one,' she whispered. 'You really don't want to be in here.'

She heard a breeze coming from somewhere and the sound of dried leaves being blown around outside the kitchen door. She looked at the door. It moved slightly, just millimetres, but it moved. Then it was motionless again. She considered her options. The wire was obviously designed to stay taught and it would loosen when the back door was opened. The small timer told her that the blast was not planned to be instantaneous, but probably after 2 or 3 seconds when the person was well inside. But the door was open that half inch. Why wouldn't they close the door? Got to get out, she thought, got to get on the phone. She moved backwards very slowly and turned to pick up the cat from the floor. Walking into the hallway very gently, she noticed a photograph on the wall. It was a picture of two cats; the tabby she was holding and another one, black and white, looking older. Lucky, she thought, I've only the one to pick up.

She stood perfectly still again as she heard a small noise behind her and turned her head just enough to see back into the kitchen. The black and white cat was there. And it was coming in the back door.

'Christ!' she said as she flung herself onto the floor of the hallway, threw the tabby towards the front door and covered her head. The device did its job. The back door was blown out into the garden, cupboards were torn from the walls, the whole kitchen shook and she felt the shock wave as it passed over her. The intense noise pushed her ear drums inwards and made her eyes water. She waited, as she had been taught, until it was all quiet; about 10 seconds, before getting to her feet. The back of her hands were cut and she could smell her hair that had been singed. 'Holy shit,' she whispered as she reached for her phone.

Delaney interrupted his conversation with Brandon Jones to pick up his phone. It said *Sally Calling*. 'Hello Sally; don't tell me, you've been held up.'

'Tom, Jesus Tom I think someone has just tried to kill me.'

'Where are you?'

'In a house in Germaine Street, number 4, Bloody hell, Tom it was a bomb.'

'Are you okay?'

'Yeah; just.'

'Get outside, sit down and wait there, we're on our way.' He didn't wait for an answer. 'With me, Brandon, move your arse.'

Within two minutes they were en route. Delaney made some phone calls and Jones used all his advanced driving skills to get them there in 12 minutes. Sally was sitting on the small brick wall in front of the house, some neighbours were gathering to find out what had happened and an ambulance pulled up just behind Delaney's car. Jones made his way over to the crowd to keep people away and clear the way for the ambulance crew. Delaney went over to where Curtis was.

'Well, you're alive,' he said, 'so you must have been quick.'

'There was a cat, I just, oh forget it, Jesus, Tom, what is happening?'

'I'll take a look inside, wait here.'

He went to the rear of the house to view the scene. Contrary to what she had been told, Curtis followed him. 'I saw the device,' she said. 'It was only one stick, just enough to kill the person coming in without leaving massive damage or causing a fire.'

'Mm, well the bomb boys are on their way. We'll find out where it came from. Come on. I'll get you to a hospital.'

Other officers had arrived by now and Jones drove Curtis to the hospital. Delaney advised the incident officer and explained his role in it all. The incident officer did not know about TOLA and it took a while for Delaney to explain. The officer checked for himself to make sure by phoning his superintendent.

Delaney was offered a lift back to his office and Maggie was waiting for him with a coffee already on his desk. Jones phoned him an hour later from the hospital to let him know that Curtis was okay and he was taking her home. When they had been at the hospital, they had called in on Taffy Burton to see how he was and they were also pleased to report that he was recovering nicely.

'Right thanks, Brandon,' Delaney said, 'when you get to Sally's place, don't go in until I get there. We need to make sure her place is alright and assuming it will be, we can talk with her there and try to find an answer to all this.'

'Yes, sir, I'll wait in the car until I see you.'

When Delaney got there, they were waiting outside and Jones got out of the car. Delaney leaned into the car to speak to Curtis. 'Stay here.'

'I'm okay, you might need…'

'Stay here.'

The two men checked over the house and the gardens. They knew that her house would be wired into the MI5 database and that anyone entering would have had a swarm of agents onto them in minutes. Jones fetched Curtis from the car and they went inside.

Rocky was standing in the hallway wagging his tail; he had met Delaney before and knew his smell and he soon settled down when he was sure they were all present and correct.

'Right,' said Delaney, 'let's have a drink and sit down.'

Jones poured three drinks from Curtis's cabinet and they sat. Curtis started to cry.

They let her, for a while, and said nothing. After she had wiped her face and taken a drink Delaney spoke to her. 'I think I know where we should be looking.'

'You mean,' Curtis said softly, 'where we should be looking for the person who's behind all this?'

'Yes. Brandon here did some bloody good work and we've found a safe deposit box in Paris.'

'Did you get authority to access it, sir?' said Jones.

'Yes. Are you both ready for this?'

The other two looked at each other and Jones spoke first. 'I reckon we are.'

'The deposit is ninety million dollars.'

'Ninety million?' asked Curtis, 'That's the exact amount that was never recovered from the Farrah brother's case that Marcus dealt with.'

'Damn right it is,' confirmed Delaney.

'Did you get the details of the box number?' asked Jones.

'Yes, the box is rented to someone called Toobun.'

'What box is this?' asked Curtis.

Jones explained to her. 'I found a letter that was sent to someone about a safe deposit box in Paris. The letter was from a Swiss bank and the boss here got access to the details.'

Delaney finished his drink and continued the story for Jones. 'Brandon found a letter in Marcus's apartment that he had obviously stolen from somewhere. It was from this bank in Geneva, and it just said 'dear sir' no name, and it was confirming that they had received instructions and all that jazz, the usual stuff. I found out who registered the box from our man in Paris. It was in the name of Toobun. The deposit was ninety million, so it's got to be the Farrah brother's heroin money.'

Delaney paused for a response but did not get one.

'Go on,' said Jones.

'Well I think that whoever killed Marcus, now believes that Sally is still investigating the case, albeit in her own time. And whoever that is, they want her dead because they have the ninety million at stake and they don't want to lose it.'

Curtis shook her head as she spoke. 'But you thought the grenade attack at your office was for you, Tom.'

'Then I did yes, but now I think it was for you. And I also think this back door bomb thing was for you as well; who asked you to go there?'

'I got a call from Toronto this morning. They asked me to check out the address because a top class informant who lived there had gone missing.'

'What was this informant's name?'

'Oh you wouldn't know him; it was just a CSS thing.'

'What's his name?'

'Bradshaw, Micky Bradshaw.'

Delaney fell silent for a moment, got up and poured himself another drink before turning to Curtis. 'Micky Bradshaw died three weeks ago from cancer.'

'But,' Curtis gasped. 'I was asked to go there by headquarters in Toronto, why...'

'Wait a minute, who was the instruction from?' Delaney interrupted.

'The assistant to the top man.'

'And when you say the 'top man' you mean the Head of the CSS, the chief honcho.'

'Yes,' confirmed Curtis. 'It's not done casually; they have to give me a code and I have to cross reference the code in my ops manual and phone them back. Everything was correct. The instruction came indirectly from the Head of CSS. I've known him for years.'

'And what is his name, Sally?'

'Well surely you know and anyway...'

'Bloody hell,' said Delaney. 'Why do I have to repeat my questions all the time; what is his name, Sally?'

'Pierre Bouton.'

Delaney breathed out heavily. 'Thank you. Pierre Bouton.'

'What is it, Tom? Tell me.'

Delaney looked at her and then at Jones who raised his eyebrows in anticipation.

'I'll tell you both as the penny hasn't dropped yet. The Head of the CSS is Mr Bouton. The owner of the deposit box in Paris is Mr Toobun.'

There was a moments silence as Jones and Curtis looked at each other. Curtis leaned forward and looked downwards. 'Bouton, Pierre Bouton, this is not a coincidence is it?'

Delaney shook his head. Jones leaned forward. 'Bloody hell, sir, what the hell is going on?'

'It all fits,' said Curtis. 'The name; it has to be him. Me being sent to a booby trapped house. And Bouton told me a couple of days ago that I could stay a while longer to sort things out. Perhaps to give him more time to hit me. The grenade attack on you, Tom, it was meant for me, not you. The hit on Marcus, they must have known he was still into the heroin case. But how did they know? Bouton deals with the CIA and that Jerome guy you mentioned, I know he does, I've seen memos. He must be the one behind all this, maybe with Jerome. Both of them would have people killed for ninety million; they're always giving out orders like that, and no one would be suspicious. But how did they know Marcus was snooping and how did they know I was looking as well?'

'I've thought about that,' Delaney said. 'There has to be someone here, who works closely to us, or you. The information was given to them by someone we know here in London. We must have someone here who is being paid a lot of money to send information to Pierre Bouton, or Charles Jerome.'

'Not from our team, sir, surely.' Jones queried.

'Not sure, I'll work on that one. You get back to Paris Brandon and help Stephen out for a while. Ask him to send all the information about the secure box back with you. Sally; you get a few things together and get to the Hawton Road safe house. I'll get two men to meet you there. Stay indoors until you hear from me.'

'How can I when we need to...'

'Just do it, Sally, I need you out of harm's way, now let's get on with it both of you, move yourselves.'

Two hours later Curtis was in the Hawton Road safe house with just a few belongings and her dog Rocky. The house was an old and damp with large rooms and open fireplaces. She turned the heating to high, and switched on the water heater. Someone had made an attempt to supply food and the fridge was full of microwave meals, milk, cheese and soft drinks; not a jar of coffee or a tea bag in sight.

Jones was on a flight to Paris to fetch back the necessary evidence himself and Delaney, having spent some time at his office talking to Special Branch, was on his way home.

He was surprised to find Angela there who had finished work earlier than usual and was putting out a few nibbles to go with the wines she had poured for them both. Delaney put a jazz CD on and relaxed while he thought through the happenings of the last few days.

'Trouble?' asked Angela.

'Err, yes, trouble. But I'll sort it.'

The word *treason* crossed his mind. Then another word, *greed.* Of course, he would sort it out, but not quickly. His gut told him that.

The next morning, Delaney used any powers he had to get a meeting with the heads of MI5 and MI6, the Home Secretary and the Foreign Secretary. The whole story of Marcus Hanson and the Farrah brothers and the ninety million dollars was explained to them. They were told of Sally Curtis's involvement and the attempts on her life, about Charles Jerome and Pierre Bouton. Phone calls were made to the very top in the States and Canada and he was confident that Bouton and Jerome would soon be in his grasp. Thursday afternoon would be interesting.

8

The Eastern States Drugs Committee had been busy and Charles Jerome had been working later than usual when the phone rang. He would have ignored it, but it was the blue phone which usually meant it was someone important. It was.

'Charles hi, Martin Zimmerman here, glad I caught you.'

Congressman Martin Zimmerman was the head of the Eastern States Presidential Security Council. Not many people could override his decisions and when he asked someone in the CIA to do something, they did it.

'Congressman, hello there, long time no speak.'

'Yeah, hey Charles, I need you to go to London. This is a big one and if you get this one right, there's a heck of a lot of brownie points coming your way.'

'Okay, tell me,' said Jerome, frowning.

'Our boys in Barcelona have picked up a drugs baron. They're working with Scotland Yard and have said they could do with your expertise on heroin numbers. The guy's being taken to London in two days, Thursday, and I think you should go. It could be useful for us and we could use a few favours being owed to us.'

'Hey no problem, jeez if I can help I will, sir.'

'I told my colleagues you would, Charles. The meeting is at Scotland Yard, Thursday 17.00 hours. They'll take you to MI6 from there. Do you need me to arrange a car?'

'No no, that's fine, I'll arrange it from here, sir. Who am I meeting?'

'Sir Adrian Lusher from MI5 will see you there.'

Pierre Bouton got home that night at about eight. He lived with his wife Sandra and she had just got back herself from her job in downtown Toronto. Bouton had always been an ambitious man and had not really been concerned with being unpopular on his way through the ranks. He had been quite ruthless and did not have time for 'amateurs'. His bald head with a scar above his ear and a look of strength had always made him seem quite awesome to his colleagues.

They were talking through their days' events when the door bell rang. Bouton opened it slowly. But all his experience through the years had not prepared him for this one. It was his boss, the Canadian Security Secretary Josh Michaels with two of his body guards.

Michaels moved forward slightly to prompt Bouton to make way. 'Pierre.'

'Secretary, what a surprise.'

'Can we come in?'

'Sure sure come along in, I'm sorry, you took me by surprise.'

The three men filed in and remained standing. Sandra offered them a drink. They declined. Secretary Michaels got straight to the point.

'Well, Pierre; I needed to speak to you about this one face to face. It was too tricky to try to speak on the phone. Has this house been checked over by our surveillance boys lately?'

'Yes, sir, just last month.'

'Great, now then; have you heard of Sir Adrian Lusher of MI5 in London?'

'Yes, I err, I think I have.'

'Well he's asked for your help. Something about a drugs gang in Barcelona and heroin being taken to London. They've got these guys in Scotland Yard and there's a big pow wow on Thursday. They need your help and input from the heroin angle of things. They don't have anyone with the same knowledge as you and have asked if you would help, and err, well I told them you would, Pierre.'

Bouton looked at his boss with disdain. 'Well I guess I will then. But I hope you won't take this the wrong way when I say it would have been nice to be asked rather than told.'

'I know, I know, but I couldn't risk speaking on the phone and we do owe the Brits a few favours. Now, here's your ticket. A car will pick you up from Heathrow; the meeting is at Scotland Yard 17.00 hours Thursday. You check in to Sir Adrian, okay?'

'Yes, I guess, okay, sir.'

The three men left as quickly as they had arrived.

9

Delaney was preparing the necessary paperwork for Jerome and Bouton's visit when his phone rang. He glanced down at his handset to see that Curtis was phoning him.

'Hello, Sally, okay?'

'Tom I've just been speaking to Brandon, something about a meeting tomorrow?'

'Mm, not sure why he mentioned it, because I don't want you there.'

'Why, what's it all about?'

'Like I said; I don't want you there.'

'Christ, Tom! If this is about Marcus and Jerome and Bouton, I have a right to be there!'

'Sally, I am sorry. I am not allowing you to be there. It has all been set up with a lot of hard work and I don't want the possibility of anyone seeing you before they arrive. You will not be there.'

His phone went dead. 'Hello?' He left it as it was. She was a good agent and he trusted her. She could go to the Home Secretary or MI5 to complain – after all, TOLA was a 'company' a 'supplier of services' and Delaney had to do as he was told when the chips were down – but he had been given permission to oversee things on this case. As far as any perpetrators knew, he was a diplomat working for the government. And his years of experience helped to get support from most quarters. Very few people were more experienced or knowledgeable.

Thursday arrived and it was very wet. The sort of wet that makes you put the windscreen wipers on the double fast setting. Charles Jerome touched down at Heathrow 12 minutes early, courtesy of British Airways. He made his way to the car hire desk and hired himself a Lexus. He always did it this way rather than relying on prim and proper English chauffeurs or taxi drivers who would talk to him about football and golf and how the weather would 'brighten up later'.

He drove to Scotland Yard and was allowed in the private visitor's car park they reserve for foreign agents. A smartly dressed woman showed him the way to the interview room, explained that someone would be with him shortly and left him with the coffee and biscuits. He wasn't happy about being left to wait, but hey, this is Britain, he thought.

Pierre Bouton touched down about 20 minutes after Jerome. The Air Canada flight had also been early. He found the car and driver that was waiting for him. The driver was a large red headed man and Bouton could see by the shape of his jacket that he was armed.

'I've been asked to get you straight to Scotland Yard, sir,' said the driver, 'if that's okay with you?'

'Of course,' replied Bouton. 'Are you a police driver?'

'Yes, sir.'

'Good, well I trust you'll get me there quickly then.'

They arrived at the Yard some 50 minutes later and the driver opened the door for his passenger. The same woman that had accompanied Charles Jerome to the interview room was there to greet Bouton and she showed him up through the premises to the same room.

As they were approaching the room, the woman turned back to speak to him.

'I do apologise, sir, but the people who need your help and who are meeting you today are running just a little late and they have asked that you wait in here. Please help yourself to coffee, tea and biscuits.'

Shaking his head in disappointment, Bouton replied. 'Okay, but I've come a long way, you know?'

She opened the door and showed him in. He saw another man looking out of the window speaking on his mobile phone. The woman left the room, closing the door behind her.

Bouton waited for a moment. He thought he recognized the man at the window from behind. The man turned away from the background light of the window. Putting his phone in his pocket, he looked at the newcomer in the room.

'Pierre.'

'Charles, I thought it was you; what the hell is going on?'

'Search me, I just…'

'Charles shut up. Don't say another word.'

'Don't say another word? You're joking right? This is Scotland Yard buddy; we were being taped as soon as we got here.'

Silence followed for half a minute. They looked at each other and started to realize why they were there, together. Jerome made his way casually over to the door. It was locked.

'What the…'

'Not another word, Charles.'

In another room on the same corridor, a group of men were listening to what was being said. Their expressions were serious and they all looked closely at the CCTV and watched the astounded looks on the faces of Jerome and Bouton. Most of the top players were there. – Sir Adrian Lusher, Head of MI5, Commander Mike Herbert, Head of MI6, Louis Hooper, Special Branch, and Delaney's own Stephen Landers. Martin Hamilton, British Home Secretary, was also present and it was he who interrupted the silence. He looked at Adrian Lusher. 'Is Delaney alright to do this, Sir Adrian? I mean, are we legal; he's not a government employee strictly speaking.'

Lusher was always confident; some said, too confident. He came across as being right, whenever he spoke. 'Yes Home Secretary, it is alright. Delaney is not doing the formal arrests.'

Mike Herbert gave the thumbs-up sign. 'Sir Adrian is right. If all else fails, we can call it a citizens' arrest.' The attempt at humour did not work, but Herbert's relaxed character was not shaken by the looks he got.

After watching Jerome and Bouton for a few more minutes, Delaney turned to his colleagues.

'Okay, let's do it.'

They made their way to the interview room, opened the door and filed in. A Special Branch Agent locked the door behind them and stood guard outside.

Bouton and Jerome were sitting next to each other at a large oak table. Jerome again opened his mouth too soon. 'Well good, we've been waiting far too long. Now how can we help?' Bouton looked at him pitifully. Did he seriously think he could still pretend now?

'Gentlemen,' Delaney said. 'Sorry to keep you waiting. Let me do the introductions before we start.'

Lusher and Herbert sat down opposite the two visitors in the only two remaining chairs. Delaney stood behind them, Landers to his left, Hooper to his right, closer to the door. Hamilton took up a position leaning against a wall, looking out of his depth.

'My name is Delaney.' He turned to gesture to his colleagues in turn. 'Also in the room are Sir Adrian Lusher, Head of MI5, Commander Mike Herbert, Head of MI6, Louis Hooper, Special Branch and Stephen Landers. Stephen works for our Paris section. He has close ties with the Gendarmerie and lots of information at his fingertips; including information about secure box numbers in Paris.' As he said this last sentence he made sure to look at Bouton. 'Can I also introduce you to Martin Hamilton, Home Secretary. I believe you both know our Foreign Secretary, Mr. Spires, but he couldn't be with us today.'

As is often the case when so many clever people are gathered in one room at an awkward moment, no one spoke.

Delaney continued. 'Before I go on, do either of you want to say anything?'

'Damn right I do, you bastard!' said Jerome. 'What the hell is this? Either I leave this room right now or you're out of a job, mister! I'm making a phone call.'

As Jerome went to reach for his phone, Delaney stepped forward to be closer to him. He looked at him with a motionless, yet angry, face. 'No you're not. You're going to listen.'

Jerome backed down. Delaney continued. 'We're all here to see that everything is done properly and to make sure you both know that we mean business. You see, we know. We know about the Farrah brothers deal with you both. We know about the ninety million in Paris that you were going to share with the Farrah brothers. We know about the hit on Marcus Hanson because you knew he was still poking around in the case, and we know about the attempted hits on Sally Curtis. Now, do either of you have anything to say? I mean we could sit here all night, but do we need to?'

Bouton shook his head. Jerome spoke again. 'What in god's name are you talking about?'

Mike Herbert leaned forward at the table. He looked at Jerome, hesitated and then at Bouton. 'I take it you're both aware of the closeness that exists between MI6, FBI and the CSS?'

'Sure,' said Jerome, 'and don't forget my outfit, the CIA; we do some great work between us.'

'Mm, and there is also the inter-action whenever we need it,' said Herbert. 'Like listening to phone calls and intercepting mail if any of us are suspicious.'

Delaney looked at Landers who walked up to the table. He took out a small tape player from his jacket pocket, placed it on the table and switched it on.

'Well I guess you know why I'm calling?'

'I guess so, but I thought you might have phoned before now.'

'Maybe I should have done. 'So, tell me, it was you who ordered the hit on Hanson right?'

'It was me. Via a third party: someone just happened to available in Munich.'

'Was that necessary? The guy hadn't been involved for six months, he was on another case.'

'Yes but he had started to trace back to our case and was doing a bit of leg work for himself. He was taking it personally. I couldn't take any chances. And he was

being helped by his CSS girlfriend; she might have to be next.'

'Your choice. Just make sure you keep everything clean.'

'Don't worry, you'll get your 45 million, and long before the Farrah brothers are released. We just need to leave things say, another 12 months while things are still being forgotten about.'

'You're damn right I'll get my money, but just be careful. Forty five million each is a lot of money and I don't want it to get messy.'

'It's already messy, but we can handle it.'

'Good, and what the hell was that rocket attack on the Brits all about? Don't tell me that was your doing as well.'

'Let's just say an over enthusiastic hit man; crazy bastard, but he's good. Probably the most expensive in Europe.'

'Okay, but this is about getting rid of a few people, not frigging Apocalypse Now. How many enemies do you want for crying out loud?'

Bouton stood up and kicked his chair against the wall. 'Okay, switch it off!'

Landers gathered up the tape player, switched it off and put it back in his pocket. Jerome had turned pale, sweat dripping from his eyebrows. Bouton turned and hit Jerome hard on the side of his face. 'You god damned moron!' You always said the calls were safe!'

Jerome straightened himself up and took out a handkerchief to wipe the sweat from his forehead and the blood from his mouth. He looked at Bouton who was holding his head in both hands up against the wall. 'And you were so damn right all the time eh, Bouton, you...'

'Okay, stupid. Stop there,' said Bouton. 'None of us says another word at all, starting right now.'

Delaney looked around the room. 'Would anyone else like to ask any questions?'

Adrian Lusher told Bouton to sit down. As Lusher started to speak, Jerome looked up at the ceiling and Bouton was staring at Delaney. 'Not sure I need to say anything, but you both disgust me. All over the world we are trying to fight crime together. Millions of pounds; millions of man hours by dedicated, hard working agents, and people like you betray us, for money. You're nothing but stinking low lifes. Just like the people you deal with. Your greed is astounding. You should both be hanged, slowly.' He turned to Delaney. 'Right, Tom, get them in here.'

'Get who in here?' asked Jerome. Delaney opened the door; two more men entered. The first one introduced himself as he looked at Bouton. 'Pierre Bouton, my name is Grafton from the Canadian Division of Interpol. I am here to escort you to Boston where you will be charged with, and stand trial for, murder, deception and treason. Come with me please.'

The second man then spoke while looking at Jerome. 'Charles Jerome, my name is Poole. I work for the American State department. You too will be taken back to Boston where you will face the same charges. Do either of you have anything to say?'

Neither man said anything further. Bouton continued to stare at Delaney. They were both handcuffed to their escorts and led towards the door. On the way out, Jerome looked at Sir Adrian Lusher. 'Up yours,' he said to him as he was taken out. Bouton paused for a while when he was passing by Delaney. His escort, Grafton, allowed him to. Bouton looked deep into Delaney's eyes. 'Very good, Mr Delaney; very good. But perhaps you need to look closer to home as well. Maybe even a little higher up.'

No one in the room acted upon the comment as the door was shut.

Delaney received the usual 'well done' from everyone. He said he was indebted to Mike Herbert for the information about the phone call, and they agreed to meet up for a drink sometime soon. The Home Secretary was the first to leave, saying that his driver would be getting impatient; he had to get to a meeting at Whitehall. Herbert put a hand on Lusher's shoulder as they left. 'Do you think this is finished now?'

'No,' said Lusher. 'I didn't like Bouton's last remark.'

'Me neither, keep in touch.'

Everyone went back to their duties and to prepare statements for the press.

Bouton and Jerome were taken down to the waiting cars. The doors to the first Jaguar were opened and Grafton and Bouton got into the back, still handcuffed. The second Jaguar pulled up and when Poole and Jerome were seated, both cars took off at a good speed.

The two car convoy made its way through the traffic towards Heathrow. When the cars had travelled a few miles, Bouton turned to his guard, Grafton, in the first car. 'Where are we going?'

'A location near the airport, sir. You will be questioned here before flying to Boston tomorrow'.

'Why here?'

'Can't say; it's just my job to get you there'.

'Where?'

'Can't say, sir'.

In the second Jaguar, Jerome was looking out of the window; a stunned, ashen face. His escort Poole looked at him. 'Soon be there, sir. You okay?'

Jerome didn't speak.

The first car came to a stop at some temporary traffic lights. A youth wearing a hi-visibility vest looked up from his work as the two shiny dark blue Jaguars took his eye. Bouton muttered something about British road works. The second car pulled up behind, leaving plenty of space between them. Jerome turned to Poole and pointed to the car in front. 'You know that guy up ahead is the real bad guy in all of this? He was the one whose idea it was. I just joined in for the money.'

Poole glanced at him briefly and then continued to look forward, his thin chiseled face looking indifferent. Jerome continued. 'And when I say money, I mean a lot of it; an awful lot of it. Enough so you and the driver here will never have to work again.'

Jerome looked in the rear view mirror to see the driver looking back at him. 'What do say driver? A couple of million okay for you?' The driver looked forward, ignoring the remark. Poole shook his head and held up a hand. 'Just leave it there please, Mr Jerome; no more talk.'

Jerome looked around him. 'I guess if I was to try this door, it would be locked, right?'

'No, sir, it's not locked,' said Poole. He looked at Jerome as though he was looking at a crack dealer who had just lied to him. They're on about the same level, he thought, except the crack dealer wouldn't have his team mates killed. 'It's open, sir; go ahead if you want to. Then I'll shoot you in the back, you son of a bitch.'

Jerome stared back at him hard. 'I don't think you would young man.'

'Try me.'

Both cars were still stationary. Jerome tried the handle of the door. It was not locked. He opened the door half an inch and looked across again at Poole. Then he closed the door. 'Huh, okay fellah, you win. Maybe I should have…'

Wherever it came from, the first bullet smashed through the window and into the side of Jerome's head. The second passed through his neck and hit Poole in the shoulder. Two more bullets followed, almost decapitating the driver; the inside of the windows now, dripping red. Two more huge crashes sounded out as bullets tore through the rear windows, Poole taking two or three more bullets in the back and neck as he tried to dive out of his door.

The driver of the first car saw it all in his mirror. 'Down now! Down!' He pushed his foot down hard as Bouton and Grafton covered their heads. The car smashed through the temporary barrier, accelerating hard. They got about 30 metres. The rifle propelled grenade hit the car just behind the rear seats, near the double fuel tanks. It tore through the rear bulkhead and exploded, ripping off the two rear doors, dismembering Grafton and Bouton. The blast lifted the car upwards and forwards about 20 metres and it came to rest on the trench that was being dug by the youth, burying him beneath its mangled remains. A woman on a bicycle caught the full pressure of the blast and was hurled through a nearby shop window. Other pedestrians were thrown to the ground and when the blast had expended, the screams started. The heat from the blazing wreckage started to crack shop windows and a man with his back on fire rolled on the floor in an attempt to extinguish himself. Drivers of other vehicles sat stunned as they observed the scene. Everything seemed stationary and lifeless, save for the screams and the black smoke rising from the wreckage.

Forty yards away, a dirty, grey van that had been parked in a side street adjacent to the road works, moved slowly away as its back doors were being closed. It had been parked there for some time. A day earlier the CCTV's in that area had stopped working.

10

In Delaney's office, Jones and Wyatt were going through the case, reviewing what had happened. Brandon Jones was the zealous one. He did most of the talking. He had enjoyed being Delaney's right hand man because Burton was laid up in hospital but he wished it had been for another reason. At the age of 35, he thought he was ready for a step up the ladder and the last few days had given him a chance to prove it. He did not know that Delaney had already considered this and had decided that Jones needed a few more years under his belt.

Jones' optimistic, lively disposition went well with his looks and the smart attire. His thin face, brown eyes and constant thin smile, made him easy to look at and this had often fooled his adversaries; 'you don't have to *look* hard, to *be* hard,' he had once told someone.

Ben Wyatt was earthier. He was a few years older than Jones, but was satisfied with his position in life. Like the police constables that get into a certain job and stay there for years, not wanting promotion, happy to serve. His chubby, face with blue eyes and auburn eyebrows was not the sort of face people looked twice at, which was a help in his line of business. The strong nose – with a scar, courtesy of a knife wielding Nottingham youth – suited the solid chin and neck. Delaney had grown tired of repeating himself when questioning Wyatt's dress sense but had decided he was good enough at his job to accept the odd pair of dirty jeans and un-ironed denim shirt now and again.

Delaney joined them having watched Jerome and Bouton being driven off some fifty minutes earlier. Wyatt poured him a coffee as he explained what he and Jones had been discussing. It was Jones who wanted to conclude the review. 'Well, it just shows that, as you've said before sir; no one is incorruptible or beyond temptation, let's admit it, ninety million is a lot.'

'Yes it is, Brandon, but you still spend your entire life looking over your shoulder.'

'Doesn't matter either way,' Wyatt added. 'Fact is, they are criminals of the worst kind. We should bring back hanging. I'd pull the lever; gladly'.

The phone on Delaney's desk rang. The digital read out said *Lusher*.

'Sir Adrian Lusher,' Delaney said to his men with a smile. 'Probably phoning to say well done.'

'Yeah right,' said Wyatt in his blasé manner.

Delaney leaned over, touched the answer key and put the phone on speaker. 'Sir Adrian. Good evening.'

As head of MI5, Sir Adrian Lusher was well known for his quiet voice. This time though, he was angry. 'Well?'

'Well what? Delaney replied.

'Bouton and Jerome!'

'What about them?'

'You don't know do you, Delaney? About Bouton and Jerome and their escorts and drivers.'

Delaney looked at Jones and Wyatt. They looked back with worried faces. Delaney spoke again. 'What is it, Adrian? Sorry, we haven't heard anything.'

'They're dead man, they're dead! The whole frigging lot of them! Hit on the way to the airport, rifle fire, grenades, six people, two cars, one member of the public, dead!'

The three men looked at each other again and seemed to draw breath simultaneously.

Delaney was ruffled. 'We'll get onto it straight away,' he said. 'Do MI6 and the Americans and Canadians know yet?'

'No no, too soon, the whole thing happened just minutes ago. My people will take care of that. The escorts and the drivers Delaney; those poor bastards. I want who did this, and so will every section leader in British Intelligence. And you know what this means don't you? It means that whoever had them hit was probably higher up the ladder than they were!'

'Not necessarily, ninety million is a lot. Anyone who had a share of that coming would have been pretty angry not to get it.'

'But, Delaney that's just it; no one could have arranged such a hit at such short notice. No one even knew we had brought them to London.'

'Someone knew. They must have done. I need to find out who.'

'Yes yes, well do so then for heaven's sake before anyone else gets blown apart!'

Delaney looked puzzled as he spoke to the phone again. 'We will do, but I trust MI6, MI5 and Special Branch will do their bit as well.'

'Meaning what, Delaney?'

'Meaning that all of us need to throw what we can at this,' said Delaney. When there was no reply from Lusher he continued. 'And I'm working on the authority of the home office. You may have been knighted but you report to Martin Hamilton, the Home Secretary, and so do I, that makes us equal, so please remember that in future.'

The phone went dead.

Delaney looked at his colleagues. 'Any ideas?'

Wyatt spoke next. 'Jerome was one of the top narcotics men in the States. Bouton was head of CSS. For someone to kill these people, and four of our boys in such a way, they need to be damned ruthless. People are as ruthless as that because either, *a,* it's in their blood or *b*, a lot of money means a lot to them.'

'But it can't be the money,' said Jones, 'killing Jerome and Bouton, wouldn't make any difference to that; and we retrieved the money from the box in Paris didn't we?'

'I don't think so,' said Delaney. 'I'll contact Landers again. Time we started to make some phone calls gentlemen.'

Jones and Wyatt got themselves seated at their desks. Wyatt was to phone Sally Curtis to let her know of the bizarre events and Jones started calling in a few favours from some of their more reliable informants. They needed to know where all of this weaponry was coming from.

Delaney phoned Stephen Landers. He was still at his hotel, not due back in Paris until the next morning. 'Stephen, it's Tom.'

'Hi, Tom, I was just about to phone you. You know then?'

'Yes. How do you know?'

'How do I know? Get this. I'm staying at the Ramada Jarvis on Bayswater Road. I heard it all. I knew it was a hit; I've heard those noises before. It happened a couple of streets away. When I went out to have a look, I recognised our cars; just. They made a mess of them. Someone out there knows his stuff.'

Delaney delayed his answer as he thought about what Landers had just said. 'Yes, well you were right. It was our cars. And our men.'

'Do you want me to postpone my return to Paris to help out?'

'No, get back there please. But tell me, that box in Paris, the ninety million.'

'Yes?'

'You did tell me there was ninety million in the box didn't you?'

'Yes. Well, in a few boxes, ninety million takes up a lot of space.'

'Did you get permission to keep the boxes?'

'No, I'm still working on that. The Gendarmerie invented the saying, Red Tape.'

'Quite. Okay thank you, Stephen. Have a good journey. Perhaps if you could confirm everything for me when you get back.'

'Of course, Tom, of course, au revoir old boy and err, I hope you get the bastards. I knew Grafton by the way; he was on an Interpol course with me a while back; he had a wife and three children. We have a bad apple amongst us, Tom.'

'Say again?'

'Think about it; who knew we had Jerome and Bouton? And who knew they were taken away in the two cars?'

'Not many of us.'

'Right, Tom. *Us* being the operative word.'

The following morning, Delaney, Wyatt, Jones and Curtis gathered in the office again. Curtis, Jones and Wyatt sat in the old leather chairs spread out around the room. Delaney half sat on his desk, a newspaper in his hand. He looked at Sally and spoke quietly to her. 'Well, so what do you think about your Mr Bouton?'

Curtis shrugged her shoulders. 'He's not the first and won't be the last.'

'No, I'm sure your right. So team, what ideas do we have?'

Jones as usual, was the first to speak. 'We need to sit back and consider all the possibilities don't we, sir?'

'Yes, I think we do, Brandon. Go on then, you first.'

Jones pulled himself up in his chair and half crossed his arms, one finger on his chin. 'Right, let's go back a few days. One, Marcus was shot. We don't know who did that yet. Two, we had the grenade attack on us here. Then you remembered the Farrah brother's case that Marcus had worked on, and we realised that someone else had the ninety million drugs money when the Farrah brothers were put away. Three, we found out about the deposit box in Paris and who rented it; Bouton. Four, we collared Bouton and Jerome and before we can get them back to their countries to be dealt with, someone takes them out. So, who would want to do that?'

'Must be for money,' said Curtis, 'ninety million is a lot.'

'But they haven't got the money, we have. We did get access to the box didn't we?'

Delaney interrupted. 'So if they didn't have the money, the only other reason to kill Jerome and Bouton would be to stop them talking.'

'Exactly,' Wyatt joined in. 'That's what I think. They were killed to shut them up. And whoever organised it must have had a bloody good reason. A full on hit like that is serious stuff by serious people.'

'Serious people like the Farrah brothers.' Delaney said.

'Of course,' Wyatt replied. 'Even locked up they could arrange a hit.'

Jones and Curtis nodded in agreement. Delaney stood up and took the newspaper he was holding to Curtis. 'Well people, I think they did arrange the hit. Just for spite. That's the sort of people they are. Now; being from eastern Canada, Sally, I bet you can speak French can't you?'

'Yes, of course.'

'Good, have a look at this newspaper.'

'It's Le Figaro,' she said.

'Yes, it is. Translate for Ben and Brandon here, what the headline on page two says.'

Curtis opened the paper and turned to page two. There was a pause for a while as she was taking it in and double checking what she had read. She looked at Delaney first. 'Why didn't you tell us this five minutes ago?' she said.

'I wanted your ideas first. Go on; tell these two what it says.'

Curtis looked at Jones and Wyatt and then back at the paper. *'Paris bank hit by gang – haul estimated at 150 million dollars.'*

Jones and Wyatt looked at each other and said nothing. Delaney sat back down, looked at them both and then spoke to Curtis again. 'Have a look through the rest of the article will you and see if you can spot anything else that might be useful.'

'Of course, excuse me.' She took up a seat at another desk and started to read the article in full.

Delaney addressed Wyatt and Jones before they had gathered their thoughts and got over the shock. 'Right guys; let's see where we are now. And yes, by the way, the bank that was hit, *was* the one with the ninety million in a deposit box. Brandon, you first; how did you get on with those phone calls you made to the informants?'

Jones took his note book from his jacket pocket and started to go through the notes. 'Right, you both probably remember Chalkie McPhail; he gave us some of the information on the Houseman case in 2007. Well his cousin, another snout, according to him, told him that the Farrah brothers tried to do a deal with some of our people as well as the USA Narcotics people and the Canadian Secret Service. They were going to name the two people who turned a blind eye on some of their drug dealings in return for some kind of amnesty.'

'The *two people* would have been Jerome and Bouton then,' said Delaney, 'go on.'

'I spoke to MI6 and apparently that was true but the deal was turned down. McPhail reckons the Farrahs gave instructions for the hit on Bouton and Jerome. No reason to disbelieve him, he knows how the Farrahs work, he did a job for them himself years ago before they went big time.'

Curtis had finished reading the rest of the article and pulled her chair up towards the others. Delaney looked at her, eyebrows raised. 'Anything else?'

'No not really, it was the deposit boxes that they targeted at the bank, so I think we can safely say that the ninety million was what they wanted.'

'Okay thanks,' said Delaney. 'Go on, Brandon.'

'Right, sir, well there was something else that came out of my chat with McPhail. Apparently some of the big drug gangs are really missing the Farrah brothers since they were put away; word is that someone is planning to get them out.'

'Any ideas who?'

'No, but McPhail thought it might be soon, because of the big amounts of income being missed out on.'

'Where are the Farrah brothers?' asked Wyatt.

'Separated of course. One is in Nottingham, John, the younger one of the two, and Alan, the older one, the decision maker, is in Manchester.'

Delaney frowned slightly and said, 'So if someone is going to try to get them out, they could try for both of them or just Alan, the decision maker.'

'But I remember,' Curtis joined in. 'Marcus always said that the Farrah brothers were inseparable and always ran things together. Not sure you're right about it just being Alan; I think they would go for both.'

Delaney looked at her. 'How much did you learn about the Farrahs from Marcus?'

'Not that much, you know what it's like; none of us really talk to our partners, wives or boyfriends about our cases much do we? But I do remember him saying about the Farrahs' being close. He told me about some of their connections as well, just like we said a few days ago, they dealt with people in London, Cologne, Nairobi, Chicago and Toronto. The last two being the reason that Jerome and Bouton were involved.'

'Okay,' Delaney said, 'So they had Jerome on the payroll in Chicago and Bouton on the payroll in Toronto. You know what my next question is don't you?' He looked at all of them in turn.

'Yep.' Wyatt joined in, 'Who is on the payroll in the other three places?'

'Mm,' Delaney replied. 'Who indeed; and we have to assume that whoever was, or is, on the payroll in London is the same person who betrayed us and gave out enough information to someone for them to arrange hits on Marcus, our offices, Sally at the safe house *and* Bouton and Jerome.'

'Right,' said Jones, 'but for someone to have access to all that information, to know what we're doing and where we are *and* to want to keep Jerome and Bouton quiet, must have to be pretty high up, yes?'

'Very high up,' replied Wyatt, 'high enough to know what Special Branch and MI6 were doing as well. Don't forget they've also been involved.'

Delaney sighed and stood up. He walked over to the window. The window that had been blasted out a few days earlier. The street below was busy; hundreds of people going about their everyday lives. He wondered how many of them actually thought from time to time about what goes on in offices like this all over the country to keep them safe and to stop things getting worse. He remembered a quote from a Sheriff in America many years ago when he was asked by a reporter whether or not he was winning the war against drugs and terrorism. The Sheriff had replied. 'No, we're not winning. But I hate to think what it would be like if we weren't trying.'

The other three said nothing. They could see that he wanted silence for a while. Delaney turned without looking at them and sat down in his chair, his elbows on the desk, and his forehead in his hands. After a while he looked up. 'Right, Sally, will you talk to your people in Toronto, make sure it's okay for you to continue working with us for a while, hopefully it will be. Let me know what they say. Brandon, you get down to Paris, see Stephen Landers and get as much information as you can on the bank job. Stephen or someone there must have an inkling as to who pulled it off, or at least some sort of confirmation that it was the Farrahs who gave the instructions. Ben, we have to consider the other places as well as London. Get yourself down to Cologne and meet our contact there. Brief him over the phone before you go, he might already know about the Farrah's contacts over there anyway. Okay everyone?'

They all acknowledged simultaneously.

'What about you, sir?' asked Jones, 'You working alone as well?'

'I'm going to tidy up some paper work from some other cases. Then I'm going to see Taffy in hospital, and then I'm going home. I won't be around tomorrow; I'm going to visit Alan Farrah in Her Majesty's Prison Manchester.'

11

When Delaney arrived at the hospital he was pleased to see Taffy Burton looking much better. He had been in hospital for nearly two weeks and the medical staff and nurses had treated him like a hero. Burton smiled at his boss when he saw him. 'Hello, sir, good to see you.'

'Hello you old trooper, how are you?'

'Oh I'm better, as you can see; they're letting me out tomorrow.'

'Good, what about working, I'm sure you're missing it!'

'I am actually, in all seriousness, can't wait to get back, the doctor says about two weeks, as long as I take the first few weeks easy.'

'Sure, well you can do some of my back log of paperwork for me.'

'Err, right, sir, if I must.'

Delaney pulled up a chair to the bedside and told Burton about all the events of the last few days. Burton had read some articles in newspapers and some of his friends who had visited had also told him what they knew. He was keen to contribute. 'If you're sending Ben to Cologne, sir, tell him to ask for Michael Donner. He's the second in command out there. Remember I had to go there last year? The man in charge in Cologne is Muhler; a miserable sort, I didn't get much from him.'

'Yes I remember, good call Taffy, I'll tell Ben.'

Delaney's mobile phone rang. A nearby nurse called to him. 'No phones please!'

'That's an old wives tale isn't it these days?' he replied.

'No it's not so…'

Delaney ignored her and looked to see who was calling him before answering. 'Hi, what was the answer?' After a minute he spoke again. 'Good. Can you meet me at my place in about an hour?' Another brief pause followed. 'Okay, see you then, I'll tell you how you can help.'

He put his phone away and looked over to the nurse to apologise, but she was looking down at her paperwork shaking her head. He looked again at Burton. 'That was Sally. She can stay here for now, but will probably have to go back to Canada next month.'

'How has she been holding up, sir?' asked Burton.

'She's okay, Taffy. She's tired, but we all are. None of us expected all this to happen.'

'No, bloody hell, what a mess.'

'Yes, that's one way of putting it.'

Angela was upstairs when Delaney got home. She heard him come in and called down to him. 'Hi! Be down in a moment.'

'Hello, I'm coming up to get changed anyway.'

He got out of what he always called his 'uniform' – the jacket, tie and smart shoes – and got into his favourite slacks and loose fitting shirt. As he was doing up his shirt, Angela came from the en-suite, naked apart from a towel around her head. She had a good body, but Delaney always thought that she was shy of letting him see it for some reason.

'Okay?' she said as she kissed him on the cheek.
'Mm, You?'
'Yeah, tired though, I must have typed up about 30 of your colleagues' police reports today'

He smiled. She sat down on the edge of the bed and started to apply her body lotion as she always did, starting with the legs. He looked at her admiringly. 'Want me to do that for you?'

Her hands started to move more slowly as she continued the task. He sat down on the bed next to her and moved his hand onto her leg. She kept looking down and then started to breath slightly heavier. 'Okay then.' She said. Delaney lifted her up and laid her on the bed. He applied the lotion to all parts of her body. She stayed on the bed. He took off his slacks and shirt and they made love.

About thirty minutes later, they were making their way downstairs as the doorbell rang. Delaney remembered the call he had had at the hospital from Curtis. 'That'll be Sally Curtis, the Canadian? I asked her to pop in for a while so I could talk to her about something. Don't mind do you?'

'No, of course not, I'm doing a chilli; it can easily be kept warm.'

'Thanks, sexy legs.' He tapped the back of her thighs and went to answer the door.

Curtis was ushered politely into the living room. Delaney introduced her to Angela. 'Angela this is Sally, the lady from Canada who's been working with us just lately.'

Delaney then turned to Sally. 'Sally, this is Angela.' He noticed a certain look in the eyes of both of the ladies. The two women paused for a while looking at each other. Curtis walked confidently over to Angela and shook her hand. 'Great to meet such an understanding lady; he must be a nightmare to live with!' she said.

'Charming!' uttered Delaney.

'He can be,' said Angela. She smiled at Delaney, thinking about the last 30 minutes. 'But he has his good points.'

Delaney kept things moving. 'Okay you two, that'll do. Well, have a seat, Sally, it won't take long, I just wanted to explain a few things, now I know you can stay with us for a while longer.'

Sally took up a seat near the coffee table and Delaney sat opposite her on the sofa.

'I'll leave you to it, Tom and go and finish the chilli,' said Angela.

Curtis looked uncomfortable. 'Oh no, I'm going to be in the way aren't I?'

'No you're not, you carry on, I'm used to it,' said Angela as she smiled and went through to the kitchen.

Delaney offered Curtis a drink which she refused and they both sat back in a more relaxed frame of mind. Curtis was keen not to keep him too long. 'Right,' she said, 'you said you wanted to see me, so go ahead.'

'Yes, okay, I'm pleased you can stay with us for a while longer. I think you could be very useful.'

'I'm always useful, Tom.' She smiled.

'Yes of course, but this time you could be the king pin for solving this whole operation.'

'Right. Go on.'

'Who knows you Sally, in our lot I mean, TOLA, Special Branch, MI5, MI6; who actually knows you?'

'They all do. They know of my involvement with Marcus and the Canadians as well as how I've been working with you.'

'No they don't. They don't know you. They know your name, but they haven't seen you.'

There was a few seconds silence as Curtis thought through events and Delaney let her. She leaned forward in her seat. 'You mean, they know my name, but they haven't met me.'

'That's exactly what I mean. All the meetings me and the guys have had with any of them, you haven't been there. And furthermore, as far as they know, you went back to Canada after we had arrested Jerome and Bouton.'

'Yes, okay, you're right, go on then, spit it out.'

'What?' said Delaney innocently.

'Your idea you old devil, you've had an idea haven't you?'

'Yes, sorry, I won't dwell any longer. Will you go undercover?'

Curtis paused and then slumped back into the chair and sighed heavily. It was as if she was expecting it. But it still wasn't easy. She had been undercover before and she had been successful. On one operation, with Marcus as her back-up, she had almost been raped. It was her quick thinking and tenacity that had got her through it, even though it had involved killing an innocent person as well as the gang leader and one of his girls. She had refused a bravery award from the Canadian Government.

Delaney decided to let her speak first. He got up and moved towards the kitchen. 'I'll be back shortly,' he said, 'just have a think about it.' He spent a couple of minutes in the kitchen pouring him and Angela some wine. They clinked glasses and he said to her quietly, 'won't be long, we'll be going through all the details tomorrow.'

'Doesn't matter anyway, it'll keep.' She said pointing her head towards the large pan of chilli on the cooker.

Curtis was standing up when he went back into the room. 'Why don't you take a bit longer to think about it?' he said to her, 'come and see me tomorrow.'

'You realise that I'll have to clear it with my people in Toronto.'

'Err, actually. I, already have.'

She looked at him and couldn't think of what to say, but she had to say something. She walked towards the front door to leave without looking at him as she said, 'You bastard.'

He said nothing.

As she opened the door, she turned to face him. 'And the answer is yes. See you tomorrow. And it had better be good.'

The following day she was still annoyed with him. She was waiting for him in his office when he arrived. He looked at her and smiled. 'Coffee?'

'No thank you; water.'

He poured her a cup of water from the cooler and pulled his chair around from behind his desk to sit in front of her. He looked at her, as he often he did, with admiration. Her dark eyes were looking into his, and her young, flawless complexion made him wonder how a woman looking like this, could be so tough and adventurous? They broke the mould when she was born, that was for sure, he thought to himself. His emotions started to get the better of him, like a father looking out for his daughter as she was growing up. He coughed quietly and took a sip of his coffee, hoping she wouldn't notice his weak spot.

'Sorry I swore at you last night,' Curtis said.

'I deserved it. I should have spoken to you before Toronto, not the other way around.'

'I guess it's just typical of you though, Tom. You have this something that allows you to do improper things and still come out of it being liked.'

'Sorry.'

'So you should be. You bastard.' She said quietly, this time with a small smile on her face. 'Right let's get to it. What did you have in mind?'

He sat back, feeling a bit more relaxed and laid out his plans for her.

'Brandon should be in Paris by now and Ben in Cologne. I'm hoping they'll find out some good stuff that will help, but meanwhile, there's no reason why we can't get things moving here.'

'Okay, I'm listening.'

'It could have been someone very high up in any of the intelligence agencies who had Jerome and Bouton killed. It could have been the Farrahs. It could have been both, working together. I think it was Jerome or Bouton who had Marcus killed because he was too close to something. I think Marcus was still working on the case unofficially, Sally. That's why they had him taken out.'

'All things considered, you're probably right.'

This was typical of her professionalism, he thought. He continued. 'This afternoon I'm going to see Alan Farrah; I made the appointment on my way here. I'm going to show him this picture.' He took a photo out of his pocket and showed it to her. It was a picture of Curtis. She looked at the picture. It had been taken about two years ago for an undercover operation in Canada and showed her supposedly enjoying a bar-b-cue in someone's garden. Two weeks after it had been taken she had been almost raped and hanged.

She turned the photo over. On the back it said, *just for you my darling, love Melanie XX.* She passed the photo back to Delaney, without speaking.

'Do you remember why it was taken?' he said.

'Yes, the Monroe case; nasty business. Alan Farrah knows the Monroes. He was at one of their parties. I was Melanie Leeder, a kind of gangster's woman. We got Monroe, but the Farrahs got out of the way before it all kicked off.'

'I understand it got a bit tricky for you towards the end.'

'Damn right it did. Are you about to ask me what I think you are?'

'Yes. I want you to be Melanie Leeder again.'

12

Earlier that morning, Ben Wyatt's plane had touched down at Cologne Airport ten minutes early at 06.35. Delaney had told him to contact Michael Donner, as Taffy Burton had advised. To Wyatt's surprise there was a car waiting for him. The driver had been waiting at the arrivals gate holding up his sign that said *'BIBLIOTHEK'* the German for library, which was the word used to greet all assignees from British Intelligence, including TOLA.

The driver explained to Wyatt that he was to drop him off at the meeting point. The meeting time was 07.30 and after about an hour they were approaching a small market square with restaurants, shops and tourists, already waiting in cues for their tour coaches. The driver said to Wyatt, 'This is the Fischmarkt, sir, fish market? Yes?'

'Yes, I saw the sign, very nice it is. Is this where I will find Donner?'

'Yes, sir, he is here.'

The driver pulled up near a café. The coffee smelt good and the outside tables were already filling up with tourists and people on their way to work who had stopped off for their coffee and pastries. The buildings around the square looked, well, fun, Wyatt thought; four and five stories, painted yellow, blue, pink and green, their tall narrow peaked roofs intersecting the blue skyline. The tables outside the café were covered in orange and red table cloths and the cushioned chairs were green and yellow. The driver pointed to a man sitting at a table near the door of the café, away from the road. He smiled and nodded at Wyatt without saying anything. Wyatt thanked the driver and made his way towards the table. The man waiting for him stood up and introduced himself. His English was faultless. 'Good morning, Mr Wyatt, good to meet you. I am Donner, Michael.'

'Hi, Michael, Ben Wyatt, nice to be here, makes a change.'

'Been to Cologne before?'

'No never,' said Wyatt as he looked around him. 'Is all of Cologne as nice as this?'

'We don't do too badly for quite a big city, but of course we have our poorer suburbs and enough organized crime to keep me busy anyway.'

Donner ordered coffee and pastries for both of them. His phone rang as the waitress was walking away and he answered it, excusing himself. Wyatt took the opportunity to assess his foreign colleague. He was about 45, with short cut dark brown hair and a well trimmed, full beard. His narrow spectacles were high on his small nose and the brown eyes seemed to be taking in everything, albeit subconsciously. The pronounced muscles on his hands and forearms were evidence of a regular gym goer or weight lifter. A minute later he had finished his phone call. 'Sorry, Ben, another matter.'

Wyatt waved his hand politely as if to say, that's fine. Donner returned his phone to his jacket pocket and resettled himself in his chair. He looked at Wyatt and hesitated before speaking. 'So, how can I help? I understand you are looking into some case or cases related to the Farrah brothers.'

'Yes, you know of them?'

'I think, Ben, most intelligence services in Europe know of them.'

'Right, well, it all started about four weeks ago when one of the Canadian Secret Service boys we were working with got killed, in Munich. His name was Marcus Hanson. His partner Sally Curtis is still working with us. We tracked down a large amount of money that was linked to a drugs deal that the Farrah brothers got put away for. It's understood that they had links with someone in Cologne.'

Donner nodded in acknowledgement. 'They did indeed have links here, Ben, go on.'

'Well they also had links in Chicago and Toronto, and the two people concerned were brought back to London to be charged and arrested but…'

'But they were hit, shot. The car bombed or something?'

'Right. You must have heard of it then?'

'Yes we did,' said Donner, nodding.

'And they were very close to the top,' continued Wyatt, 'so we think that whoever had them killed was also someone senior, probably to stop them talking. Either that or it was the Farrah brothers in revenge. Either way we have two things to sort out. Getting the people who killed Marcus Hanson, who are probably the same people who killed the guys from Chicago and Toronto; as well as the drivers and guards, and getting back the ninety million that was taken from a bank in Paris, just as we were about to have it retrieved for the courts.'

'And maybe,' said Donner leaning forward, 'stopping the people in Cologne from being killed as well.'

'Yes. Chances are that someone in Cologne and Nairobi were also on the payroll.'

'I personally would say it was the Farrah brothers who did these killings,' said Donner. 'Just to make a point. They are pretty ruthless I understand.'

'Yes, it seems so. I personally have not dealt with them.'

The waitress appeared from the doorway. She set down two pots of coffee and a selection of pastries. Donner smiled at her in acknowledgement and put some money on her tray. She smiled back and turned to walk to another table. Wyatt looked around at her and Donner could see he was admiring her legs. Wyatt turned to face Donner again and raised his eyebrows.

'What is it about you British men,' Donner said, smiling. 'You can't seem to pass a female without, err, I think the word is letching?'

'Maybe,' Wyatt said, also smiling. 'Not sure it's just us though. Anyway, an E-mail on my Blackberry when I was on the way here, said that you could maybe take me to someone who might be able to help.'

Donner took a photo from his jacket pocket. As he did so, Wyatt could see the shoulder holster; full. He handed the photo to Wyatt and waited for a comment. The photo was of a man in a wheelchair. About 50; shaven head, large nose, strong jaw and small eyes that could hardly be seen under huge white eyebrows. He was wearing a T-shirt that had across its front *Kenya National Parks*. Kenya, thought Wyatt, could that be the Nairobi connection? He frowned and looked at Donner. 'Is this the man you're taking me to meet?'

'No; I thought that it would get you thinking, that's all, Ben. But the man I am taking you to meet knows the man in the photo and what he does for a living. He may be able to give you some information that will help.'

'Okay, so let's finish the coffee and get on with it.'

'No hurry my friend. He only lives a couple of kilometres away and he is quite old. I do not think he will be going anywhere early this morning, or any morning.'

The coffees and some of the pastries finished off, they made their way towards a small road leading off the square. Donner walked in a relaxed manner, almost too casual for Wyatt's liking. He was observant, always looking up as well as around him. Wyatt of course did not know where to look. He was not on home turf. After some time they turned into a large park. Wyatt noticed a sign that said Frankenwerft and they crossed a busy road. Another sign then said Rhein and he realized where he was. The river was wide and grey. A large white tourist river boat swept slowly and quietly past, empty now, probably on its way to its first pick up of the day.

Donner looked at Wyatt as they walked on and pointed in the direction the boat was going. 'Just down here, another one hundred metres.'

Wyatt nodded.

Some small boathouses lined the river, set amongst trees. A path led them to what looked like the oldest of the boathouses, painted blue, but not recently. The windows were covered in lace curtains and the door was an old plywood sheet with a knob on it. Donner knocked on the door four times. Nothing happened. After a minute, he knocked again. The door was opened by a tall man. Wyatt guessed between 80 and 90. His face looked quite frail, but his deportment was proud and straight. The black framed spectacles were crooked on his face which somehow went with the old cardigan that was leaning the same way.

He looked at Donner and then Wyatt, slowly. The door was opened wide and he pointed to two chairs near a window which looked out onto the river. Donner said something in German to the old man and Wyatt waited for a moment before speaking. 'Will you be translating then?' he said.

'Wait a minute please.' Donner replied.

'Sorry.'

The old man looked at Donner and pointed to a chair. Donner got up and moved the chair closer to Wyatt. The old man sat in it and looked at him. 'No young man, he will not be translating. I am not German.'

Wyatt nodded and smiled. 'My apologies, sir.'

Donner did the introductions. 'Mr. Hoetger, this is Ben Wyatt, the British man I told you about. Ben this is Joseph Hoetger.'

Wyatt put his hand out towards Hoetger who responded and shook it gently.

Hoetger looked into Wyatt's eyes and spoke quietly. 'You are looking for information Mr Wyatt? Donner tells me it is a very nasty case and many people have already been killed.'

At that moment Wyatt realized the old man's accent was South African. 'Yes, sir,' he said.

The old man shook his head in a grieving way and then spoke again, this time to Donner. 'Did you show him the photograph?'

'Yes I did,' replied Donner. He took the photo from his pocket and handed it to the old man. 'This one. I think you said it was taken just a few months ago.'

'Yes that is correct,' replied the old man, before looking at Wyatt again. 'Now, Mr Wyatt, do you have any specific questions for me?'

Wyatt pulled himself up in his chair. 'Not really, sir, I didn't know about the man in the photo until Michael here showed it to me. Michael said that you would be able to explain who it is,'

'Very well, Mr Wyatt. That is correct.'

The old man passed the photo back to Donner. He rested his hands between his legs and looked down as he spoke, without looking at either of them. 'You should remember what the man in the photo looks like Mr Wyatt. It may help you in the future. That man is now 48 years old. He was brought up in a small town in Kenya, about 30 kilometres from Nairobi. His best subjects at school were mathematics and geography. He left Kenya when he was 22, although he likes to go back whenever he can. He moved to England because he wanted to be in the British Army. He did very well and made it to the rank of Sergeant. In 1981 he almost lost both his legs in a Belfast bombing. He is paralysed from the waist down. He was fit though and survived it well. When he realized he would spend the rest of his life in and out of a wheelchair, he became bitter, very bitter. He is very tough Mr Wyatt. Remember that.'

Wyatt then looked at Donner. 'Michael, you showed me the photo of that man and now Mr Hoegter here is explaining to me how tough he is. Are you both going to tell me that this man is still active, and that he's working for the other side?'

'Oh yes, Ben,' said Donner, 'He is active, he is on the other side and there is more than a remote possibility that he may be just *one* of the men you need to go after. Before he kills again. And he will.'

Wyatt looked at the old man. 'And Mr Hoetger, are you now going to tell me what this man's name is?'

Hoetger moved his hands from between his legs and folded them in front of him. He looked up at Wyatt.

'He has many names, Aldo Biolli, Charlie Trent, Lance Plater, to name just a few. He usually changes his name every few months. Mr Donner here still does not know where he gets his identities and passports from, do you Mr Donner?'

'No.' Donner said. 'We don't.'

Hoetger unfolded his arms and looked at the floor again while speaking to Wyatt. 'Well whatever name he is using now, Mr Wyatt, he is using it in Britain. He has been there for two weeks. And in case you haven't worked it out yet, he is right now, probably the most successful hit man in Europe.'

Wyatt sat back, sighed and wiped his hands outwards across his eyebrows. Wait until Delaney hears this one, he thought. After a brief pause Donner stood up as though to leave and Wyatt followed his lead. The old man tried to stand also but could not.

'Stay there, sir,' said Wyatt, 'no need for you to get up. And thank you very much for this. Do you mind if I ask you if you were once in the service sir?'

'No I was not.'

Wyatt looked quizzically at Donner, who said nothing.

Turning back to look at the old man once more, Wyatt went to shake his hand. 'Well, thank you anyway, sir. I am intrigued to know how you know so much about this man in the photo though, whatever name he is using now.'

The old man then looked at Wyatt in a way he had not seen before; cruelly, impatient. 'Well, Mr Wyatt, whatever name he is using it will not be his real one. His real name is William Hoetger. He is my son. And Alan Farrah's cousin.'

Donner led the way back towards the town centre. They paused for a while on a small bench outside a pastry shop. Donner fetched two coffees in paper cups. Wyatt spoke quietly, so passers-by could not hear him. 'Well, that's what I call quality information.'

'Yes. Mr Hoetger got in touch with us just a few days ago. He was tired of the killing his son was doing. He told him never to contact him again, but he didn't tell him that he was going to inform us. I hope his son doesn't find out, Ben, or I think maybe he would kill his own father,'

'Right; so is this William Hoetger the Farrah brothers Cologne contact?'

'No. Just their cousin. Their Cologne contact was a Heidi Mayer. She was found dead yesterday. Shot five times. Her body had been dumped in a field. Our coroner said she was actually killed about two weeks ago.'

'Two weeks? Mr Hoetger said his son went to Britain about two weeks ago.'

'Yes.'

'So presumably, this William Hoetger had an accomplice, I mean, he's in a wheelchair, and she was dumped in a field.'

'Yes,' repeated Donner.

'Do we know if this accomplice went with him to Britain?'

'No he did not go with him.'

'Sure?'

'Very sure, Ben. I shot him dead last night.'

Wyatt nearly choked on his coffee. Donner continued. 'We had been following him for a while, he realised it and tried to board a train to Belgium. He would not stop when I told him to. I shot him.'

Wyatt said nothing for a few seconds. He finished his coffee and spoke to Donner as he looked down at the pavement. 'So the Farrah brother's Cologne operator was killed by a man in a wheelchair; their cousin, with the help of an accomplice. You shot the accomplice dead; and the wheelchair hit man; real name William Hoetger, has been in Britain for two weeks.'

'That is about it my friend. And Marcus Hanson was killed in Munich, just over two weeks ago.'

'Are you thinking what I'm thinking, Michael?'

'Yes. Hoetger takes out Hanson, travels here to Cologne and takes out Mayer. Then he goes to London; you know the rest.'

'Bloody hell. This is going to get interesting.'

'And nasty, my friend, you and your colleagues need to be very careful.'

13

In his cell in block G, Alan Farrah was reading the last few pages of his book about medieval weaponry. He had waited for this day for a long time. There had been months of planning. The final piece of the plan had been put into place at lunchtime, when the chef on his payroll had slipped a tablet into his serving of peas. He had put the tablet in his pocket to use when the time was right.

He nodded slowly and said to himself, 'amazing, fascinating,' as he read the last sentence in the book and closed it carefully. 'I might just take this with me.'

He had managed to narrow the field somewhat over the last two weeks. His cousin, William had, as usual, been very efficient. The instruction to kill Hanson had come from Pierre Bouton and all Farrah had to do was pass that instruction onto his cousin. That got rid of someone who wouldn't let things go. So, as William was not far from Cologne, why not get rid of the Cologne contact; that would mean more money for the others and the Cologne contact probably would not be of much use on future plans. It was the deaths of Bouton and Jerome that had been the icing on the cake. But this troubled him; because their murder was not instructed by him. Someone else had given *that* order; and he didn't know who. He still had some useful people on his payroll. People who could make sure that he got away with as much as possible. All they needed was a couple of million now and again. Their dishonesty and greed astounded him.

He looked at the clock on the wall. The prison governor had told him that he would be having a visitor this afternoon. He knew of the visitor and what he did for a living. But it really did not matter to him. Not today.

He filled the basin with cold water, sunk his face into it for half a minute then wiped himself with his dry hands. He turned around, picked up the chair he had been using for the last 18 months and threw it against the wall. When it didn't break completely, he picked up what was left and threw it again.

Tom Delaney's driver from the Greater Manchester Police turned the car into Southall Street and up to the entrance of the prison. Being part of the HMP's High Security Estate, the prison had a comprehensive method of entry for visitors. Even Delaney, there with permission of Scotland Yard, was not exempt. The Gatehouse staff welcomed him and recorded his details in the Gate Book. From there he was escorted to reception where he met the Governor, Andrew Tonge, who led him to his office.

'Tea or coffee, Mr Delaney?'

'No thank you, Governor, I'd rather get straight on with it.'

'Sure; I have reserved a private interview room for you, I'll take you there myself.'

The Governor took Delaney down some corridors and through numerous barred doors painted green. Hospital type coloured lines on floors led the way to various departments. The interview room was large; there was a small table to one side of the room, away from the door. Three chairs were placed near the table and another to the side of the door. Along one wall was a wide narrow window, with bars on both sides of it. A single fluorescent tube above the table provided light.

Governor Tonge asked Delaney to take a seat and pointed towards the prison guard that had followed them in. 'Simpson here will have to stay with you, prison rules and all that.'

'Of course,' replied Delaney as he eyed Simpson; an overweight man with a moustache and the look of someone who had done this on many an occasion.

'Right,' continued Tonge, 'I'll get Farrah brought in now then.' Simpson shut the door as Tonge left.

Delaney smiled at Simpson. 'Been in the job long?'

'Thirteen years, sir.'

'You must have dealt with a few hard characters in all that time then.'

'Yes, sir, suppose I have. You get used to it. Not sure if that's a good thing or a bad thing.'

'Yes, see what you mean. Have you had any dealings with Alan Farrah?'

'Escorted him a few times; only internally though; the medical centre and the visitors rooms. He spends a lot of time in the gym.'

'How often does he need to go the medical centre?'

'Quite a bit actually. I think he has some sort of stomach problem.'

'Doesn't blame the food does he?' Said Delaney jokingly.

Simpson allowed himself a small laugh. 'Oh they all do that. I think it's quite good myself.'

Delaney smiled and nodded but didn't continue the conversation. He was concerned with what Simpson had said about Farrah's trips to the medical centre. Four minutes later Governor Tonge returned with another prison officer and Alan Farrah. Simpson looked at Farrah and pointed to a chair that was opposite where Delaney was sitting. Farrah sat down and looked at Delaney. After a few seconds, he stood up and offered his hand to Delaney, who did not respond. He had decided to play this one in his 'hard' mode. 'Sit down Farrah; I'm not here for nice crap like that.'

'That's not very nice,' said Farrah. 'I mean for a diplomat; you are a diplomat aren't you?'

'Perhaps, amongst other things.'

Farrah sat back down and looked around the room and at Simpson rather than Delaney. He looked quite fit. Not all that tall with a clean shaven face with short-cropped, greying hair. The shallow-set, large eyes were almost fish-like. Not, Delaney thought, a prepossessing man.

Farrah looked at Delaney. 'So who are you then?'

Delaney was not sure why he had asked this question. Strict rules dictated that Farrah would have had to have been told exactly who he was going to see and that he had the right to refuse if he wanted to. Remembering to stay in his hard mode, he did not answer. He decided to move in quickly. Seconds later he stood up walked around the other side of the table and half sat on it next to Farrah. Simpson moved slightly, nervous of Delaney's actions. Farrah's ugly eyes stared at Delaney. 'Getting a bit close aren't we? Fancy me do you?'

Delaney kept his poker face. He stood up again, went back to his seat and folded his arms as he spoke. 'So, why did you have Jerome and Bouton killed?'

'Who?'

'Charles Jerome and Pierre Bouton. Were you angry at them for getting all of the ninety million?'

'What ninety million?'

'The ninety million you made from heroin smuggling, and maybe even with a bit of human trafficking thrown in.'

'I was convicted for drugs crimes. That's why I'm here. You know that. But if you want to play games, go ahead.'

'No game, Farrah, just some questions.'

'Right then, next question.'

'Okay, did you also arrange to have the ninety million, and a bit more, lifted from the bank vault in Paris?

'No.'

Wrong answer, thought Delaney. It should have been 'what bank vault.' He stood again and walked across to stand under the long narrow window so Farrah had to turn to see him. 'Come on, Mr Farrah, people like you can arrange to have anything done while you're inside. What's the next instruction you're going to give?'

Farrah looked at him and smiled. 'Hmm, haven't decided yet.'

'Right, last question, who did you hire to kill Marcus Hanson?'

Farrah paused for a while before replying. 'Well as I'm in here for a long time and not guilty of that one, I suppose there's no harm in me telling you. It was someone else who hired Hanson's killer, not me. You may even know him.'

'Right. So with Hanson out of the way, Bouton and Jerome could stay out of trouble. That's why you had those two killed; you were inside and they were going to get your ninety million.'

'Don't know about that one.'

'No, of course you don't.'

Farrah got up from his chair quickly. Simpson moved forward and shouted at him. 'Sit down!'

'No, I won't sit down because this meeting is over. The rules don't allow for you to insist that I stay.'

Simpson looked at Delaney. 'Sir?'

'Fine, let him go. He clearly knows the rules.'

As Farrah walked towards the door, Delaney took a photo from his pocket and held it up in front of him. 'Do you know this woman?'

'No, who is she?'

'Her name is Melanie Leeder and we hear she is wanting a piece of the action as pay back for you helping to get her ex into jail.'

'Who's her ex?'

'Monroe et al; the same Monroe you were involved with in Canada.'

'Old Monroe eh, got put away didn't he?' asked Farrah in an innocent manner.

'Yes he did and Melanie here was one of his girls.'

'Never seen her before, but tell her where I am won't you, she looks good.'

Delaney could see in Farrah's eyes that he did recognize the woman in the photo and that he was lying.

Simpson knocked on the door and two officers walked in and led Farrah out. Delaney decided to try a 'last minute' question. Just as the door was being shut he called out 'Hold on.' The officers turned with Farrah who stood in the doorway. Delaney got close to him and said, 'The ninety million by the way, didn't your people tell you that we had recovered it?'

Farrah moved towards Delaney quickly. Simpson's fist came round and landed in Farrah's stomach, stopping him in his tracks.

'Okay' said Delaney. 'Get him back to his cell.'

The officers led Farrah away. Simpson used his radio to inform the Governor that the meeting was over.

Delaney had lied about the ninety million being recovered, but he knew he had to rattle Farrah. The more he was on his back foot the better.

Governor Tonge arrived back at the interview room and asked if everything was satisfactory. Delaney glanced at Simpson and told the governor that everything was fine. The same police driver that had delivered Delaney was waiting for him at reception and within an hour Delaney was in a queue for his flight back to London.

Within that same hour, Farrah had returned to his cell. He had also swallowed the tablet that the chef had slipped into his peas at lunch time. It was an emetic that would work quickly. As he felt himself feeling more and more nauseous, he shouted out loud through the door. 'Oh god! Someone! I'm bad, my belly again! Ahh!'

The nearest officer to his cell attended and saw him lying on the floor holding his stomach. Another officer then arrived and they pulled Farrah up onto his feet. Farrah gasped and went down again. 'Better get him to the medical centre again,' said one of the officers.

'Yeah, okay. Come on Farrah, you can walk. What's happened to the chair? Did you break it?'

Farrah screamed out in agony again. 'I can't walk you bastards! I'm in agony here!'

'Okay, we'll get you a wheelchair,' said one of the officers, gesturing to his colleague.

The medical centre only had one other person being treated. The other four beds were empty. Farrah was wheeled in and helped onto a bed. He was groaning constantly. A young doctor approached his bed just as he was about to be sick. Perfect timing, thought Farrah. He threw up all over the doctor's forearms and hands. He groaned again as he spoke. 'He hit me; he hit me in the interview room!'

'Who did?' said the young doctor.

'The screw, the screw who was by the door, he's ruptured my spleen! Ahh!'

The young doctor asked the officers to stay with Farrah and ran back to his desk to make a phone call. Farrah groaned, a little quieter this time so he could hear what was being said. The doctor returned and spoke to the officers. 'It seems there could have been an altercation, but the guard has left for the day. He could be right about the spleen. Can one of you call for an ambulance?'

The officers looked at each other and frowned. One said, 'Just fix him up here, doc, I thought you did minor operations in here.'

'We do, but the spleen is not like the appendix! This could kill him! Get the ambulance.'

'We'll have to ask the Governor first.'

'Okay, do so.'

Governor Tonge entered the medical centre two minutes later. Farrah noticed him come in and started to groan louder again. Tonge took the young doctor to one side. 'Spleen you say. Are you sure?'

'Not a hundred percent no, but the pains and the sickness all point to it. It could be something minor, but I'm not sure I would want to wait for as long as the tests will take to find out.'

The Governor shook his head. 'Damn.' After a short pause he confirmed. 'Alright.'

He issued instructions to the two officers. The ambulance arrived very quickly and Farrah was loaded into it. One officer sat with the driver up front, the other with the paramedic and Farrah in the back.

The ambulance moved quickly out of the prison onto Southall Street and on towards Charter Street. The paramedic was looking at Farrah. 'You'll be okay, it won't take long and all of those experts at the hospital can put you right.'

The prison officer moved away from them both to give them more room. He looked at the paramedic. 'Where are we going, the infirmary?'

'Yes of course, the good old MRI.'

About five minutes later, the officer looked out of the side window and turned to face the paramedic again. 'You'd better tell your mate driving that he's just missed a turning; he should have gone down Hathersage Road.'

'It's fine, he knows another way, probably quicker.'

The prison officer knew that there was not another way that was quicker. The paramedic could see the look of doubt on his face.

Farrah began to groan again. The paramedic stood and nudged his way past the officer. 'Excuse me, I need a special pain killer from that cupboard.'

The officer moved his legs out of the way. The paramedic reached into the cupboard, as though feeling for a bag or box. 'Ah, here it is.' As he spoke, he turned quickly, he was holding a small pistol with a silencer on it. He brought the pistol up and shot the officer three times in the chest. Farrah jumped up and kicked the officer out of the way as he was dying. The paramedic knocked hard, three times, on the back of the driver's compartment. The officer sitting next to the driver turned his head as though to look through to the back. 'What does that mean?'

'Trouble,' said the driver.

'What do you mean, is the patient at risk?'

'No, you are.'

'What?'

The driver pulled into a small quiet side street. The observation hatch behind them opened and the officer was shot in the head twice, the force throwing him into the windscreen. The driver got out of the cab and walked around to the rear of the ambulance. He opened the doors; Farrah and the paramedic got out and closed the doors behind them. They all walked slowly down the street for about 30 metres. An old man got out of a Ford minibus and opened the sliding side door. The three men got in. He drove them out along the A56 towards the M60. At the first exit, he left the motorway and headed for an industrial estate. At the bottom end of a quiet cul-de-sac on the estate, he pulled into a small warehouse. A man waiting at the warehouse door closed it after them. They got out of the minibus and into an old Ford Ka. As the Ka was driven out of the warehouse, the man who had been waiting for them set fire to the minibus, closed the warehouse door and made his way quietly and slowly on a bicycle away from the area. As the four men in the Ka approached Hyde some twenty minutes later, the paramedic's mobile phone rang. 'Yes...course it's me stupid...What have you got for us...Right.'

He turned to the others. 'Mich has got a Range Rover for us, false plates, Simmons Street, just down here.'

The driver turned right into Simmons Street and they moved quickly to swap cars. The Range Rover was unlocked and the keys were in the ignition. Within minutes they were heading south. 'Not down the motorway,' said Farrah, 'go down through Derbyshire, the A6, then through Leicester and Bedford.'

'Right boss,' the driver replied. 'Where are we ending up then?'

'Go from Bedford, down the M11, over the bridge and towards Dover.'

'Dover?'

'Yes, Dover.'

The paramedic looked to Farrah. 'What next then, Alan?'

'I'll tell you when we get to Paris.'

14

Sally Curtis was getting impatient. That same afternoon, she had decided to drive to Paris to meet Brandon Jones to see if she could help – against Delaney's wishes.

As instructed by Delaney, Jones had gone to Paris to find out as much as possible about the hit on the bank where the ninety million was being kept. He had met Stephen Landers, their Paris contact, at Orly airport. Landers drove like a racing driver through Paris and pointed out some of the landmarks on the way. His 'office' was a small shop on Rue du Mont Thabor on the Right Bank in Tuileries. The windows were covered in blinds and a small sign said the shop was closed due to relocation. In the back room of the shop, Landers' dusty old desk stood alone in the middle of the room with a modern bright red office chair that did not go with it. Two more chairs occupied corners of the room and three large filing cabinets stood in front of a back door. Jones had asked him why. 'I would have thought that was your second exit'.

'No,' replied Landers, 'this is.' He went over to a corner of the room and poked a stick up towards the ceiling. A loft hatch door came down automatically followed by a ladder. Jones was impressed. 'Crikey, very good, where does that lead to?'

'The upstairs room next door; we own that as well. It's been empty for years. From there I can use a fire escape that leads to the back alley.'

After a quick briefing, Landers had taken Jones to the scene of the bank robbery. It was just a bank, Jones had thought, no special features, no doorman, seven service windows, easy for any professional outfit to hit. Landers had agreed. It was getting dark when Landers drove them to a small hotel and found Jones a room. They rested a while in the hotel bar and swapped stories over a few beers. They were both keen to talk about how things had changed for them since joining TOLA.

'It's the boss that keeps it all together; he's quite a guy,' said Landers.

Jones agreed. 'Yeah, he's done some great work; I think this thing with Marcus and Sally though, is getting to him.'

'How so?'

'Well, he seems to be going the extra mile on this one; less delegation, more doing things for himself.'

'Right; I wouldn't know, stuck here in Paris.'

'We need you out here though, Stephen; at the very least, we need you to translate!'

'Yeah, right.'

Jones moved his weight around in the soft armchair. 'Do you miss the air force or Interpol?' he asked Landers, as a waiter put down two more full bottles.

'No, not really. Sometimes I think I should have stayed in the RAF longer; the pension would have been nice. But with the amount we get paid now, it's not such an issue.'

'Got a woman out here then?'

'Had a couple; one of which was 'well connected', but not right now.'

Jones didn't pursue the issue. Landers leaned forward for a drink of his fresh cold beer. 'What about you? Family alright?'

'Mm, pretty much. Harry is ten now; wants to join the same regiment his old man was in.'

'Do you want him to?'

'Sure why not? Do him good.'

'And Maria?'

'Yeah, she's fine thanks mate. Still organising the local writers club and the car club.'

'Maybe I should get married; settle down; collect trolleys at Waitrose or something.'

Jones laughed. 'I don't think so; you'd be bored stiff!'

Their conversation continued a while longer. Landers told Jones what he had in mind for the following day and excused himself, conscious that they both needed to get some rest.

As Jones was leaving his hotel the next morning for his second meeting with Landers, his mobile phone rang. He could see who it was calling him, but he didn't know where she was.

'Hi, Sally.'

'Brandon; okay?'

'Yeah sure; you want to know how I'm doing?'

'Yes, but I want to help as well. I'm here.'

'Where?'

'In Paris, driving towards the centre, just coming through Riquet. I came through the tunnel.'

'Err, right. Does the boss know?'

'Not yet, I'll tell him when I get to Landers place.'

'Okay, see you there.'

Jones snapped his phone shut and smiled as he spoke to himself. 'What a woman.'

After greeting Jones and Curtis at his office, Landers offered them a coffee. – 'But not here, come with me.'

They walked down Rue du Mont Thabor and turned right towards a large park area. Landers led them towards a small gateway. 'Here we are; Jardin des Tuileries, there's a small stall that sells coffees and cakes just in here. We can sit for a while. Better than that old shop eh?'

'Just a bit,' said Curtis, 'especially on a beautiful day like today.'

Landers supplied the coffees and they sat down, as joggers, business professionals and loners went about their daily routines.

Curtis was still impatient. She didn't give the men a chance to talk about unrelated matters, especially the stylish, slender women that were walking past.

'Right you two, what have we got then? And don't look at me like that, Brandon; it's only the same question Delaney will ask you tomorrow.'

She was right. The men looked at each other. Jones waved a hand towards Landers. 'Go ahead, Stephen, you might as well tell her what you told me.'

Landers stood for a while to crush his empty espresso cup and deposit it in a bin. He sat back down closer to Curtis. 'Okay,' he said as he settled back. 'Well the money that was taken was about 150 million. I'm certain that particular bank was hit because it was the one with the ninety million in the vault, as well as other things, but it's the cash they wanted. I spent some time with my pals in the Gendy and it all points towards a gang that has done previous work for the Farrah brothers. The Gendy thought they had them, in an old farmhouse near Chablis, but something went wrong. They'd had a tip off from someone, but when they arrived the place was empty except for one dead body. It was thought that one of them was injured in the getaway and they finished him so he wouldn't hold them up or talk.'

'They are a nice bunch aren't they?' said Curtis.

'Yeah, well anyway, they slipped the dragnet of the Gendy *and* the French Secret Service. A couple of nights ago a national news programme said that the Paris police were looking for them in Marais, a suburb of Paris, but yesterday Le Figaro said they were last seen in Lyon. So, basically, no one knows where they are and it looks like they've gotten away with it.'

'How sure can we be that it was the Farrah brothers they were working for?' asked Curtis.

'Probably about 95 percent sure,' replied Landers. 'But there is one thing that we may be able to work on. Apparently, according to a chap in the Gendy, the last time this gang pulled off a big one like this, they were led by another person, a different gang leader, quite ruthless by all accounts.'

'What's so odd about that, they're all ruthless aren't they?' said Curtis.

'Yes. But this guy was in a wheelchair.'

Jones joined in. 'A wheelchair! Bloody hell what next.'

'Well,' said Curtis, 'that wouldn't surprise me at all considering all the other things that we've discovered over the past couple of weeks.'

15

Alan Farrah looked around him at the other men in the Range Rover as they approached Dover. The driver, Mich, was getting on a bit now, he thought, but was still one of the best. The first job he had done for the brothers was in Derby, some 20 years earlier. His driving had been nothing short of genius as he left the chasing cars standing and got them lost in the side streets. Farrah watched him as he drove. His eyes never left the road. You could tell him his mother was a whore and he would not flinch; he would just look ahead, concentrating on his driving. He had a few more years left in him, Farrah thought, but not too many. Mich's perfectly weathered, handsome face made him look fit, but Farrah knew his reflexes were slowing down. They joked sometimes that Mich had had his free bus pass for four years and never used it. Mich saying, 'That'll be the day; I'd rather walk or nick a motor.'

The 'paramedic' was Dick Hobson. He had worked for the Farrah brothers for 14 years. The son of a shopkeeper, he had always been in some kind of trouble and the Farrahs had recruited him when he had been left without an employer; who had fled to Morocco when Inland Revenue had questioned his dealings. He didn't have a single cell of empathy or remorse in his body. A couple of years earlier, Alan Farrah had been threatened in a meeting with a rival gang, and he had told Hobson that he was upset, 'Very upset.' Three days later, the man who had threatened Farrah had been found in his garden, pinned to a tree with his garden shears through his throat. Farrah had said to Hobson later, 'You need to calm down a bit, mate. But thank you.' Hobson did not calm down and remained as he was; unfeeling, not caring. And most people would not argue with his 6'4" frame and his arms about as big as some men's thighs. The only thing that worried Farrah sometimes was Hobson's limited intelligence and common sense.

The man who had driven the ambulance was Mark Ashby. Not quite as mean as Hobson, but a good worker. More efficient, more intelligent. He did what he was told without saying a word. He was ten years younger than Hobson, and it showed when it came to stamina and thoughtfulness. For a bad guy still in his late twenties, he was remarkably mature and his well groomed looks and sense of dedication made him stand out from the crowd within criminal circles.

As the Range Rover made its way down the A2 towards Dover, Farrah tapped Mich on the arm. 'Pull over here, Mich, this superstore car park will do.'

They came to a stop in the far corner of the car park. Farrah looked around at Ashby. 'The money, let's have it.'

Ashby pulled out a bundle of money from his inside pocket and handed it to Farrah who counted it. He took about half of it and handed it to Mich. 'Here Mich, there's about two grand there, take it. I want you to get back to London. The other boys will need your skills to get my brother out of jail.'

'But, gov I…'

'Just do it, Mich. Please. And anyway things might get a bit hairy down here and I don't want to lose you.'

Farrah turned and looked at the other two as he continued, jokingly, 'these two clowns I can do without.'

'If you say so, gov. You sure you'll be okay?'

'Sure.'

'Okay, I'll get myself a car from here, shouldn't be too difficult.'

'Right, go on then, get on with it. Mark, take the wheel.'

Mich got out of the Range Rover and started to look around at the shoppers and their cars. A young woman was parking her Saxo not far from where they were. He waited until she had gone into the main entrance of the store and strolled over to the car. About two minutes later, with the help of a small generic key and a by-pass clip, he was in the car and on his way back up the A2 to London.

The other three men in the Range Rover drove towards the Dover Docks.

PC Simon Tibbs was on his way to work. He had stopped as usual, to get himself a couple of sandwiches and a bottle of his favourite cola from his local superstore. He put his purchases away in his rucksack and reached back to gather the seat belt. It was then, out of his right hand window, that he noticed the Range Rover. He thought he recognized the man in the front passenger seat, but he wasn't sure. Then, when the driver had got out and approached the Saxo, he knew he had to think quickly. He reached for his mobile phone. Dead battery! Damn! As the Range Rover pulled away he noted the number and ran towards the store entrance. He went straight to the nearest payphone and dialed up his station. 'Sue its Simon Tibbs, put the Sergeant on, now!'

Back in Paris, Jones, Curtis and Landers were looking through their case notes trying to piece together all the small bits of knowledge they had so far. Jones looked at his phone as it rang. It was Delaney.

'Hi, boss.'

Delaney's voice was quiet but disturbed. 'Brandon, are you still in Paris?'

'Yes, sir.'

'Good. Got a car?'

'No, but Sally...'

He realized what he had said and hesitated before continuing. 'Sally has sir, she's with me now, and so is Stephen.'

'Sally is with you?'

'Yeah, she came over to help.'

There was a silence. Curtis looked at Jones and shrugged. Jones pointed the palm of his other hand upwards. Landers smiled. With nothing being said, Jones enquired, 'Do you want to speak to her, sir?'

'Yes I bloody do'

Curtis took the phone from Jones as she raised her eyebrows. 'Hello, Tom.'

'Hello; so you decided not to take my advice and stay in the safe house then?'

'Yes. Sorry. But we need all hands on deck don't we?'

'Maybe; that doesn't mean you can go against my wishes, especially without asking me.'

'Tom, I'm sorry, but can you remember please that I work for the CSS, not you. I'm working *with you* to help;

not *for you*. I don't want to have to remind you again, which of us is the customer.'

'Yes, you're working *with* me, but I still out rank you by quite a way, when we're working together on an international case; whether I'm a government employee or not. Don't do it again. Put Jones back on.'

Curtis did not want to push her luck. But she was angered by the way Delaney had spoken to her. Delaney could send her back to Canada any time he wished. She decided it would wait until she saw him again, face to face. She handed the phone back to Jones who was smirking, knowing that Delaney would let her off. The smirk soon left his face as Delaney started to speak again.

'Brandon, listen carefully. Alan Farrah has been busted out of the nick on an ambulance scam. It's pretty certain he's on his way to France with two of his top men. He was spotted in a car park near Dover by a local bobby. Chances are he's headed for Paris to get his ninety million from whoever lifted it for him. You need to get every bit of information you can from Stephen and the three of you will have to take the lead out there. Check all the small coastal airfields as well as the airports and ask Stephen to enlist what help he can from the Gendarmerie.'

'Right, sir, we're on our way. Do we know who's with him?'

'The local chap wasn't sure, but from the limited description we have, it could be Hobson and Ashby.'

'Dick Hobson and Mark Ashby?'

'Probably.'

'Crikey, I'd better get Stephen to brief the Gendarmerie on exactly what sort of characters we're dealing with then.'

'Might be wise. Keep me informed and err, look out for Sally, yes?'

'Yes.'

Jones flicked his phone shut and looked at Landers. 'Alan Farrah; he's out and on his way here.'

Landers knew what that meant. He looked at Curtis and then back at Jones. 'I need to tell my mate in the Gendy.'

'Yeah, the Commander said you would need to involve them. So, where do we start; at the airports?'

'No,' said Curtis, 'to obvious, they wouldn't use the usual transport; we need to check the coastal airfields and small fishing ports.'

'She's right.' Landers confirmed. 'We'll go in my car and I'll make some phone calls on the way.'

Curtis nudged Jones on the arm as they made their way to Landers' car. 'The Gendy?'

Jones whispered to her. 'It's Stephen's nickname for the Gendarmerie.'

Mark Ashby had driven towards Dover docks as Farrah had instructed, but then his instruction had changed. 'Go past the docks, Mark, and out towards the west side of Dover,' Farrah had said, 'I'll tell you where to go.'

A few miles out of Dover, Farrah spoke again. 'Turn right here, towards that farmhouse.'

Ashby swung the Range Rover swiftly round a corner and down a small dirt track. Dick Hobson leaned forward from the back seat. 'I recognize this; the 99 job, right?'

'Right,' said Farrah.

Farrah and Hobson had been there before, in 1999 when they were fleeing the country after killing three people as they snatched five million pounds from a bank distribution depot.

As Ashby approached the farmhouse Farrah told him to turn left towards an old aircraft hangar. On the side of the hangar were the words, Jewel Crop Sprayers, in large white letters that had almost faded away with time. Farrah told Ashby to blow his horn four times. The hangar doors opened as they approached and two men stood waiting for them. The smaller of the men pointed to the right and Ashby steered the vehicle inside the doors and parked it in the right hand corner of the hangar. A small single engine Cessna was parked in the hangar. Farrah told everyone to relax for a few hours until it got dark.

It was approaching 11pm when the pilot walked quickly into the hangar, jumped into the Cessna and started it. He beckoned to the three men to get on board. Farrah, Hobson and Ashby ran to the aircraft and scrambled aboard as quickly as they could. It moved slowly out of the hangar, turned right and within minutes was tearing along the old runway. Farrah leaned forward and held the pilot's shoulder. 'Bingo, you old bastard,' he shouted, 'how are you?'

'Great, Alan, you?'
'Yeah, suppose so, a bit of bother as usual'
'Well I'll soon get you over the water'
'I know you will, mate. Did Mich get the money to you?'
'He did; very generous of you. Now sit back and let me concentrate'

Farrah laughed as he sat back, the pilot pulled back on the controls and the aircraft was airborne, heading for somewhere in France.

16

Delaney knew he needed to get to France. As he arrived at home, Angela had started to pack his bag. She kissed him on the cheek and held his arm. 'I've got most of it ready; you just need to finish off.'

'Thank you, I should be back in a couple of days.'

'Okay. Where to this time?'

'Paris; got a flight from Stansted in about three hours.'

Angela looked at him with concern. 'Is it about that prison escape in Manchester?'

'Yes, been on the news has it?'

'Only for a while, wasn't that Farrah man the one you were going to see?'

'Mm, anyway it's a long story.'

Angela was quiet then. She knew when to stop asking.

Delaney's driver pulled up outside Stansted departures an hour before the flight was due to depart.

'There we go, have a good flight.'

'Thanks,' replied Delaney as he got from the car, hold-all in hand. He checked in for the flight and sat down to wait. Half an hour later, the double espresso had done its job but a toilet break was needed. He also took advantage of the fresh cold water in the washroom. The coldness on his face was refreshing and as he looked in the mirror, he wondered how much longer he could go on doing this sort of work.

Another man, short and sturdy, walked into the washroom and made his way into a cubicle. After just one minute, the man came out of the cubicle. Delaney was adjusting his tie as he felt the barrel of a gun being pushed into his back.

'Don't move. Stay dead still.' The man said.

Delaney could tell this man was good, but not special. He had given Delaney the benefit of the mirror. The man spoke again. 'Turn around slowly, into the cubicle behind us.'

When he knew the position was right, Delaney lifted his right leg sharply up behind him, catching the man in the groin. As he did this he swung around and elbowed the man on the chin. The gun went off and a bullet shattered the mirror, Delaney's left fist came round next, landing on the man's stomach. Locked together with the gun between them, they fell to the floor; the gun went off again, the bullet burying itself into a cubicle door. A third shot followed. The man slumped to the floor still holding onto Delaney who freed himself from the grip that was loosening. The gun was on the floor and Delaney grabbed it. He thought quickly; there would be another man somewhere, acting as a back-up or look-out. He dragged the groaning man into a cubicle and shut the door before going into the next cubicle further away from the entrance door. He left the cubicle door a quarter open so the other man would think it was empty.

After a few more seconds, sure enough the other man came in. 'Tony?' he said, 'you there?'

Delaney sat still on the toilet seat, feet up. He heard the first man groan again and the second man forced open the cubicle door. Delaney couldn't wait to find out if the second man was armed; he knew he had to be pro-active. He lowered his feet quietly to the floor, looked down and shot the second man in the foot through the bottom of the cubicle divider. The man let out a cry as he fired his gun down at the floor near to where Delaney was standing. Delaney jumped up onto the toilet seat and fired a second shot over the top which hit the man in the shoulder. The man cried out again and fell. He jumped down, ran around to where the two hoodlums were and grabbed the second man by the lapels.

'Who sent you?'

The first man groaned again and shook his hand at the first man.

'Who sent you?' Delaney repeated.

The second man managed a small smile through his agony. 'Never tell you, never tell you.'

Delaney let him drop to the floor, stood up and leant against the wash basins; this time no mirror to look in. He was still getting his breath back when two policemen burst in. He held his hands high and shouted, 'Code four! Code Four!' If the officers knew their stuff, he thought, they would know that he was working for the Home Office.

One of the policemen shouted back while he aimed his gun at Delaney, 'ID! Now!'

Delaney reached into his pocket and produced his card. 'Here, here it is, now get your procedures sorted out quickly because I have a plane to catch.'

The policeman looked into the cubicle. Both injured men were unconscious but looked alive. He looked again at Delaney's card, and then at Delaney. 'Do you know who they are, Mr Delaney?'

'I think you'll find that they work for a man called Farrah, the older one is called Tony.'

'You mean Alan Farrah, sir?'

Delaney had forgotten that these days, airport police were well briefed Special Branch officers. 'Yes, Alan Farrah, I'm on my way to Paris to try and catch up with him.'

Ninety minutes later Delaney's plane was starting its descent into Charles de Gaulle airport. It was 9.30pm. During the flight he had been thinking of his encounter at Stansted. How did they know he was there? How did they know him by sight? And as they were relatively amateurish, did that confirm that Farrah's professionals, Hobson and Ashby, were still with him, in France, just as he had thought?

Some 40 kilometres away, Stephen Landers was heading away from Paris towards the coast, with Curtis and Jones as his passengers. He had decided to try for Le Touqet. There was a small airfield there that was only open during the day and it had been used before by other criminals fleeing Britain. The small planes could land at night and passengers could easily get away from the area by using local unfenced fields and tracks.

The suburban roads around the airfield area were quiet. It was 10pm. They drove around for a while and came to rest in a large open area where they could get good all round, low level vision. Jones reached for his phone as it buzzed quietly. It said *Delaney calling.*

'Hello, sir.'

'Hi, Brandon, where are you?'

'A small airfield near the coast sir, Stephen says it's been used before.'

'Well tell Stephen he's too late.'

'How's that, sir?'

'Farrah and his men were seen at Dover two or three hours ago and it's only about 30 minutes across the channel by plane.'

'They could have waited until it was dark. I think we should wait for a few more hours.'

'Okay, give it until midnight and if nothing turns up get back to Paris. Tell Stephen I'll be at his office early in the morning.'

'Right, sir.'

'Is Sally still with you?'

'Yes; do you want a word?'

'No, just tell her not to get seen if anything happens tonight.'

Jones finished the call and relayed the conversation to his colleagues. Curtis explained to them that Delaney did not want her seen because she may have to go undercover. They both asked her for more details, but she decided to keep the story to herself.

Time went slowly as they sat waiting in the car. It was cold; the engine had been turned off so they could listen for sounds. At about 11.30pm Stephen turned around to both of them. 'Well, shall we call it a night then?'

'Not sure,' said Jones.

'Give it a bit longer,' said Curtis, 'I'm going to look around again.' She got out of the car and rested her elbows on the roof as she peered through the night binoculars. Nothing. Not even birds. A noisy motorbike could be heard in the distance, but that soon faded away. Some light from the half moon shone on the wide open fields and small bushes and trees. The wide roads and low level fences made it easy to see to a good distance. When it was just past midnight she got back into the car. 'Okay, boys, back to Paris it is then.'

Landers pulled the car onto the road and drove slowly back towards the main streets they had come through.

'Stop!' shouted Jones. Landers stopped and turned off his lights and engine in anticipation. He looked at Jones who was pointing through the side window. 'There,' said Jones, 'just above that tree line; a light.'

As Landers and Curtis looked in the direction Jones was pointing, they could see a light. It looked like a light that would be on the front of a small aircraft, and it was heading their way.

'It's getting closer.' said Curtis.

'Yes,' replied Jones, 'but why this way? The airstrip is back there.'

'Well, we'll soon know,' said Landers as he pulled the car off the road and parked behind a large truck that had been abandoned by the driver for the night.. The aircraft got closer and lower, it's course not altering. They watched as it got lower and slower.

'Bloody hell,' said Landers, 'this is a first!'

'What is?' asked Curtis.

'They're going to land on the road!'

All three of them stared at the aircraft as it came down. The road was wide and quiet and they began to realise it was possible. A car suddenly appeared from nowhere and parked about 50 metres from where they were. Curtis grabbed the binoculars again and wrote down the number of the car. The plane came down, slow, quiet, straight, and landed. It came to a halt near the car and two men eased themselves out of the side door, stepped onto the wing and jumped down. Some bags were thrown to them and a third man jumped down. They all got into the car, carrying a bag each.

'What do we do?' whispered Landers, 'we can't follow them with that plane there.'

'We wait. See what happens.' Jones replied.

They watched the car move off slowly and quietly back in the direction from which it had come. The plane, engine still running, turned slowly, accelerated and was airborne again in under a minute. Landers started the car. 'Right,' he said, 'let's see if we can latch onto that car.' He drove swiftly in the direction the other car had gone. Luckily the moonlight was enough for him not to use his headlights. At a junction he turned towards the Paris road. Curtis pointed to some old signs on the side of the road that looked like they had just been thrown down. The reflective writing on two of the signs was visible. Landers looked at them a tutted.

'What do the signs say?' said Curtis.

Landers looked at her in his rear view mirror, smirking. 'They say *road closed, no entry.*'

A few kilometers further on they could see the back of the car that had collected the men from the aircraft. Landers kept his distance but even that was tricky, as the roads were so quiet. It was only a matter of time before the driver up ahead would realise he was being followed.

17

As Landers, Jones and Curtis followed the car towards Paris, Jones thought about Delaney. What would he want them to do? The car in front started to slow down. Landers was worried.

'What do you think you two? They could be on to us.'

Jones knew that Delaney would not want things to be rushed. He kept his eyes on the car in front as he spoke. 'Leave it. Pull off. We can't take the chance; we can let your friends in Paris know that they're heading that way.'

Landers looked at Curtis in the mirror. 'Sally? What do you think?'

'I agree,' she said, 'we can call Tom and tell him what's happening. He'll soon tell us what to do.'

'Okay,' said Landers, and he pulled the car off the road into a small lay-by. The car in front carried on towards Paris. Jones reached for his phone. 'I'll call Tom, see what he says.'

In his hotel in Paris, Delaney wasn't sleeping much and it did not surprise him when he saw Jones' name on his phone as it rang.

'Brandon, what's new?'

Jones explained what had happened during the last hour. Delaney thought for a while. He told Jones what had happened at Stansted. Jones listened with interest and only spoke when he knew Delaney had finished.

'Okay, sir, what do we do now then?'

'Get back to Paris. On your way get Stephen to check out the car number. Chances are it's stolen anyway, but you never know. And tell Stephen to tell his mates in the Gendarmerie not to intercept the car. When you get back here hopefully I would have thought of the best way to approach this blasted mess.'

Jones relayed the phone call to Landers and Curtis. He swapped seats with Landers and drove the car slowly in the direction of Paris while Landers made his phone calls. His Gendarmerie contact confirmed that the car was not registered anywhere in France and they had some men covering almost every road into Paris from the north-east.

An hour later as they were approaching the outskirts of the capital, Landers' phone rang. It was his contact coming back to him. After a few minutes of listening and being very quiet, Landers ended the call with a disappointing sounding '*merci.*'

'Well?' asked Curtis.

Landers sighed slightly and answered. 'They found the car, abandoned. No sign of anyone. It had been completely emptied of all items. Looks like a vehicle switch. Trouble is, the roads will soon be full of cars heading into Paris; lots of them with four people in. They're either already in Paris, or waiting somewhere, ready to go in later, either way, we've lost them.'

Two hours later Curtis, Jones and Landers were sitting in Delaney's hotel room waiting for him to speak. The small two-star establishment was old and ornate and the armchairs creaked as they moved in them. 'Coffee?' asked Curtis.

'Yeah, for all of us,' said Delaney. 'We're all yawning.'

Curtis ordered two pots of coffee. A breeze blew through the French doors leading to the small balcony; the lace curtains and thin paisley drapes wrapped themselves around the arm of a nearby chair.

Having discussed the events of the night, Delaney wanted to make sure they were all singing from the same hymn sheet.

'Right, we need to achieve three things, correct me if I'm wrong. – one; recover the ninety odd million dollars, two; get Farrah back into jail, and three; find out who's close to us who is feeding information to Farrah. Whoever it is probably fed information to Jerome and Bouton before they were killed. Probably in return for a lot of money, and we can't let whoever it is continue to do this because they might be informing Farrah about other future cases as well.'

'Might not be for money, they could be distant relatives or something,' suggested Curtis.

'Maybe, but all of the home office and intelligence departments check all people don't they before employing them?'

Blank looks.

'Do they?' said Jones 'I don't know. And anyway how do we know Farrah is getting his information from someone on the inside? Could be a group of people who tail us closely.'

'No sorry, Brandon, I don't buy that,' Delaney said. 'They couldn't follow all of us *and* get information to their colleagues so quickly. My little episode at Stansted, Jerome and Bouton being blown up and that booby trap bomb when Sally visited that house; it's just too much; they would need a small army of men. Somehow, the Farrahs' et al have been given information from a distance, by someone who always knows what is about to happen.'

'I agree,' said Landers 'but what do we do?'

'You go back to your office, Stephen,' said Delaney, 'we'll need almost permanent connections with the Gendarmerie and no one does that better than you. In fact you had better start to involve your Interpol friends here in Paris as well. Keep us informed about what's being achieved, if anything, and we'll keep you informed.' He turned to Jones and Curtis. 'Okay you two?' They nodded in unison. 'Right, Brandon; you get back to London and join forces with Ben. Remember, while he was in Cologne, he found out about that hit man who supposedly works from a wheelchair, although I'll believe it when I see it. Talk to anyone and everyone. Someone must know some more about him and if he *is* working for Farrah, we need to get a step ahead of *him* as well. Okay?'

'Okay, sir, but what about you, you can't work here on your own, these bastards are deadly.'

'I'll decide when I can work on my own, Brandon, not you. Besides, I won't be on my own.' He looked at Curtis. 'This woman here is a top Canadian Secret Service operator, or had you forgotten?'

Jones looked at Curtis, who had raised her head in that confident style that women used when they walked into rooms of strangers. 'No, I had not forgotten,' he said 'but this will need more than two of you.'

'Oh don't worry, Brandon, I'll be straight on the phone to you and Ben if we need you to get back here. Remember you'll only be an hour's flight away.'

The experienced Landers decided to jump in, in case Jones laboured the point. He got up and tapped Jones on the shoulder. 'Quite right, Tom; come Brandon, I'll share a taxi with you, let's get on with it.'

When Jones and Landers had left, Delaney asked Curtis to join him for breakfast in the hotel. 'Fancy a coffee and a croissant? Say about 8 o'clock?' She yawned and accepted the offer.

'Mm, that'll give us a few hours to sleep.'

The small restaurant was quiet and warm. They sat at a table in the corner away from the few other guests. Delaney shrugged his shoulders as he took up his first croissant. 'Just fancy a bacon sandwich, but I suppose, when in Rome and all that.'

Curtis smiled knowingly. 'With all the butter in that thing, a bacon sandwich would probably be healthier. Mm, this coffee is gorgeous.'

After a couple of coffees, Curtis sat forward during a moment of silence. 'Go on then, Tom, tell me what you have in mind.'

'About what?'

'About me going undercover again, as Melanie, remember?'

'Yes, I was thinking about that last night. First thing we have to do now though is find Farrah again. Any ideas?'

Curtis reminded him of the Monroe case. She had infiltrated the gang of Bruce Monroe three years earlier. He was a Canadian arms dealer who bought guns from the Belgian manufacturers and sold them to the Toronto and Vancouver mafia. She had presented herself at a party being held by Monroe in Vancouver as a corrupt personal assistant to Pierre Bouton, the head of the Canadian Secret

Service. Delaney and his Overseas Liaison team were involved because Monroe had links to the Farrah brothers, who would help Monroe get the arms to Canada from an airfield in England. The Farrah brothers had been at the same party.

During a visit to England, Monroe was to meet Alan Farrah to discuss future shipments. Delaney's team and some operators from the CSS, including Curtis, had raided a meeting at a club in Bristol just as some money was being handed over. The whole conversation, including details of mafia buyers had been recorded by a listening device on a table lamp. Everyone had been grabbed and arrested, except Farrah. It was later discovered that the owner of the club was on Farrah's payroll as well as the police's. He had cleared a back entrance and an old tunnel leading from the basement of the club in return for a cut of the money Farrah was going to get from Monroe. Farrah wanted to get Monroe out of the picture and do the arms deals himself. They were very lucrative.

Monroe was put away for life for illegal arms dealing and aiding the mafia. Alan Farrah's brother, John, took over the operation and they made enough money out of the deals to buy three villas, one in Florida, one in Spain, the other in France.

As Delaney listened to Curtis's recollections, he realised he had forgotten about the villas. 'Don't suppose he would go to the villa in France now would he? Too obvious.'

'Yes, far too obvious,' Curtis replied. 'Stephen knows where the villa is though if you want to check.'

'Yes, why not; nothing to lose. I'll phone him later. Do you think Farrah will remember meeting you at that

Vancouver party? When I showed him your photograph in the nick he hid his recognition very well if he did.'

'Well, given the way I made myself up that night, and the short dress I was wearing, not to mention the jewelry, I certainly hope he does remember.'

Delaney paused, not quite knowing what to say. 'You always look good anyway,' he said, as he put his hand on top of hers. She tilted her head to one side and smiled.

Delaney moved his hand away. 'Sorry, I've embarrassed you. Now then, let's see how we can get you to Farrah. Of course we have to find him first. Come on, drink up and let's get going.'

About eighty metres away from the hotel, a pair of binoculars was trained on the hotel dining room where Delaney and Curtis were sitting. The observer could not make out exactly where they were, but he knew they had to pass the window again to leave the dining room.

Six minutes later they did so.

The observer put down his binoculars and picked up an old British Army issue rifle. He pointed the rifle towards the hotel entrance, adjusted his sights accordingly, and waited.

18

Delaney finished packing his few travel belongings and phoned down to reception to ask them to have the bill ready. He met Curtis in the small foyer and settled the bill. Curtis phoned Stephen Landers to ask how he had gotten on with the gendarmerie. 'Anything yet, Stephen? Tom and I are just leaving the hotel.'

Landers sounded concerned. 'No, nothing on Farrah or where he might be, but listen, be careful, okay? Has Tom told you about William Hoetger?'

'Who?'

'William Hoetger.'

'No, should he have?' she said as she looked at Delaney.

'Yes. Do you remember me telling you and Brandon about the hit man in a wheelchair?'

'Yes, the one who was in charge of the bank raid?'

'Mm, well his name is William Hoetger and a grey van with odd wheels has been spotted in Paris. Word is he works out of this van with the help of a driver.'

Curtis needed to involve Delaney. She asked Landers to hold on and looked at him as he was putting away his credit card and the hotel receipt.

'Stephen says a William Hoetger is in Paris.'

'Hang on,' said Delaney. He moved away from the reception desk and beckoned to Curtis to hand over her phone to him.

'Where is this information from, Stephen?'

'A Gendy snout. One of their officers was told last night, but the snout ran off before saying where it was he saw Hoetger.'

'Right. Well, he won't be on foot, that's for sure.'

'No, sir; very funny, but word is that he has a driver and works from the back of that Renault van. One of those modified vans with a ramp that takes wheelchairs in backwards.'

'Okay, Sally and I will be careful. He might be here covering Farrah's backside. And I guess this van is just like all the other Renault vans in Paris. There must be thousands of them.'

'Yep,' replied Landers.

'Right,' said Delaney, 'well thanks for that Stephen. Sally and I are going to make our way towards Grenoble. Farrah has a villa there doesn't he?'

'Yes he does; I'll SMS the address to you.'

'Thanks, Stephen; let's move then.'

'Okay, be careful both of you, yeah?'

'Yes, you too.'

As they gathered up their belongings, Curtis questioned Delaney's decision. 'Not sure about Grenoble; too obvious surely.'

'Maybe. Or maybe not. Farrah might want us there. He would know where we are and would have the upper hand because he knows the lay of the land. He would flee elsewhere while he got his men to take care of us.'

'Still say it's too obvious.'

'Right; and your alternative suggestion was?'

Curtis put a finger to her lips. 'I'll tell you later.'

They made their way out of the hotel and looked around before they walked down the steps leading to the pavement.

William Hoetger held his rifle very steady. Using the remote switch, his driver lowered the blackened rear window a few inches. As Hoetger looked through the lens, he hesitated, adjusted the angle and relaxed his muscles. He would not recognise the woman, but he had been shown photos of Delaney. He felt nothing; no guilt, no nerves. It did not matter who these people were to him as he briefly focused on their faces. A man and a woman that he had to kill; nothing else. As Delaney and Curtis reached the last few steps leading to the pavement he breathed out slowly and took aim.

Little Claude Mullier was as quick as usual that morning as he raced around the corner of Rue de Gulle. His new bicycle was even quicker and he had it mind to beat his own record on his daily journey from home to school. But there was not usually a Renault van parked around the corner in Rue de Gulle and he smashed into the side of it at some speed; just as Hoetger was pulling the trigger. The shot missed Delaney by three inches and hit the hotel door smashing the glass into pieces, Curtis jumped to the left of the steps, Delaney to the right, both emptying their shoulder holsters. Hoetger shouted to his driver to get out of there and the van started to move. The driver saw the young boy getting up off the pavement. Claude Mullier stared at his bicycle as the van drove over it. People around the hotel were scurrying away as Delaney shouted to Curtis. 'See anything!'
   'No, could have come from anywhere!'
   'Get back inside!'

'You too!'

'Yes yes, just go!'

The hotel staff were shouting at Delaney, but he couldn't understand them. Curtis asked in French where the back door was and a frightened young girl pointed to a corridor. They ran down the corridor and out of a back door leading into an alley. After a quick check in each direction they ran to a side street. A taxi driver was standing by his open car door, Delaney shoved him into his driving seat and Curtis shouted her instruction. The Taxi sped away in the direction of the train station.

The police had acted quickly and had sent officers down to the scene. Claude Mullier was by now, sitting on the curb next to his bicycle, crying. The distraught young boy had been looked after, but he had no recollection of the van number, not even its colour.

Delaney phoned Landers to tell him what had happened. Curtis called Brandon Jones who had just arrived back in London. He had already made contact with Ben Wyatt and couldn't believe the coincidence of Curtis phoning. 'I was just about to phone you, Sally, are you and the boss heading for home?'

'No, Grenoble. Farrah has a villa there and Tom thinks he will go there for some sort of showdown.'

'Well he won't.'

'Oh. What do you know?'

'Three people looking like Farrah and his buddies were seen at Calais. From the description I have, I would say there's a ninety percent chance it's Farrah. We have the car number and everything. If it was them, they will be landing at Dover in half an hour.'

'Christ! What are these guys doing!'

Delaney butted in. 'What is it?'

'You will not believe it.'

'Try me.'

Curtis ended her call to Jones and relayed the information to Delaney. He shook his head and swore. 'Right,' he said, 'when we get to the station we had better get the north bound train then, instead of the southbound.'

The Eurostar train came to a stop in London at 12.30. Curtis and Delaney had both slept for a while on the journey. They made their way back to Delaney's office to meet Jones and Wyatt who were waiting for them. Jones had got back to London as instructed and met up with Wyatt to go through possibilities and start to talk to their usual snouts. Wyatt was always the one with more reliable information for some reason and it was he who had contacts at Dover.

'I can confirm, boss,' he said, 'it was Farrah at Calais; he arrived in Dover a few hours ago.'

'Right, where is he now?'

'Err, don't know sir.'

Delaney looked at Wyatt and raised his eyebrows as though to ask a question without speaking. Wyatt continued. 'The Dover police tried to get hold of him. He was recognised by a customs lady. Obviously to them he's an escaped prisoner and an operation was launched at the dock gates, but it all went wrong. Two policemen have been shot, they're not dead, and one of Farrah's boys was hit in the arm.'

Curtis stood up and raised her arms in disgust. 'Oh come on! What is going on? If this had been in Toronto the CSS would have this guy back behind bars now, or dead!'

Wyatt folded his arms and scowled at Curtis. This was a side of Curtis he or the others had not experienced before. 'Hang on, you; let's not get disrespectful,' he said, 'you're the visitor here remember; piss off back to Canada if you're not happy with things.'

'Oh that's crap!' said Curtis, 'You shouldn't have let this happen.'

Delaney looked at her and said quietly, 'Well, please forgive us for our shortcomings.'

'Yeah, well damn your shortcomings! I'm going to get things moving myself!'

She started to walk out of the room. Delaney raised his voice. 'Where the hell do you think you're going?'

She turned; her eyes wide. 'Look, Tom, I stayed here to help, remember? I don't report to you. I know people and I have ideas. Ideas that none of you have asked me about. I'm out of here, I'll be in touch.'

'Sally, we need to work as a team.'

'Damn the team, Tom! This whole thing is taking too long! I am no closer to getting the people who killed Marcus after two god damned weeks!' She carried on walking out and slammed the door.

Wyatt raised his eyebrows and smirked. Jones got up to run after her but was halted by Delaney. 'Leave her, Brandon.'

'We can't leave her, sir; she can't work alone against these people.'

'She won't do, we'll catch up with her when we need to.'

The casual Wyatt got up and looked out of the window. 'There she goes, she doesn't look happy,'

'No, well, maybe she's right, eh?' said Delaney. 'So far this hasn't been our most successful job has it?'

Wyatt and Jones saw the look of anger on Delaney's face. A look they did not see very often.

Curtis made her way back to the safe house in the pool car she had signed for an hour earlier. She was angry. Her lover Marcus had been murdered. Jerome and Bouton had been arrested and they had been killed. They would not be punished for their part in a drugs deal worth ninety million. The ring leader of the whole affair – and countless others – had escaped from prison, killing god knows how many people. One of the best hit men in Europe was wandering around various countries getting away with it and all of the time someone who was close to Delaney's team was probably bent. Bunch of god damned amateurs, she thought to herself. Well maybe they need a kick up the backside from the Canadian Secret Service; I'll show them how to get results!

She arrived at her new safe house to find her dog Rocky being looked after by a Special Care Officer. They were employed by British Intelligence to care for people and families in safe houses. Rocky had the usual down trodden look on his face that said, I know you are not staying. The Care Officer explained that he had taken Rocky for a walk and that he seemed happy enough. Curtis fussed him for a while and packed. An hour later she was on the M1 motorway heading north. She was still angry.

A car up ahead would not move out of the way. The pool car had sirens and the alternate flashing front lights and she used them. She knew she was breaking the law doing it, but she was in a hurry.

She was on her way to Nottingham. When she had been waiting for the pool car she had recalled that Alan

Farrah's brother, John, was in jail in Nottingham. She was thinking hard as she drove. Nottingham was not a high security jail. Why was someone like John Farrah sent there? Why would Alan Farrah come back to England? To spring his brother out of jail perhaps?

Two hours later she was booking into the Sherwood Hotel on the northern outskirts of Nottingham, a couple of miles from the jail. She unpacked her bag carefully, as it contained a few extras this time. – Wig, jewelry, shoes. She thought hard about how she had acted as 'Melanie' when she had first met the Farrah's at that party in Vancouver and decided it would not be too difficult to get into character again.

The following morning she woke early and emptied two coffee sachets into a cup. The morning visitor session at the jail started at 09.30, when she wanted to be there. Most relatives of inmates visit in the afternoons. She applied the same heavy eye makeup, thicker foundation and crimson lipstick that had been used previously. The look was completed by a medium length blonde wig. As she looked at herself in the short skirt and high heels, she realised that it was actually quite pleasing that she still 'had it', and allowed herself a quick smile. The spectacles would have to go. She replaced them with contact lenses. Another careful look in the mirror and a double check against the photo on her 'Melanie Leeder' drivers licence, and it was done. By 08.45 she was leaving her room, her gun in a bag. The gun would have to be left in the car, along with the *genuine* ID card. The hotel receptionist was not the same one that had booked her in the night before, so there were no quizzical looks as she left.

Nottingham jail looked like so many others as she approached it. The large timber doors, red brick arch and old, black, worn out roof. She had parked her car a couple of streets away. Only three more people were waiting by the visitor's door. At 09.25 they were sent through to a waiting room and gently body searched before being taken to another room for an ID check. A tall slim woman prison officer came over to Curtis. 'Name.'

'Melanie Leeder.'

'Visiting?'

'John Farrah.'

'Not seen you before. Are you related?'

'Just an old girlfriend. I haven't seen him for ages.'

'You American then?'

'Canadian.'

'Why see him now then?'

'Mind your own business.'

The woman looked at her with a superior smile. 'Cute.' Her eyes then settled on Curtis's body and her legs. 'Mm, very cute you are.'

The four visitors were told to go through to the meeting room. Curtis could see John Farrah sitting at a table in the middle of the room. It was three years since they had met. He looked older but not unfit. She wondered what made these people exercise and keep fit when they were inside. Maybe it was just something to do. It surprised Curtis that Farrah spoke first.

'Well well, the gangster's girl from Toronto.'

Curtis finished settling herself in the chair and smiled at him. 'Well, I'm flattered you remember me, Mr Farrah. It's been a while.'

'Now how could I forget you my love, especially looking like that. How is Mr Monroe, the arms dealer?'

'I see prison hasn't taken away your charm,' said Curtis, 'but I am not here to discuss Monroe.'

'No? So, what brings you here? Someone must have sent you. Wasn't my brother was it?'

'No. I came all by myself, to help you.'

He looked at her quizzically. 'Why would you help me?'

'Well, let's just say I have a soft spot for rich men, even if they are criminals.'

'But you could get any rich man you wanted. Why me?'

'I guess it depends what you call rich. One million or ninety million.'

Farrah paused, looking angry. 'What do you mean, ninety million?'

Curtis went for the kill. 'I can help you Mr Farrah, help you a lot. But you start giving me bullshit and I can make sure you never get out of here.'

Farrah sat quiet for a minute staring at her. She leaned forward, her elbows on the table and spoke quietly. 'I mean the ninety million you and your brother had lifted from the bank in Paris, or was it a hundred and fifty million? The money you got from the drugs deal that involved Charles Jerome and Pierre Bouton from the American and Canadian intelligence services. Do you want me to continue?'

'Why not?'

'Okay. It's simple really. You get out of here and you and your brother get the heat taken off you. I get ten million.'

Farrah sat back, crossed his arms and looked up. Soon after he leaned forward onto the table to be as close as he could to her without prompting the guard. 'Now I think you should stop insulting my intelligence and tell me who you really are.'

Curtis threw her final punch. 'Sally Curtis, Canadian Secret Service. I used to work for Pierre Bouton and now I'm working with a group of people who do work for the government to get your brother back in jail and retrieve the hundred and fifty million.' She sat back to give him time to digest what she had said.

He sounded disturbed when he spoke again. 'Okay, so how long have you been bent?'

'Long enough.'

'And why?'

'You must have a rough idea of what people like me get paid. Ten million would keep me happy for a while.'

19

Delaney had had a good night's sleep. He had sent Jones and Wyatt home with instructions to get some rest and come to his house at 10am. He was worried about the way Curtis had stormed out of their meeting. It was not like her and it almost seemed like a nervous reaction to something. Someone was passing information to Farrah and he could not rule out anyone at this stage. But surely, Curtis was not the informant.

Angela came up behind him at the kitchen table and kissed him on the head. 'Right darling, I need to go, I'll leave you to your meeting with the boys. Why don't you sit them down in here and have toast and coffee or something?'

'No, too informal, we'll use the office.'

'Okay, I need to go because we're moving to a new office, remember I told you?'

'Oh yes, that's today is it?

'Yep.'

'Is this all part of the cost savings to do with you civilian secretaries?'

'Yes, we're only down the road though. Our boss said it didn't really matter where we work with all the I.T. available these days.'

'Quite. Okay; drive carefully.'

'I will; see you later; I'm just going to get some papers from the office on my way out. Oh and err, happy birthday darling, the cards on the mantelpiece.'

'I forgot, thank you.'

She returned to him and kissed him again. He felt embarrassed for some reason and he was always conscious of being ten years older than her. 'Not getting too old for you am I?'

'Don't be daft; not on this mornings' performance anyway my 55 year old silver haired lover!'

Delaney admired her as she walked out and then he settled himself at his desk. The home 'office' was the conservatory. The dark brown leather chairs surrounded the slate coffee table which was the permanent home for the computer and documents.

Jones turned up at exactly 10am. Delaney told him to help himself to coffee and take a seat. Ten minutes later, Jones was just about to reach for his phone when Wyatt turned up.

'Sorry I'm a bit late, sir, I've been somewhere.'

'Get yourself a coffee. This place you've been to; was it useful?'

'It was.'

'And is it related to our current troubles?'

'It is.'

'Right. Well unless you want me to throttle you, Ben, I suggest you tell me and Brandon about it.'

'Yeah right boss; you'll like this. The attempted hit on you and Sally in Paris, it was William Hoetger.'

'How do you know?'

'Micky Shapiro told me.'

'And who the hell is Micky Shapiro?'

Jones butted in. 'An old time driver; he did runs for quite a few gangs in Manchester; right, Ben?'

'Right; he knows a lot about what goes on and he's still in touch with some of the bad guys he ran for.'

'That sort of information doesn't come cheap,' said Delaney.

Wyatt looked apprehensive. 'Err, no, boss, that's a thousand the business owes me.'

Delaney nodded slowly. He wondered how a nuisance and a mischief like Wyatt kept surviving. Then he realised he knew the answer. Wyatt survived because, like everyone else, he did not go by the book all the time, and it got results.

Wyatt continued. 'Hoetger works from the back of a van and has his own driver.'

'We already know that,' said Delaney.

'Yes, but listen, the driver was in touch with Micky Shapiro to ask a favour. Apparently he helped them to swap vans somewhere and he heard them mention Nottingham.'

'And you know why don't you?' said Jones.

'John Farrah?'

'Yeah, he's in Nottingham jail.'

Delaney interrupted them both. 'I've just realised boys, Nottingham jail is for low risk prisoners; how come a Farrah brother is classed as low risk?'

'Don't know,' said Wyatt, 'that's the Home Secretary's choice; but Hoetger is on his way there.'

'By the way,' said Jones. 'Why did Alan Farrah go to France just to come back again?'

'To retrieve his money,' said Delaney. 'He'll keep it with him now, whatever happens.'

'Right; what do we do now then?'

'Go to Nottingham. What else?'

20

Alan Farrah opted to drive the dirty blue car himself. It was a normal looking car; common and inconspicuous, which was just what they wanted. His contact just outside of Dover had met them as planned to swap vehicles. His staff were still with him. Dick Hobson had caught a bullet in his arm in Dover as they were escaping from the police and customs people, but it had gone straight through and he had suffered worse in his time. Constant pressure on the area for a couple of hours would do. Mark Ashby rested on the back seat next to him.

Farrah looked at them both in his rear view mirror. They had their faults, he thought, but they had also got him out of some pretty bad situations. He decided to give them a million each when all of this was over. The northbound M1 was busy. A couple of times he slowed down as they were passed by a police car, but his Dover contact had thought about things and the car's windows had been blacked out and the number plates were legal – registered to a man in Kent. When he saw the sign that said, Nottingham 42, he knew they would make it in time for the afternoon visitor session at the jail.

He was determined that his brother John was not going to stay in prison. He had a few ideas of how to get him out and John had already been given the options; via their letters with code words in them that only the two brothers knew. As Alan Farrah turned off the motorway near East Midlands Airport, he thought about his brother's history and how he was lucky to be alive. John was four years younger, not as clever, and that was probably the reason why they had had so many close shaves. The first big job they did together was a drugs deal for some Polish mafia men. The Farrah brothers knew some secret and quiet ways in and out of England better than most and top gangs would pay good money for an easy uninterrupted route. The Polish people had links in Canada and it was in Vancouver that the Farrahs made their name as go-betweens for some of the top bosses.

But it was also in Vancouver that John had got sloppy and talked too much in a bar. Unfortunately for him some local Canadian Mounties frequented the same bar and John was followed to his hotel. It was the quiet Mark Ashby, who had accompanied them on the Canada trip, that spotted John being followed into the hotel. As John got into the lift, the two Canadians took to the stairs and Ashby followed them. Just as John was about to enter his room the two men approached him and pinned him up against the wall. Ashby stabbed one of them in the back and grabbed the other one as he turned, but he was a big man and somehow they fell to the floor, the big man on top. John Farrah kicked him in the head and he rolled over, giving Ashby just enough time to re-grip his knife and plunge it into the man's side two or three times.

Hearing the ruckus, Alan Farrah opened his door, silenced gun at the ready. He fired twice at each fallen man to make sure. Twenty minutes later, with the two dead men pulled into a janitor's cupboard; they were on their way to the airport. When John Farrah had apologised on the way, his brother had hit him hard on the jaw without saying anything.

Still, he thought, after all that, he is my brother; and if I can get him out of prison and we can both get back to France or Spain to enjoy our 100 million, we can put all this stuff behind us. But he knew deep down that this would not be his last job. He knew he had become too greedy, wanting everything, regardless of who got hurt. Sometimes he hated himself for being like that; but that was where he was. He wasn't going to change now. He looked back in the mirror; Hobson was asleep. Ashby was cleaning his 9mm Browning. 'You okay, Mark?'

'Course I am; it's all the other ones you need to worry about, not me?'

Farrah smiled and thought, he was probably right; maybe Ashby would end up being like him, whether he wanted to or not.

Farrah and Hobson waited in the car as Ashby signed in for the afternoon visitor session at Nottingham jail. After the usual drills, Ashby found himself approaching the table where John Farrah was sitting. He had never liked his boss's younger brother. He thought of the times he had saved his skin without so much as a thank you.

John Farrah looked at him with nervous eyes as he spoke. 'What are you doing here? Where's Alan?'

Ashby huffed and shook his head before replying. 'He's outside with Dick Hobson. He has a well known face you see, and he escaped from jail two days ago, someone would probably recognise him don't you think?'

'Oh yeah. Well what's the message?'

'He wants to know which option you want to go for.'

'Right. Tell him the green option.'

'Okay. Anything else?'

'Yeah. Tell him I had a visitor. Melanie Leeder.'

'Who's she?'

'You nearly met her yourself Ashby, in Vancouver a few years ago, she was Monroe's girlfriend.'

'You mean the Monroe we kind of, replaced, on that arms deal?'

'Yes, tell Alan she wants to see him and tell him she may not be Melanie Leeder.'

Ashby raised his eyebrows. 'What do you mean?'

'Just tell him.'

'Okay.'

'Right, now just talk about the weather or something, the guards will think it was just a visit to pass on information if we're too quick.'

Ashby nodded and spoke for a while about a few news items. A guard walked past their table slowly and paused before walking on.

Back at the car Ashby told Alan Farrah and Hobson what John had said. Farrah spoke knowingly. 'I thought he might say the green option, no bloody sense of adventure.'

'What is this *green* thing then?' said Ashby.

'It's the gardening; he gets to work in the prison garden twice a week. Trucks are coming and going all the time and the gates are opened and closed every few minutes. Easy really.'

Ashby looked away for a moment. The thought of his boss thinking something which involved his brother was easy, amused him. 'Oh yes, and he said that Melanie Leeder has been to see him and she wants to meet you, and she may not be Melanie Leeder.'

'Is that all he said?'

'Yes, that was it.'

'Right, let's find a hotel or something. We need to stay here for a few days so John can tell us his gardening schedule. Mark, you visit him every morning for the next three days and he'll find a way of getting the information to you.'

'Will do.'

'Good, let's go, you drive, Mark.'

Ashby drove out of town towards Mansfield. It started to rain and Farrah was almost in a doze when his phone message tone rang out. The message read; *I'll be with you later*. It was from William Hoetger.

The Nottingham Prince Hotel to the south of the city was busy when Delaney, Jones and Wyatt booked in. After settling themselves into their rooms, they met in the bar. It was packed with businessmen and women on overnight stays, some with their mobile phones to their ears, some operating laptops. The dark wood panelled walls and the gold coloured lamps did not suit the modern tables and chairs. Bar food was being served to tables and in a far corner, a dozen men sat watching football on a screen that was far too big for the room. Delaney told the other two that he was expecting someone else. Wyatt gulped down the last of his first pint and smiled. 'That'll be Sally then will it?'

'Yes, Ben, it will.'

Jones, nursing his lime and soda, glanced at Wyatt before speaking to Delaney. 'You okay with Sally, sir? She seems to be getting somewhat impatient and restless and that can put her in jeopardy, as well as us.'

'I know that, Brandon. She's been up here for a day longer than we have though, so let's just wait and see what she has to say first.'

'Speak of the devil,' said Wyatt. Curtis was walking towards them. She looked good as usual, but the wiser observation of Delaney could see the stress in her eyes. She sat down in the remaining empty chair around the circular table and looked at all three of them as she spoke. 'Tom, Ben, Brandon, how are we all then?'

'Well I'm okay, Sally,' said Jones, as he got up from his chair 'let me get you a drink.'

'Thanks, dry white wine.' She looked at Wyatt. 'Okay, Ben?'

'Mm, yes thank you.' His reply was aloof.

'And you, Tom?'

Delaney rested his glass on the table. 'Yes I am, what about you, what have you been up to?'

Curtis looked at them both and then over her shoulders. 'I've been to see John Farrah.'

Wyatt stopped drinking and looked at her with surprise. Delaney raised one eyebrow and looked at her with admiration. 'As yourself, or as Melanie Leeder?' he asked, smiling.

'Who?' said Wyatt.

Curtis ignored him and looked at Delaney. 'As Melanie Leeder.'

Delaney said nothing. She had said exactly what he had wanted her to say.

When Jones returned with the drinks, Curtis explained to him and Wyatt about Melanie Leeder and where it had all begun. They were both experienced enough to know it was all possible and believable.

'And what about John Farrah? I take it you have a plan,' asked Delaney.

'Yes I do.'

'Okay tell us and we'll see if we agree.'

Curtis gave Delaney her confident, arrogant look as she spoke. 'He remembered me from Vancouver. I told him I wanted to meet his brother Alan. He asked me why. I said that I could help them because of my contacts in Canada and here. As far as they know, I'm just a good time girl with contacts in the international criminal world. They will need help to launder all that money they have. John will tell his brother that I'm asking around and Alan Farrah never could resist me.'

'But no contact as yet, with Alan?' asked Delaney.

'No, it was only about 12 hours ago that I visited John.'

Wyatt joined in. 'So what happens when Alan Farrah contacts you?'

'Well, with everyone's help we should...'

'Hang on,' interrupted Wyatt, 'you didn't need our help when you stormed out of the office yesterday; now you do.'

'Oh come on, Ben I....'

'No, bollocks, you come on; we work as a team, everything that is happening now would have come about anyway, the only difference is that we would all have known at the same time, it's called teamwork, or don't you practice that in the CSS.'

'Look I was angry okay,' replied Curtis, 'I lost it yesterday, but you're not getting an apology. I'll still go through with this, with you, or without you.'

'Well I rest my case,' said Wyatt as he lay back in his chair and raised his arms. 'Fine, you can do it without me anyway.'

Jones looked at Delaney in an attempt to ask him to intervene. Delaney shook his head. He actually wanted the argument to continue because he thought there was something that Curtis was not telling them.

After a dull moment Curtis looked at Jones. 'And you Brandon? Are you with me?'

Jones gave the correct sort of answer that Delany admired him for. 'It's not whether I'm *with* you or not Sally. I may, or not, disagree with the way you have gone about this, but I take my orders from Tom, not you.'

Delaney stood up. 'Right well, if we pull together and pool all of this anger, we should have Farrah and the money quite soon. Good night. I want all of you out by my car at nine in the morning.'

He went to his room and made tea before phoning Angela. 'Hello, how did the move go?'

'Oh fine, they got some strong young lads into do the shifting and we were settled at our new desks by about three this afternoon. You okay?'

'Yes, I think so.'

'Only think so? This case is getting on your nerves isn't it?'

'Mm, maybe, anyway I'm on my mobile as usual if you need me.'

'Okay. Nice hotel?'

'Not bad, the Nottingham Prince, just out of town, it was easy from the motorway.'

'Good, okay then, phone me again when you can. Love you.'

'You too. Bye then.'

There was an uncomfortable feeling coming into Delaney's head and he was concerned about the immediate future. He remembered having the same feeling twice before. Once outside the Libyan embassy many years ago and once at Stansted; as he was waiting for the hostage negotiators to do their job. It had been a long haul up the ladder, he thought to himself. His melancholy thoughts were interrupted by the telephone.

'Hello.'

'It's Taffy, sir.'

'Taffy, how are you?'

'That's why I'm phoning, I'm okay. I Came out of the hospital this morning. Supposed to be on light duties working from home.'

'What do you mean, supposed to be?'

'Well I did nip into the office a while ago to check E-mails and other things.'

Delaney knew he would be wasting his breath if he told Burton not to work. After six years of working together he knew him too well. 'Okay Taffy, just be careful. Why don't you go home to Cardiff for a couple of days?'

'No time sir, I've had ideas, be in touch.' The short answer was typical of Burton, thought Delaney, as the phone went dead.

Wyatt had not stayed with Curtis and Jones when Delaney had left; he ordered another drink and took it to his room. Jones and Curtis stayed in the bar a while longer talking about events and what they thought would happen. Curtis told Jones he could go and watch the football if he wanted to; she wouldn't be offended. 'I have no time for football,' he said, 'the way people get infatuated and manic over it, astounds me.'

'Wow,' said Curtis, 'Do you put the toilet seat down as well?'

'Yes, I do actually.'

'Hey, you ever get divorced, Brandon, let me know.'

'No chance of that, my marriage is what I live for; which is why Maria wants me to pack this job in; emphasis on the word *live*.'

Curtis excused herself and said she would see him in the morning. He sat alone for a few minutes before taking a quick walk around the hotel and settling in his room to phone his wife.

Some twenty miles away on the other side of Nottingham, Alan Farrah answered the door of his hotel room. The look of William Hoetger was the look he had remembered. The mean eyes looked up at him in the shadow of the white eyebrows. He looked malnourished and tired. Hoetger maneuvered the chair into the room and parked himself near the window. Farrah closed the door and picked up the phone. 'Two chicken sandwiches, two beers... yes... room 25, thanks.'

Hoetger ran his hands over his bald head and stared at Farrah. 'You owe me a lot of money, Alan.'

'Yes I know. You always get paid, eventually, don't you?'

'Yes. Yes I suppose you do look after me.'

'And anyway; how many bloody tries do you want at getting this Delaney bloke?'

Hoetger shrugged his shoulders and wheeled himself back away from the window before answering. 'Yes, I think perhaps this target has not been my easiest.'

'Well, see how easy this is,' Farrah answered as he chose an apple from the fruit bowl. 'I know where Delaney is staying tonight; all you need to do is be there in the morning when he leaves.'

Hoetger did not reply. Farrah moved across to the window and looked down into the street. A Ford van was parked across the road with the driver at the wheel. He smiled a little as he spoke. 'I see you got the van swapped then. Is Michael still doing the driving for you?'

'Yes.'

'You deserve a new vehicle; let me buy you one, when you've taken out Delaney.'

'I would prefer some cash; the vans have to be specially adapted and I should change them more often anyway. A new vehicle is already being arranged for me,' said Hoetger as he moved himself closer to Farrah. 'Just tell me where Delaney is if you know.'

'A hotel, other side of town; the Nottingham Prince.'

'Right, see you tomorrow.'

Farrah watched him as he wheeled himself towards the door. He had known many bad people, most of whom were so hard they would kill their own mother for money. Some had. But Hoetger was a one-off. More heartless than anyone else he had ever met. The wheelchair creaked as its occupier turned to look at Farrah again.

'Don't forget my money, Alan. Goodnight.'

21

The following morning in the car park of the Nottingham Prince Hotel, Delaney felt restless as he waited for Jones, Wyatt and Curtis. Something was not right. He did not know exactly what, but he knew something was missing in his chain of thoughts. He opened his car door as he saw Jones approaching. 'Thought you might be first, Brandon, seen anything of the other two?'

'Yes; Sally's on her way; I've just seen her in reception, no sign of Ben though.'

Curtis looked nervous as she approached. 'Sorry, they had trouble swiping my card.'

'Right,' said Delaney, 'let's get going.' He looked at Jones and nodded towards the hotel entrance. 'Go and see what's holding Ben up, Brandon, he's not usually late.'

Michael Turner parked the Ford van in the opposite corner of the same car park. Some tall hawthorn bushes obscured the vision to and from the main parking bays. Blackbirds were making various calls and a break in the clouds allowed a small patch of sun to rest on the trees. He looked around him and pushed a button that was to the right of the steering wheel. The blackened windows in the rear doors of the van lowered quietly and slowly.

Hoetger reached for his old rifle that was at the side of his wheelchair and attached the silencer. Farrah's information had been correct. This time he *would* earn his money. It was pleasing to him that as he looked down the barrel; he could see the silhouette of Delaney.

Wyatt remained as still as he could. Five minutes earlier he had been looking out of his hotel window. A van had entered the car park and parked up in a corner. The car park was not busy; most of the guests by this time had left, so why park in a corner away from everywhere? He thought. Perhaps the driver was meeting someone else and was going to leave the van parked there all day, as people do. It was then that he had remembered what had been said about vans being swapped and he noticed the blacked-out windows, but he had left his mobile phone in the car and Delaney and Jones were already out there. The young hotel receptionist had almost cried when he had told her to open the back door and say nothing. He moved quietly from the back door to the corner of the building from where he had a side on view of the van.

As he raised his handgun in the direction of the van, he could just make out the silhouette of someone holding a rifle through the blackened windows. But Hoetger shot first, just as Delaney reached for the car key he had dropped on the car floor, the bullet smashed through two windows narrowly missing him, he stayed down, Wyatt's shot was put off by the crack of Hoetger's rifle; it ricocheted off the van roof, Curtis knelt down and emptied her shoulder holster in one swift movement and fired two shots towards the van. Three or four more shots came from the van, one going straight into the petrol tank, the others into two of the car's tyres. Curtis threw herself down on the floor and fired again, Wyatt stood and emptied his magazine into the van as it accelerated away. Running from the hotel entrance, Jones cut across the corner of the car park in the direction of the exit. The van accelerated and ploughed its way through some bushes to avoid the exit road where Jones was standing. He ran across the exit, through some bushes and came out 20 metres behind the van as it raced away. He fired twice, smashing one of the back windows. Hoetger, his rifle still raised, waited until the van was on level ground. He fired once and Jones was thrown back as the force of the bullet hit his chest. Delaney rolled out of the car and kept himself low as he shouted instructions. 'Ben, get over to Jones, see how he is! Sally, get to your car now!' Curtis moved quickly but it was only as she started to drive towards Delaney to pick him up that she realized she had four flat tyres.

Delaney had moved away from his car and the leaking petrol tank. When he realized the situation with Curtis's car, he ran towards the hotel entrance. As he ran he shouted over to Wyatt. 'Ben! Tell me!'

Wyatt looked up from where he was kneeling next to Jones and gave his boss the thumbs down sign. The hotel manager was running down the corridor towards reception. Delaney grabbed him. 'Your car keys now!'

'They're in my...'

'Get them, now!'

Thirty seconds later Delaney was running towards a VW Golf, Curtis chasing after him. The hotel manager held his hands on his head as he watched them speed away, cutting into the traffic without looking.

Wyatt shouted to the manager. 'Dial 999! Sod the car!'

The manager, now turning white, ran back inside. Wyatt looked down again at Jones and put his ear close to his mouth.

Nothing.
He held three fingers to the side of Jones' neck.
Nothing.

'There! I see them!' Curtis shouted to Delaney. 'Just in front of that minibus!'

By now they were two miles away from the hotel and had been lucky in deciding which road to take. Delaney accelerated harder. He had to cut in front of other vehicles as they blew their horns in anger, not realising just what was happening. He could see the van as he came alongside the minibus. 'Stay back!' shouted Curtis. 'He'll take another shot at you!'

'Okay, okay,' said Delaney.

Then the minibus moved to the right; no signal, no warning, it just moved to the right and pushed the VW Golf into the central reservation barrier. Delaney held the wheel tight as the car came to rest squashed between the minibus and the barrier. Curtis was thrown forward onto the airbag. They could hear the screech of tyres as cars behind them shuddered to a halt.

Delaney looked at Curtis to see she was lifting her head. Unable to get from the doors sandwiched between the minibus and the barrier, they crawled out of the back of the hatchback, other drivers watching the situation in disbelief. As they stood together catching their breath, the minibus driver approached them. 'Bloody hell,' he said, 'you okay?'

'Yes we are. Do you have passengers?'

'No, just me, luckily. The steering; it just sort of stopped working; I couldn't do anything.' He turned his attention to Curtis as she lifted her head and looked at him.

'What about you, miss? How are you?'

Curtis straightened herself up, took a deep breath and looked at him. After a few seconds she clenched her fist and hit him hard in the face. He went down, blood pouring from his mouth. A nearby onlooker shouted to her. 'Eh I saw that! I'm a witness!'

Curtis walked towards the woman looking like she was going to throw another punch.

'Leave it, Sally!' shouted Delaney. 'Leave it.'

Back in the hotel car park, an armed response vehicle came to a screeching halt. Wyatt reached for his ID card and held it in the air. 'Agent! Home office! Man on the ground is deceased!'

When the armed response team had verified everything, they relaxed their status and cordoned off the area. Thirty minutes later, another police car pulled up. Delaney and Curtis got from the car and walked over to where Jones was being put on a stretcher, his face covered. Delaney looked over to where Wyatt was sitting on a car bonnet. Wyatt looked at Delaney and raised his head in acknowledgement. Curtis walked over to Wyatt and sat next him. 'This would have been even worse, Ben, if you hadn't spotted the van,' she said, not looking at him. 'All of us could be dead if not for you.'

'You sound like you're saying, it's only Brandon so that's okay.'

'No, I...you did what you could; so did we. Brandon was a brave man doing what he did.'

'Yeah, well, it's still shit isn't it. Those bastards better be good at hiding.'

Delaney watched them both as they made their way towards the hotel entrance. The ambulance pulled away and he watched it until it was out of sight. In the foyer, he apologised to the hotel manager and told him that he would be fully compensated. 'Thank you,' said the manager, still looking shocked. 'Sorry about your colleague. The other two went that way.' He pointed towards the bar.

Delaney got to the bar just in time to hear Wyatt talking to the breakfast waiter. '…well today my friend, you're opening the bar early.'

22

Sir Adrian Lusher answered his mobile phone as he was arriving at MI5 headquarters. It said *Fisher calling*. 'Morning, Fisher, what is it?'

'It's TOLA sir; they've been at it again.'

'At what?'

'We had a call not long ago, sir, from special branch attachment in Nottingham. It seems that the man they are after for the killings of Jerome and Bouton had someone make a hit on them. One of them is dead.'

'Delaney?'

'No, sir, not Delaney, one of his operatives.'

'Okay, Fisher, thank you. Be at my office in about 40 minutes please.'

Lusher asked his PA to pull the file on Delaney. '…And his department, Carol, TOLA; The Overseas Liaison Agency; I want to see what we have.'

Sitting at his desk, he went through the files. All the information was there; CV's, finished operations, current operations, successes and failures. But the file had not been updated for some weeks and there was no information on their movements since the death of Jerome and Bouton.

The waiter had opened the bar as Wyatt had instructed. He had poured them some drinks and Wyatt told him not to go far away. 'Some guests are still having breakfast,' said the waiter.

Wyatt looked at him. 'I don't give a shit who's having breakfast. I told you not to go too far away.' The waiter swallowed, nodded like a scolded child, and stayed behind the bar, pretending to do something.

Sipping their drinks, Wyatt and Curtis looked at Delaney, as he answered his phone. The look on his face told them it was a phone call he did not want.

'Hello.'

'Delaney?'

'Yes.'

'Just one moment please, I have Sir Adrian Lusher for you.'

Delaney expected a call from someone, but not Lusher. 'Hello, Adrian.'

'Hello, Tom, I understand you have lost one of your people.'

Delaney was pleased he had remembered his manners after their last phone call and had called him 'Tom' and not just, Delaney. He hesitated for a moment before answering. 'Yes I have, you wouldn't have known him.'

'You may be surprised at who I know; was it one of your main men?'

'Yes.'

'Jones or Wyatt?'

Delaney frowned. 'It was Jones.'

'Oh dear, well bad luck old boy; look, I was phoning to see if you needed help, I could have some of my men sent up to you.'

'Thank you, Adrian, but it's too late. We need to re-think and re-group for a while.'

'Okay, if the Home Secretary phones I'll assure him that things are still progressing. The last time I spoke to him he was asking how close we were to recapturing Farrah.'

'Did he say he wanted to hand this job over to Special Branch?'

'No; he wants it to stay with you; something about having more flexibility.'

'Thank you, bye for now.'

Yet again, Delaney found he had some unanswered questions as he put his phone back in his pocket. Lusher obviously had a file on him and his team, which was plausible and understandable. Jones and Wyatt would be in that file as key members of the team. But why had he offered help? He had not done that before, especially going as far as to offer some more men. And why offer to reassure the Home Secretary if he were to call? If the Home Secretary wanted to know what was happening, he would phone Delaney direct, as he had in the past. It seemed Lusher was, for some reason, becoming more helpful.

His thoughts were interrupted by Wyatt. 'Okay?'

'Yes, Ben, he just wanted to offer help really.'

Wyatt curled his mouth down. 'Well, there's a first.'

'Mm, isn't it just.'

Curtis had finished her drink and was sitting forward with her head in her hands. Wyatt put his hand on her shoulder and looked at Delaney. 'What now, sir?'

Delaney sighed. 'We'll need to get someone back in London to sort out the arrangements for Brandon and then…'

'And then get these scum bags!' Curtis said as she raised her head. 'Jesus Tom, I swear I'll get the bastards.

First Marcus and now Brandon; not to mention all the people along the way. Where are we going wrong?'

Delaney decided not to answer.

A police officer came towards them and addressed Delaney. 'Excuse me, sir, message from our traffic boys who tried to pick up on the trail of the van. It's been found burnt out on an industrial estate near the M1.'

'Right, thank you officer,' said Delaney. 'Can you ask someone to get me two hire cars please; good ones.'

'Right away, sir.'

Wyatt beckoned to the barman for some more drinks. Delaney stopped him. 'One will do this time in the morning Ben; we've got work to do.'

'Like what?' asked Curtis.

'Like getting you closer to Alan Farrah,' said Delaney. 'Remember, you're our ace up our sleeve, Farrah doesn't know you're with us and neither do the other departments. As far as they know you're held up in a safe house or back in Canada.'

'And Hoetger?' asked Wyatt.

Delaney thought for a while before answering. 'He can wait. We need to concentrate on Alan Farrah. That's where all the blasted instructions are coming from.'

Curtis nodded her head. 'Right, let's get on with it then.'

As they got up to leave, Wyatt walked across to the waiter who was still trying to look busy behind the bar. He took out a ten pound note and put it into the waiter's hand. 'Sorry mate,' he said, 'have a drink on me when you finish work.'

The young man looked at him in awe. 'Are you like, undercover agents or something then?'

'Something like that mate.'

'Wow.'

'Hmm, yeah,' said Wyatt as he walked away slowly. 'Wow.'

They were looked after very well by the local police force. A day later Delaney and Wyatt were waiting in the lobby of another hotel; two hire cars were ready outside. Wyatt did not realise, as Delaney did, who the blonde woman was walking towards them. Curtis was now Melanie Leeder; a blonde with heavy makeup and a tight fitting dress. As Wyatt was admiring her legs, as she moved closer to him.

'That's good, Ben, you didn't recognize me did you?'

'No I did not, where are the glasses?'

'Contact lenses now.'

They moved out into the car park. Delaney took two bunches of car keys from his pocket. 'You take the Subaru, Sally, we'll have the Mercedes.'

'Crikey, these must be costing a fortune,' said Wyatt.

'Yes, Ben, they are, but I'll let the Home Office worry about that. Now, Sally; are you sure you know what to do?'

'Yes I'm sure.'

Alan Farrah stayed in his hotel room that day, as he had the day before when Hoetger had tried another hit on Delaney. His men were close by and he could control things from there without venturing out too much and showing his face.

His brother John was allowed to make one phone call a day from the prison and it was 10am when the phone rang. They were both well versed on exchanging information without giving away what they were really talking about.

'Hello?' said Alan Farrah.

'Can I speak to Mr. Porter please, it's John Farrah.'

'Speaking.'

'Hello Mr. Porter, it's about my mother, you said you could arrange for some flowers to be freshly picked for her birthday.'

'Yes of course, what time would you want them delivered?'

'Two o'clock this afternoon if that's possible.'

'Of course it is, how is she these days?'

'Not too bad thank you, Mr. Porter. And remember my friend, Melanie, would like to meet you sometime.'

'Of course, sir, send her along when she has the time. I have to go now.'

As John Farrah put the prison handset back onto the wall, he looked around to see if anyone was watching. They were always told that the screws could not listen into phone calls, but no one ever really believed it. And if someone *had* been listening, they would not have known what *fresh flower* meant, or what was happening at *2 o'clock*.

Curtis had been impressed at Delaney giving her the Subaru. It was fast. She made her way to HM Prison Nottingham, hoping to get to see John Farrah in the late morning visitor session. She had mixed feelings as she drove through the traffic. Brandon had been such a good man, a bit stuffy and by the book sometimes, but a good man. His wife would be devastated. The feelings of grief were sometimes over-ridden by the learning experience she was having getting to know the powerful characteristics of the Subaru. 'We'll get these low lifes Brandon,' she said to herself, 'just for you and Marcus.'

The visitor's room at the jail looked no different as she walked in. John Farrah had been told he had a visitor minutes after putting the phone down to his brother, and he was waiting. 'You again eh,' he said to her as she sat down. 'You must be desperate.'

'Desperate for what?'

'To meet my big brother.'

Curtis put on her hard face as she replied. 'Like I said, I can help you both, it's your choice.'

'Yeah well, you're in luck. Big brother says you can go and see him.'

'When?'

'Today.'

Curtis held back her feeling of satisfaction. This had been easier than she had expected. She took the chewing gum from her mouth and placed it on the table, licking her lips. 'Where is he then?'

'Sherwood Hotel, about five miles north of here, room 25.'

'Thank you, John,' said Curtis, 'I'll go and see him now then.'

'Make it quick, he's got a little job to do this afternoon.'

A prison guard was hovering around their table and Curtis decided to leave straight away. She punched in the name of the hotel into the car's satellite navigation and made her way north. The hotel was large, and set back near some woods on the outskirts of Sherwood Forest. A large sign pointed towards the hotel while another said *this way to Robin Hood's hideout.*

She walked into the hotel reception. The receptionist asked if she could help. Curtis, putting on her arrogant film star look, said, 'no thank you,' and carried on walking towards the lifts. Room 25 was at the end of a corridor next to a fire escape. Duly noted, she thought, as she put another piece of chewing gum in her mouth.

To her surprise it was Alan Farrah that opened the door, not one of his men, and he was alone. He pretended not to be impressed by the way she looked and opened the door wide so she could walk in easily.

She took a few steps forward and turned to look at him. 'Well Mr. Farrah, you do remember me don't you?'

'Yes, I remember you. The Monroes, Canada. You were one of their tarts.'

'Well, that's your word Mr. Farrah, not mine.'

Farrah did not offer her a drink or a seat, which she was quite pleased about as she did not know if she would need to make a quick exit or not. She stood near the window and looked out for a while before turning to face him, leaning against the window. The sight of Brandon Jones on a stretcher with his face covered, flashed through her mind. Farrah walked around for a while, sometimes passing close to her. His wide, shallow eyes and tough, weathered face were abhorrent to her. He sat down and looked at her, rubbing his forearms and adjusting his crotch. 'So, what is it you want Melanie? And John tells me you may not be Melanie Leeder by the way.'

'I'm not. My name is Sally Curtis.'

'And have you always been Sally Curtis?'

'Yes, Delaney and his men think I'm only here as Melanie.'

Farrah put his hands behind his head and sat back in an over confident manner. 'If I believe you, how can you possibly help me?'

'I can get Delaney and his crew off your back, not to mention MI5.'

'MI5? What have they got to do with it?'

'Don't under estimate yourself, Mr. Farrah. When someone like you has as much effect as you do with all the lost money and the killings, all the British Intelligence departments will have you on their 'to do' list.'

'Including you.'

'No, not including me. I'm CSS, Canadian Secret Service.'

Farrah looked surprised as he bent forward. 'Ah the CSS; you know that your boss had one of your boys taken out don't you, because he was getting too close.'

'Too close to what?' Curtis asked, not wanting to give away how much she knew.

'Too close to the truth and the 90 million dollars.'

'Yes, well, Mr. Farrah, that's why I'm here, I want a good piece of that 90 million.'

The look on Farrah's face told Curtis that he was not going to dismiss the idea. She pushed harder. 'Just think, Alan, a man like you would not miss ten million and in return for that, you and John get to live the rest of your lives unhindered.'

'How can you guarantee that? How do I know you haven't got other ideas? You could take the money and then tell everyone where we are.'

'Yeah right!' said Curtis, 'and then have your hit man pursue me for the rest of my life.'

The conversation was stopped by Farrah's phone ringing. 'Yes, who is it?'

Curtis turned and opened the window to look out, in order to make out that she was not interested. But she could hear Farrah clearly; 'Right....did you organise the other van?....Glasgow!....bloody hell.... Call me tomorrow.'

Curtis waited until Farrah had finished his call before turning around. She had done enough for now. 'Time I was gone, Alan, they'll be wondering where I am. As far as they know I was just visiting your brother in jail.'

'Why don't you hang around, my little brother could be with us soon.'

'No thanks, let me know what you decide.'

She walked confidently to the door, opened it and walked out. She hoped that Farrah had not noticed how much she was sweating. The fact that he had not tried to stop her was good, she thought. And the phone call; it had to be Hoetger.

She got into her car and drove about 3 miles before parking in a large lay-by where she had good vision. Her hands were still sweating as she phoned Delaney. 'Tom, I think Hoetger is in Glasgow.'

'Why the hell do you think that?'

'Something John Farrah said when I was talking to him.'

There was a pause. She could hear Wyatt saying something in the background.

'Okay, Sally,' said Delaney, 'meet us back at the hotel.'

'Will do, I can't wait to get out of these awful clothes.' She was about to put the phone down as Delaney spoke again.

'And why did it take you so long by the way, you have just been to see John Farrah haven't you?'

'Yes, just John, there was a hold up at the jail because of some visitor causing trouble.'

'Okay, see you soon.'

Curtis made her way out of the lay-by and headed back to their hotel.

Delaney and Wyatt waited for a few minutes and then took the same route. Curtis had not seen the Mercedes they were sitting in, parked up on the same side of the road a few hundred metres behind her.

23

The hotel dining room was quiet as most guests had already eaten and the only other people there were an elderly couple sitting in the opposite corner to where Delaney, Curtis and Wyatt were having lunch. Curtis told them about her visit to the prison, but not about her visit to Alan Farrah.

'So it went okay,' said Delaney, 'but he didn't tell you where his big brother was.'

'No,' said Curtis as she reached for her drink to hide the fact that she was swallowing hard.

Wyatt remained silent, eating his club sandwich.

'I've just thought of something else,' said Curtis.

Delaney raised his head enquiringly.

'He said something about his big brother having a little job to do this afternoon, so even if he was going to agree to see me it wouldn't be today.'

'I'll have a think about that one,' said Delaney. 'How about we all get some rest?'

'Agreed,' said Wyatt.

They finished lunch and went to their rooms. Curtis removed her disguise and showered, scrubbing more than usual as if to get the stench of the Farrahs off her. Delaney had phone calls to make to old friends in Scotland. Whichever Farrah she got the information from, he was confident that Curtis was right about Hoetger going to Glasgow.

When Wyatt had been in his room for five minutes, he threw some cold water over his face, washed his mouth out and made his way to reception. The lady behind the desk looked up as he approached. 'Can I help you sir?'

'Yes please, can you get me a taxi?'

'Of course, going to where?'

'Nottingham jail.'

The gate man watched Wyatt on the CCTV as he got out of the taxi and walked towards the entrance. Wyatt knocked on the huge black timber door. A voice from a speaker said, 'Yes please.'

Wyatt looked up at the camera as he reached for his ID card. 'I would like to see the Governor please.'

'You need an appointment.' said the grey box.

'I haven't got time for appointments,' said Wyatt. He held his card towards the camera. 'Get a close up of this. My name is Wyatt, British Intelligence. Tell the Governor I need to see him now.'

There was silence for a few minutes. Just as Wyatt was getting impatient, the huge door opened. Two prison officers stood in front of him. The smaller of the two smiled and said, 'come with us please Mr. Wyatt.'

They led him through some archways and in between two chrome posts. An alarm sounded. Wyatt knew what was coming and stood still. Being the only one, it would seem, who could speak, the smaller man asked Wyatt if he had any metal items on his person.

Wyatt opened the left side of his jacket slightly to reveal his shoulder holster and handgun. 'Only this,' he said, 'and it's staying there.'

The officers looked at each other for a moment, before one of them went into an office. Wyatt saw him make a phone call and noticed his surprised look as he put the phone down. He emerged from the office, nodded and said, 'Okay.' They led Wyatt through a maze of corridors and eventually into a room with a large, old fashioned desk in the middle of it and a filing cabinet in every corner.

The Governor was a big man with a gentle air about him. He asked Wyatt to sit down.

'Good afternoon, I'm Asher. This is of course, a little out of order, Mr. Wyatt,' he said.

'I know, Mr. Asher, but I knew any sensible Governor would realise that someone like me wouldn't turn up without good reason.'

'Quite. So how can I help?'

'One of the inmates, John Farrah, it's about him.'

'Thought it might be,' said Asher.

'Why did you?'

'Because I always wondered why he ended up here. You know we're not high security don't you?'

'Yes,' said Wyatt. 'Are you one of those prisons that still listen to outgoing phone calls?'

'That's not strictly allowed, Mr. Wyatt, as you probably know.'

'I didn't ask if it was allowed, I asked if you still did it.'

Asher looked undisturbed. He smiled and said quietly, 'yes we do.'

Some minutes later they were listening to a taped telephone conversation between John Farrah and a 'Mr. Porter.' Wyatt listened intently to what was being said and made a mental note of certain phrases. - *'Hello Mr. Porter, it's about my mother.... you said you could arrange for some flowers....picked for her birthday...yes of course, what time would you want them delivered?....two o'clock this afternoon...and remember my friend Melanie would like to meet...'*

Asher turned the tape off. 'There you are Mr. Wyatt, any questions or observations?'

Wyatt stood up and began walking around the room. 'Yes,' he said 'John Farrah's mother died two years ago.'

Asher said nothing, thinking that Wyatt may have been disappointed he didn't know about Farrah's mother.

'What time is it?' asked Wyatt.

'One forty nine.'

Hobson and Ashby drove the truck down Mansfield Road in the direction of Nottingham Jail. The small tipper truck had other motorists winding up their windows; the fresh compost on the back of it was *very* fresh. Hobson drove steadily and sensibly. Ashby checked the shot gun at the side of his seat. The entrance to the prison garden was 100 metres away from the main entrance and for the last two days, the compost had arrived at exactly 2 p.m.

Alan Farrah followed them in his Range Rover and stayed well behind. As they approached the prison garden gates, he pulled into a side street and parked up facing the main road and the prison. It was 1.51 p.m.

The young prison guard opened the outer gates to the garden. 'Ah, what a smell!' he said. 'Where are the other blokes today then?'

Hobson leaned out of his window. 'Daft sod broke his leg last night, tripped on a branch or something walking his dog. Do you want it in the usual place?'

'Yeah, but pull in first so I can close the outer gate.'

The young officer was not experienced enough to realise that when Hobson had said, 'do you want it in the usual place', he was actually planting into the young man's mind that he had been there before, but of course he had not. He had no idea of where the 'usual place' was. Hobson pulled forward so the officer could close the outer gate. Ashby jumped from the cab and approached the man. 'Here, let me get that for you while you deal with the inner gate.'

The officer agreed.

Ashby closed the gates and banged the catches against each other to make it sound like they were closed. The young man started to open the inner gates while Hobson inched the tipper truck forward slowly.

Asher had poured tea and waited before speaking again to Wyatt. 'Any other questions Mr. Wyatt?' A noise came from outside. It was the noise of an air brake being used on a truck. 'That sounded like a truck,' said Wyatt.

'Yes, probably the compost delivery we get some days.'

'Compost?'

'Yes, for the prison garden.'

Wyatt tapped the top of his head repeatedly while he was thinking hard. Then he turned quickly to face Asher. 'Where is Farrah now?'

'In the garden, as he is every other day.'

Wyatt bolted for the door. 'Sound the alarm and show me the way to the garden, now!'

Asher, stunned, said 'What are...'

'Picking flowers, 2 o'clock! Think about it! The only thing being picked is John Farrah, move your arse!'

The young prison officer had just opened the inner gate when the alarm sounded.

'Damn!' said Hobson. He put his foot down and headed straight for the young man. The guard dived out of the way, but hit his head on a boulder nearby; he was stunned but not unconscious. Ashby ran from the outer gates and kicked him in the head. Fifty metres away John Farrah began to sprint as Hobson turned the truck around. Ashby jumped back into the cab and grabbed his shotgun. Another prison officer ran after Farrah but dived behind a shed as Ashby let off a shot from his window. Wyatt was now on the scene, followed by three men. He stopped short when he saw the shotgun pointing out of the truck window. The three men carried on running towards the gates, and Wyatt noticed Farrah getting near the truck. He pulled out his gun and shouted. 'Down! Down now!' The three men hit the ground, Ashby's shotgun rang out again, but he was too far away to hurt anyone seriously. Wyatt knelt down, breathed out and took aim. He fired twice. Farrah took both bullets in the back just as he was about to jump into the back of the truck. Wyatt fired two more shots at the truck; he heard someone in the truck shout 'go go!' and the vehicle raced away in the direction of the main road.

Alan Farrah had heard the gunshots. He reversed his Range Rover further back down the side street. Hobson turned into the side street and he and Ashby jumped out and into the Range Rover. Farrah drove quietly and slowly down the side street and onto another main road. They parked the vehicle and walked down to a bus stop. They stood waiting for the bus just as anyone would. A police car raced past them heading in the direction of the prison.

Wyatt, still holding his gun, walked up to John Farrah. The force of the bullets in his back had thrown Farrah to the ground and his face was buried in mud. Wyatt turned him over with his foot. Farrah's eyes were open and he choked on the mud and his own blood as he looked at Wyatt. It was a look of hatred as Wyatt waited for him to die.

Governor Asher was standing at the side of them by now, he started to say something and Wyatt told him bluntly to shut up. Asher walked away and started to give out instructions to his stunned officers. Wyatt kept looking at Farrah. Then he kicked him hard in the gut. 'That's for Brandon Jones you bastard. And I make that one-all.'

It was 6pm by the time Wyatt got back to the hotel. He walked into reception to find Delaney and Curtis sitting near the window looking at him. An hour earlier they had had a visit from the local CID who had explained what had happened at the prison.

Wyatt looked at them both without speaking.

'Just a wild guess, Ben,' said Delaney, 'but I bet you could use a drink.' He walked through to the hotel bar and Wyatt and Curtis followed.

Wyatt explained what had happened and how John Farrah had died. Delaney did not say too much. Wyatt had been in the wrong by going it alone, but Wyatt was Wyatt, and a telling off did not seem appropriate, after the death of Jones.

Curtis however, was not so benevolent. She waited until Wyatt had finished his story. 'And what about Alan Farrah? How do we get him now John's dead?' she said.

Wyatt was taken by surprise. 'You what?'

'You heard.'

Delaney told them both to keep their voices down. Curtis continued. 'John Farrah was going to tell me where his brother was, what do I do now?'

'Try harder. You're too quick to question what we do, like I said before, if you don't like it, piss off back to Canada.'

Curtis looked to Delaney for support. She did not get any.

'Come on, Sally,' said Delaney. 'Ben has just taken out one of our main enemies. It may hold up progress for a while but if it hadn't happened today, it would have happened in the not too distant future. Anyway, after a short spell of grieving, Alan Farrah will be probably be glad not to have the burden of his little brother on him.'

Curtis got up and shook her head. 'I'm not so sure Tom, he *was* his brother, and I think the hardest of people still care for their families. I'm going to my room to make some phone calls. I know a few people who may be able to help us if we are going to Glasgow.'

'Who said anything about Glasgow,' asked Delaney.

'I thought we would go after Hoetger; remember what John Farrah said to me?'

'Well, as much as I would like to catch up with Hoetger,' said Delaney, 'if he is up there, wouldn't it be a good time to find Alan Farrah first, as we think he's in this area?'

'Of course gov, you're right,' said Wyatt.

Curtis looked at Wyatt with a clenched mouth and left.

Wyatt replenished the two drinks and sat closer to Delaney. 'Why didn't you tell her that we saw her at that hotel?'

'Perhaps I should have asked her, I just thought maybe she might not be telling us because she doesn't want anything jeopardized. She was undercover remember.'

'Yeah; do you think it's a possibility that Alan Farrah was in that hotel?'

'Yes I do.'

'So if he *was* there, why didn't she tell us?'

'I was wondering that myself, perhaps she's playing for both sides.'

24

Angela Casey switched off her bedside alarm. The green digital figures said 06.30 and she needed to be at work for eight o'clock. All the civilian secretaries had been asked to be in the office a little earlier because there were some new assignments coming through from Interpol and they had to be checked, de-encrypted and in some cases, translated. The recent office move had also affected procedures, and people were still getting used to new I.T. and security systems.

The well rehearsed morning tasks of hair washing and makeup were soon sorted out and the muesli and yoghurt tasted as good as usual. As she switched on her phone it bleeped to tell her there was a text message. *Won't be home for another couple of days, will ring you later. Xx.* She answered – *Okay. XX.*

Delaney was often away. She had become used to it but he kept in touch and she had the contact details of all of his staff and she knew she could phone anytime if she needed to. His job though, was certainly not a *normal* one and she would never phone him unnecessarily, especially in the daytime.

When she arrived at the office, one of her colleagues was already there.

'Morning, Michelle, early bird again I see,' said Angela as she took off her coat.

'Morning, Angela, I got the earlier tube. You should see all this stuff coming in from Europe; you'd think all the police forces have been saving up work to send in all at once.'

'Has Daniel been in then?'

'Yes he was here when I got in, he's gone upstairs.'

Daniel was the I.T. manager and it was his job to get things started up each morning and check for viruses and verification codes before anyone could receive messages.

'I would get yourself a cuppa before you sit down if I were you,' said Michelle. 'You won't believe the amount of assignments coming in, and most of them need translating.'

Angela, Michelle and two other women could translate from French and Italian. Assignments would sometimes come in a mixture of languages because the originator of the work had tried to translate into English, with varying degrees of success. Angela could see what Michelle meant as she tapped her 'receive' button. There were a total of 23 assignments that had been allocated to her.

She started to sort through them. Each assignment came with a priority code, five being high, one being low. Seven had been given a high priority rating and she moved those to the top of the list and started to go through the code fives; three from Hong Kong and four from France. One of the French communiqués surprised her that it was a code five. She had seen similar information come through before. Some of the intelligence staff based in France liaised with the Gendarmerie and the information they sent was a mixture of answers and observations from both parties when they had worked together. It usually came through as code two's or three's to be passed onto the named party. This particular communiqué took her eye when she noticed the recipient's name.

Item: Farrah 3479
Agents: Landers 12107/deVille909G
FAO: Delaney 666/121
Confirmation – Farrah's villa near Grenoble empty.
Confirmation – Hoetger masterminded bank raid.
Confirmation – Gendarmerie questioning two men in Auxerre. Found spending stolen money.
For information, - Delaney and Overseas Liaison Agency only. – send to private box 666.

She zipped the document as they always did and sent it to box 666. Only two people could access 666; Delaney and his second in command, Taffy Burton. Knowing he was away in Nottingham and that it would be another day at least before he read the message, she decided to text Delaney to let him know.

The atmosphere around the breakfast table in Nottingham was not good following the previous day's events. Delaney was finishing his coffee as Wyatt sat down with his second helping of sausages and bacon. Curtis gave Wyatt her usual breakfast look of 'I hope you know what that is doing to your heart' as she nibbled on her fruit and yoghurt. Wyatt was getting increasingly impatient with her. 'Problem?'

'No, you eat that stuff if it's what you really want.'

'I will, and after I've finished I'm going outside to have another cigarette, okay?'

Delaney, smirking, looked at both of them and got up to leave. 'Well whatever both of you are eating, get on with it; I want you both outside ready to go in twenty minutes.'

Thirty two minutes later Delaney was giving his instructions. 'Right, Sally you're with me in the Subaru, you drive. Ben, you follow in the Mercedes, Our wonderful back-up people couldn't get us onto any flights this morning so we're driving.'

'Where to?' said Curtis.

'Glasgow, we should be there for early afternoon.'

Curtis raised her hands in despair. 'And what about Farrah? Do we just leave him here?'

Wyatt couldn't resist jumping in. 'Leave him where? Know where he is do you?'

'No but if he's in the area we...'

'He was in the area, yesterday,' said Delaney.

Curtis was silenced because she was not expecting this and Wyatt said nothing because he knew Delaney wanted to continue.

'Alan Farrah was at the hotel you went to yesterday morning, Sally,' said Delaney. 'Last night I had the local boys go in for him but he had gone. There was no sign of him, or his men. According to the hotel manager he had left about thirty minutes after he had been visited by a blonde woman. From what they told me, I think he left without thinking, unusually for him, because there were a few notes scribbled on a piece of paper, something about charter flights. He had used the hotel phone to make calls as well. One number was East Midlands airport, another was a car hire firm in Glasgow.'

Wyatt looked at Delaney with admiration. It was times like this that reminded him why he liked working for him.

'I got a call from Taffy as well by the way,' continued Delaney, 'he's out of hospital, on light duties.'

Curtis stood motionless, not knowing what to expect next. Delaney looked at her and pointed his head towards the car door. 'Get in; we'll talk on the way.'

William Hoetger looked out of the train window as it made its way into Glasgow. His driver, Michael Turner, had already started to gather up their belongings; paying particular attention to the new package they had collected en-route from Manchester.

They had left the rifle and handgun they had used in Nottingham, to burn with the van, and Hoetger had contacted an old army friend in Manchester who had done very well for himself since he started dealing in arms and weaponry 'for the discerning'. The dealer had supplied them with Smith and Wesson firearms; two 9mm handguns and a 15R rifle. 'You'll like this one, William.' The dealer had said to Hoetger. 'It's accurate and easy to take apart.' Hoetger had told him, it had better be for what it cost.

Turner opened the compartment door as they approached the Queen Street station and wheeled Hoetger out into the corridor. He slung the few bags they had over his shoulder and Hoetger held the sports bag containing the weapons on his knee. The new van that someone had arranged for them was parked in a disabled bay and a young man greeted them when he noticed the wheelchair. 'Mr Johnson?'

'Yes, that's right,' said Hoetger.

'I have your vehicle for you. I'll just run through all the controls and then...'

'That's fine,' said Turner, 'I know how everything works.'

When the papers were signed he used the rear tail-lift to get Hoetger into the vehicle. It was brand new with all the latest gadgets and Hoetger wondered if this one was going to end up wrecked as well. They made their way to Bearsden and booked into the hotel on Milngavie Road that Farrah had reserved for them. The ground floor room for disabled guests was well appointed and Hoetger settled himself in. Turner took the room next door.

A short while later there was a knock on Hoetger's door. He pressed the two buttons on his phone that put him straight through to Turner and let it ring twice, which was the signal for Turner to come at once. The young hotel employee holding the package looked surprised as Turner approached her. 'I'll take that for Mr. Johnson,' he said. The girl handed a package over to him just as Hoetger opened his door. Satisfied that the package was getting to the right man, the girl said. 'It's just arrived by courier.'

Turner guessed what might have been in the package; he handed it to Hoetger and went back to his room. Hoetger closed his door and wheeled himself to the side of his bed. He opened the package at one end and emptied the contents onto the bed. A quick count told him there was about £50,000. The note with the money was brief, as usual.

This is for J and B. hope the van is Okay. – A.

'Well?' said Delaney as he put his foot down getting on to the northbound motorway.

Curtis did not turn to look at him as she answered. 'Sorry,' she said. Delaney, eyes on the road and his mirrors at all times, said, 'I want a reason as well as an apology.'

'I couldn't be sure, Tom.'

'Sure of what?'

'That you would let me go and see him alone. I thought if I told you, you would want back-up and all that stuff and would want to nail Farrah there and then. I wanted to get closer to him before I involved you all, I didn't want to jeopardise getting a complete result.'

'What do you mean, complete result?'

'Getting the lot, Farrah, Hoetger *and* the money. I just wanted to be sure I could sell myself to Farrah before I let you know, maybe I was afraid of failure.'

Delaney looked in his mirror again and he could see Wyatt behind him, following sensibly, not too close. 'We're all afraid of failure in this job, Sally, whether we realise it or not, but the chance of failure increases even more when we try to go it alone. Why do you think Ben and I followed you when you left the prison? We were just looking out for you.'

Curtis, satisfied he wasn't going to scorn her too much, asked her own question. 'But why didn't you and Ben do something when you followed me there. You must have realised I was meeting Farrah senior.'

'I was pretty sure it was Alan Farrah in the hotel, although not a hundred percent sure. Ben wanted to go in, but I said no.'

'So why did you say no?'

'For exactly the same reason as you gave me a minute ago, I wanted a complete result.'

Curtis opened her mouth more. 'You hypocrite! You talk about not going it alone and then leave me with Farrah, alone, when you're a few metres away! In case it jeopardized *your* complete result'

'Well, yes, simply because we were just that; a few metres away.'

Curtis was silent then, not wanting to push her luck too far. Delaney kept his eyes on the road as his phone rang. 'Get that will you.'

Curtis checked his phone. 'It's a text message from Angela,' she said.

'Okay, read it to me.'

She read the message slowly to him. *'assignment info from Landers, gendarmerie have two men, villa empty, sent to your inbox.'*

Delaney nodded in acknowledgement. 'Right, I'll phone Stephen when we get to Glasgow.'

At Carlisle services, where they stopped for a break, Wyatt received a call from one of his 'helpers'. Delaney asked him what was wrong when he saw the quizzical look on Wyatt's face.

'It was about Hoetger, gov, apparently his reason for going to Scotland has nothing to do with us or Farrah.'

'Go on.'

'Well, he reckons Hoetger has another target, something about a bent barrister.'

'Gee this guy gets around,' said Curtis.

'How reliable is this source, Ben?'

'Reliable enough, he's the one that knew about Hoetger going north with a new driver.'

'Right,' said Delaney. 'Sally and I will get on the road again. You make some phone calls from here, Ben. Tell the local boys in Glasgow and the London office what we're doing, and then catch us up.'

Wyatt had caught up with the Subaru about 30 miles from Glasgow. It was approaching 4pm when they booked into the Holiday Inn on Stockwell Street overlooking the river. They all spent the last part of the day phoning local Glasgow contacts but no one had heard anything about an imminent hit. Curtis received an important piece of information from the local transport police; the CCTV cameras at Queen Street station had picked out a man in a wheelchair. Delaney decided that his first phone calls the next day would be to car hire companies; not many of them hired out wheelchair friendly vans.

25

Michael Turner was pleased when Hoetger had said that he wanted him to do the next job. It had been a while since he had made a hit, but he was still quite fit for his 49 years and he could remember how to handle a good rifle.

'Who is it, Mr. Hoetger?'

'A solicitor called Cox. Here are the details; a room has been booked for you.'

Turner studied the details that were handed to him. 'Looks pretty straight forward. When?'

'Tomorrow morning. Its nine p.m. now, if you leave soon you can be in the guest house in an hour.'

The taxi driver looked at Turner in the mirror. Right, he thought, let me see if I can figure out what this one does. 'Hello, sir, welcome to Glasgow.' He said in his tourist friendly voice. 'Where to?'

'Calvechie Guest House, do you know it?'

'Aye, I know it.'

'Thank you.'

The driver looked again as he pulled away. Definitely a tourist he thought, probably about forty five to fifty, well travelled, perhaps a writer or some kind of trouble shooter that was sent to sort out legal or medical problems by an insurance company. His black hair was greying at the sides. A little greasy. He had not shaven for a few days. His sunken eyes looked intelligent and calculating.

'Here on holiday, sir?' The driver asked.

'Yes, just for a few days,' said Turner.

'Your first time in these parts?'

'First time for many years.'

The taxi was soon approaching the guest house. Thinking of his tip, the driver put on his tourist voice again. 'Well here we are then, sir; it only takes a wee while to get here. Now, would you like a hand with your luggage?'

'No thank you, I just have the one sports bag.'

The guest house was small but well looked after. The room which had been booked for him was clean, but the owners had been a little too free with the air freshener. The strong smell of lavender made him cough slightly. The chintz of the furniture and the patterned wallpaper with a dado rail, made the room look like it needed a refurb. He drew back the lace curtain at the window a few inches. Across the road and slightly to his right was the building he was most interested in. Its old grey walls made it look like it had been imported from Aberdeen, as none of the surrounding buildings were like it. The first floor office windows all had their blinds pulled down and lights were out. He opened the sports bag and started to lay out its contents on the bed.

There were four parts to 15R Rifle. It was known to him as the RHV and he had used one before. The butt clicked nicely into its mechanism and the short barrel, which had only just fitted in the bag, also connected perfectly. The scope clicked onto the top of the rifle with a reassuring, solid clunk. A Bauer silencer completed the assembly. The small tripod was unfolded and set up easily. He laid it under the bed with the small box of spiral tipped bullets. It was ten p.m. He rested, and was asleep 20 minutes later.

The alarm clock went off at the side of Turners' bed. It said 6.05 a.m. He arose quickly feeling fit and sober. The water was cold and sharp as he put his head under the tap and threw the water over his arms and neck. He pulled the 15R rifle from under the bed where he had left it and mounted it on the tripod. The bullets slipped into the magazine easily. It held 12 although he hoped he would only need one. With the curtains open, he could see the office windows across the street that had been shut with blinds drawn. Lights were already starting to go on and some blinds had opened. He pulled back the lace curtain a couple of inches, sat back and waited.

The offices that Michael Turner was watching were occupied by Cox, Cox and Kitchener, Solicitors. Senior partner Andrew Cox had started the business 30 years ago and still played a full time role in running the business as well as taking on new clients. His specialty had always been Health and Safety Law and many cases had involved helping the Health and Safety Executive and the Scottish Environmental Protection Agency. He made his son David a partner when he became fully qualified. David had worked in the business for seven years and was doing very well. He specialised mainly in matrimonial cases, but recently had taken on a few clients who needed help setting up businesses and dealing with employment law. The third partner, Johnnie Kitchener had worked with Mr. Cox senior for many years and was always there to handle anything given to him. Although as he had gotten older, he had become a bit more choosy and was now tending to take a back seat more and help with the running of the business and the mentoring of the 'juniors'.

David Cox arrived at work earlier than usual that day at 6.30. His father and Johnnie Kitchener had organised a golf day for some clients and David was keen to get to work earlier than the juniors; as his father would have done. He walked vigorously up the stairs to his first floor office. Susan was already behind her desk. Susan Cradley had worked as a secretary in the practice for 20 years. Mr Cox senior referred to her as 'the old stalwart'; not a title she was ever keen on.

David acknowledged her presence as he passed her desk on the way to his office. 'Hi, Susan, didn't think I'd be here before you'

'Aye and you'd be right with that one, Master David' She sometimes called him this as though they were in a Dickensian play, and he hated it but indulged her as he knew his father wanted him to.

'Right, a coffee if I may please and then I'll prepare for the first appointment', said Cox as he hung up his coat and took his usual position at his modern desk. Susan was already on her way to the kitchen. 'Aye, right enough, you get on, I'll get you your coffee'.

David lifted the blind behind him and opened the window before sitting back down. He preferred sitting with his back to the window as he was too easily unsettled by the busy Glasgow street which always had plenty of distractions and noise.

Turner had a clear sight of David Cox through the lens of his 15R. He moved the gun around, looking through the scope to take in the rest of the office and check that no one else was there. Through the scope he could see the books on the shelves and a picture of a woman with two young children, smiling, buckets and spades in hand. He slowly moved the rifle around again and eventually aimed it directly at the back of David Cox. He would go for the upper back. He knew the bullet would go straight through to the heart and probably come out the other side of him, eventually resting in some furniture somewhere. He moved the lace curtain another few inches so he could see more easily. It exposed him more, but at this time in the morning, with most of the street still asleep, he accepted the risk.

Just then he couldn't believe his luck. Coming down the street with full blues and twos was a fire and rescue vehicle. The noise of the sirens bounced off the buildings and covered the whole scene with a deafening screech. He took his final aim just as the vehicle was approaching. But in a millisecond he saw David Cox raise his head. Susan had brought him his coffee and as she approached his desk she looked up, over the shoulder of Cox. The reflection of a blue flashing light had bounced off something and had caught her eye. The she was gazing directly at Michael Turner.

'Great timing lady. Shit' Turner said as he pulled the trigger. David Cox died instantly as his blood splattered over Susan Cradley. Trent aimed again and pulled the trigger again. The bullet hit her in the head and she was thrown back against the wall. He had to, he thought; she saw his face even if it was partly hidden behind the rifle. Job done, he packed the 15R away.

At the reception desk, the elderly lady smiled at him. 'Everything okay there for you?'

'Yes, great thank you, I'm on my way to Skye today. How much do I owe you?'

'Just the room rate will be fine, sir if you're not stopping for breakfast'.

'No no, that's good thanks, £55 was it?'

'Aye, Please'.

He handed her the money in cash. She seemed concerned and looked at him again. 'Now you be careful out there, there's all sorts of things going on what with fire engines rushing around and all. Always is these days, always is. Still, you'll be well out of the way on Skye'.

'Indeed', said Turner 'Indeed. Well, goodbye and thank you again'.

'Not at all, Mr err...' she looked down at the hotel register and then back up again. '...Mr. Lister, not at all.'

He walked out onto the street and turned towards the city centre down a side street. A young man came from a doorway. Above the door it said Azzerro's Restaurant. He was carrying a tray of old food and a bag of waste which he tipped into a small council skip, leaving the lid open. As Trent walked past the skip, he threw the sports bag into it. He paused for a while at the end of the street and looked back. No one else was around. The young man came out of the restaurant again and threw another two bags of waste and a crate of empty bottles into the skip and closed the lid. Turner smirked as he turned to make his way back to Hoetger. It had become a sunny morning and he decided to walk the four miles back to the hotel on Milngavie Road.

The big brown Clyde River moved slowly. Delaney watched it from his hotel balcony. Yet again he was feeling tired and yet again he wondered how many more years he wanted to continue chasing criminals or protecting people that most of the public had never heard of. As he reached the hotel reception, Wyatt and Curtis were waiting for him and he explained that he wanted to go and talk to car hire companies in the city that had wheelchair vans available. They left the Mercedes at the hotel and Curtis said she would like to drive the Subaru. Delaney agreed and they made their way to Avis rent-a-car on Craighall Road. The traffic was busy and the journey was slow. Curtis looked at the car clock that said 07.00. 'We should have left it a bit later for the rush hour to die down,' she said.

'Too late for that suggestion now,' said Delaney.

The traffic was moving slowly along Craighall Road. Curtis was concentrating on getting in the right lane, Delaney was checking his phone messages and Wyatt was looking around generally at everything that was going on. It was his first time in Glasgow and he was taking in the different scenes, buildings and shops.

'Avis is just down here,' said Delaney. 'When we get there I want to ask about…'

'Stop the car!'

Curtis slowed down; Wyatt had meant what he'd said. She pulled into a small lay-by outside a newsagents shop and looked at Wyatt in the mirror. Delaney turned slightly to talk to Wyatt over his shoulder. He knew him too well to know that he wouldn't say something like that without cause. 'What is it, Ben?'

'Just stay here,' said Wyatt. 'In a second, a man will walk past on your left.'

They waited and said nothing. A few men walked past the car. 'There,' said Wyatt. 'The one wearing the dark blue jacket.'

'What about him?' asked Delaney.

'It's Michael Turner, also known as Andrew Lister, also known as Stevie Holden; he's one of the best drivers and hit men in the business.'

Curtis stayed quiet and put the car into first gear to await instructions. Delaney kept his eyes on the man while he spoke to Wyatt. 'How do you know?'

'I know; he did some jobs for John Balfour, the fraudster, and he was the one that my snout said had been given the job of working for Hoetger.'

Delaney trusted Wyatt enough to make a decision. 'Get out and follow him; Sally and I will stay in the car and keep you in sight.'

Wyatt got out of the Subaru and started to walk about 50 metres behind Turner. Traffic permitting, Curtis drove the car slowly; pulling in if they got too close. A few blocks further on, Turner stopped to look inside a café. He walked in and sat at a table facing the window. Wyatt stayed back and looked to see if his colleagues had realised. They had. He decided he would wait for Turner to have his breakfast or coffee. He knew Turner by sight, so why wouldn't Turner know *him* by sight?

Turner dialed his short code number four while he was sipping a coffee. 'It's me, Mr. Hoetger, I'm on my way back and the job is completed.'

Hoetger sounded satisfied. 'So you haven't lost your touch then?'

'No, course not. I'm just having a coffee; I'll be with you again by about eight.'

Wyatt threw away his cigarette as Turner came out of the café 20 minutes later. Turner looked to his left and then to his right.

Wyatt was looking at him.

He was looking at Wyatt.

He started to walk away and Wyatt followed. Delaney watched Turner from the car and told Curtis to get a little closer. Someone in a large bus blew their horn at Curtis as she was crawling by the roadside holding up the traffic. Turner turned to see what was happening. He paused and looked at the Subaru, then looked to see that Wyatt had stopped to look inside a shop window. Delaney recognized the motion straight away. It was the motion of a man reaching for a gun from a shoulder holster without making it too obvious. Delaney held out his right hand to Curtis. 'Stop.'

Curtis stopped the car and looked back to see where Wyatt was. Delaney by now had his handgun at the ready. Turner raised his gun and aimed at the Subaru, but suddenly spun around and changed his aim to Wyatt. Delaney was not in a mood to shout warnings; not after losing Brandon Jones. He shot twice; the first bullet hitting Turner in the leg, the second in the shoulder. Seeing he was not grounded, Delaney fired again, the bullet hitting Turner square in the chest, throwing him back through a shop window. Shoppers and commuters ran out of the way as they screamed and Wyatt sprinted up to Turner who was lying in the shop window covered in blood and glass. Curtis got out of the car and got to the scene seconds after Wyatt and Delaney. Turner was dead; his eyes wide open, looking at nothing. Wyatt was smiling and after a while his smile turned to a small laugh. While Curtis was asking people to move on, Delaney looked at Wyatt. 'Something funny?'

Wyatt pointed to a blood covered sign at the side of Turner's head.

'Assistant needed – apply within'

Delaney took a deep breath. 'Well, it's Hoetger that needs an assistant now.'

'Yeah,' said Wyatt. He looked again at Turner. 'I make that two-one; to us.'

26

The sun shone down on the countryside of Montague de Lans near the village of Claix, just south of Grenoble. Alan Farrah was in a reflective mood as he looked out over the early morning dew clad fields. He had not gone to Glasgow.

The call logs from the hotel in Nottingham and the flight details he had left in his hotel room were meant to be found. It would be difficult for Delaney to resist going to Scotland, hoping that Farrah *and* Hoetger would be there. It gave Farrah enough time to organize transport in the opposite direction. His contacts had been reliable as usual and the short helicopter flight from Nottingham to Lowerstoft had been well handled. From there, another 'old mate' had taken him and his men Ashby and Hobson, on a fast boat trip down to France.

The only reason he had returned to England was to spring his brother out of jail. The bundled rescue attempt and subsequent death of his brother, John, had not really upset him. He had grieved for a while when he thought of some of the things they used to do together as children, but not for long. His brother had not been very clever and he always knew that he would out live him. If it wasn't someone in the prison who shot him, it would have been someone else, and probably not long after. He knew he had grown bitter and indifferent to these things that happened around him and he wondered for a while why he wasn't sad about losing his brother.

But lately, he had changed a little. Sometimes he found himself feeling sorry for those around him that been injured or killed. Recently he had admitted to himself that he would always be greedy and would never really feel remorse. But subconsciously, maybe John's death had affected him. For a second, he considered how good it would be to retire; perhaps soon.

Hobson was sitting near the window. He and Farrah had just finished double-checking the money and Ashby had put it away. They got the exact count to $148m. Ashby strolled back into the room and sat down as he looked at both of them. 'I've put half of it in the cellar, in the old vat, and the other half in the garage behind the work benches.'

'What about the keys?' asked Farrah.

'Both doors are locked and the keys are in my pocket.'

'Right, you keep hold of them then.'

Pops walked into the room. 'Pops' was the name they had given to the old French man who lived nearby. He kept a watch on the villa when Farrah was away. He probably realized they were criminals but 500 francs a week, cash, was enough to keep him quiet and it supplemented his income from his fruit stall nicely. He would ride to the villa on his bright blue bicycle, do some work, and ride back. Hobson spoke to him first. 'Hello, Pops, what is it?'

Pops spoke slowly. 'There is message. Telephone, you see?' He pointed to the telephone on the side table. Farrah looked at Hobson and Ashby with disappointment; they had not checked for messages. The old man left the room. Ashby pressed the playback button on the telephone and they listened to the messages.

Click. 'Message one.'

'Alan, it's Hoetger. Michael Turner is dead. He was doing a job for me and they caught up with him. I can get another driver to get me back to France, but when I am there I will need one of your boys. Okay? It will take me a couple of days to get to you'

Click. 'Message 2.'

'It's me, I can confirm that Hoetger, or his man, got rid of David Cox, so you can forget about his share. Don't forget to put my share to one side will you.'

Not recognizing the voice of the second caller, Hobson motioned his head towards the telephone. 'Who's that then, boss?'

'Just another bent colleague. You'll meet him when he comes for his share,' said Farrah.

'Who's David Cox then?' asked Ashby.

Farrah hesitated before answering because he was not sure he wanted to tell them. 'Well guys, if you must know he was a solicitor who worked for me. He helped me forge documents and get over legal stumbling blocks now and again, but he was getting too greedy.'

'How greedy,' said Hobson. 'He wasn't after a portion of our share was he?'

'Possibly, but he's dead now so forget it. Both of you.'

Hobson wanted to push the point and find out who it was that left the second message, but the tone of Farrah's voice changed his mind. Instead, he looked at Ashby. 'There you go then, Mark, a nice little job for you, looking after Mr. Hoetger when he gets here.'

'Piss off, you can do it. You're always telling me what a good driver you are.'

Farrah cut them both short. 'Okay that'll do. It'll be my decision anyway. You can do one thing though Mark;

organize a van for him will you, there should be somewhere in Grenoble that can provide one, failing that you'll have to get one from Lyon.'

Ashby nodded. Hobson smiled.

Stephen Landers pulled his sun visor down as he drove south. The early morning sun was pleasant enough but the roads around Voiron were unknown to him so he was driving cautiously. His main contact in Marseille had told him that Farrah's villa near Grenoble was empty, so he had sent that message to Delaney, but one of his Gendarmerie friends had said that they thought it was occupied. He needed to check it out for himself. If he was going to let Delaney have new information, he needed to make sure it was correct.

He made his way to the west of Grenoble and through Fontaine and Seyssins. A small sign said, Claix 5km, and he pulled off the road and parked up behind a small truck in a lay-by. The detailed map told him that the Farrah villa was about 2km as the crow flies and he decided to walk across the fields and approach the villa from the west. As it was a hot day, he used his lightweight jacket to cover his shoulder holster, phone in one pocket, binoculars in the other.

The tracks to the sides of the fields were dry and uneven as he pushed on in the direction of the villa. A young girl was walking her shabby looking terrier dog and he exchanged a quick *bonjour* with her as they passed each other. As he got closer to his destination he paused to check the map again. Concealing himself in a small copse he looked carefully in the direction of the villa. It was surrounded by large conifers and tall poplars. He would need to get much closer.

He followed a small timber fence that was overgrown with hawthorn, alongside a large field. When the fence line came to an end there was about 100 metres to the trees surrounding the villa. He ran to the trees and squatted down to wait. No motion, no sounds. After ten minutes he crawled through the tree line and took out his binoculars. A brief scan from left to right revealed no movement in the grounds of the villa.

Mark Ashby pressed the remote control for the garage door and drove the Citroen out towards the roadway. He had the address of a car showroom in Grenoble that possibly had the sort of van they were looking for.

Landers followed Ashby through his binoculars and waited until the vehicle was out of site. Looking back towards the villa, he could now see Farrah and Hobson as they strolled out onto the patio and sat down at a small wooden table. Seconds later, an old man brought them out a tray of what looked like coffee and pastries. Farrah said something to the old man and he went back inside as Hobson filled their cups. Landers took out his Blackberry phone and started to take photos. This was just what he wanted. He could send the photos to Delaney.

The old man came from around the side of the house and rode off on a bicycle in the same direction as Ashby. As Landers watched Farrah and Hobson, he was surprised at how relaxed they looked. Surely they did not think that the intelligence services did not know about the villa. Perhaps Farrah had under estimated Interpol and the Gendarmerie.

Then, he held his breath. Something was behind him. He turned slowly. It was the young girl he had passed earlier with her dog. She stared at him and asked him what he was doing. His French was not good enough to be able to say 'bird watching' or 'hunting' so he tried to wave her away. She ignored him and hesitated for a while as she looked around and said, 'you are English?'

'Yes,' said Landers quietly. 'You speak English?'

'Of course, monsieur, everyone in my class speaks English.'

'How do you know I am English?'

The girl pointed to his map which was by his side. Landers looked at it to see that it had folded itself inwards revealing the English writing on its cover.

'Very well,' said Landers. 'You must go now and leave me. Take your dog with you please.'

The girl nodded politely and turned to leave. Suddenly a large pheasant took flight from a nearby group of bushes. The dog barked and the girl shouted something in French.

Hobson and Farrah both stood up and looked in the direction of the noise. The girl ran away from Landers as she called her dog to her. She realised that maybe she should not be there; and as she ran, she called back to Landers, 'Pardon Monsieur!' Landers dropped to ground level again and stayed perfectly still.

Farrah moved to the edge of his patio and looked in the direction of the noise. Hobson went into the house and emerged again holding binoculars. He trained them towards the trees.

'See anything?' asked Farrah.

'No, probably just a bit of wildlife and a local's dog.'

'Mm,' said Farrah, unconvinced.

They watched for a couple of more minutes before returning to their seats.

Landers left it a good ten minutes before he moved again, slowly crawling backwards. When he was sure he was out of sight of the villa, he stood up, brushed himself off and walked back in the direction of his car. As he was approaching the car, the young girl was there again, sitting on a fence near the lay-by, her dog, now on a lead, sitting with her. He got into his car as she sat smiling at him. He paused for a while before starting the engine and smiled back at her. It was strange to him that such a beautiful young girl, with what was obviously such a nice disposition, probably lived with her idyllic family in the village somewhere, not knowing just how ruthless one of their neighbours was.

27

The morning had turned wet and windy in Glasgow. The Strathclyde police had insisted on interviewing Delaney and Wyatt although they knew who they were. Michael Turner was not known to them so it took a while for Delaney to explain what it was all about. He had got them on his side though and a few police patrols had checked out hotels and guest houses to see if they had had two guests; one in a wheelchair. Curtis stayed in the background and checked out a few hotels for herself.

Delaney's phone bleeped twice as he was leaving the police station with Wyatt. He pressed a few buttons and Wyatt saw the look on his face. 'What is it, gov?'

Delaney passed his phone to Wyatt. 'It's a photo, taken a few minutes ago.'

Wyatt looked at the photo of Farrah and Hobson sitting at the table on the patio in France. 'So this is from, don't tell me, Landers,' said Wyatt.

'Yep.'

'And it's in France, at Farrah's villa.'

'Yep.'

'Right, so let me guess, that's where we're going next?'

'I suppose it is, Ben. Farrah is taking the piss, and he is starting to make me angry. Those flight details he left in his hotel room where obviously a red herring.'

As they stood on the pavement, Curtis pulled up in the Subaru and lowered her window. 'Get in,' she said. The two men got into the car and she drove off in the direction of Bearsden. 'Well?' said Delaney.

Curtis explained to them where she was going. 'I phoned a hotel that had two guests last night, one was in a wheelchair and the receptionist remembers them taking delivery of a package. By the way she described them, I think it was Hoetger.'

At the hotel, the receptionist showed them the two rooms that Hoetger and Turner had used. 'His name was Mr Johnson, the one who was in the wheelchair,' said the receptionist.

The room had been cleaned. Delaney asked where the rubbish from the bin would have been put and they were shown out through the back of the hotel to two large bins. Wyatt knew what was coming. 'On you go then, Ben,' said Delaney as he pointed to the bins. 'The latest bags should be on the top.'

'Yeah right,' said Wyatt as he started to pull bags of waste from the bin.

Curtis started to open some of the bags as Wyatt threw them to the floor.

'By the way, Sally, take a look at this,' said Delaney. He took his phone from his pocket, accessed the photo of Farrah and Hobson and passed it to her.

'France?' she asked.

'France,' said Delaney. 'Perhaps we should have driven south from Paris that day after all, instead of coming back here.'

Curtis muttered something to herself and then paused. 'Wait.'

'What is it?' asked Wyatt.

She had unfolded a piece of paper from one of the bags. 'What do you make of that?'

She passed the paper to Delaney. It was a small hand written note.

This is for J and B. hope the van is okay. – A.

Wyatt stopped looking through the bins and Delaney handed him the note. Wyatt read it two or three times before asking, 'So what is the *This*?'

'Probably money,' said Delaney. 'It was a payment for the hit on J and B, Jerome and Bouton. The *van* probably means that someone ordered a van for him and his driver to collect when they got here.'

'And the *A*?' asked Curtis.

'Alan; Alan Farrah,' said Wyatt.

Delaney took the note back from Wyatt and put it in his jacket pocket. 'Looks like it. Okay you two; decisions. What do we do now?'

'France,' said Curtis. 'If Farrah is at his villa, the money must be there as well.'

'Stay here and get Hoetger,' said Wyatt.

'You're both right in a way,' said Delaney. 'But the chance of Hoetger still being in Glasgow is a slim one. What puzzles me is Farrah. Surely he doesn't think we don't know about his villa. Why would he go there?'

'And why doesn't the Gendarmerie or Interpol just go and get him?' asked Curtis.

'He hasn't been there long enough,' said Delaney. 'Remember they want him and the money all at once. Remember also that he still has contacts in other countries. Interpol will want the lot f them, at exactly the same time on exactly the same day. They'll time it right so that every operator in each country goes in simultaneously.'

'Not forgetting something else,' said Wyatt.

Curtis looked at him for the answer, but he did not respond.

'Quite so,' said Delaney. 'We still don't know who it is that's giving information to Farrah. Enough information to keep him one step ahead of us. Perhaps that's why he's comfortable in his villa. He will be told if we get close.'

'So how do we get close without everyone knowing?' asked Wyatt.

Delaney looked at Curtis, put his head on one side raised his eyebrows. Wyatt saw the interaction between them and said, 'what?'

Curtis shook her head and then looked at Wyatt. 'I think he means that Farrah will get a visitor to his villa. A certain Melanie Leeder.'

They drove back to London. On the journey down, Delaney phoned Maggie Phelps to book three separate flights for the following morning. All flying to Lyon, but at different times.

It was 8 p.m. by the time they arrived and the hire cars were dropped off for the hire company and the Nottingham police to sort out. They caught cabs back to their homes and would meet up again the following morning.

Ben made his way to his local, The Flying Pig. After a quick chat with some other fellow operatives who had been on a fraud case, he walked to his apartment, poured himself another scotch and fell asleep.

Curtis arrived back at her safe house to find her dog Rocky waiting for her. There was a note on the table from the 'helping hand'.

Rocky okay. Has been out for a walk. No sign of anyone snooping. I'm outside in the van, two doors down.'

She took off her shoes and her shoulder holster and let them fall to the floor at her side. Rocky jumped onto the sofa at the side of her. They were both asleep within minutes.

When Delaney got home, he too had been left a note. He vaguely remembered getting a text message from Angela and the note confirmed it for him.

At office. Had to go back in and work late. New assignments coming through. Should be back by 12. Xx.

He cut up some cheese, poured a red wine and sat down. Unlike Wyatt and Curtis, he did not sleep. He knew the next few days were going to get unpleasant and his guess was that he, and probably the others as well, would be in jeopardy. He thought about Brandon Jones, William Hoetger, Alan Farrah and the money. After he had poured a second glass of wine, he took a piece of paper and a pen and started to list the possible names of anyone who could be the person giving information to Farrah. The list was longer than he thought it would be -

Wyatt - not impossible but very unlikely.

Curtis – she had lied about seeing Alan Farrah in the hotel.

Jones – no, his death had confirmed that; or had it?

One of his men's informants? – Again not impossible, but too many to consider.

Landers – not impossible but unlikely.

Someone in another department; but who and why?

Stephen Landers arrived back in Paris that evening and stayed in his office. He was sure Delaney would get himself and his team back to France once he had seen the photo of Farrah and Hobson. But he, like Delaney, was not about to sleep. He phoned Delaney.

'It's Stephen, Tom.'

'Stephen, how are you?'

'I'm good, you?'

'I've been worse.'

'Did you get the photo?'

'Yes, thanks for that. I think.'

It took Landers a while to realise that Delaney was being sarcastic. 'Oh yes, well, I didn't think you'd be too pleased, but at least you know where he is.'

'Yes, I do, Stephen, but why is he there? It's too easy and too obvious isn't it?'

'I thought that, but then I thought maybe Farrah had underestimated us all.'

Delaney considered this idea for a while but dismissed it. 'I don't think Farrah would underestimate us; he is a villain, and part of the scum of this earth, but he's not stupid. He knows who we are and how good we are *and* what our shortcomings are.'

'Right,' said Landers. 'So why would he go somewhere we know about?'

There was a moment's silence. Landers was waiting for an answer to his question. Delaney suddenly realized that Landers was one of the people on his short list.

'Good question, Stephen, why do you think he went there?'

'The money. It has to be there. The two men questioned by the Gendarmerie lived in Lyon. That's not far from Grenoble and Farrah's place. Maybe they did a bit of work for him and he paid them in cash without thinking.'

'Perhaps,' said Delaney. 'Anyway, we can discuss it better face to face. I obviously need to get to France, and I'll bring Ben and Sally with me. We should be with you later tomorrow. Did you hear about Brandon by the way?'

'Yes I did. The last time he spoke to me, he was saying how his wife wanted him to pack it in. Anyway; right, I'll meet you at the airport if you text me your flight number.'

'Okay, see you tomorrow.'

It was after midnight when Delaney put the phone down. He thought about Stephen Landers sending him the photo of Farrah and Hobson. It had been taken and sent to him using a mobile phone. The picture was a little grainy so he would have had to zoom in, which means it was taken from a distance. It was not a close up. If Landers was close to Farrah, he wouldn't need to take a photo from a distance. Landers should probably be taken off his short list. But not yet.

The front door slammed, helped by the wind. Angela walked in and kissed Delaney on the cheek. 'Sorry,' she said. 'I didn't really want to work late on the day you arrived back, but its double time. Think of the money.'

'No that's fine; I've been working and thinking anyway. Have you eaten?'

'Oh, Tom, it's too late to eat now anyway, let's go to bed. Did you get the message I sent you from Landers?'

'Yeah.'

'I know I really shouldn't have done, but I wasn't sure when you would be back. And I've had another look tonight while I was there. No more messages from France tonight, just Italy and Denmark.'

'Were they all from Interpol people?' asked Delaney.

'Mostly. One was a message for one of your men.'

'Oh?'

Realising what she had said, Angela continued. 'Now, Tom you know I shouldn't say.'

'But you will say won't you. For me.'

Angela huffed and sat down. 'One of the Italian messages was for Ben Wyatt, something about a man being stopped at the French Italian border with a van full of guns and a wheelchair. Anyway, I've been working so I'm wide awake. Are you tired?'

'Yes, but…'

Angela stood up and walked over to him. She sat on his lap and kissed him. 'But nothing,' she said. 'Come with me.'

Mark Ashby had arrived back at the villa at 7 p.m.

'Why the hell has it taken you so long?' asked Hobson.

'It's taken me a long time because I got it right, okay?'

'Sure it's okay, Mark, just asking.'

Farrah smiled at the two of them. 'What have you got, Mark?'

'A Citroen C7; all the mod-cons. Tail-lift, the lot. I waited until they confirmed everything. It was in their Lyon showroom. It's being delivered to us tomorrow.'

'Well done mate,' said Farrah. 'How did you pay for it?'

'I didn't.'

The smile left Farrah's face. 'What do you mean, you didn't?'

'I didn't pay for it. I told them I wanted a one week trial and if I was happy with it we would buy eight of them for our reps.'

'Reps?'

'Yeah, on the way I stopped off at one those machines that make instant business cards.'

Hobson and Farrah looked at each other. Ashby continued. 'Easy really; they think I'm the managing director of a holiday company with my own villa. And by the way; the guns and old-what's-his-names new wheelchair is on its way to us. I had a phone call from our man on the Italian border; the bent customs man you paid off. He let the driver through not long ago so he should be with us in the morning.'

'What happens then?' asked Hobson.

Farrah laid out his ideas to them. 'Hoetger should be with us by then. That will give us maximum strength and fire power if anything goes wrong. Dick, I want you to drive Hoetger.'

'Me? I thought Mark was doing the driving, that's why you sent him to choose the vehicle.'

'No, I want you doing the driving,' said Farrah. 'And that's an end to it.'

Hobson looked at Ashby who shrugged his shoulders as Farrah continued. 'Mark, you'll be driving the Jaguar, with me as your passenger.'

'What Jaguar?' asked Ashby.

Farrah took some keys from his pocket and tossed them to Ashby. 'The XJ8; it's parked in the barn at the back. Get it checked over and make it ready for a long drive. The tank is full and there are two cans that are full in the boot as well. Pops took care of it for me.'

'I bet he loved that,' said Ashby.

'Yes I think he did,' said Farrah. 'Now listen, both of you; there is only us three now and one other who gets a share of the money. He's coming to the villa in a few days time. I'm going to pay him off and he will leave. I've told him I won't be in touch with him again once he's been paid. You two get one million each and when we get to where we're going, we split up and don't make contact again for six months. By then I'll have other projects on the go. Questions?'

'Who is this other person then boss?' asked Hobson.

'He's the one that's been giving me information on the movements of MI5 and Delaney's lot.'

'How much is he getting then?' said Ashby.

'Ten million.'

'That's a big chunk.'

'It's worth it. He could be useful to us again in the future, but he doesn't know that yet.'

'And what about Hoetger?' asked Hobson. 'He must be getting some of it as well.'

Farrah ignored the question and continued with his instructions. 'Mark, when you get to the barn, you'll see some other cans of petrol. Bring them back in here. We're going to torch this place when we leave. Right, you have about two days to do what you like, but don't wander too far. Questions?'

'One more question from me please,' said Ashby. 'Why wait two days? Why not go now and leave the money for the others to collect from somewhere?'

'Because I'm still waiting for our new passports.'

'Oh right, and what sort of passports might they be?'

'Spanish.'

Hobson stood up. 'And one question from me,' he said. 'What about Hoetger, Alan? You didn't answer me before.'

Farrah looked at Hobson and then towards Ashby. He waited for a moment, deciding if he should tell them. 'Hoetger is not getting any more money. He's becoming too well known and too much of a liability. When we get out of here, we're going to lose him on the way to Spain.'

'Lose him?'

'Yeah, kill him.'

Ashby folded his arms and sat back. 'Fine by me, boss, do you want me to do it?'

'If you want to.'

Hobson walked towards the patio and lit up a cigar. 'I'm just going to sit outside for a while,' he said.

'I'm going to check out this Jaguar,' said Ashby as he threw the keys up and caught them again. Farrah reached for a book from the shelves and sat in a large leather chair in the corner.

Out on the patio, Hobson was looking out over fields as the sun was setting. He looked over his shoulder to see that Farrah had settled down to read. Kill Hoetger eh? He thought to himself. Easier said than done.

28

Gatwick airport was busy as usual as Delaney, Curtis and Wyatt sat together drinking coffee.

'What time is your flight, Ben?' asked Delaney.

'9.15.'

'And yours, Sally?'

'9.40, but I'm going via Paris.'

'Good, well I'm off at 9.30 via Strasbourg so we have enough time to go through things.'

'Why the separate flights anyway?' asked Curtis. Delaney tried hard not to answer, but Wyatt wasn't so careful. When he saw Delaney was not going to answer, he leaned forward and looked at Curtis. 'Don't you know anything in the CSS,' he said with a smirk on his face. 'It's like a sort of spread bet. They're out to kill us remember, especially the boss here. If we were all on the same flight arriving at the same time, they could get all of us. This way, if they got one of us, it still leaves the other two.'

'Very clever,' said Curtis. 'So why are we sitting here together now?'

'Ah, she's got you there, Ben,' said Delaney.

'No she hasn't. We're safe here because this is the departure lounge. No one in here would have a gun or any other weapon because everyone has gone through the scanner. Why do you think they brought us through another door?'

Curtis folded her arms and sat back in a defensive position. Delaney looked at Wyatt as if to say *was that necessary*. He told them both to sit closer to him.

'Right, Sally, tell me again what you're going to do.'

'Yes, I've been thinking about it,' she said. 'I guess the best way to approach Farrah is with a gift. He won't even listen to me unless there's something in it for him. I need to offer my services for free *and* give him something to look forward to.'

'Like what?' asked Wyatt.

'Like money. He can't get enough of it; that's what I've never understood about the criminal classes. With the money he has now he could lose himself somewhere and never have to try again.'

'They just need to do what they do, it doesn't matter how much money there is, it's never enough,' said Delaney, 'go on.'

'Farrah thinks that Melanie Leeder has links with some VIP's in the drugs trade. I'm going to offer him a piece of the action. I spoke to Stephen Landers early this morning; he's getting me some 'in' money. I'll tell Farrah it's a down payment for future services rendered. My contacts in Canada want him to do some work for them and this is a good-will payment.'

'Why would you do this for Farrah?' asked Delaney. 'That's the question he will be asking himself.'

'I'm doing it for my share of the money, to keep me in houses and toy-boys.'

'Sounds plausible,' said Wyatt. 'Just.'

'Well we need to get close don't we?' Curtis continued. 'We don't know if the money is there or not.

Nor do we know who it is who's feeding him the information about us and other departments.'

'It's a gamble,' said Delaney. 'I'm not a hundred percent comfortable with it, but we can't keep chasing this guy all over Europe for ever, and this is a way of getting close.'

They all looked up at a television monitor as an announcement was made. 'That's me,' said Wyatt. 'See you in Lyon.'

Curtis waved a hand as Wyatt left them. 'Be careful,' she said. Wyatt turned and acknowledged her.

'Another coffee, Tom?' she asked Delaney.

'Yes, thank you.'

A few minutes later Curtis was looking at Delaney as she made her way back with the coffees. He was looking at a small piece of paper in his hand.

This is for J and B. hope the van is okay. – A.

Her return took him by surprise, he expected her to be longer. 'What's that?' she asked.

'It's that note that we found in the hotel skip in Glasgow where Hoetger was staying, I was just studying it again.'

'Anything in particular?'

'Only that we all thought the *A* was for Alan, seems obvious, but it doesn't have to be. It could the first letter of a surname.'

'I think you're trying to find something that's not there, Tom. It has to be Alan Farrah. Who else would do that for Hoetger?'

'Mm, suppose you're right,' said Delaney. He did not actually suppose that she was right at all, but he wanted to end the conversation. He could think about it again when he was alone. His phone rang and as he looked at it, Curtis noticed a pleased look on his face. 'Hello, Taffy…yes not too bad….it's today is it?' Delaney's look changed. '….right, well, look err, thanks for being there, did someone arrange flowers?...okay, see you soon.'

Curtis watched as Delaney's look changed to a despondent one. 'How's Taffy?' she asked.

'I think he's recovering well.'

'Is it Brandon's funeral today?'

'Yeah.'

'That's quite soon isn't it?'

'Mm, I think his wife wanted it that way.'

'We should have been there, Tom.'

Delaney leaned back, sighed and put his hands behind his head. 'Yeah.'

Another announcement was made and they left to board their separate flights.

Maria Jones was not crying.

It had been 5 days since she had received the phone call from Delaney. There were 24 people in the crematorium, mainly family; brothers, sisters, sons and daughters. As she followed her husband's coffin through the large doorway, her son, Harry, held her hand tightly.

The dirge played loud, as though not to apologise for the noise and she wanted to tell them to switch it off. The reverend looked calm, thoughtful and gracious as he beckoned them to the front row. Maria looked at him as he started the proceedings. What do you know, she thought; with your gracious words and your look of sympathy and your smug 'God will accept him' speech. Her thoughts were interrupted as her son squeezed her hand again.

Now, she was crying.

Taffy Burton was sitting three rows behind her. He had been out of hospital for four days and was officially on 'light duties' working from home. He had phoned Delaney to let him know he was out and Delaney had asked him to attend the funeral. Flowers had been sent from 'the department'.

There were no hymns, just two prayers and two readings, and Burton felt a lump in his throat when one of the readings ended with '...and so farewell, we will meet again'.

The congregation gathered around the floral tributes. The sunshine was warm and the breeze caused the labels to flap around, so people had to hold them steady to read them. Burton waited until he saw that Maria had read the message from the department. As she turned, her eyes met his and she looked at him with a face that he had seen so many times before. It was a face that asked, why? He moved closer to her. 'Hello, Mrs Jones, I'm Taffy Burton, we did meet once.'

'Yes, I remember,' she said. 'You must thank your colleagues for me, for the flowers.'

Feeling somewhat ashamed that he could not think of anything original to say, Burton put his hand on her arm and offered a kind smile. 'If there is anything we can do, just call us won't you.'

'Yes, thank you. I may need some help; there are still some of Brandon's belongings at your offices.' She looked around for a moment. 'Tom Delaney not here then?'

'No, Ma'am. Urgent business. Sorry.'

'I understand,' she said. 'People like me have to don't we? It's a shame though; Brandon thought a lot of him. He would have liked him to be here.'

'Indeed, and I know Tom thought a lot of Brandon, he was one of the best.'

'Aren't they all Taffy? Aren't they all?'

Burton acknowledged her gracefully and stood back as other mourners approached her. He decided to leave. No one else knew him and his time would be better spent doing just what Brandon's widow wanted. He made his way back to the office.

With everyone out on a 'job', the office was empty when he arrived. Maggie, the records and reports lady, was sitting in her small office with her head buried in some paperwork. He did not disturb her. Neither he, nor any of his colleagues, kept much at the office. They all had their own desks in a room next to Delaney's, and they had access to a locker room if they needed it.

Burton went through the two draws of Jones's desk. There was nothing unusual; pens, note pads, stationary and a couple of E-mails he had printed off; one from the payroll department about holiday pay and one from a holiday firm, confirming a booking. The departure was in three weeks time, flight to Florida, two adults, one child. Burton closed the drawer, hesitated, and then kicked the nearby chair away with such a force it landed against the wall a few metres away.

The locker room was cold and damp. Jones's locker was not locked. Taffy started to take out what was there and put it into a bag. He would take it to Brandon's widow himself in a few days. Apart from the usual spare shirt and shoes there was a folder with a couple of pieces of paper in it. He needed to make sure it wasn't sensitive and looked briefly at what was written. He was surprised to find that both pages were actually Sally Curtis's CV. Her personal details, religion, education, references and even details of two assignments she had been given earlier in the year. It was the second of those assignments that caught his eye. Two months before Marcus Hanson had been killed she had been sent details of a Canadian drugs ring and two addresses in London had been hand written on the back of one of the papers. He took both pages and photocopied both sides of each before putting them in one of the draws of his own desk. The photocopies he kept with him. A bit of home work, he thought to himself; but why would Brandon have had Sally's CV in his locker? And why would he write down two addresses on the same piece of paper? He finished putting a few more items in the bag and labelled it *Maria Jones,* ready for him to take to her in a few days.

Wyatt's flight landed at Lyon at 10.30. Landers was waiting for him.

'Hi, Ben, good flight?

'Yes fine, the other two are coming on separate flights.'

'Yes I know, Tom text me to let me know.'

'Have you got us some cars?'

'Yes just the two, as per Tom's instruction. We might as well wait for the others to arrive, come on let's eat.'

They settled in a small cafe near the arrivals lounge and Landers explained how he had got close to the villa.

They both agreed that the 150 million must be at the villa and that it was not going to be long before Farrah went elsewhere.

'What do think Tom has in mind then?' asked Landers.

'Probably getting Farrah and the money as quickly as possible,' said Wyatt as he squeezed the large hold-all that he had placed between his feet. 'You should see the firepower I've got in here. The other two are carrying as well. They had to get us through special gates, here as well as at Gatwick.'

'Speak of the devil,' said Landers. Wyatt turned to see Curtis approaching them. She put her hold-all on the ground at Wyatt's feet. 'Hello boys. Watch that for me, Ben, I need the ladies.'

Two hours later, when they had had multiple coffee refills, Curtis looked at her watch. 'Shouldn't he be here by now?'

'Yes I was just thinking that,' said Landers. 'His flight was the same time as yours wasn't it?'

'Roughly, but it was coming via Strasbourg.'

'Probably just held up on the transfer or something,' said Wyatt. 'He would let us know if there was a problem.'

William Hoetger was watching the French countryside go by as his 'temporary' driver approached Reims. His contact in London had sent him Julie Brewer. She had arrived at Glasgow some five hours after Hoetger had made the call to request a replacement for Michael Turner. Hoetger was surprised when he had been told his driver was to be a woman. This was a first for him, but he soon felt reassured once Brewer had gone through her history on the drive down to Portsmouth. She was talking too much, he thought, but he did learn a lot by picking out the more important snippets of information. Especially the bit about Micky Black.

'Yeah, Micky Black is my dad, do you know him then?'

'Yes I know him, well *knew* him anyway.' said Hoetger. 'He retired to Brazil didn't he?'

'Yeah that's right, four years ago now.'

'I thought you would have gone with him.'

'No not me, Will, I married a boy from Manchester see, and dad couldn't keep all of us.' She had called him 'Will' as soon as they had met. He did not like it, but there was something about her, and he did not feel like telling her not to, for some reason.

As they approached Reims, for whatever reason, she started to tell her tales again. He looked at her long blonde hair in a pony tail and the tattoo on the side of her neck. Her large brown, heavily made up eyes looked attractive in the rear view mirror as she glanced at him occasionally. 'My dad did a job once, in Reims, you know.'

'Did he?' asked Hoetger, hoping it wasn't going to be a long story.

'Yeah, he nearly got shot by one of them national police blokes, the Gendarmer.'

'You mean Gendarmerie.'

'That's them, anyway, it was a van full of bullion and we got about 12 million Euros worth.'

'We?' asked Hoetger, intrigued.

'Me, dad, little brother Simon and big brother James. Right mess it was, I ended up having to shoot one of the bullion drivers in the back. Cheeky bastard tried to walk away, cool as a cucumber. Then the other one shot Dad in the arm and Simon had to grab him and stick him. He was quick though, got him right in the throat.'

'But you got the bullion and you got away?'

'Only just, Will. Like I say, a right mess.'

Hoetger thought about their destination and he remembered saying to Farrah that he would need one of his men to drive for him once he got to Grenoble. He was not sure now if that would be necessary.

He looked into the rear view again to see that she was looking at him.

'So where do I head for now then, Will? We'll be through Reims in half an hour.'

'Follow the signs to Troyes, then Dijon.'

'Dijon eh, Will? Mustard and all that.'

'Yes. Mustard and all that.'

29

The second flight that Delaney had taken from Strasbourg had been delayed and it was early afternoon before he got to Lyon. Landers, Wyatt and Curtis were waiting for him in the car park. They needed to head south as soon as possible.

'Who's driving what?' asked Delaney looking at Landers.

'I was going to lead the way sir, in the Mazda,' said Landers. 'If you would like to follow in the Cherokee?'

Delaney looked at both vehicles quickly and turned to Curtis. 'Sally, you drive the Cherokee, I'll come with you. We can talk on the way. Ben, you go with Stephen.'

'Okay, sir,' said Wyatt. Within minutes they were heading south east towards Grenoble.

Delaney looked at Curtis as she drove and then turned to see what was on the back seat. 'I take it that Melanie Leeder is in that bag,' he said.

'Yes she is, wig and all.'

'How do you want to play it?'

'I thought you might have an idea actually.'

'I haven't thought of any specifics, we just need to get you in there.'

Curtis nodded as she concentrated on the road signs and watched Landers and Wyatt up ahead. 'I think maybe we should park somewhere close to the villa, where we can see who comes and goes for a couple of hours.'

'I agree, but we need to go straight there. It'll be dark by the time we get there and you need time to get changed.'

Some time later, Landers pulled into a shopping mall as they approached Fontaine to the west of Grenoble and Curtis followed. They parked away from the busy area and gathered around Landers as he spread out a map on the bonnet of the Cherokee. 'Right,' he said, studying the map. 'The villa is here, near a village called Claix. We will probably find somewhere to stay in the village as well. This road is slightly higher than the ground where the villa sits so you can see the front of the property, but not the rear.'

'Will there be somewhere where we can watch the entrance from a distance?' asked Delaney.

'Probably; and it's not a busy road.'

'Good, any ideas anyone?'

'Yeah,' said Wyatt. 'Why don't we just order an Air Force jet and blow the bastards apart?'

None of the others responded. Delaney continued. 'Right, Sally, there'll be toilets and washrooms around here somewhere. You should get changed.'

He then looked at Wyatt and Landers. 'We'll drive to Claix and find somewhere to stay, and then Sally and I will drive out to watch the villa. If we get chance for her to go in, she can do.'

They double checked their firepower as they waited for Curtis. Delaney took the driver's seat of the Cherokee. Landers and Wyatt waited in the Mazda. 'By the way,' said Landers. 'I liked the bit about the air force jets, if only we could eh?'

'Mm, if only. Mind you if we…'

'Bloody hell,' interrupted Landers. 'That's not her is it?'

Wyatt looked in the same direction. It was Curtis. He remembered seeing her in the hotel reception in Nottingham. 'Yep, that's her. Melanie Leeder, gangster's mol.'

'Crikey!' said Landers. 'That's amazing.'

Delaney had also seen her. He got from his seat and opened the back door of the Cherokee. 'Put your belongings in here, out of sight,' he said.

She threw one bag into the vehicle and kept one with her. 'What's in there?' asked Delaney.

'Make-up, spectacles and a Smith and Wesson if you must know.'

Landers and Wyatt watched as she came round to get into the passenger seat, revealing her legs as she climbed in. 'Put your tongue away, Stephen,' she said, 'it's just part of the job.' Landers smiled and started the Mazda. Delaney started the Cherokee and put it into gear ready to follow.

'Wait' said Curtis. 'Something I've forgotten.'

Delaney paused before pulling off. She got from the vehicle, went to the rear, picked something out of her other bag and got back in again.

'What is it?' he asked her.

'My chewing gum; it's a big part of the character.'

'Where now, Will?' asked Julie Brewer.

Hoetger gathered himself from his doze. 'Err, Lyon, then follow the signs for Grenoble.'

'So when we get to this Grenoble place, Will, then what?'

'I collect some money; a lot of money. And you get your wages.'

'Is that all? I thought I might see some action from all the stories I've heard about you. Who are we going to see?'

'Alan Farrah.'

Brewer straightened up in her seat. 'Alan Farrah! You know Alan Farrah?'

'Yes I do.'

'Well, and here's me thinking that this was just another job. Tell you what, Will; if I get to meet him you can keep my wages. It would be worth it just to get on his side. He pays serious wages, and I mean serious.'

Brewer's voice drifted away from Hoetger's thoughts as he considered what was ahead of him. Farrah owed him a lot of money. But he still hadn't taken Delaney out of the picture. Perhaps when he did, Farrah would pay the big money he had promised. Would Farrah pay him off and tell him to forget about Delaney? Or would he still want more? Brewer was right, he thought, Farrah does pay good wages, but he expects more than most. This time the money may just be enough to retire with and make way for some of the younger eastern European hit men that were making their names these days using poisons and injections.

Landers parked the Mazda outside a small hotel in the village of Claix. Delaney pulled up behind him. 'Stay here please,' said Landers, 'I'll go and see if they have enough rooms for us.'

Wyatt waited and watched as Delaney followed Landers into the hotel. Curtis walked around for a couple of minutes to stretch her legs before settling on a wooden bench set into stones in the middle of the town's market place. She looked around her. A small dog on a porch, two young girls talking to each other as they walked past, and a young child sitting with her terrier dog; both of them staring at the visitors.

Delaney and Landers came from the hotel a few minutes later and confirmed that they had somewhere to sleep. 'Ben,' said Delaney. 'You stay with Stephen here and get our bags in for us. Sally, you and I will take a drive up to that road that overlooks the villa.'

Landers parked the Mazda in a small side street and beckoned to Wyatt. 'Come on Ben, I noticed a bar a couple of streets away, we'll check in and go for a beer.' He looked at Delaney. 'If that's okay with you, sir?'

'Why not? You two have a beer; we'll keep in touch by phone.'

Curtis walked back to join them when she heard what was happening. As Landers entered the hotel he turned to look at her. He wanted her. She had always fascinated him but professional etiquette had taken over any ideas he had had. But looking at her dressed up as Melanie Leeder had been enough to make him think twice. As he checked in, he felt guilty. It is shallow of me, he thought; but that did not change his feelings.

As Curtis climbed into the Cherokee, Delaney put it in gear and moved off. The road to the villa was twisting and dark, as the sun set on the countryside. Four kilometers later, Delaney slowed and pulled into a farm track entrance. 'There,' he said. He pointed to a medium sized, modern style villa with its lights on and a patio area to its left. A small track between two fields could be seen leading to the main road at a point a few hundred metres from where they were parked. Curtis checked the map on her lap. 'That's it. What do we do now?'

'Wait and watch for a while. It's early yet.'

Delaney pointed the Cherokee towards the villa, switched off the engine and sat back. Curtis got out of the vehicle and rested against the front of it, binoculars in hand. As she watched the villa, Delaney found himself doubting her. He wasn't sure why, but something was concerning him. He trusted her ninety nine percent. But he wanted to have one hundred percent trust – in everyone. Fifty minutes passed before they saw any movement. 'A car,' said Curtis. 'Someone has just started a car.' They watched as a dark coloured car left the villa and headed towards the road. 'It's coming this way,' she said.

'Just stay still,' said Delaney. 'They won't see us in this light with these thick hedgerows.'

The car, with two men in it, went slowly past them and headed towards Claix.

Curtis moved out to the road to look at the rear of the car as it left their sight. 'Looks like one of those sports cars you Brits love so much.'

'It is,' Delaney confirmed. 'Jaguar XJ8.'

Ashby and Hobson had decided to make the most of what Alan Farrah had called 'two days to do what they like'. The Jaguar needed some running time so they had decided to take it for spin down into Claix and have a few beers together. They had left Farrah alone. Hoetger would be with him soon and he did not seem worried or even aware when they had told him they were going out for a while. The book Farrah was reading dropped to his lap as he fell asleep.

There had been silence for ten minutes when Curtis got back into the Cherokee. 'It's got to be now, Tom, surely.'

Delaney nodded. 'Right. I'll drive you down there. You tell him I'm your driver and you told me to stay in the car and watch. Tell him I'm armed.'

He drove onto the road in the direction of the villa. There were no gates or cameras. He parked near enough to the front door to see what was happening, but far enough away so he was shadowed by a tree and Farrah would not recognize him. Curtis got from the vehicle as soon as it stopped, walked to the front door of the villa and knocked on it. Farrah had stirred with the sound of the vehicle and had already looked out of the window. He looked through the spy hole in the door before opening it. 'Well well, you get around,' he said as he looked Curtis up and down.

'Of course I do, Alan. I can't help myself; I go to where the money is.'

'I thought you said in Nottingham that you wanted to help me get rid of Delaney and some MI5 nuisances.'

'I also said that that would cost you. I'm just about to get rid of Delaney. It's time you gave me a first installment.'

Farrah stood back from the doorway to let her in. 'If you were a man young lady I'd be saying now that you had balls.'

'I haven't, but my driver out there has, so no funny business.'

'Come in young lady, come in,' said Farrah smiling.

She walked in and sat down without being asked and looked at him in a determined way. He sat on the left hand arm of her chair and put his right hand on her knee. 'Drink?'

'I think so. I'll drink to my new found fortune.'

'What fortune would that be?' he asked as he poured the drinks.

'Oh, just the ten million you're about to give me in payment for getting rid of Delaney and his incompetent helpers.'

'And where do I get ten million from?' he asked as he passed her a glass of wine and sat down opposite her.

'Alan, my dear Alan, everyone that matters knows it was some of your men that snatched the 150 million from Paris. You did it to get your drugs money back didn't you?'

'Drugs money?'

'Yes, drugs money. The money from the heroin transfers that Jerome and Bouton helped you to cover up in exchange for a few million each. Is the money here?'

Farrah looked nervous as though he was thinking how the hell she knew all this. He paused for a while before putting his drink down and moving over to look out of the window in the direction of where Delaney was waiting in the Cherokee. 'You're very confident Melanie,' he said. 'Just like you were in Vancouver all those years ago.'

'I've learned a lot, Alan; I know what I'm worth. You give me ten million and Delaney will be dead within 24 hours, and who knows, I may even decide to stay on and be your personal assistant.'

He looked at her as she intentionally crossed her legs. What he did not know was that she was very nervous and if he had confirmed that the money was there, she would have shot him dead. But she needed confirmation that the money *was* there. Farrah paced up and down for a while, occasionally glancing at her, sometimes out of the window. She decided to end it there before he had time to think. 'Well, you clearly are not in the mood, either that or you don't trust me, which I guess, is understandable. I'll be back in the morning.'

She rose from her chair and walked towards the door. His mood changed suddenly. He raised his glass in the air, hesitated and smashed it against the wall. 'Why do I put up with bitches like you?'

She tried to remain calm. 'Because you need bitches like me, Alan. By the way, if you look after me, I might have something for you in return.'

'Like what?'

'Like a down payment for future services rendered. My colleagues in the CSS may need someone like you.'

Farrah walked up close to her. 'Mm, I'd almost forgotten you were CSS, Sally Curtis; how do you get away with it?'

She said nothing as she turned and walked out, closing the door quietly behind her. Delaney started the engine when he saw her walking towards him. He leaned over and opened the door so she could get into the vehicle quickly. 'What did he…'

'Just get me out of here, Tom, he scares me.'

'Is the money there?'

'Can't be sure.'

Not wanting to arouse suspicion, he drove slowly away in the direction of the gates. They were a few hundred metres away on the road back to Claix when Delaney pulled over to the side of the road. 'Get down!'

Curtis dropped down below the line of the dash board. A vehicle went past them in the direction of Farrah's villa. They sat back up and Delaney turned to see the rear of the vehicle. 'Hoetger,' he said.

Stephen Landers put two small beers in front of himself and Wyatt, as he sat down and sighed. 'There we go, Ben, enjoy, we've earned it.'

After checking into the hotel they had walked down to the outskirts of the village to a small bar. A few locals had paused for a while when they had entered, but they soon blended into the atmosphere and after a few minutes, people had forgotten they were there. Wyatt finished his beer and looked out of the dirty window. 'No sign of Sally and the governor yet.'

'No, they'll be okay. We'll spot the Cherokee when it passes. They should come straight past here on the way to the hotel.'

Wyatt pushed his glass towards Landers. 'Same again please.'

'Why me again?'

'Because you speak the lingo and I can't be bothered to try.'

Landers smiled and did as he was asked. He knew of Wyatt's reputation as a straight talking hard man. A few more people had arrived since their first drink and he had to shuffle past a few locals to get to the small bar. He ordered two more beers and looked around him as the landlady poured the drinks carefully and thoughtfully. Then he noticed two men leaning against the end of the bar about 20 feet away. He turned his head away and paid for the drinks. Wyatt was leaning forward in his seat, looking like he knew exactly what Landers was about to say. 'I know, I've clocked them as well,' he said as he took a beer from Landers.

'Is that who I think it is?' asked Landers.

'Yes, Hobson and Ashby; Farrah's men.'

'So that means that Farrah was probably on his own when Sally visited him tonight.'

'Probably. Just continue to chat normally; they don't know us, remember.'

Landers looked surprised. 'But we have to take them surely; we can't let an opportunity like this go.'

'Mm, difficult isn't it. But we don't know what the situation is with the governor and Sally yet.'

Landers nodded and moved his chair around slightly so he could see out of the corner of his eye if Hobson or Ashby were to move. Wyatt had told Landers that the two men would not know who they were, but he wasn't a hundred percent sure. He didn't want Landers to make a panic decision. He reached for his phone to send a text message to Delaney *'Hobson and Ashby here'*. Seconds later his phone received a message in French. He passed his phone to Landers. 'What does that say?'

'Vodafone France - Message not sent'

Wyatt sipped his drink and sat back. As he watched Hobson and Ashby, he thought of some of the things they had been involved with. He did not hate them, he thought, but he was not sure why. Ashby was still quite young, probably no more than 35 or so, but his reputation for being a quiet, but hard thug, had soon spread after certain officials or rival gang members had crossed him. As Ashby tilted back his head to finish a drink, the large tattoo of serpents on his neck could clearly be seen and his manner seemed educated yet brusque as he spoke to Hobson.

Dick Hobson was the old timer of the two. Wyatt noticed how he was much more observant than Ashby as he was listening and talking. Pictures of a man with garden shears through his throat had stuck in Wyatt's mind for a while after being told that Hobson was the killer. He remembered Delaney telling him about Hobson's wife. She had been shot dead by a police marksman when she had tried to attack a young WPC with an axe. And she was the nice one of the two, he thought. He wondered if Landers would be up to it if the evening ended up being two against two.

Headlights suddenly appeared through the window of the bar and were quickly switched off. Wyatt kicked Landers who was looking towards the door and spoke quietly to him. 'Get out there and stop them coming in, these two will recognise him.'

Landers got to the door just as Delaney and Curtis were opening it. He moved into the line of sight between Ashby, Hobson and Delaney, and put his hand on Delaney's chest. 'Turn round now, you too, Sally.'

Delaney and Curtis responded quickly, knowing that Landers would do something like this for good reason. All three moved into the shadows between the light of two windows. Landers waited until he was sure no one else was about to come outside. 'Ashby and Hobson, sir; they're both in there.'

'Wyatt too?' asked Delaney.

'Yes, he's watching them from just underneath this window here.' He pointed to one of the windows next to them.

Delaney looked at Curtis. 'You get out of here, Sally, they may recognise you too. Get back to the hotel and get back to being Sally Curtis. I'll phone you if we need you.'

Curtis, still shaken from her meeting with Farrah, started to walk back to the centre of the village. Landers moved closer to Delaney. 'Ben said not to act, sir, because we didn't know the situation with you and Sally.'

'Well you do now; Ben will know what to do.'

Wyatt waited for ten minutes before getting up. He walked over to the door with his handkerchief up to his face pretending to cough. He thought he saw Ashby and Hobson look up briefly but he was not sure. Outside, he joined Landers and Delaney in the shadows and whispered to Delaney as he looked around. 'Did Sally find out if the money was at the villa?'

'No; not for definite.'

'We can't move in on these two then can we, gov; Farrah will know it was us.'

'I think he probably suspects already that we're not far away. You're right, Ben, we need to be careful, but why not lessen their chances while we have the opportunity?'

Wyatt read the mind of his leader and tilted his head to one side. 'Why not, sir.'

Landers looked at both of them in turn. 'You mean reduce their numbers by one.'

'Yes,' said Delaney, 'that's what I mean. Any ideas?'

'We need to separate them,' said Wyatt.

'Fat chance,' said Delaney, 'they're not amateurs.'

Landers looked carefully through the dirty window. 'They're still standing at the far end of the bar,' he said. 'What about starting a fight with the locals? They're bound to join in.'

'Might work, we could…'

'Shh.' Wyatt's voice was sharp. 'Someone's coming.'

Unable to hide the fact that they were there, they huddled together and chatted quietly as though they were sharing a story. A small man walked past them wearing a long coat and holding a briefcase. His attentive face looked at them briefly as he passed. They waited until he had gone inside before they continued.

'I don't like it, too many people,' said Wyatt.

'You're right,' said Delaney. 'You and Stephen take the Cherokee back to the hotel; I'm going to wait around for a while.'

'Come on, sir, you can't...'

'Just do it, Ben.'

It was thirty minutes later when Ashby and Hobson left the bar. The small man with the briefcase was with them. Delaney had positioned himself behind a row of cars on the opposite side of the street. The night was dark and quiet and he could hear their voices clearly. The small man looked around carefully and held a hand to his mouth.

'To repeat gentlemen, tell Mr Farrah that his contact apologises for the delay, but he is sure that Mr Farrah will understand. He will join you all in a couple of days; and please tell Mr Farrah that he will still want his share.'

'How did you know we were here then?' asked Ashby.

'I watched you leave the villa and drive towards the village. Where else would you be going?'

'You've been watching the villa?'

'Only for a short while. Who is the woman?'

Hobson put his hand on Ashby's arm to stop him talking. 'That's enough chit-chat you two.' He looked at Ashby. 'Come on, let's get back.'

The small man walked away still holding his briefcase. Delaney watched as he crossed the road and made his way back in the direction of the village centre.

Then he crouched lower behind the roof line of the cars as Hobson and Ashby got to their vehicle. Hobson told Ashby to get in and wait as he turned around and walked to where Delaney was crouching. Delaney heard the footsteps of Hobson come to a halt. He rose slowly until he could see Hobson through the back window of a parked car. Hobson was holding a gun with two hands, taking aim; but not at Delaney. The thud of the two silenced rounds was unmistakable. Fifty metres away the small man fell to the ground. Hobson walked up to him and removed the briefcase from his clenched fist. Delaney froze as Hobson walked back to the Jaguar, Ashby started the engine. 'What did you do that for?' asked Ashby.

'The money lad, the money.'

'What money?'

Hobson opened the briefcase and poured bundles of cash out onto Ashby's lap. 'This money; he had obviously just been paid by someone to deliver that message to us. He was insignificant. We got the message and we can deliver it to Alan. We don't need the minions getting in our way.'

The Jaguar drove off in the direction of the villa. Delaney straightened himself up and walked back to the hotel. Nice people, he thought to himself, but who paid the small man that cash to deliver a message. It had to be Farrah's informant and perhaps he would be on his way to collect his share of the money. Then Delaney recalled some of the conversation. - *he*. The man had said '*he.*'

Perhaps it was time to remove Curtis from his short list.

30

Taffy Burton phoned Delaney at 7 a.m. 'Not too early, sir?'

'No, Taffy, you know it isn't. How was the funeral?'

'Same as usual, I didn't stay too long.'

'Right; I probably wouldn't have done either. How are you doing?'

'Oh I'm just about fighting fit again.'

Delaney paused, doubting Burton's optimism. 'Got something for me then?'

'I think so; it's a strange one really.'

'Go on.'

'I was bagging up Brandon's belongings for his wife. The usual stuff; papers, spare clothes and all that. Then I found a folder that contained Sally's CV.'

'Sally Curtis's CV?'

'Yes, and he had scribbled a few notes on the back of it about some of Sally's recent assignments.'

Delaney understood the notes; anyone could quite easily be making notes about a colleague, but why the CV and where would he have got it from. 'Go through the CV for me briefly Taffy will you; just the main points.'

'Right,' There was a pause as Burton settled back and opened the folder. 'Sally Alison Curtis, born Toronto 1975, went to school in Thunder Bay, then University of Quebec; good grades I think sir, reading this, not sure about their education system. Joined the Mounties in '97, promoted to drug squad in Toronto in '99 and err, looks like the Canadian Secret Service in 2002. Highest solve and arrest rate, two years running. Worked undercover in Vancouver, and that's about it, sir. That's probably when she and Marcus Hanson started their work in England with us, when we got to know them.'

Delaney scribbled down a few notes as Burton was speaking. He found himself underlining Curtis's middle name. 'What sort of things did Brandon write down, Taffy? You mentioned he made some notes on the paper.'

'A few things about our meetings and the odd phone number. There's one line that took my eye though; it just says 'Hanson, no assignments', looks like it was scribbled down in a hurry.'

'Right thanks, Taffy, not sure if it means anything; Marcus certainly didn't speak to me about problems or assignments.'

'Right, well I'll leave that with you.'

Delaney put the phone down. Eight hours earlier he had decided to remove Curtis from his short list of suspected internal informants. As he prepared himself for the day ahead, he reached into one of his trouser pockets and again pulled out the note from Hoetger's hotel in Glasgow.

This is for J and B. hope the van is Okay. – A.

Breakfast at the villa near Claix started with a smash and a clatter.

Alan Farrah hurled his plate at the wall just to the side of where Hobson was sitting. 'You stupid, unintelligent fool!'

'He was a nobody, Alan,' Hobson said, 'a greedy little man just carrying a message; we can make better use of this.' He reached down and emptied the contents of a briefcase onto the floor. Farrah looked at the money lying in bundles.

'Oh well fantastic! There must be ooh, a few thousand there! We have 148 million you imbecile!'

Ashby had watched as Hobson explained to Farrah what had happened the night before. He waited until Farrah had stopped shouting. 'We couldn't be sure the small man was genuine, Alan. Dick had to shut him up. He found us, and the villa. If we…'

'Shut up, Mark!'

Ashby stayed silent and continued to eat his breakfast. Hobson sat still waiting; he knew Farrah had not finished. Farrah walked closer to Hobson and slapped him across the face. Then he swept Ashby's breakfast off the table onto the floor. 'Get out, both of you.'

Hobson stood up slowly and approached Farrah. 'Come on, Alan, it was just…'

'Get out! Both of you!'

As Ashby and Hobson made their way to the door leading out into the garden, another door opened. Hoetger was being wheeled into the room by Julie Brewer. Hobson turned and looked at them. He and Ashby knew that Hoetger was due to join them, but the girl was unknown to both of them. He looked at her; her scruffy shorts and sleeveless vest revealed a figure that was well proportioned but too muscular for a woman. 'Who the hell is she?'

Brewer did not give anyone else a chance to answer. She let go of the wheelchair and stood to one side of it as she stared at Hobson. '*She* is Julie Brewer, and *she* doesn't take shit from anyone.'

Farrah sat down and poured a coffee, then looked at Brewer. 'These two men are Dick Hobson and Mark Ashby, Julie, and they're just about to leave.'

Ashby tugged on Hobson's sleeve. 'Come on, Dick; let's get out of the way for a while.'

As they both walked through the doorway Hoetger shouted out. 'And I won't need either of you to drive for me! Julie here will be driving me.'

Farrah looked at Hoetger who nodded to him. Then he looked at Ashby and Hobson as he drank his coffee. 'You heard the man. Get some fresh air and be back here in 30 minutes, we have a briefing to do. We need to leave earlier than we thought because of your shenanigans.'

Hoetger wheeled himself closer to Farrah as Brewer poured him some coffee. 'The weapons, Alan; did they arrive alright from Italy?'

'No; they must have been stopped at the border, which means you don't get your new wheelchair either.'

'So what do we do for fire power?'

'Relax; there's enough here. We'll take it all with us.'

Wyatt was waiting by the vehicles outside the hotel enjoying his second cigarette when Landers and Delaney joined him.

'Ben, I want you to drive the Cherokee, I'll be with you,' said Delaney.

'Me and Sally in the Mazda then, sir?' asked Landers.

'Yes please; changing travelling partners will help us all to sing from the same hymn sheet. When Sally gets here I'll go through my ideas.'

Curtis arrived a few moments later. Delaney spread a road map out over the bonnet of the Mazda. 'Now then,' he said. 'We have to assume that Farrah, Hobson and Ashby will be leaving the villa. Hobson's decision last night to kill the man with the briefcase would not have gone down well with Farrah. He will be panicking and he won't want to stay in one place too long.'

'So why don't we just raid the villa and take them?' asked Landers.

'Because I want them all, Stephen, and I mean *all* of them. Farrah, Hobson, Ashby, the money, the informant; *and* Hoetger.'

'Hoetger?' said Curtis. 'How do you know he's with them?'

'I just know, Sally; I knew when I saw that vehicle last night when we were leaving the villa; call it old man's intuition.'

'And the informant that keeps letting Farrah know where we are?' asked Wyatt.

'Not sure, Ben, he or she might be with them, but I would guess not. Not yet.'

'*She*?' said Curtis.

'Yes, Sally, *she*. It could be a woman just as well as a man. Now then, let's have a look at Farrah's possible routes out of here.'

31

'We're going to Spain. Anyone who doesn't want to come, leaves now.'

Farrah looked determined as he spoke to the four people in front of him. Hobson answered first. 'I'm with you boss, you know I am.'

'Me too,' said Ashby.

Hoetger hesitated. 'Payment, Alan; I want payment, now, *and* when we get there; you will owe me more by then and considering what lies ahead of us, you need me.'

Farrah smiled. 'Sure, William, I'll get Mark to get you some cash if you insist.'

'I do.'

Farrah looked at Ashby and pointed to the door. 'You heard him, Mark, bring him 50,000 from the garage, and while you're there put the rest of it in the Jaguar.' Ashby left without hesitation.

'And you my girl?' asked Farrah, looking at Brewer.

'You mean I can come with you? Bloody hell Mr Farrah, you bet I want to come with you!'

'That's settled then, now listen; Mark will drive the Jaguar, me and Dick will be in the back. Julie, you drive William in the new C7 that Mark got you. Stay close to us. We go from here, across country to Valence, then down to Orange and Nimes, Montpelier and Narbonne. I want to be near the Spanish border by tonight.'

'Brilliant!' said Brewer. 'Wait until I tell my brothers!'

Hobson shook his head. 'Your brothers?'

'Yeah, my brothers; problem?'

Hoetger explained. 'This may be news to you, but she has pedigree.'

'Really,' said Hobson. 'I thought she was a mongrel.'

Brewer did not rise to the remark. Hoetger looked at Hobson and Ashby. 'The brothers she is talking about are Simon and James. She is Micky Black's daughter.'

Hobson remained quiet. Micky Black was good, he thought, but that didn't mean *she* was.

An hour later, Farrah had just finished spreading petrol over furniture and curtains when his phone rang. 'I thought you might be phoning, don't you want your money?...okay....Why pay that man to deliver a message when you could have phoned?...I see....Is Delaney close?.....Right, thanks again, see you in Spain.'

He looked out of the window to see that the others were waiting for him by their vehicles. One match was enough. The curtains flared up in a mass of flames, black smoke was coming from the upholstery and windows started to crack. He looked around one last time as he paused at the doorway. 'Blasted shame,' he said to himself.

Wyatt parked one kilometer away from the villa. 'Look sir,' he said as he pointed to a large plume of smoke coming over the horizon.

'The smoke looks new,' said Delaney, 'it's not very high, get a move on, Ben, we may be able to see which direction they're heading in.'

Wyatt accelerated away and behind him Landers followed. As they got closer to the villa, Delaney pointed to a small road. 'There, go down there, it looks like a small track that goes west, probably to Valence, they wouldn't take the main roads for the first few miles.'

Wyatt turned sharp right and put his foot down; he was pleased to see that Landers was keeping up with him. 'Don't go mad, keep it on the road,' said Delaney.

'I will, don't worr...Shit!'

As they went round a corner, Wyatt stamped on the brakes hard. They came to rest about two inches from a tree that was lying across the track. Not far behind them, Landers swerved and the Mazda came to a halt just to the right of the Cherokee. Everyone looked at each other to make sure they were all okay. The two drivers stayed with the vehicles, Delaney and Curtis jumped out and emptied their shoulder holsters as they looked around.

Nothing.

Curtis started to talk but Delaney held a finger to his mouth. Fifty metres away an old man walked from the trees, got onto a bright blue bicycle and rode away. He had an axe in his hand. 'That bicycle was resting against the wall of the villa when we visited last night,' said Curtis.

'Right,' said Delaney, 'let's get these vehicles turned around then and get back to the main roads, I'm not messing about trying to pull trees out of the way. Stephen, get on to your Gendarmerie mates and see if they can pick up on where Farrah might be heading. Tell them they're looking for a JaguarXJ8, probably accompanied by a large van or people carrier.'

Landers acknowledged the instruction and asked Curtis to drive so he could make the phone calls. Wyatt was back on the main road within seconds, Curtis following behind, but not too close.

As they made their way south, Landers finished his phone call and looked at Curtis as she was driving. He had liked her since their first meeting in London, but this *like* had almost turned into lust, he thought to himself. He admired the way she carried herself, her dark and intelligent eyes, the legs he had seen when she was 'Melanie Leeder' and her confident, sometimes assertive manner. It would of course be extremely unprofessional of him to make advances towards her. Then Curtis spoke to him. 'So how did you end up working for Tom, being posted to a permanent position in France?'

'The main reason was that I spoke French; a little. I didn't even apply for it. When I was working for MI5, I got a phone call out of the blue from Delaney about two years ago. The idea was that I would work for TOLA *and* MI5 as a source of information on French related cases.'

'So how come you know so many people in the Gendarmerie after just two years out here?'

'Ah well, there lies the other reason they asked me to come out here.'

Curtis took her eyes off the road for a second to look at him. 'Which is?'

'I once lived with a French girl in Lyon. Her father would often entertain us at his large house near the city centre.'

'So?'

'So her father is Simon de Ville, second-in-command of the Gendarmerie.'

Curtis looked impressed. 'And are you still seeing this girl?'

'No, basically I just wasn't rich enough for her, but we still say hello now and again. The last time I spoke to her she was on her way to New York; she does fashion photography.' He turned to look out of the side window and Curtis decided not to continue with any more questions. The vehicles came to stop briefly at a small road junction and she took the opportunity to look longer at him. She had been impressed with him when they had first met. She liked his quiet, sturdy character. He always looked well groomed and his strong, but somehow polite manner was attractive to her. She found herself looking down at his chest and stomach as he was looking out of the window. When he turned his head she looked away and the traffic started to move again. He turned to face her, sensing she had been looking at him. 'So what do you think Tom has in mind for tonight? Another little C rated hotel somewhere?'

'Probably,' she replied. 'I'm sure he'll let us know when he wants to.'

As they approached a large supermarket mall, Wyatt pulled off the road. Curtis followed and parked at the side of them. Delaney got out of the Mazda and walked round to speak to Curtis and Landers. 'Give me your mobile phones.'

They handed their phones to him; he put them in a bag and then reached for his own phone. With Wyatt's phone also in the bag he walked towards the large store. They watched him as he hesitated for a while and reached for each phone in turn, removed the sim cards and threw the phones into a litter bin. Curtis looked over at Wyatt. 'I suppose you're just going to say he knows what he's doing.'

'He does. Think about it.'

Fifteen minutes later Delaney appeared holding a bright red bag. He handed a new phone to everyone in turn. 'Pay-as-you-go. You can have your old sim cards back when this is over.' The tone of his voice was such that none of them challenged him.

'Blimey, sir,' said Wyatt, 'your credit card must be close to its limit.'

'It's not actually, Ben, just as well eh?'

Delaney was pleased none of them had challenged his decision. He was almost sure that the informant was none of these three, but he needed to make sure. If they were going to phone anyone, they would need numbers and very few people remembered numbers once they had put them on their short-dial. Anyone wanting to phone them, would not get through. New numbers could easily be exchanged, but what he did not tell them was that he was going to repeat this exercise again tomorrow.

The phone line that had a direct connection to and from the Foreign Office did not ring very often at MI5. When it did, it was always for the head of the department, Adrian Lusher or his second in command.

Andrea Beecham acted as an office manager for MI5 *and* PA to the Home Secretary, whose office had been put in the same building for security reasons following recent terrorist scares. As she answered the phone, she looked at the diaries of the main players who could expect a phone call. She knew that these calls invariably meant someone having to change appointments.

'Blue line, Mrs. Beecham speaking.'

'Mrs. Beecham this is Linda Scott, PA to the Foreign Secretary, is Sir Adrian Lusher there please?'

'He is, one moment please.'

Mrs. Beecham put the line on hold and rang Lusher. 'Foreign Office for you; I'll put them through and then I have to get back to the Home Secretary.'

'Thank you, put them through.'

Lusher waited for the call to come through.

'One moment please, Sir Adrian, I have the Foreign Secretary for you.'

There was a long pause. Lusher waited for his caller to speak first. 'Sir Adrian?'

'Yes Foreign Secretary, how can I help?'

'Do you know anything about those Overseas Liaison people chasing all over Europe to get that Farrah man?'

'You mean Delaney's people; yes I do.'

'Why didn't they leave it to MI6 and Interpol? I've got top men from France phoning me about people being shot in small villages and villas being set on fire. None of my people can get through to them and the only one who knows anything and who's still here, is apparently in hospital.'

Delaney had told Burton not to report that he had been discharged from hospital. He had seen him as an unknown extra man that he had up his sleeve.

'Chiefly because it involves the Canadian Secret Service,' said Lusher. 'A CSS man was killed and another CSS operative is helping them. You may remember the killing of their top man, Pierre Bouton, after he had been arrested.'

'Yes I do. Why is this Delaney chasing these people? Shouldn't it be MI6?'

'Yes it should be Foreign Secretary, so why are you phoning me, I'm MI5?'

'Yes, Lusher, you are, so perhaps this Farrah man shouldn't have been able to get as far as he did.'

'I'm sorry, Foreign Secretary if you feel MI5 have failed in their duties, but that is a matter you should take up with the Home Secretary. It is he that I report to, not you.'

'Oh I will, Lusher, I will. God knows what all of this is costing the tax payer, let alone the body count.'

'As you say sir, it is not good. I am a knight of the realm by the way, so I would appreciate it, if in future, you addressed me as Sir Adrian and not just Lusher. You might also bear in mind that Delaney's TOLA is employed by all of our departments, for when we need to break the rules now and then; they are officially just diplomats. Goodbye sir.'

As Lusher put the phone down he stood up quickly and kicked his desk. Yet again someone had blamed one of the intelligence agencies for the short comings of the government, he thought to himself. Years and years of under budgeting on prison security. Forming one department and then another, cross communication everywhere, what did they expect. I wasn't one of the best officers to come out of Sandhurst and I didn't fight wars for this country and end up with medals and a knighthood to be told that I was not doing a good job by some grammar school kid.

He picked up the phone to Mrs Beecham. 'Get me MI6 please, Andrea...no, wait, get me Superintendent Taylor at Interpol.'

Larry Taylor had been a good ally to Lusher over the years. If MI6 wasn't telling him what he wanted to know, he knew he could rely on Larry. Mrs. Beecham put the call through.

'Sir Adrian, how are you?'

'Fine fine, Larry, and you?'

'Well yes I think so, doing one's best and all that.'

'Quite. Listen, Larry; are you still in touch with your colleagues in France regularly?'

'Mm, quite regularly, need a favour?'

'Oh I'm just trying to help MI6 and the Foreign Secretary, not sure why, but I am. You know Tom Delaney don't you and his Overseas Liaison lot?'

'Vaguely, Sir Adrian, he has a reputation for not being the best at communicating with other departments, but I get to know what he's up to sometimes. Last I heard, they were trying to get that Farrah man who escaped. God knows why, I wouldn't have thought it was in his remit.'

'Right, I don't think it is. If I knew where he was in France I could send some of my people over there to help him bring this job to a close and that would get the cabinet members off our backs; well, on this issue anyway.'

'Leave it to me, Sir Adrian, one of my contacts in France should know something, I'll come back to you.'

'Much obliged, Larry, good to talk to you again.'

Lusher put the phone down and re-dialled.

'Put me through to the Home Secretary please, it's Lusher.'

There was a pause and a few clicks before someone spoke. 'Sir Adrian, I thought you might be calling.'

'Hello, Home Secretary. I've just been speaking to the Foreign Secretary and I didn't like his tone.'

'I see, and what was all that about?'

'Delaney again; it seems he blames me for Delaney having to chase all over Europe after this Farrah man.'

'Well you are domestic security, Adrian.'

'Exactly, so he should be calling MI6, not me. Anyway, I'm going to France.'

There was a brief moment of silence and Lusher thought he could hear someone click their fingers. 'Okay, Adrian, but why?'

'To help Delaney, and then perhaps when we have Farrah and his cronies, everyone will shut up about this mess. I have national terrorist threats to sort out; I sometimes wonder why I'm asked to bother with drug smugglers.'

Lusher did not wait for a response. He put the phone down and tried Andrea Beecham again. 'Get me a flight to Lyon will you, Andrea, preferably leaving in about two or three hours. And get Larry Taylor again and ask him to talk to his French colleagues; I'd like some news on Delaney.'

32

The road to Nimes was quiet and in the most part, straight. Wyatt slowed down and drove carefully, always keeping Curtis in sight behind him. Delaney told him to stop for a while and the two car convoy pulled off the road near a small copse. Curtis and Landers wandered over to the first vehicle. 'My SIM card that you have, sir,' said Landers, 'that's the number the Gendy have. If they're trying to get hold of me they...'

'I know, you'll have to phone them; that's one of the reasons I wanted to stop for a while. It's no good going further than we have to.' He handed Landers his card.

'Thanks, Tom.'

Delaney walked away from them in the direction of the copse. 'I'm going to phone home while you do that.' He rested against a tree and dialled his home number. As he waited for it to be answered he looked around at the landscape and at the others, who were standing by their vehicles talking. Angela answered the phone and he concentrated on the conversation.

'Hello, how are things?'

'Oh alright,' she answered.

'You sound a bit fed up.'

'I'm okay, just tired; we've had quite a bit of work coming through the last two days, I'm doing a late shift tonight.'

'Right; any new communiqués from France by any chance?'

'No I don't think so, I was transferring assignments from Italy mainly yesterday, something about a Naples drug ring. Where are you anyway, I'm missing you.'

'South of France, heading towards Nimes, not really sure what's going to happen next but we'll probably be a few more days. Have any other people been in touch?'

'Someone did phone from Interpol, they asked if I knew where you were? Of course I said no, I didn't know where you were anyway.'

'Who was it?'

'I think he said Larry someone, a superintendent.'

'Yes I know him, Larry Taylor; he has a reputation for getting information when others fail. If he phones back put the phone down.'

There was a pause and Delaney sensed something was bothering her. He asked her again if she was alright and she sighed heavily. 'Oh I just get tired of working sometimes, and I wish we could spend more time together.'

'Well when this nasty bit of work is out of the way, we can have a few days off and go up to Scotland or somewhere like that for a few days if you like.'

'Mm, alright, sorry to burden you with my thoughts anyway, I'm sure you have enough on your plate without me telling you that I'm fed up.'

'Don't be silly,' said Delaney, 'It's understandable, I'll be back as soon as I can be, I miss you too you know.'

'I'm sure.' she said, 'Don't worry about me, I'm fine, really.'

As he finished the call, Delaney noticed Landers coming over to him. 'The Gendy say they have had a sighting, sir; an XJ8 near the centre of Nimes. They want me to phone them back if we want it intercepted.'

'Thanks, don't phone them back yet. Did they give you a detailed location?'

'Yes, not far away actually, about 40 kilometres south of here. No other vehicle with it though, just the Jag.' They walked back to Wyatt and Curtis who were standing away from the vehicles, Curtis leaning on a small fence. Delaney asked them to gather round.

'The Gendarmerie has spotted an XJ8, probably Farrah's,' he said.

'Travelling on its own,' confirmed Landers. 'One driver, two passengers in the rear.'

'Keep a sharp eye everyone,' continued Delaney. 'This could mean that Hoetger and his driver are ahead of them as an advance party, or behind them, playing at tail end Charlie. If it's the latter, he may not be far from us. We'll change drivers, I'll drive the Cherokee up front, Sally; you're with me. Stephen, you drive the Mazda. I want Ben with you, observing.'

The rain had started to fall in London as Angela Casey sat at her dressing table preparing to go to work. She was to start at 5pm and work until about midnight depending on what work came in from other forces and departments. The phone call from Delaney had made her feel better, but just a little, she thought. The afternoon seemed to be turning colder and she reached for her coat as she opened the front door.

'Ahh, oh my god!' she screamed. Two men were standing in front of her. One of them smiled as he looked down at her. 'Sorry if we startled you,' he said, 'we were just about to knock.'

Angela looked at them with displeasure. 'Right, well what is it? I'm on my way out.'

The smiling man looked at his shorter companion who was removing his tweed cap, and then back at Angela. 'No you're not, love.'

He hit her hard in the face; she was thrown back with the force of the punch, blood streaming from her nose. Both men walked in and shut the door behind them. Angela was struggling to her feet and turning in the direction of the back door. The shorter man kicked her and she fell forward, holding her hands over her face. The two men hesitated for a while as she turned and looked at them, her hands still in front of her. 'Please!' She said. 'Take whatever you want! There's money in the kitchen drawer, some jewellery upstairs.'

The tall man was still smiling. 'Well,' he said, 'you're obviously not as clever as you look.' He kicked her legs as she tried to fold herself up for protection. She yelled out; he kicked her again. As he continued to kick her, the other man hit her across the head which made her drop her guard and her hands fell to the floor. He hit her twice across the face and then thumped her neck as she cried out. The tall man stood back. He had stopped smiling now. 'Don't overdo it,' he said to the other man, 'we might need to do a re-visit. Save some damage for another day just in case.'

His accomplice looked annoyed. 'Spoil sport; I'm giving her a good beating; that's what the man asked for,' he said as he turned and kicked his victim again hard in the head.

'That's enough I said!' the taller man shouted.

'Piss off!' came the reply as the short man hit her again in the head.

The two men turned to leave and closed the front door behind them.

Angela lay on the floor, reeling in agony and crying. She tried to cry out for help but could not find strength in her lungs. She tried to crawl to the telephone, but every bone in her back and legs was aching and she could not reach out with her arms. Her vision became blurred, her head started to roll and a minute later she was unconscious, blood coming from her nose, mouth and forehead.

As Delaney approached Nimes, he asked Landers to phone his Gendarmerie contact again. Landers made the relevant notes during his conversation and advised Delaney. 'They can meet us when we get close; apparently the Jaguar is parked outside a cafe.'

'Are the men in the cafe then?'

'They're not sure, they lost sight of the vehicle for a while and when they found it again no one was with it.'

'Right, where to?'

'Turn right just down here, down the D999 and go towards the town centre, then left at St. Baudile. There's a cathedral and they'll meet us in the car park next to it.'

They approached St. Baudile 14 minutes later; Wyatt and Curtis close behind them. A large cathedral stood in the middle of an open area, it's two huge pointed spires reaching upwards, its grey brown colour looking old but well maintained. There was a small car park just in front of it and three or four broad shallow steps led to the entrance. A clock set against a small round ornate window above the arched doorway had stopped, probably some time ago, Delaney thought. It had that stationary look about it. Sitting on the steps were two Gendarmerie officers. Landers had explained what vehicle they would be in and as they approached the two officers walked towards the car park and gestured to an empty space. As they got from the car, the two men greeted them.

Landers did all the talking and then translated for Delaney. 'They're both quite senior, sir; it's unusual; normally they work in pairs of an inspector and a lower rank. We will need to take instruction from this gentleman.' Landers put out a hand in the direction of the older of the two officers. 'Inspector Caron.'

Caron shook hands with Delaney and nodded politely. Delaney acknowledged. 'Hello, Inspector, this is very good of you to help us like this.'

The inspector spoke cautiously in English, though with authority. 'Monsieur we can help, we must, and we do not like these people in our country.'

Landers said something in French to the inspector and the officer pulled out a small street map. He explained to Landers where they were going and Landers relayed it to Delaney as they got into their vehicles. 'We follow them; they'll signal when they want us to stop.'

'Right,' said Delaney. Then he looked at Wyatt. 'Stay close, Ben.'

The unmarked Gendarmerie car pulled away and Delaney followed. They were heading for the centre of Nimes. A few minutes later a hand was raised from the window of the leading car and they pulled into the side of the road opposite a small central park where a sculptured fountain spewed water into the sunlight. Some people were sitting on the edge of the pool eating their lunches and talking. Delaney looked carefully around and then checked his rear view mirror. Wyatt had pulled up behind them and he nodded in recognition.

'The Gendy boys will stay in their vehicle, sir,' said Landers. 'They won't show their uniforms in cases like this. I'll go to them.' He got from the Cherokee and walked to the passenger side of the vehicle. After a couple of minutes he returned and got back into the Cherokee. 'The Jaguar is just around that corner, but still no one in it; suggestions?'

Delaney thought carefully. 'Sally and I have to stay in the cars, they know both of us. You go and get Ben, find a cafe table somewhere where you have sight of the Jaguar and we'll sit it out for a while. Will the inspector want to hang about?'

'Normally they would yes, but they may move further away, probably park somewhere on the road in the direction that the Jaguar is pointing.'

'Right, confirm that with them then and go and sit down somewhere with Ben. Tell Sally to stay with the Mazda, ready to drive.'

When an hour had passed, Wyatt and Landers ordered more coffee as they watched all around them. 'Don't like it,' said Wyatt.

'Too long you mean?'

'Yeah, it's getting on for six o'clock. They may have stopped for lunch, in which case they wouldn't still be here. If they stopped for an afternoon break, it wouldn't have been this long; and why here, in the middle of a town?'

'Good call, Ben, good questions. Shall I phone Tom?'

'Yes, see what he thinks.'

Delaney answered his phone just after he had observed Landers dialling. 'Hello, Stephen; something happening?'

'No. Ben and I think something is wrong, it's been too long.'

'Yes I was just beginning to think that myself, give the car a walk past will you.'

Landers finished the call and looked at Wyatt. 'He wants a walk past.'

'Right, I'll do it.'

Wyatt moved casually away from the cafe table and walked towards the Jaguar. He stood next to the vehicle for a while and looked around him. He could see no one in any of the shops or cafes that might have been Farrah or his gang. He looked into the car and walked around the other side so he could see all areas inside it. Landers watched him for a while and as Wyatt summoned him, he paid the cafe bill and gestured to Delaney. Curtis saw the movements, left her car and joined Delaney as he left the Cherokee and they started to walk towards Landers and Wyatt. They all stayed well away from the Jaguar and Wyatt came to them. 'Ben?' asked Delaney.

'Vehicle switch, boss. Has to be; the car is empty, no papers, no notes, no maps, no food and drink. Nothing.'

Guessing that something was wrong, the Gendarmerie officers had left their vehicle and were walking up the street towards them, attracting attention in their uniforms. Delaney tapped Landers on the arm as they approached. 'The boot, Stephen,' he said.

Landers spoke to the officers and the younger one returned to their vehicle and brought back a metal bar, curved and flattened at one end. He forced the boot open and stood back. Inspector Caron and Delaney looked inside. Nothing; completely empty.

Wyatt then tried one of the doors; it was open and a quick look inside again confirmed that there was nothing in the car. He slammed the door shut. 'Bastards! Told you boss, they've switched cars, for crying out loud!'

'Looks like it,' said Delaney. Landers perched himself on the car's bonnet and sighed, Curtis raised her hands and let them drop down. 'Now what?' she asked, looking at Delaney.

'Hoetger,' said Landers. 'If he's still with them, he will have some sort of van transport, it's our only chance.'

'Yes, it probably is,' said Delaney. 'Speak to the inspector about it will you.'

Landers explained to the Inspector that they now needed to find another vehicle, probably a van or people carrier which was adapted for a wheelchair. The officers then shook hands with Delaney and Landers and rejoined their vehicle. As they drove away, Delaney noticed that the inspector was already on his phone. Then he noticed the other three, looking disappointed and annoyed. He began walking back to the Cherokee. 'Come on you lot, we'll stay here for the night. The beers are on me. No one's going to find a van overnight, let's get to a hotel.'

After a few minutes driving around, the two cars came to rest outside the Hotel Kyriad on Rue Roussy. Only three rooms were available so Wyatt and Landers shared while Curtis and Delaney had their own rooms. Delaney settled himself in and ordered a sandwich and a beer from room service. Still with numerous things in the back of his mind, he decided to phone Taffy Burton to see if he had any more news about Brandon Jones's notes.

'I'm very relieved that you have phoned, sir.' said Burton. 'I've been trying to get you.'

'Sorry, Taffy,' said Delaney, sensing something was wrong. 'I got new phones for us all to minimise unwanted interference. Something happened?'

'It's Angela, sir; she didn't turn up for work this afternoon. When her station Commander phoned your home there was no answer. He phoned me and I went round there. Sir, she's in a bad way, looks like a real good beating up she's been given by someone. She's in intensive care now and under permanent observation, but stable.'

Delaney stayed silent for a while, not knowing what to say. Burton waited for it to sink in before speaking again. 'Shall I organise a flight for you, sir?'

'Yes, thank you, Taffy; Ben can take over down here. Call me back on this number with the details. Where are the main injuries?

'They kicked her head a few times by the sound of it; but they're not operating, so chances are she'll be okay.'

'Right, thanks.'

Delaney put his phone down and buried his head in his hands. His face was hot and red and he clenched his fists across his forehead. How many years have I been doing this, he thought to himself, and how many times have I played it by the book? Two wrongs don't make a right, you're no better than them if you do that. He paced around the room for a while. There was a knock on the door. A young boy came in and placed a sandwich and a beer on the dressing table. Delaney threw the sandwich at the wall, smashing the plate. He took a deep breath and drank down the beer in one.

Curtis was in the room next door and when she heard the noise she rushed round to check on things. 'Tom?'

He was looking around the room, as though he was trying to decide what to pick and throw. 'It's Angela. They've got to her; beaten her up.'

'Oh Jesus, Tom.'

'Taffy is organising me a flight, Ben will have to take over. Go and fetch them both will you, Sally, and we'll go through ideas.'

'Why Ben? I can take charge. You might need him back in London at some point if there are people over there to deal with.'

'Thanks, Sally, sorry, but my call okay. I've got Taffy back at home. Ben will be in charge.'

An hour later, Delaney had briefed them about what to do and Landers had organised a Gendarmerie chauffer to Marseille. Burton had booked a flight for Delaney from Marseille to London, arriving about 08.15.

One hundred metres away from the Hotel Kyriad, Julie Brewer looked at her watch. It was 06.15. She had dropped Hoetger off at another small hotel in Nimes and had been watching the Kyriad for several hours. Earlier they had observed Delaney and his men as they had realised that the Jaguar had been abandoned. Hoetger had then told Brewer to watch for Delaney and the other three and let him know when they left the hotel. As she spotted movement at the hotel entrance she phoned him. 'They're coming out now, Will, only two men with her though, not three.'

'How old do the two men look?'
'Thirtyish.'
'Good, it's worked.'
'What's worked?'
'Delaney has gone back to London; that evens it up a bit. He must have left in the early hours. Get back here and pick me up. We'll join Alan and the boys as agreed, near the border.'
'Yes, but what do you mean, Will? What has worked?'
'I called in a favour from two old friends in London. They put Delaney's girlfriend in hospital. I thought he might go back home for that.'
'Nice one, Will, see you soon.'

33

The Gendarmerie were very efficient; Delaney's driver got him to Marseille in time for the flight and the Airbus 380 made good time; getting to Heathrow early. Delaney had tried to sleep on the plane but it was impossible. The thought of Angela being attacked was constantly on his mind. How many times had loved ones or friends been punished because of what he did for a living? Perhaps it was time he retired, he thought, but, how many times had he said that before? The woman sitting next to him looked up as he muttered to himself subconsciously; 'I'm getting angry now.' He realised he had just spoken out loud and smiled at the woman for a second before continuing to look out of the window.

Taffy Burton was well prepared as usual and had arranged for a quick arrival process for Delaney when he got to Heathrow. The airport police allowed Burton special access at arrivals. Delaney looked weary as he looked at Burton waiting for him, with a car. 'Take a seat, sir; I'll drive you to the hospital.'

'Thanks, Taffy, good work.'

They drove away from the airport, passing the waiting cues of traffic going in the opposite direction. Delaney was looking out of the window when he spotted something. 'Slow down, Taffy, I know that car.'

Approaching them, going in the direction of the airport departures area was a large Daimler. Delaney looked carefully as the vehicle passed him. Sitting in the back seat, reading a paper was Sir Adrian Lusher.

As Burton approached the hospital, he glanced at Delaney. 'I'll wait here for you, sir.'

'Thanks, and while you're waiting Taffy, get on the phone will you. I want to know if any of the Heathrow flights around now are going to Lyon or Marseille and if they are, I want passenger lists.'

Delaney could see Angela as he approached the ward. A young nurse offered him tea as he sat down at Angela's side. She was asleep. The last time I visited this place, he thought, Taffy was lying in here with tubes coming out of his face. Now it's Angela. Her swollen lips and bruised face made him shiver with anger. Brown pus was leaking from a stitched wound on her cheek. He squeezed her hand gently. Someone approached him from behind and he looked around to see a large Asian lady with fine porcelain skin. 'Hello, I'm Doctor Hague.'

Delaney stood up and moved to one side as they shook hands. 'Tom Delaney, how is she?'

'She's not too bad under the circumstances Mr Delaney, she will recover but it may take time.'

'How long?'

'Oh she should be up and about in a week or two.'

'Is it alright for me to sit with her for a while?'

'Of course, but I doubt she will be awake again today.'

Delaney looked hard into the eyes of the doctor. 'She's had head injuries, doctor; any chance of brain damage?'

'The x-rays don't show any, but we'll look again in a few days.'

Sitting next to Angela, Delaney thought seriously again about whether or not he should retire. As he looked at her, he had strange mixed feelings of anger and melancholy. Someone had given instructions to have her beaten up. Who? Why? Was someone in England out to get him *and* Angela? Or did the instruction come from France; perhaps to get him back in England and out of the way. He looked up at the monitor at the side of the bed. How many times had he done that? Too often. Angela remained still and her breathing seemed calm and regular. He kissed her on the forehead and left, making sure to dry his eyes before he got outside.

Burton had just finished his phone call when Delaney got back into the car. 'Got anything about those flights, Taffy?'

'Yes sir, Maggie back at the office has done some finding out for me; three flights in that direction, two to Marseille and one to Lyon. Passenger lists will be on your desk by the time we get to the office.'

They arrived at the office an hour later and Delaney went straight to his desk. He looked through the passenger lists. Sir Adrian Lusher was not on them. Burton looked out of the window and yawned.

'I'm surprised you want to stand there, Taffy,' said Delaney.

'Sir?'

'The last time you stood there, you were nearly killed.'

'Yes, I see what you mean. Those lists any good?'

'Not really. Can you see what other flights left Heathrow about the same time?'

'Yeah, I'll do it here, it's just as quick using the internet.'

Burton settled himself down at a desk as Delaney sifted through some other papers. A large brown envelope took his eye because it did not have the 'received' stamp on it. Inside was just one small piece of paper with just one hand written sentence on it. *Retire Delaney, or we will visit her again.*

He left Burton to his computer and walked down to Maggie's office. She looked up as he entered. 'Where did that brown envelope come from, Maggie? The one with no 'received' stamp on it.'

'It was left at the front desk; by a lad on a bike apparently.'

'Okay thanks.' Delaney returned to his office. The 'lad on a bike' drop had been used before. He began to get an idea who might have sent it. Burton was still studying a website.

'Won't be long now,' he said, 'just checking a few more destinations.'

Delaney located himself behind Burton and looked at the screen. 'By the way, Taffy, did you ever find anything out about those notes that Brandon had written on Sally's CV?'

'Yes I did; all very innocent, Maggie knew as well; apparently he was trying to get her a job in MI6.'

'MI6? She must be trying for a transfer then from the CSS.'

'Probably, sir, I suppose she may *still* be trying.'

'Maybe.'

Delaney returned to his desk, searched his in tray, and found Curtis's CV that Burton had left there for him. As he looked at it he was reminded of what Burton had told him over the phone – *'Sally Alison Curtis, born Toronto 1975...'*

Alison.

Once again he found himself taking that small piece of paper from his pocket.

This is for J and B. hope the van is Okay. – A.

'How about this one sir?' said Burton, interrupting Delaney's thoughts. 'About an hour after we left Heathrow there was a flight to Barcelona.'

'That's a possibility; get me another passenger list will you.'

Ten minutes later a passenger list was coming through on the fax. Delaney picked it up. Burton watched him as he screwed up the fax and through it in the bin.

'Lusher, Taffy; Sir Adrian Lusher, head of MI5, was on that flight.'

'Maybe MI5 have a job that has links with something in Barcelona.'

'Yes, and maybe not, I doubt if he would go himself and it would probably be MI6 anyway, not his lot.'

Burton switched off the computer and stood up, gathering his coat. He knew an instruction was just about to be given out. 'Come on, Taffy,' said Delaney, 'we're going to see the Foreign Secretary.'

As Burton pulled the car into King Charles Street, Delaney phoned an old friend; Linda Scott, PA to the Foreign Secretary. 'Linda, its Tom Delaney.'

'Tom hi, lovely to hear from you; how can I help?'

'Well I'm hoping the Foreign Secretary is in, I need an urgent word with him.'

'Yes he is in, just a second I'll check his diary, I wouldn't do this for everyone you know.'

'I know you wouldn't, sorry to be a pest.'

Burton parked the car. It was a few minutes before she came back on the line.

'Not looking good, Tom, he has an appointment in an hour and then goes off to Westminster. By the time you could get here he'll probably be on his way.'

'Any chance of a meeting now then, before he leaves; just ten minutes.'

'Now? Where are you then?'

'Just outside.'

'Tom Delaney you old fox; wait a minute.'

Burton smiled and looked for a permanent parking space. 'You've done that before then I gather.'

'I just know he's always there for the first hour; bit of a gamble though.'

Linda Scott came back on. 'Come up now, Tom, he says you can have the ten minutes, but no more.'

Delaney remembered the Foreign Secretary's office from a previous meeting. It was still the same; wood panelling that was old, a desk that looked like it would have been used by Churchill and the ubiquitous pictures of the royal family. Foreign Secretary Jeremy Spires stood up as Delaney entered, shook his hand and offered him a seat. 'Mr

Delaney, you get about a bit; the last time I heard you were chasing around France after that man Farrah.'

'Indeed, Foreign Secretary, and who told you?'

'MI5 told me, I understand their leader is not happy with you right now.'

'Perhaps; but I have a job to do, and sometimes that job takes me overseas.'

'Yes, Delaney, but why not leave it to Interpol or MI6?'

Delaney decided not to answer. Previous meetings with the Foreign Secretary had shown him that he was in fact, quite weak on taking charge of the conversation. He changed the subject. 'Forgive me, Foreign Secretary, but I don't want to exceed my ten minutes. Do you know why Sir Adrian Lusher has gone to Barcelona?'

'Of course I don't; he reports to the Home Secretary, not me.'

'Precisely, sir, he reports to the Home Secretary because he is responsible for home security affairs, so why go to Barcelona?'

'If you want to know that, you should ask the Home Secretary.'

'I will sir, thank you.'

Spires looked perplexed. He looked at the clock on the wall. 'Anything else? We could have had this conversation on the phone.'

'Yes sorry, but I was passing anyway. There was one other thing sir, I wonder if you could have a word in the right ear, I could do with some help from MI6 in the next couple of days? I may need a few people.'

Spires looked surprised and put out. 'No; we have too much going on with these terrorist threats, you'll have to make do.'

'It wouldn't be a big commitment, sir, just one more man would be a help.'

'No. Now, is there anything else?'

Delaney stood and leaned over the desk to shake hands. 'Very well, sir, thank you for your time.' He turned quickly and left the room.

Burton started the engine as he saw Delaney approach. 'Any good?'

'Not sure, Taffy, I just wanted to sow a seed really.'

As Burton drove them back to the office, Delaney made another phone call to Linda Scott. 'Hello, Linda it's me again, just wanted to say thanks very much for arranging that meeting at such short notice,'

'Mm, you old thing,' she replied. 'As I said, I wouldn't do that for everyone. How was it anyway?'

'Fine, but I forgot something while I was there, any chance of a word with him?'

'No; he's on the phone anyway.'

'Let me guess, to the Home Secretary.'

'Perhaps, take care, Tom.' The phone went dead.

Delaney knew the 'perhaps' meant, yes. His seed sowing had been successful.

34

Wyatt had just passed a sign for Perpignan when he pulled the Cherokee over into a rest area. Landers and Curtis pulled up behind him. They stood by the vehicles for a while before sitting together in the Mazda. 'Anything from your Gendy mates, Stephen?' asked Wyatt.

'No, I tried them again about 20 minutes ago, there's nothing new. The Jaguar has been towed away to their garage in Marseille for forensic investigation, but they've had no sightings of Farrah since they left us in Nimes.'

Curtis looked up from the map on her lap. 'According to this, I reckon we're just about an hour from the border at the most.'

'I know,' said Wyatt. 'We'll get a bit closer and wait for some information. The Gendarmerie has people all over the place. They must spot something soon.'

'I say we get over to Spain now, and then we can brief the border police. Farrah's mob has to go through the border at Le Perthus if they're going to Spain.'

'Unless they fly,' said Landers.

'Exactly, another reason to get across the border now and find out where the small airfields are,' said Curtis.

Wyatt held up a hand. 'Hang on you two, I'm not starting to chase all over Spain as well as France until we know where Farrah is. This bloody job has taken long enough as it is.'

'So what,' said Curtis. 'These are serious criminals; who cares how long it takes.'

Wyatt pointed his thumb at himself. 'I do, and so will Tom, we need to get the local boys to help us as much as we can. They know the territory better than we do.'

'Apparently not,' said Curtis. 'They lost Farrah, Ashby and Hobson and can't find them again, and Hoetger is nowhere to be seen either.'

Wyatt took a deep breath. 'They still know more than we do about the territory and the possible routes Farrah can take. We wait.'

Before Curtis had a chance to reply, Wyatt got out of the vehicle. He moved away and rested against the Cherokee. He looked back at the Mazda to see Curtis remonstrating to Landers, presumably about his decision. He reached for his phone as it started to ring. It was Delaney.

'Hello, boss.'

'Ben; you and the other two, okay?'

'Yeah, I think so, we haven't heard from the Gendarmerie though, so we don't really know if Farrah is still heading this way, we're about an hour from the border.'

'Right, well based on what I've found out in the last hour, I think you should gamble. Give the Gendy another couple of hours and if you don't hear from them, make your way to Barcelona.'

'Okay, will do. What do you know then?'

'Nothing too concrete, but I'm guessing that Interpol or MI6 may be involved and Lusher of MI5 is flying to Barcelona as we speak.'

'Right, we'll give it two hours and if we don't hear anything we'll get across the border and make contact again when we're on our way to Barcelona. And how is Angela, sir?'

'In a bad way, Ben, but she'll get through it according to the experts.'

'Good, I'll let Stephen and Sally know.'

'Okay, be in touch. Oh and Ben; even if you get the chance, don't take Farrah and his men until you clear it with me. I want the lot; him, the money *and* his man on the inside.'

Wyatt went back to the Mazda and related his conversation with Delaney to Landers and Curtis. He told them they would wait for two hours. 'You two may as well stay in here, I'm going to get a couple of hours of sleep in the Cherokee. Let me know straight away Stephen if you have any contact from the Gendarmerie.'

'Of course I will, there must be some news soon surely,' said Landers.

'I doubt it,' said Curtis, as she looked disapprovingly at Wyatt.

As Adrian Lusher made his way through the customs area at Barcelona airport, his phone rang. He looked to see that it was the man he reported to; the Home Secretary.

'Home Secretary, hello.'

'Sir Adrian, what on earth are you doing in Spain?'

'I've come to help someone out sir.'

'Who?'

'Delaney and his Overseas Liaison Agency; they're after that Farrah man.'

'Oh come on, Sir Adrian, you're MI5, let MI6 look after these things.'

'I normally would, but this is important. Most people blamed me for Farrah's escape anyway, so maybe I should be involved. I'll be back in England in a couple of days, Home Secretary. By the way, how did you know I was in Spain?'

'The Foreign Secretary told me actually, Sir Adrian.'

'I see, did he say how he knew by any chance?'

'Yes, Delaney went to see him to ask for more men and he mentioned that you were heading for Barcelona.'

Lusher stayed silent, not wanting to talk too much about his plans. After a while his caller spoke again. 'Anyway, get back here as soon as you can please, Sir Adrian, your job is domestic security, not all these complicated overseas things.' The phone went dead. Lusher wheeled his case out of the terminal, reached into his jacket pocket and put 200 Euros cash into the hand of a waiting taxi driver. 'Get me to Tossa de Mar please, quick as you can.'

Landers looked at Curtis as they were waiting for news of any sightings from the Gendarmerie. 'Well that's one hour gone, Sally; looks like we might be going to Spain.'

'I think we should have gone anyway. Farrah doesn't hang about. He probably has a meeting planned with some other crook on the Costa del Crime, as you Brits call it.'

'Perhaps, but Ben's in charge.'

'Mm, well I'm giving him and Tom another day and if we still don't have Farrah, I'm going solo.'

Landers tilted his head to one side. 'Your call I suppose, as you don't officially report to us.' She did not speak but kept looking at him. A few seconds later he put his hand on her shoulder. 'Listen,' he said, 'if ever you fancy it, perhaps we could meet up when this case is tied up; socially I mean.'

She looked at him again and put her hand on top of his on her shoulder. 'Thanks, why not?' she said. He kept looking at her; she did not turn away. He moved his hand down to her thigh. 'Can I kiss you?' he asked.

Curtis did not reply but she found herself wanting him as she put both of her hands around his neck and kissed him, hard. Landers' head moved down and he kissed her nape passionately. She took off her spectacles and laid them on the dashboard, caressed his head in her hands and kissed him again. One of her hands moved down and started to unbutton his shirt as he moved his hand between her legs. She opened her legs slightly. Her hand moved from his shirt to his groin and she pulled back as she felt how aroused he was. 'We can't, not here.'

Landers pulled away also. 'No, you're right. Sorry.'

'Don't apologise, Stephen, these things just happen. The answer is still yes to that date.'

He looked at her as she reached to put her spectacles back on. 'Not sure I can wait that long, Sally. I want you.'

'I think you've already demonstrated that,' she said. They smiled at each other and started to laugh, but their temporary joy was interrupted by the sound of Landers' phone.

Curtis watched him and listened as he took the call. 'Bonjour....yes.... right....when?....okay... merci...thank you....yes that is good.... merci.' Curtis turned to see Wyatt approaching. He had slept for an hour but had been awaken by a huge gust of wind that rocked the car as a large intercontinental truck rushed past. 'Anything yet?' he asked Landers.

'Yes, they just phoned.'

'Have they sighted Farrah?' asked Curtis.

'No,' said Landers, 'they've sighted Hoetger.'

Wyatt and Curtis looked at each other. 'Well about time,' said Curtis.

'How come the Gendarmerie knows what Hoetger looks like?' asked Wyatt.

Landers explained. 'They didn't, but they knew he travelled in a van or people carrier with a driver. They spotted a Citroen being driven by a woman with a wheelchair passenger behind her, took a photo of them both from long range, sent it Interpol, and Interpol confirmed who it was. It sounds like it's definitely Hoetger.'

'What about the woman driver?' asked Curtis.

'Don't know,' said Landers, 'never heard of her; someone called Julie Brewer.'

Wyatt stared at Landers. 'Are you sure they said Julie Brewer?'

'Dead sure; know her?'

Wyatt nodded his head and looked down. As he raised his head to speak to them, he was smirking. 'I know her.'

'Well come on then, tell us' said Curtis.

Wyatt was counting on his fingers.

'Bad news, right Ben?' said Landers.

'Well I reckon she must have killed about two of us and six or seven innocent bystanders. Her old man is Micky Black, robbery with violence, gold bullion smuggling, kidnapping, protection racket, the lot really. She has two brothers, Simon and James, who like to think they're in charge, but the old man is still the boss. Last I heard he was in Brazil or somewhere like that with the millions he had after a gold bullion heist not far here; somewhere in France anyway.'

'And the woman?' asked Curtis.

Wyatt looked at Curtis as he considered what he was about to say. He wondered what would happen in a one-to-one showdown between her and Brewer. 'Put it this way, about two years ago, a rival gang tried to kill her dad. They failed, but a few days later, she went to see the gang. The police found carnage. She had shot two men dead and stabbed a woman in the breasts and throat. In another room they found the gang leader with his head just about blown off. She had shot him, cut off his genitals and posted them in a gold box to his ex-wife.'

'Pity she's not on our side,' said Curtis.

'Mm, but apart from that, she's okay,' joked Wyatt.

'Perhaps we need to get serious,' said Landers. 'I haven't told you where they are yet.' His colleagues looked at him. He held up a finger at waist height and pointed in the direction of Spain. 'About two kilometres ahead of us.'

The other side of the Spanish border Mark Ashby was driving slowly in the direction of La Jonquera. The old Mercedes van was no substitute for the abandoned Jaguar, but it was inconspicuous. The first half of its cargo section had four seats fitted into it; Farrah and Hobson occupied two of the seats. The back half was empty, save but a few bags full of clothes, money and weaponry.

'Get through La Jonquera, Mark,' said Farrah, 'and look out for an old church on your left. That's where I said we'd wait for Hoetger.'

Ashby listened carefully as he glanced down at the shotgun that was on the seat beside him.

'That was easy anyway,' said Hobson.

'What was?' asked Farrah.

'The border; they didn't even look in the back of the van.'

'Probably wouldn't have been a problem if they did.'

'Why's that?' asked Ashby.

'This border is a right little money spinner for the guards. A couple of thousand Euros and we would have got through anyway.'

Ashby spotted an old derelict church some ten minutes later. It stood back from the road and a short track leading to it was strewn with old beer cans and empty plastic wine bottles. A stop-off point for kids en-route to nowhere, he thought. He pulled the van around the back of the church and parked close to its wall in the shade. Hobson and Farrah got out through the back doors and looked inside the church through an old cracked window. There was nothing inside but a few overturned benches, more empty beer cans and the ashes of a small fire on the floor. Hobson pushed the rear entrance open and they went inside. 'A bit smelly, but at least it's out of the sun,' said Farrah. 'Good vantage points too.'

He looked out of a side window and then opened the front doors. From there they could see the road and the track leading up to the church. No one could approach in a vehicle without them knowing.

Julie Brewer was about an hour behind them. Hoetger had fallen asleep as she approached the border checkpoint. A young Spanish customs man put out his hand. She handed him the two passports. As the young man looked at Hoetger, Brewer put her finger to her mouth. 'Shh, very important man, you wake him, he tells the commissioner, they are best friends.' He handed the passports back to her and stood back smiling. She smiled back and drove on as she spoke to herself. 'Idiot. A bit of alright though.'

Hobson called out as he saw the Citroen pulling off the main road. 'They're here!'

Ashby stood up from his position in the shade and went to Farrah who was sitting in the back of the van, reading. 'Do you want me to do it here, boss?'

'Do what?'

'Kill Hoetger, you said that he was becoming a liability and that when...'

'Too early, we may need him. Until we know that Delaney is gone for good, we should probably keep our maximum resources.'

Brewer parked in front of the church, opened the back door of the Citroen and lowered Hoetger to the ground. He used his electronic control lever to manoeuvre himself across the rugged surface and came to rest in front of Farrah who had walked around from the rear. 'William; you made it then?'

'Of course we made it, Alan. We watched them all as they stood, bemused in front of the Jaguar and then we followed them to a hotel. The odds have been reduced by the way; I arranged a little something that would get Delaney scurrying back to England.'

'Like what?'

'Oh just a, how can I say, a *physical* message for him.'

Farrah knew what sort of *physical message* he was talking about but did not ask for details.

'Right; hungry boys?' said Brewer. She opened the side door of the Citroen and pulled out two bags of what looked like groceries. Hobson went to help her. 'I'm getting to like you young lady, I'm starving.'

Within minutes they were all tucking into bread, cheeses, cold hams and wine. Hobson started to doze as he sat with his back against the church wall.

'William,' said Farrah, 'come in out of the sun and I'll explain what I have in mind for tomorrow.' Brewer stayed clear. She could see that Farrah did not want anyone else there. She picked up a half bottle of wine that Hobson had let drop to his side and went to the rear of the church to speak to Ashby.

'Hello handsome; brought you some wine.'

'Not for me; not good for you in this heat anyway.'

She kneeled in front of him so her cleavage was on full display. 'I can think of something that *is* good for you.'

'Go away, you're not my type.'

'You mean you prefer boys?'

'No, I mean I prefer women. Women with class, with style. Not young stupid unprepossessing louts.'

Brewer sat back. 'Oh really, clever bastard. What does unprepossessing mean anyway?'

'Look it up in a dictionary when this is all over.'

She got to her feet, picked up the wine bottle and stared at him. 'It might not be the only thing I do when this is all over. By the time I've finished, Mr Farrah will want me more than he wants you.'

Ashby watched her walk away. She sat down on a small piece of dried out grass and began to finish off the wine.

With the news of the Hoetger sighting, Wyatt, Curtis and Landers had moved fast. Wyatt made the decision that it would be quicker and less complicated in one vehicle. They left the Mazda where it was. Landers called in a favour and the local police had it removed back to Lyon. Wyatt phoned Delaney to make sure he concurred with their plan. He did. Curtis drove the Cherokee as fast as conditions and safety would allow. Wyatt and Landers took the back seat and made the most of being passengers by checking and cleaning guns and familiarising themselves with the road map and the terrain. They were disappointed not to have sighted Hoetger's Citroen as they approached the border crossing. Landers made another phone call to the Gendarmerie and told Curtis to flash her lights as they approached the border guards. A guard standing by his motorcycle pointed to the outside of the crossing and Curtis moved over to go down the unoccupied lane. They were through the border in seconds.

'Don't tell me,' said Curtis, 'another favour.'

'Not really, my mate at the Gendy has done this before. He radios the French side who talk to their Spanish counterparts. As long as they have the vehicle make and number, they'll let it happen, they trust each other.'

'Good stuff, Stephen,' said Wyatt. 'Put your foot down Sally, they can't be that far ahead of us now.'

The wind picked up as they left La Jonquera behind them. Sand and dried earth was being thrown over the carriageway. Curtis slowed down. 'I'll take it a bit slower;

the visibility is not so good, and we don't want to miss anything.'

Wyatt and Landers kept a close eye on the surroundings. The road was quiet with just a few vehicles going in each direction.

'Stop, now!' shouted Landers.

Curtis pulled over and stopped on the soft sandy verge. She and Wyatt looked to the left in the same direction that Landers was looking. 'Down there, see that church?' said Landers.

Two hundred yards from the road was an old church. A small track they had just passed led to it between bushes and knee-high grassy areas. Curtis took up the binoculars that were by her side and focused them on the church. 'Gotya!' she said.

'The vehicle?' asked Wyatt.

'The vehicle; take a look.'

Wyatt put the binoculars to his eyes, hesitated and then passed them to Landers as he spoke. 'A Citroen people carrier, doors open, tail lift on the ground. This is where it gets interesting folks.'

Ashby heard the Cherokee before any of the others. He moved into the church via the rear door to see Farrah and Hoetger huddled over a map. 'We've got company.'

Farrah got to his feet quickly and grabbed the rifle that Ashby was throwing to him. Hoetger wheeled himself back and looked out of the front window.

'Where the bloody hell is Dick?' asked Farrah.

'Out here, just waking up,' said Hoetger.

Hobson woke up as the vehicle was driving slowly towards the church. He got to his feet and fell into the front door of the church. Farrah could see that he was not alert. 'Dick, get out to the rear, get yourself a weapon from the van and watch the back, Mark, you stay here with me. Where's Brewer?'

'Last I saw her she was out the back, asleep, with an empty bottle in her hand.'

'Bloody hell!' said Farrah.

'She'll soon come round when it all kicks off,' said Hoetger.

Farrah knelt down at the side of Hoetger to look out of the window. The Cherokee was being driven towards the church at a crawling pace, one person at the wheel, and no sign of passengers. It came to a halt about 40 metres away from the church. Curtis turned it around so it was facing the road again and got out of the vehicle. She moved to the front so that she was partly shielded by the bonnet and shouted towards the church. 'Alan! It's me, Melanie Leeder!'

Farrah said nothing.

Curtis shouted again. 'Only this time, Alan, I'm here as Sally Curtis, remember? When we met in Nottingham I told you I just wanted a slice of the cake. And at the villa, I mentioned a payment that I had for you.'

Farrah went to the open doorway. He stood half-in, half-out and called to her. 'Get back in the vehicle, turn it around so it's side-on to me and open all the doors.'

Curtis did as he asked. She knew he wanted to be sure that no one else was in the vehicle. There was no one else in the vehicle; Wyatt and Landers had made their way quietly on foot, one to the left of the church, the other to the right. As Curtis spoke again, Wyatt was lying in the dried grass with a rifle trained on Farrah from his position on the right, and Landers was lying in a shallow hollow with his Pistol pointing at Hobson who was crouching down next to the Mercedes van at the rear of the church.

'You see, Alan! I'm on my own. The other three don't know I'm here!'

Farrah moved back away from the doorway.

'What do you think, boss?' asked Ashby.

'She's lying. If she was on her own she would have driven up close. The only reason she's staying at that distance is that someone else is here watching. Check out the back.'

Ashby moved slowly out of the rear door to see Hobson crouching at the side of the van. He moved backwards into the church again, still looking around. 'Dicks got the back covered.'

'There must be at least one more out there somewhere,' said Farrah.

'Delaney won't be there,' said Hoetger.

'Right,' said Farrah. 'Let's get at least one of them out of the equation.'

He moved back to the door and opened it a little more. 'Well, Sally Curtis! Start walking. This way.'

Curtis walked towards the church. She stopped when she was about 10 metres away. Farrah started to walk towards her. As he got close, he grabbed her arm, swung her around and held her in front of himself as a human shield, looking from side to side. 'Whoever else is out there!' he shouted, 'you leave, now!'

Wyatt stayed perfectly still; his rifle still trained on Farrah. He could have shot him without harming Curtis, but it was not without any risk at all and that would only have taken one of them out. He needed to see more faces before he started to reduce numbers. To the rear, Landers had heard Farrah and he started to make his way quietly towards Hobson who was looking towards the church because of the voices. Within a minute he would be on him. He crawled slowly, pausing every few seconds. As he got closer he stood up in readiness, his pistol pointed at Hobson.

Thud! The fence post came down on Lander's head, hard; he was thrown to the ground as he started to spin, the scenery swirling around him. Then the post came down again, this time on his back. He felt a kick to his side as he passed out. Hobson spun around to see what was happening.

'You're too slow, Hobson, he nearly had you.' Brewer was standing over Landers, still holding an old fence post.

'Where the hell did you come from?' asked Hobson.

'Same place he came from; back there. I've been watching him.'

Hearing the noise, Ashby rushed out to see what was happening. He looked at the scene without saying anything, having realised what had happened. Brewer looked at him and remembered what he had said earlier. 'I might not be a woman with style, but I'm better than this bloke,' she said, looking at Hobson with disdain.

'Stay here then and guard the back if you're that good,' said Ashby. 'Dick, you'd better get in here.'

Farrah had dragged Curtis back into the church and thrown her to the floor. As she started to pick herself up, Hoetger moved his wheelchair so that one of the wheels ran over her hand. 'Aah, you son of a bitch!' she screamed. Ashby walked over to Farrah. 'Brewer got one of them outside when he was trying to creep up on Dick.'

'Right,' said Farrah, 'we're out of here before we let them get a foothold and more of their troops arrive. Dick, bring the van round to the front and tell Brewer to get round here and get William loaded up. Mark, you're with me in the back of the van.'

'What about her?' asked Ashby, looking at Curtis.

'She's coming with us. Insurance.'

Curtis kicked Farrah in the leg. 'The hell I am you pig!' Farrah swiped her across the face with his rifle butt, she fell back, blood streaming from her temple.

Wyatt, still remaining perfectly still, watched as Farrah emerged from the church holding Curtis in front of him. Then Brewer brought Hoetger out and loaded him into the Citroen. She closed the back doors of the vehicle as Hoetger was reaching for a gun at his side. They drove off towards the main road. The Mercedes van, being driven by Hobson, came to the front door. Farrah threw Curtis into the back and climbed in himself. Ashby jumped up into the van and sat down facing outwards, leaving the doors open, his gun aimed at anything or everything as they drove slowly away.

Wyatt edged himself up slightly and took aim. He couldn't kill anyone, that would be the end for Sally, he thought. He aimed at one of Ashby's legs hanging out the back of the van. The bullet hit just above the ankle and Ashby screamed out in pain. Farrah dragged him inside and slammed the rear doors shut. Hobson slowed down but Farrah shouted at him. 'Keep going! Don't slow down, that's what he wants you to do!'

The van reached the main road, turned left and caught up with the Citroen being driven by Brewer. Farrah tapped Hobson on the shoulder. 'Get in front of her, then she can follow us; she doesn't know where we're going.'

Wyatt dropped to the floor again as he heard a noise from one side. Landers was stumbling towards him, his head covered in blood. He looked around to see the vehicles had gone before stumbling again. 'Sally?' he said to Wyatt in a weak voice.

'They've taken her with them; I told you this was going to get interesting.'

Landers nodded and smiled slightly through the blood on his face. 'So you did, Ben. So you did.'

He was still nodding when he hit the ground.

35

Burton dropped Delaney back at the hospital as the evening started to approach. They both realised that Delaney needed to get back to Wyatt, Curtis and Landers as soon as he could; especially as it had been a good few hours since Wyatt had communicated. 'I'll wait for you, sir, I've nothing planned.'

'Okay, Taffy, I won't be long, and I don't think the doctor will want me to be.'

Angela was awake. Some of the tubes had now been removed and she seemed less drained as Delaney looked at her. He kissed her gently on the cheek. 'Nice to see your eyes open,' he said. She nodded slowly and tried a smile. Through her distorted mouth, she attempted to speak to him in a quiet, injured voice. 'I feel much better; the doctor thinks I'll be in for about a week.'

'Okay,' said Delaney, 'I'll make sure they arrange something for you when you get home.'

A voice from behind said, 'It's already arranged.' Delaney turned to see the doctor he had met the day before walking towards them. 'Hello, Doctor Hague.'

The doctor moved around Delaney, checked the small screen at the side of Angela's bed, and looked at him. 'I've made phone calls, home visits have been arranged for her in a weeks' time, she should be home by then, she's doing really well.'

'Right, thank you,' said Delaney. Doctor Hague patted Angela on the arm.

'Well, I'll leave you to it for a while, not too long please Mr Delaney.'

'No no, of course, just a few minutes,' acknowledged Delaney.

As the doctor left the room, Angela raised herself up in her bed with a wince. She spoke again in her weak voice. 'I saw them, Tom.'

Delaney raised a hand slightly. 'You don't have to talk about it now.'

She ignored what he had said. 'Two of them, one small, one tall. The small one had a cap on, like a beret.'

'Right, well you rest now,' he replied, 'I'm sure the local boys will ask you questions when they think the time is right.'

She nodded and her head fell back again, against the pillow. He stayed with her for a while longer, until she was asleep again.

'How is she?' asked Burton as Delaney climbed into the car.

'Better, Taffy; she'll be okay.'

'That's good to hear, are you staying here for a while longer, or getting back to Ben and Sally?'

'Depends how they're all doing, I'll phone them later.'

A silence followed that Burton had experienced before. Delaney sat quietly clicking his knuckles and occasionally wiping a hand over his chin in an impatient manner. The last time he had to deal with it was just before a raid on a house where a people trafficking gang were hiding out. The raid had been successful, although not perhaps, by the book. The silence was interrupted as

Delaney sighed heavily, crossed his arms and sat back in his seat. 'Drive to the Dog and Partridge in Horton, Taffy.'

'The Dog and Partridge, sir?'

'Yeah, it's just about the time when the locals will be getting there.'

Burton drove. His boss would explain when he wanted to. After ten minutes, they approached the back of a cue of traffic and came to a stop. Delaney looked straight ahead without moving as he spoke to Burton. 'If I said to you, Taffy, one small man wearing a beret and one tall man, what would you say?'

'The Comptons, sir; Patrick and his cousin Kevin.'

'Spot on.'

'Just a wild guess, but would they by any chance frequent the Dog and Partridge?'

'They would indeed.'

'Just as well I'm with you then. We wouldn't want you losing your temper would we?'

'Me? I don't know what you mean, Taffy. Anyway, it looks like they're the ones that gave Angela that beating.'

'But why would they, sir? Knowing she could identify them?'

'Not sure, but when we get through this bloody traffic I'll ask them. Call for back-up please.'

They were only about five minutes away from the Dog and Partridge, when Delaney's phone rang. It was Wyatt. Burton wondered what on earth Delaney was being told, because he said very little and didn't interrupt his caller.

Wyatt gave Delaney the whole story. The border crossing, the church, his shot at Ashby to slow them down, the taking of Curtis and the trip to a hospital to get

Landers' head stitched up. Delaney waited until the story was complete. 'But why did Sally end up so close to them?' he asked.

'She disobeyed me, as per usual,' said Wyatt. 'I told her to stay with the vehicle and talk from a distance but she decided to walk to where Farrah was.'

'Tell me, Ben, when she came out being held by Farrah, did she look as though she was struggling?'

'No, sir, but there was blood coming from her head.'

'And you didn't shoot to kill because?'

'Because they would have killed Sally, you know what they're like. I couldn't risk it.'

'Mm, well, we have what we have. I'd better get back to you. Is Stephen fit enough to carry on?'

'I hope so, because he's standing next to me.'

Delaney paused for a while to think. 'Right, Ben, I'm with Taffy, we just have a small job to do and then I'll arrange a flight. Where are you?'

'We're going to head for Barcelona. I found a street map of the place in the church where we had our little altercation. I called the Barcelona police and gave them a description of the vehicles that Farrah's using.'

'Okay, I'll get a flight to Barcelona; be in touch.' Delaney finished the call and threw his phone down on the dashboard just as they were approaching the Dog and Partridge.

'More trouble, sir?' asked Burton.

'Yes, more trouble; Farrah has got Sally.'

Patrick Compton had not changed much, Delaney thought, as he stood watching him. Three men were sitting together at a small table in the corner of the pub; Patrick, arms folded, back straight, his cousin Kevin, leaning forward over his beer, and another man, younger and fitter. It was Kevin who looked up to see Delaney standing there. He nudged his cousin's arm and they stood up. The younger man moved forward to stand between them and Delaney.

Patrick Compton moved the younger man out of the way. He walked up to Delaney, his chewing gum accentuating a distorted mouth and yellow teeth. 'Mr Delaney, what brings you here? I thought you had quit the force.'

Kevin Compton started to make his way behind the bar, where there was another exit door. Burton appeared to block his path. Two police officers came up behind Burton as two more entered the pub and stood either side of Delaney. Patrick spoke again. 'My my, we are getting heavy aren't we?'

'Sorry, Patrick, but this time you got it wrong,' said Delaney.

'Got what wrong?'

'You and Kevin here gave a woman a good beating two days ago.'

'Is that a statement, Mr Delaney or a question?'

'It's a statement, she's identified you. The trouble for you, Patrick, is that whoever asked you to do it, didn't tell you who she is.'

Compton stayed silent. The younger man reached into his jacket pocket, but Kevin Compton shouted at him. 'Don't be stupid lad! Leave it.'

Delaney moved forward until he was about five feet from Patrick Compton and looked at the floor. 'She is my partner, Patrick, and that was my house you went to.' He turned to look at the two officers that were with him. 'Take him, and the short one, leave the kid here.'

'My cousin has a name, Mr Delaney,' said Patrick, 'don't just call him 'the short one.'

Delaney turned again and moved back a little so he was closer to Compton. His right fist swung upwards and Compton's teeth made a loud cracking noise as they came together. The left fist then went into Compton's stomach and he fell to the floor. The younger man pulled a knife and lunged towards Delaney but he stopped in his tracks when Kevin Compton shouted 'Stay there!'

Burton took Kevin Compton's arm and led him around the front of the bar. The two officers behind the bar followed him. He pushed Kevin towards the officers and pulled Patrick up to his feet. 'Get these two out of here please; we'll talk to them later.' He then looked at the young man. 'You, leave now.'

'Why should...'

'Leave now!'

The young man hesitated, looked around and left.

An old man who was sitting at the bar started to clap his hands. 'Well done boys!' he shouted. 'Nothing but trouble that lot are.'

A large man with tattoos on his neck sitting nearby looked at the old man. 'Keep your mouth shut, Charlie.'

Delaney and Burton walked out. The Comptons were being put into separate cars. Delaney called over to the officer handling Patrick and asked him to wait. Holding a handkerchief to his blood soaked mouth, Patrick looked up. 'What now, Delaney? You bastard.'

'Who asked you to do it, Patrick?'

'Nobody you would know, you prick.'

'Try me.'

'Piss off!'

One of Compton's legs was still outside of the car. Delaney got hold of the door and slammed it hard. Compton cried out as the door came into contact with his shin. Delaney put all his weight behind him and held the door against Compton's shin. 'Who asked you to do it, Patrick?'

'Hoetger! A bloke called Hoetger! For crying out loud, you bastard!'

Back at the hospital, Angela looked more tired than she had looked a couple of hours earlier when Delaney saw her again, but she was awake. Burton had joined him and Angela looked uncomfortable as she acknowledged them both. 'Back so soon,' she said.

'I just wanted to see you were still alright,' said Delaney. 'I need to get back on the case.'

'It's okay I'll be fine.'

'Taffy here can call in on you. Did you ask the nurse or doctor to call your sister?'

'No, I don't want people fussing.'

'Well,' said Burton, 'I can call in everyday anyway.'

'Oh, you're so sweet, Taffy,' said Angela, trying to smile at him.

Delaney rolled his eyes in a gesture of light humour.

'Don't tell my enemies that will you?' said Burton.

Angela was asleep again a few minutes later. Burton drove Delaney home so he could get a change of clothes and check that everything was okay. When he checked the E-mails, an E-ticket was there for a flight to

Barcelona. Delaney asked Burton who had organised it and Burton, in his modesty, said it was just a friend in the right place. As they drove to the airport, the heavens opened up and rain drops the size of golf balls bounced off the bonnet of the car like a firework display as they caught the reflection of car lights, street lights and flashing advertising signs. As they sat in the traffic, Burton leaned his head to the right, to rest it in his hand against the window. 'Oh dear me, sir; what a mess eh?'

'Yeah, a mess alright, Taffy.'

'Do you want me stay here? I could help out there.'

'No you stay here please, and anyway according to a report on my desk, you're not fully fit yet.'

'Oh I'm fit enough.'

'Perhaps, but let's be sure eh?'

Burton decided not to labour the point. He did not want his boss any angrier than he already was. 'Sorry about Angela, sir, as though you haven't enough to think about without all this; still, we got the Comptons, I don't think you'll hear from them again,'

'No.'

Burton looked to see that Delaney was staring out of his side window. 'Something else bothering you?'

'Yes; Hoetger,'

'You mean Hoetger getting the Comptons to do what they did?'

'Yes.'

'Well, people like Hoetger know lots of bad guys that will do things like that.'

'Yes, Taffy, but you know how our details are kept out of the public eye.'

'Yes?'

'So how did Hoetger know where I live?'

The Boeing touched down at Barcelona at 23.30. One hour earlier, Wyatt and Landers had found a small hotel in Breda, about two hours away. Delaney phoned Wyatt as soon as he was through customs. 'Where are you, Ben?'

'A place called Breda. Shall I come and get you?'

'No, I'll get a car here and come to you.'

'Right, it's a small place just off the main road; you should be with us by about two.'

The Avis lady offered Delaney a Mercedes for the same price as a smaller car because of a cancellation, but he refused the offer. He wanted something less conspicuous. The Toyota was comfortable enough and the quiet roads allowed him to make good time on the journey. He was surprised to find Wyatt waiting for him at the hotel entrance.

'Thought you'd be asleep,' said Delaney.

'No chance, anyway they have no more rooms so you're in with me if you don't mind sharing with the minions.'

'I'll rough it this time.'

Wyatt led the way to the bedrooms and pointed to another door. 'Stephen is asleep, in there, so I've left him. He says he's okay but the knock on the head has affected him more than he realises I think. We're in here.' He opened another bedroom door.

'Thanks, Ben; Are you on the sofa, or am I?'

'I'll take the sofa, boss; you might find it a bit cramped.'

'Right, well let's get a few hours sleep then.'

'Good idea. The Spanish police have been amazing by the way; they say they have put extra people on the case to try to find Farrah's little convoy, so we might hear from them in the morning with any luck.'

'Let's hope so. But the small bottle of wine I had on the plane helped me to think. If we don't hear from them, I've got another idea. Time is running out, especially for Sally.'

36

Daybreak in Breda came all too quickly. The rising sun shone through the thin orange curtains as Wyatt pulled on a shirt and tapped Delaney on the shoulder as he slept. 'Seven o'clock sir.' He threw open the curtains and the light covered the room; it reminded him of a flood light being switched on at a border crossing. Delaney woke up quickly. 'Right, get Stephen up as well will you, we'll meet downstairs in half an hour.'

Wyatt went next door to find Landers already up, packing a bag. 'How are you mate?'

'Not too bad, could have done with a few more hours though.'

'Me too, Tom's here, he arrived early this morning. Have you heard from the Gendy at all?'

'No, not a thing.'

Thirty minutes later, the three men were sitting in the Cherokee. 'Right, lads,' said Delaney. 'If you haven't heard from the Gendarmerie or the Spanish federal boys, we need to think of another way to find out where they are.'

'Local police?' asked Landers.

'Possibly, doubt it though, not enough men,' said Delaney.

'By the way, sir,' said Wyatt. 'I tried Sally's phone last night but there was nothing. They probably smashed it up and dumped it.'

'Okay, let's just wait for another 30 minutes,' said Delaney, 'I might have a solution.'

He instructed Wyatt and Landers to check all of the gear and weaponry they were carrying in the Cherokee and to make themselves familiar with the local maps. Sitting alone in the Toyota, he waited for a while before making a phone call. 'Linda Scott please.'

The operator asked who was calling. Delaney mellowed his voice. 'It's a private call.'

After a few seconds, Linda Scott answered the phone. 'Foreign Secretaries office.'

'Hello, Linda, it's Tom again.'

'Tom Delaney, you do push your luck.'

'I know, sorry.'

'And before you ask, the Foreign Secretary is not in.'

'Actually, Linda it was you I wanted to talk to. I err, need a favour?'

'Well there's a surprise; go on then, be quick.'

Delaney grasped the nettle. 'Sir Adrian Lusher may be in trouble, so I wonder if you could contact Mrs. Beecham, his PA. I need to find out where he is quite quickly and I don't have his mobile number.'

'So why not phone her direct then, Tom?'

'Err; she's not really keen on me.'

'Yes, and I'm beginning to see why; I'll call you back.'

Linda Scott finished the phone call. Delaney was quietly optimistic that this was a good sign.

Wyatt tapped on the window a few minutes later just as Delaney's phone rang. Delaney wound down his window and asked Wyatt to get him a pen and paper before answering. 'Hello, Linda.'

'That's a bit presumptive of you, it could have been anyone.'

'I just guessed it was you when it said 'private number.'

'Right, this is his number, and you owe me, Delaney, *again*.'

'I know, thank you very much.'

She read out Lusher's phone number to him and he wrote it down. Then she ended the call just as quickly as she had ended the previous one. Delaney decided he had had his quota of favours for a while. He handed the piece of paper to Wyatt. 'Here Ben, take that to Stephen, tell him to get onto his Interpol friends and trace the location of that phone by GPS tracking.'

'Will do, sir, who's number is it?'

'I'll tell you later.'

The blood on Sally Curtis's face had dried up, and as she tried to open her eyes, the left one stayed shut. She forced her eyes open again, the coagulation gave way, and she could see around her. The bed cover she was laying on was pink, now with small patches of blood. To her left she saw a woman sitting on a chair looking at her. Two men were at a table near an open window. She could just make out the sound of waves breaking onto a beach. A hotel room, she thought, or perhaps a house, near a beach. She turned again to look at the woman. 'Who the hell are you?'

'Julie Brewer, that's who I am.'

'Oh yes, I've heard about you,' said Curtis as she turned to look at the two men. 'I see Mr. Farrah isn't here, so you two must be Ashby and Hobson.'

Hobson nodded. 'Correct.'

Ashby stood up, moved slowly towards the bed and sat down on it, a couple of feet away from Curtis. He raised one of his legs so that Curtis could see the blood soaked bandage. 'And when I get the bastard who did this to me, he'll be in a worse state than you are right now.'

Curtis was hurting bad, but only physically, her mind was still intact and she decided not to respond and give him an excuse to lash out at her. A door to the left of the bed opened. Curtis watched as a man in a wheelchair propelled himself quickly into the room followed by Alan Farrah. It was then that she remembered their altercation at the church and that the wheelchair man was Hoetger. I should have stayed close to the vehicle like Ben told me to, she thought.

Hoetger settled near the window. Farrah looked at Brewer, Ashby and Hobson, one after the other. 'Go and take a walk you three, give me 30 minutes at least.' Brewer walked out first, followed by Hobson supporting Ashby as he winced at the pain from his leg injury. Curtis made a mental note of this. A weak spot, she thought. The look on Farrah's face was not an angry one or an unkind one as he sat down next to Curtis and lit a cigar. 'Now then, Sally; or should I call you Melanie?'

Curtis remembered her training; never respond to the first few questions. She looked away. Farrah continued. 'When you revealed to me in Nottingham that you were actually a bent copper, I thought to myself, why would she tell me? And then later I guessed. To get closer to me; to get me to trust her. Well, you know what, it nearly worked. Why wouldn't a copper on the normal salary want to get their hands on a few million? I could have employed you full time; someone like you that knows about how intelligence services work, could be very useful; worth paying say, a million a year. But then I remembered something.' He paused to caress his cigar as he looked over at Hoetger and gestured towards him with his other hand. 'William here shot your boyfriend didn't he. And that must have really upset you. You must be aching for revenge, and how could you get revenge? By getting me as well as Mr Hoetger here. By getting me, his paymaster.'

Curtis looked at Hoetger who was looking out of the window. So it *was* you, she thought. She looked at him, sitting in his wheelchair; the ugly neck and unshaven jaw. Even from the side she could see his cruel emotionless looks and sensed his cold, thoughtless disposition. You're mine, you bastard, she thought to herself. When the time comes, you're mine.

Remaining silent, she looked back at Farrah who was drawing on his cigar. He turned to her again. 'Now, Sally, go ahead, tell me I'm wrong.'

Curtis waited for a while to give herself chance to think. Killing someone meant nothing to these people. She needed to be careful. 'You're wrong Alan. Why do you think I walked right up to you at the church? Marcus Hanson didn't mean anything to me; he wasn't even any good in bed. I've been bent for years. I can help you, if you let me; I'm sick and tired of working like I do for a pittance.'

Farrah stood up, walked away from the bed and paused for a while, saying nothing. Then he turned and walked back to where she was sitting on the bed. She looked into his eyes and spoke softly. 'So come on, what do you say? Wipe this blood off my face and we can talk properly.'

His left arm swung outwards and his fist came into contact with her face, sending her rolling sideways on the bed. He raised his left hand again and brought it down hard on the same spot. Blood poured from her left eye and she held her hands over her head. A split second later his right hand came over and he buried the lit cigar into her neck. She screamed with pain as he put his hands underneath her and rolled her off the bed. She came to rest near the wall, still screaming from the burn deep into her neck. She lay there for about two minutes holding herself defensively. When she had stopped crying out with pain, Farrah walked over to her. She unfolded her arms and looked at him in defiance. He looked down at her as he threw the cigar to one side. 'And that, young lady, is for insulting my intelligence.'

Brewer and Hobson came back when they heard the screams. 'Where's Mark?' asked Farrah.

'He's sitting down on the beach resting his leg,' said Hobson.

Farrah looked at Brewer and pointed to Curtis. 'Get her some cold water for that burn.' Brewer filled a glass with water, walked over to Curtis and threw it over her head. 'There you go my dear, cold water.'

Having seen what Brewer had done, Farrah went to the sink, soaked a small towel with cold water and went to Curtis. He carefully folded the towel and placed it on her neck where the cigar burn was. 'Here,' he said to her, 'hold that on it for a while.' Curtis watched him as he walked away, wondering where the change of attitude had come from. He went to where Brewer was standing and put his face close up to hers. Brewer looked nervous as he spoke to her. 'Get out.'

Hobson followed Brewer out of the room and they joined Ashby who was sitting on a low wall looking out to sea. The beach was quiet; just a few people trying to enjoy the breezy conditions. Ashby looked up as they approached him. 'What's happened?'

'Alan has roughed up the woman a bit,' said Hobson, gesturing his head towards Brewer. 'And this one here has lost a few brownie points.'

'Spare me the details,' said Ashby. 'Has Alan said what we're going to do now?'

'No, nothing yet,' answered Hobson.

Brewer looked to the right and stood up sheltering her eyes from the sun. 'What's that place there then?' Behind them and to the right, a huge castle loomed, its straight walls leaning back. Large turrets overlooked the beach and the sea, like guardians.

'How the hell would we know,' said Hobson.

'Sorry!' said Brewer, 'I just thought you might have been here before.'

'This bloody leg is killing me,' said Ashby.

'Thank yourself lucky the bullet didn't hit the bone,' said Hobson. 'Do you want me to get you some more painkillers?'

'No, I'd better not take too many.'

A shout came from the window behind them. It was Farrah. 'You three! Come here.'

They moved close to the open window. Farrah spoke quietly. 'I've got a visitor due any minute. Mark, you stay on the beach, but face this way and keep your eyes open. Dick, you and Brewer come and get the woman and take her to the room next door. Keep her there and stay quiet.' They all did as instructed. Hoetger stayed near the window in his chair and Farrah lay on the blood stained bed.

Curtis had been right with her guess about being near a beach. When they had taken her from the church, they had driven to Tossa de Mar, a town on the coast about 100 kilometres from Barcelona. An old acquaintance of Farrah's ran a small hotel that lay in the southern corner of the main beach and two ground floor rooms had been reserved for them. They were just a few paces away from the beach and it was the brisk breeze coming north that had stirred up the low laying surf. All the windows were open and the sound of the surf could be heard as they as they all sat and waited.

A few minutes later there was a quiet knock on the door. Farrah got to his feet and moved to a chair facing the door, pistol in hand. 'Come in.'

A tall man in a suit entered the room, threw a bag onto the bed and sat down next to it. He looked at Farrah for a while before casting an eye over Hoetger, noticing the wheelchair and the gun on the table at the side of him. 'You must be William Hoetger,' he said.

Farrah chuckled and leaned forward in his chair. 'Yes, he's William Hoetger. Allow me to introduce you, William. This is Sir Adrian Lusher.'

Lusher spoke cautiously. He could see how close Hoetger's hand was to the gun on the table and he had arrived unarmed. 'Mr Hoetger, your reputation precedes you.'

'And I too, believe I know your name from somewhere,' said Hoetger.

Farrah laughed. 'I should bloody well hope so! Sir Adrian here is the head of MI5.'

A moments silence followed. Hoetger frowned and wheeled himself closer to Farrah.

'Alan, are you telling me that this man is your man on the inside?'

'No William, I'm telling you that he's *just one* of them.'

37

'Got it sir,' said Landers.

Delaney and Wyatt looked at him, waiting for the details. Landers leaned forward from his position in the back of the Cherokee. 'That mobile phone is about 50 kilometres east of here, close to the coast. They suggest that we make our way in that direction, they can start to get a more accurate location for us, providing the phone stays switched on.'

'Right, let's get on with it,' said Delaney. 'Ben, you drive so Stephen can navigate, I'll follow on in the Toyota.'

With instructions from Landers, Wyatt headed east. He drove fast and Delaney kept up with him. 'Stay on this road, Ben, until you see a sign for Vidreres,' said Landers. 'That looks like the best road to take for the coast. Those clever Interpol boys shouldn't take long to get a more accurate location for us.'

'How do they do that anyway, I thought GPS information was a bit inconsistent?'

'It is, but the US navy tracking system isn't. There are hundreds of satellites up there you know.'

'Yeah of course, let's hope that phone doesn't get switched off then.'

'Quite, any idea whose phone it is?'

'No. Tom obviously didn't want to tell us, but he will when we get closer, I'm sure of that.'

Forty minutes later, Wyatt turned off the main road and drove through Vidreres, still heading east. 'Stay on the C35 until you see a road on your right,' said Landers. The slip road to the right was soon in sight and Wyatt turned onto a smaller road heading south. A sign confirmed their destination; Tossa de Mar. He checked his mirror, Delaney was still with them. The landscape changed as they progressed. Large sundrenched fields gave way to bushier, more barren areas interspersed with clumps of trees and small fields with huts. Then the tree line thickened and they started to climb, the road winding around dry scorched bushes that limited the line of sight. Soon, they were descending again and the trees were turning greener.

'Pull over somewhere,' said Landers as his phone rang. Wyatt pulled into a side track entrance and Delaney pulled up behind him as Landers flipped his phone open. 'Hello...yes...ola...street name please?..okay, yes...thank you.'

Delaney approached the Cherokee and opened Wyatt's door. 'Anything yet?'

'Yeah, that was them,' said Landers. 'The phone is here alright; in Tossa de Mar, somewhere on Passeig del Mar.'

'Mar means sea doesn't it,' asked Wyatt.

'I think so; it's probably the coast road or a promenade somewhere.'

'How do we look for just one mobile phone user in a whole street though?' asked Landers.

'We won't be looking for a phone; we'll be looking for those two vehicles you encountered at that church. I'll drive the Cherokee, Ben you're the observant one, sit with me. Stephen, you follow up in the Toyota.'

The road they were on led them into the town, down a straight road lined with trees, parked cars and black and white pavements. They came to a stop at a junction.

'What's your instinct, Ben? Left or right?'

'Right.'

Delaney swung the vehicle right. After a few minutes, Wyatt pointed. 'There, sir, I think that sign means, 'to the beach.' They turned left and ahead of them was a large beach. A few people were walking along the pavement, but it was generally quiet, not being the holiday season. They turned right onto the road that ran parallel with the beach. 'Well done, Ben, good instincts.'

'You reckon boss?'

Delaney smiled and pointed to a sign that said 'Passeig del Mar.'

They parked the vehicle and Delaney watched Landers pull up behind them and acknowledge the situation with a nod.

Wyatt sat back. 'What now then?'

'We wait. That's all we can do; and hope we spot one of their vehicles.'

'Delaney won't be troubling you, he's back in England,' said Lusher.

Farrah seemed disturbed. 'How do I know that?'

'He went to see one of his bosses, the Home Secretary, just 24 hours ago.'

'There are a couple of people I know,' said Hoetger. 'I got them to beat up Delaney's girlfriend. That's what sent him back there.'

'He has other people,' said Farrah. 'Like whoever it was at the church that shot Mark. They won't be amateurs.'

'So why are we waiting here?' asked Hoetger. 'Let's split the money and go; meet up in a few months time as we agreed a few weeks ago.'

'I agree,' said Lusher. 'You got out of jail, Alan, and you've got the money, I need to get back to England before they start to miss me and ask questions.'

'No,' said Farrah. Hoetger raised both arms in the air, took the gun from the table at the side of him and wheeled himself out of the room. Lusher perched on the table and opened his hands out to Farrah. 'Why?'

'Because I want Delaney as well and maybe even some more of his team. One of them killed my brother. I want freedom, the money *and* revenge.'

'Fine, your call, all *I* want is the money, so I'll take my share now and leave you to it. Two million I think you said.'

Farrah sighed and stood up. 'Okay, I'll get one of the boys to count it out. But remember, this is just a down payment. I'll need you again in the future. Don't spend any of it yet, and when you do, keep it as quiet as you can.'

'Don't worry about things like that, Alan; I've already opened an account in Cuba.'

Farrah thumped twice on the wall. Hobson came to him a minute later. 'Dick, get the money out of the van and count out two million for this gentleman please.'

Hobson frowned at Lusher. 'Don't I know you from somewhere?'

Lusher stayed quiet and Farrah smiled. 'Just get the money, Dick.'

'Alone at last, eh, sweetheart.' In the room next door, Brewer had locked the door when Hobson left. Curtis could hardly move as she sat on the floor, her back leaning against the wall. She could hardly open her eyes and the cigar burn was giving her extreme pain, no matter how hard she tried to put it out of her mind.

Brewer sat on a chair, two metres away. She leaned forward and lit a cigarette. 'Now then darlin'. I reckon that that cigar burn looks so cool; you should have one on the other side as well. And maybe even some more on your body somewhere; it could look as sexy as a tattoo.'

Curtis could only see Brewers blurred face through her half open eyes, but she was conscious enough to hear what she was saying. Don't say a word, Curtis thought to herself, not a word, don't aggravate her any more. She thought of an old mentor that had told her not to bother talking to psychopaths, it wouldn't help either way. Brewer moved the cigarette so close to Curtis's face she could feel the heat. She hesitated, then moved the cigarette to one side. There was a pause. Curtis clenched her teeth. A loud knock on the door startled them both. Ashby shouted from the other side. 'Brewer, open this door now!'

'Coming, Mark! Just girlie things and all that you know!'

Curtis started to relax her body and for one split second she forgot who she was dealing with. As Brewer got to her feet, she sunk the burning cigarette into Curtis's neck. Hearing the scream, Farrah and Lusher rushed round from the neighbouring room just as Brewer was opening the door for Ashby. 'She's fine,' said Brewer, 'just a girlie argument.'

Farrah went over to Curtis and moved her head to one side. On the opposite side of Curtis's neck to where he had sunk his cigar in, was another burn; smoke and the smell of burning flesh still coming from it. Curtis looked as though she was about to pass out. Seeing the look on Farrah's face, Brewer left the room quickly.

Farrah looked at Ashby and motioned his head towards the door. 'Get some cold water Mark and some kind of ointment from somewhere, this woman has had enough for now.'

'Who the hell is she?' asked Lusher.

Farrah frowned at Lusher in disbelief that he did not know. 'She's from Canada; works for their intelligence service. She's been helping Delaney and his crew.'

'I see; do you know why?'

'It was her boyfriend who got shot in Munich, when he was getting too close to the top men.'

'What top men?'

'Jerome and Bouton.'

'So why is she still persisting? They're both dead.'

'Probably because she wants the man that pulled the trigger.'

'And who's that?' asked Lusher, not expecting to get an answer.

Farrah stared at him. 'The man you just met in the wheelchair; don't underestimate him.'

'On your orders I suppose.'

'No; not this time; his instruction for that came from someone else.'

Curtis had only just resisted passing out. The trauma had somehow built up some kind of adrenalin and she had stayed lucid enough to hear what was being said. She kept her eyes shut and tried to remain motionless as the pain surged through her neck and head. 'You should just let her go,' said Lusher. 'She'll slow you down in her state.'

'She will also make Delaney think twice if he gets close; she stays for now,' said Farrah.

Both men started to move around as they talked and Curtis took the opportunity to move slightly and open her eyes briefly enough to see who the other man was. She recognised him instantly. Ashby came back into the room with water and a towel. 'I've told Brewer to go and buy some ointment from somewhere,' he said.

'Right,' said Farrah, 'wet the towel and put it round her neck.' Curtis felt some relief as Ashby wrapped the towel around her, but she still kept her eyes shut as she continued to listen. When Ashby had left the room, Lusher spoke again. 'By the way, you mentioned next door during the introductions, that I was *just one* of your people on the inside; who's the other?'

Farrah ignored the question.

'Well well, I don't believe it,' said Wyatt.

Delaney looked at Wyatt and then turned his eye to the same direction that Wyatt was looking in. 'Don't believe what?'

'That woman there, walking this way; the one with the earrings and the tattoo. Recognise her?'

'No, tell me.'

'Remember Micky Black?'

'Yes; ran away to Brazil a couple of years ago.'

'That's him. Well that's his daughter Julie Brewer. We'd better cover our faces in case she...'

'She's going into that shop,' interrupted Delaney, 'looks like a pharmacy.'

Wyatt raised a hand so Landers behind them could see that something was happening. Delaney started to open his door. 'She must be with them then, which probably means they're not far away.'

'Agreed, boss, what do we do, follow her?'

'No, we take her, come on.'

Seeing Wyatt's signal, Landers had now joined them. 'Something happening?' he asked.

Delaney, now out of the vehicle, waited until Landers was close to him. 'A woman in that shop, she has to be with them. Stephen; stay here with the Cherokee, open the back door and wait for us. Ben, come with me.'

Another person was exiting the pharmacy as they approached. Wyatt stayed further away as Delaney walked past slowly and back again. 'No one else in there; just her and a sales girl. We'll get her on her way out.'

'Right, but I know what she's like, just holding her arm isn't going to do it.'

'Fine, give her good punch then.'

Seconds later, Brewer was leaving the shop. Delaney was standing by the door pretending to look in the window. Just in case he was recognised, Wyatt turned away and held a hanky to his face, pretending to be blowing his nose. Brewer turned right. Seeing her reflection in the shop window, Wyatt turned when she was two feet away from him. He spun, swinging his right fist into her jaw, she reeled but went for something in her pocket, Delaney kicked the back of her leg and she collapsed, Wyatt pulled his gun, bent down, grabbed her neck and pushed the barrel of the gun into her cheek. 'Your choice, come quietly or die now.'

As soon as he saw the look on her face, he realised she was not going to submit. She hesitated and started to draw breath. Wyatt knew that a huge scream or shout would be heard by a lot of people, possibly even her accomplices. He quickly drew the gun away from her face and brought it down with all his might against the side of her mouth and then onto her neck. She was silenced and Delaney grabbed her from behind while Wyatt took her legs. They bundled her into the back of the Cherokee, Wyatt staying with her. Delaney jumped into the passenger seat as Landers started to drive away.

'Where to, sir?'

'Find a local police station; we'll dump her there and then get back here. When Farrah starts to miss her, he or one of his boys will soon surface.'

Fifteen minutes later, they were identifying themselves to the local head of police; Sergeant Gabillo. His old run down station had just two cells and one of them was occupied by a local drunk. The front office was clean but sparse with dark brown walls and a white corridor that led to the cells. There were no bars on the cell doors. They were solid wood with wired glass vision panels and run-of-the-mill keys and locks. The sergeant could speak English well enough not to hesitate. 'She will be in here, and later perhaps, the Barcelona transport will collect her. I must wait for documents you understand.'

'Of course,' said Delaney as Wyatt bundled her into the cell. She settled on the small wooden box bed and stared at them all. Blood was still coming from her mouth after Wyatt's blow to her face with his gun. She wiped her arm across her face to take off some of the blood as she turned her gaze on Delaney. 'So, I reckon you must be the man in charge. Wait until my brothers catch up with you, mister.'

'I don't suppose it's worth me asking you where Farrah is?' asked Delaney.

'Correct,' said Brewer as she looked away. They turned to leave the cell and suddenly Brewer called out. 'Hey!' Delaney carried on walking and Wyatt turned to face her again. She had gotten up from the bed and was walking towards him. She stopped short and spat at him in the face, phlegm, blood and saliva almost covering his eyes. He raised a hand.

'Ben! Save it for later.' Delaney's command was short but strong enough.

Sergeant Gabillo offered Wyatt soap and towels on the way out. He cleaned his face as Landers entered the building, having parked the Cherokee. 'Trouble?'

'No trouble,' said Wyatt. 'It'll keep.'

Gabillo put the cell keys in his drawer and offered his visitors some water. As they all stood around the water cooler, Delaney asked him if he knew of any places along the Passieg del Mar that may not be in full time use.

'There is one place I think,' said Gabillo. 'A small hotel which is not used, near the castle. The owner I think can only be seen there a few times a year. You want me to get some men?'

Delaney looked at Wyatt who shook his head. They were clearly singing from the same hymn sheet; if too many local people got involved, it would get too messy and communication would suffer. Landers answered the sergeant's question when he could see the response from his colleagues. 'No, thank you very much, we will look after things. Of course, we understand you need to be kept informed and we can assure you that no innocent bystanders will be injured. If the people we are after are here, we will wait until they have left the town before approaching them.'

Wyatt, still drying his face, arched his eyebrows and turned to leave. Delaney thanked the sergeant again and explained to him that he would arrange for two men to collect Brewer as soon as possible. Gabillo handed Delaney a card. 'Our contact details, I am here most of the time and I have two more people.' Just two, thought Delaney, I had better get Brewer collected soon.

Outside in the streets, a few people were putting up umbrellas as the clouds opened. Blue sky was still visible in the distance. 'Just a shower,' said Landers, 'follow me, I'm parked down here.' Minutes later they were parked back on Passieg del Mar and Landers was on the phone to Interpol.

'Tell them to get her collected as soon as they can,' said Delaney. 'I want her back in England; she can be kept in one of our basement cells until we get back.'

'It's the afternoon already,' said Wyatt. 'They'll be missing her by now if she was only going to a local shop.'

'Mm, well all we can do is wait. That must be the building the sergeant mentioned.' Delaney was pointing to a small two storey building, one window either side of the central door. Green window shutters were partly open and the first and second floor windows had closed blinds. Behind the building was a tall and long castle wall, interspersed with large turrets. Cars were parked in a row between the building and the beach, but there was no sign of the vehicles they were looking for. Wyatt reached for his Smith and Wesson, checked the magazine and put it back in his shoulder holster. 'I'll take a walk around the back of the place, sir, okay?'

'Yeah sure, be careful and stay in touch.'

Landers finished his phone call and leaned forward from the back seat. 'All sorted sir; they can collect Brewer tonight and get her on a plane in the morning.'

'Well done, Stephen, having you based over here for the last couple of years has certainly been worthwhile.'

'It hasn't been easy.'

'I appreciate that; now let's just keep our eyes open and concentrate.'

Ashby looked sheepishly at Farrah. 'She's probably trying to find a pharmacy.'

'Don't be stupid, Mark, she's been gone an hour. She could have walked around the whole bloody town by now.'

Farrah, Ashby and Lusher had returned to the main room. Hobson had counted out approximately two million from one of the bags in the Mercedes van, stuffed it into a small wheeled travel case and brought it to them.

Farrah noticed the pathetic look on Lusher's face. 'There you are then, Sir Adrian; two million. Thank you for your help and I look forward to using you again.'

'Right,' said Lusher, 'but let's just calm down for a while before getting into another big job.'

Ashby seemed disturbed when Lusher spoke. He wanted to kill him there and then. 'Well, what a pillar of society you are,' he said to Lusher as he nursed his leg which had started to bleed again.

Lusher stared at him. 'Don't criticise me you vagabond; if I chose to, I could finish your life tomorrow. You're probably twice as hard as me, but I'm twice as intelligent as you and history has shown that brain wins over brawn every time so keep your mouth shut and don't judge me; because one day I may be making a decision about your future.'

'Okay you two, that'll do,' said Farrah. He gestured to Hobson. 'Dick, get back next door will you and stay with the woman; I'll let you know when we're leaving.'

'We should be leaving now,' said Ashby.

Farrah nodded. 'You're probably right, Mark; we'll give Brewer another hour. If she hasn't shown up by then we'll make a move.'

Hoetger wheeled himself into the room and looked around for an answer. 'What are we doing then? And where's Julie?'

No one gave him a good answer. Ashby casually gave his opinion. 'Bloody stupid girl's probably gone for a walk along the beach.'

Farrah turned to Lusher. 'Are you going then? No reason to stay; you have your money.'

'Yes, I'm going and you...' Lusher's phone rang. Farrah knocked it from his hand as he went to answer it. 'You idiot! Have you had that switched on all the time?'

'Most of the time, what the hell do you think you're doing?'

Farrah kicked the phone against the wall and stamped on it as it came to rest. 'Tracking, man, tracking! Anyone with enough know how can track the location of that phone!'

Lusher did not respond, although he was well aware of what tracking could, or could not, be done. Ashby picked up the phone, opened it and removed the SIM card. He placed some paper in an ashtray and put the SIM card on top of the paper, which he then lit using a cigarette lighter. Hoetger wheeled himself over to the window and looked around. 'We need to go now. This changes everything; if anyone suspects this man is with us, they could be very near to us already.'

Farrah didn't waste time saying that he agreed. 'Mark; get the van out of the basement; have it ready to go in five minutes.'

'I can't drive with this blasted leg li...'

'Just do it Mark! William, get next door; tell Dick to get the woman on her feet. He'll have to drive you; we can't wait any longer for Brewer.'

As Ashby and Hoetger left the room, Lusher started to wheel the travel case full of money towards the door. He paused when he noticed Farrah staring at him. 'I've a good mind to take half of that money back from you, Lusher, for making a mistake like that.'

'You won't though, will you, Alan, because you need me and I may not cooperate if you reduce my income.'

Farrah continued to look at him for a while and then gestured to the door. 'Get out of my sight; I'll let you know when I need you again.'

Curtis was gripping the wet towel around her singed neck as Hobson pulled her to her feet and dragged her out of the door. The stairs to the basement were steep and Curtis had to grip the handrail to stop him pushing her down. Ashby had started the engine of the Mercedes van and was opening the back doors as they approached. 'Get her in the back and close the doors,' said Hobson, 'I've got to drive Hoetger; where's the Citroen?' Ashby pointed to a dark corner of the basement. 'Over there, the keys are in; but you'll have to go around the front to pick him up, there's no ramp or lift down here.'

Hobson cursed as he ran to the Citroen; the last thing he wanted to do was to be seen at the front of the building. Hoetger had already made his way to the front door and was waiting for Hobson to appear. Lusher had decided to wait until they had stopped panicking and had gone through to the room where they had been holding Curtis to wait until things calmed down.

Farrah was coming down the basement stairs in a hurry as he shouted to Ashby. 'Mark, move over! I'll drive. You get that leg raised and tighten the bandage; I don't want you fainting on me.'

Ashby had already raised the basement door and Farrah drove out and turned left. He then turned right, then left, then right. He was about half a mile away when he parked in a side street and waited. They looked around. There was no vehicle movement and no pedestrian movement. 'No one around by the look of it,' said Farrah. 'That was lucky.' He looked at Ashby. 'Keep that leg raised.'

Curtis still had shock and pain going through her body. She managed to look up at Farrah as his gaze moved from Ashby to her. After a few seconds, he turned back to his driving position and shook his head. 'Don't say a word, young lady; not a word.'

Hobson pulled up outside the front of the hotel and Hoetger made his way to the vehicle as the rear chair lift was being lowered. Two minutes later they were driving around the corner of the building heading for the town centre.

'There' Landers pointed to the Citroen.

'I see it.' said Delaney. 'Follow it and keep well back until we're out of town. Where the hell is Ben?' As they drove slowly around a corner, Landers spotted Wyatt who had started to make his way back to them. He had noticed the Citroen and then the Cherokee so he knew what to do. Landers slowed down almost to a stop as he reached back to open a rear door. Wyatt jumped in and the vehicle got back up to speed as they followed the Citroen.

Through the darkened windows of the Citroen, Hoetger, looking backwards, had seen it all. He could not be one hundred percent certain, but his gut feeling was enough for him to act. He turned his head and shouted at Hobson. 'Around the next corner, pull up. Alan has arranged another vehicle for us.' Hobson, having no reason to doubt that Farrah would have organised something as cunning as this, stopped the vehicle in a small side street. He opened the rear doors and lowered Hoetger to the ground just as the Cherokee was coming around the corner. 'Wait here,' said Hoetger, 'I know where the keys are.'

Hobson, not knowing he had been followed, folded up the chair lift. 'Be quick then. Which vehicle is it?'

Hoetger looked quickly around and chose a vehicle that was parked on the opposite side of the small street, knowing that Hobson would need to cross the road. 'That one, the large red one.' He pointed to the car.

'Right, well hurry up then!' said Hobson.

The Cherokee was driving slowly towards the Citroen as Hobson crossed the road to get to the red car. He turned to look at the Cherokee as it approached and it was then that he remembered something. The Cherokee had been at the old church they had fled from when they had taken Curtis. Wyatt was now out of the vehicle, running down the sidewalk, keeping low, gun in hand. Hobson suddenly stopped in the middle of the road, and one arm reached for the small of his back.

'A gun?' Landers asked Delaney.

'Has to be, stop here.'

Hobson raised his right hand, holding what looked like a 9mm. His left hand came up to grip his right wrist and he took slow but steady aim at the driver of the Cherokee.

'Hey.'

The voice that spoke to Hobson was coming from his right. He turned his head but his gun was still pointing to the Cherokee. Wyatt was staring at him from behind a car, his Smith and Wesson resting on the roof, pointing at Hobson. 'Don't,' said Wyatt, 'stop now.'

When he could see the look in Hobson's eyes; the look of defiance, Wyatt pulled the trigger twice, Hobson's gun went off as he was knocked sideways, blood splattered across parked cars as he dropped and the gun fell to the ground. Still alive, Hobson struggled to retrieve his gun. Wyatt walked up to him. He would have put another bullet into Hobson in most circumstances, to make sure, but when he saw Hobson's eyes and the blood coming from his ears, he kicked the gun from Hobson's hand and kicked it again in the direction of the Cherokee. Delaney and Landers were now out of the vehicle running to the scene.

Hobson was gurgling on blood as he looked up at Wyatt. He tried to say something, but a second later he was spent, his body giving way and resting, distorted, against the roadway. Wyatt took a deep breath and kept looking at his victim as he spoke. 'Poor bastard, but you're just a pawn aren't you? One of these days I'll have your boss in checkmate.'

Realising the incident was closed, Delaney looked around. 'What about Hoetger?'

Hoetger had chosen what he thought to be the back entrance to a restaurant or cafe, when he had told Hobson to stop. The back door led through a small passageway and into a busy burger bar. A few people noticed him and assumed he had come from the public conveniences to the rear of the establishment. He wheeled himself casually in between tables and out onto the street. An old taxi; big enough to put a wheelchair in, was standing empty nearby and he shouted to a man that he assumed to be the driver. The man looked old, bored and tired as he approached. Hoetger reached underneath his wheelchair, unzipped a large pocket and pulled out about one thousand Euros in twenties. He thought about what Farrah and Ashby had said earlier and about Barcelona. That was to be the next stop and Delaney and his men would not be far behind them. He stuffed the money into the old man's hand.

'Get me to the French border, as quick as you can.'

38

Home Secretary Martin Hamilton was pacing around his office with his arms folded. 'Where the hell is Lusher?' His PA, Andrea Beecham, was standing in the doorway

'We don't know, Home Secretary, his phone is still not responding.'

'How the hell can the head of MI5 have a phone that doesn't work?' There was a pause as he sat down. 'Sorry, Andrea, I shouldn't be asking you should I?'

'The technical communications department are onto it now,' she said. The last I heard was that his GPS signal had been lost in South East Spain.'

'Right, so can you please let me know when he resurfaces, wherever that might be.'

Mrs Beecham nodded politely and turned to leave the room. He shook his head at his own thoughtlessness and called after her. 'Andrea.' She looked back, put her head on one side and smiled. 'Sorry,' he said, 'I ask too much of you sometimes.'

The blue phone on his desk was ringing. He answered it to be told that a call was coming through for him from Number 10. He waited until he could hear the usual double click that told him the caller had been put through via the secure link at GCHQ Cheltenham. 'Martin Hamilton speaking.'

'Home Secretary, this is Colonel Pritchard. Cobra meeting in two hours please.'

'Very well.' Hamilton did not hesitate; Colonel Pritchard was the Aide to the Chief of General Staff. When you got the 'Cobra' call you just stopped what you were doing and got there. Cobra was the publicly known code name for the government's emergency committee. Headed up by the Prime Minister, its members included some of the most senior people in the armed forces and civil service, including himself and Foreign Secretary Spires. There had been some murmurings about a new terrorist cell operating out of Bristol and Leeds and he guessed they were being summoned to be advised on the status of the alert before the press announcement. Perhaps it was going from amber to red. He phoned through to Mrs Beecham and asked her to send for his car. The blue line rang again as he was retrieving his private folder from a drawer. 'Martin Hamilton.'

'Martin, it's Jeremy Spires; have you had the call too?'

'Yes, it has to be that new cell doesn't it?'

'Probably, see you there.'

Hamilton spoke to himself as he put the phone down. 'The Foreign Secretary as well this time? Must be the terrorists. Let's hope they don't ask for Lusher.'

Taffy Burton was breathing heavily as he stepped off the cross-trainer. His recuperation had gone well and the muscles, tendons and joints were almost back up to full strength. He stood on the scales and looked at the readout that said 100kg. Not bad, he thought, I'll soon be as thin as Ben. Then his thoughts turned to *all* of his colleagues. Delaney had told him to get well and stay in England but he knew he was now fit enough to make a good contribution to the team again. With Brandon Jones gone, that left just Wyatt and Landers, but their experience was about half what his was and as TOLA's 'second-in command' they had often looked to him for an answer.

It was raining outside as he made his way to his car. The journey to the hospital took him 40 minutes. Angela had phoned earlier that morning to say that she would be discharged from the hospital at 1 p.m. after the doctor's rounds.

As he entered the ward, she looked much better to him and was sitting up in a chair, waiting.

'Hello, Taffy; you know, you have been so good to me.'

'Not at all, my pleasure, besides; Tom gave me strict instructions to look after you, so I'm doing my job I suppose.'

'Yes I know, but this is beyond the call of duty, surely.'

Burton did not answer, but simply held out his arm for her to hold as he led her to his car. After a few paces she was walking without his support and it came to his mind that he would let Delaney know how much better she was as soon as he could. They were moving slowly in the London traffic some 10 minutes later when a news item on the car radio caused them both to concentrate.

'...the reason for the Cobra meeting is not yet known but it is thought to be linked to the recent terrorist alerts. We understand all key members of Cobra have been summoned and...'

'Looks like things might be about to happen,' said Burton.

'Yes,' said Angela. 'Did I ever tell you about the famous typing error?'

'No, what was that?'

'Well, sometimes my colleagues and I get given some pretty confidential work to do; sometimes from GCHQ at Cheltenham and on the odd occasion we get stuff from the home office; they use us because it's all to do with saving money on more staff apparently. Anyway, about a year ago some work was sent to us by mistake, and it was about a Cobra meeting. It was in the papers, remember?'

'No I don't, sorry; go on.'

'Oh it didn't amount to much in the end, it wasn't a full meeting, but we all thought at the time of how serious it could have been if it *had been* a major incident.'

'Absolutely; was that the first and the last of such a mistake?'

'So far yes, but we often joke about it when we see something marked for the 'head of the department' wondering if it could from the Bird's Nest again.'

Burton smiled, but he was not exactly sure what she meant. 'Bird's Nest?'

'Yes, you must know surely, Taffy; in the trade, Cobra is referred to as the Bird's Nest because all the members are given names of birds as codes; something to do with identification if some clever clogs is listening in.'

'Well, I never knew that.'

'You spend so much time chasing around with Tom and the others, you never have chance to sit down and read about things.'

'Yes, you're probably right, anyway let me get you home.'

The rain had eased by the time they reached Delaney's home. Burton made sure that she was comfortable with everything before he left. As he walked back to his car, he nodded to two men sitting in a small rusty old van. On the side of the van were the words XRAY ELECTRICIANS. He thought to himself that it was about time the Special Protection boys got themselves some new vehicles.

Home Secretary Hamilton had been right in his assumptions about the reason for the Cobra meeting. The terrorist cells that MI5 and MI6 had been tracking for some time had become more mobile and he and Foreign Secretary Spires had been summoned to make sure that the Interpol intelligence matched theirs. If nothing changed in the next 48 hours, the public would be told that the country would be on red alert.

Mrs Beecham was waiting for Hamilton when he returned to his office at 6 p.m. 'We've had contact, Home Secretary, from Sir Adrian.'

'Thank god, is he okay?'

'We believe so sir; he's going to make contact again when he arrives back in England.'

'Good, because the way things are shaping up we're going to need him.'

In Tossa del Mar, it had been two hours before Lusher had decided to move. He had seen too many people leave in a hurry to get away from situations, only to find that they were still caught up with everyone else. As Farrah, Ashby and Curtis had left the old hotel, he remained in the second room. When Hoetger and Hobson left a few minutes later, he walked with the wheeled suitcase to a local cafe on the beach front and drank coffee and ate pastries until he was full. Some people who looked like regular customers were surprised he stayed so long. They would be even more surprised, he thought, if they knew what was in the suitcase.

After a couple of hours had passed he walked out into the sunlight and found a shop that sold mobile phones and electrical goods. Once he had activated the Nokia, he phoned London and left a message for the Home Secretary to say that he was okay and would make contact again once he was back in London. After some negotiation, a taxi driver agreed to take him to Barcelona at an extortionate cost and a few hours later he was boarding a flight for Heathrow. The airport police acknowledged his wishes when they had established his ID and the case full of money was put into a special security chamber in the luggage hold.

During the flight he was constantly thinking about what he had just gone through and whether or not it was all worth it.

39

The Villa Esperance was bathed in a golden shade as the sun set on the hills around Gelida, west of Barcelona. Gelida Castle was the only building higher than the villa and the last drop of sunlight settled on the castle walls as Alan Farrah looked out over the red tiled roofs of the town below and the blue haze rising from the trees.

'Another drink, Alan?' the voice was quiet, as though it didn't want to disturb him.

'Yeah, thanks, Mark, How's your leg?'

'The pains gone and it's finally stopped bleeding, I'll live.'

'Is the girl keeping quiet?'

'Yeah, I checked on her again not long ago; what are we going to do with her?'

Farrah sighed and sat down at the old wooden table on the veranda. 'I don't know yet. We should kill her really; I doubt if she could ever be persuaded to change sides.'

Ashby poured another drink and put it on the table in front of Farrah. 'No word from Dick or Hoetger either, I'm getting worried.'

Their journey from Tossa del Mar to the western side of Barcelona had been trouble free. Curtis tried to stay conscious throughout the journey but the injuries and trauma to her body had been too much and she had fallen asleep. Some uneven roads occasionally woke her up but her body was too tired to respond to the requests coming from her brain. Ashby had put her in the kitchen of the villa and handcuffed her to a huge cast iron handle that was used to raise and lower an oven door that was the access to an old wood burning stove. The door was heavily hinged and Curtis knew any attempts to move it, or herself, would be futile.

Farrah took a sip from his new drink. 'Well if Delaney was close to us in Tossa del Mar, we've lost him now. I'll start to worry about Dick if we haven't heard from him by the morning.'

'And Hoetger?' asked Ashby.

'I'll never worry about him.'

'So, what now, boss? Only you, me and Dick know about this place don't we?'

'Yeah and I want to keep it that way. Trouble is, that woman in the kitchen knows now as well.'

'Doubt it, she was out for the count most of the time; she'll know she's in a villa, but she won't know where.'

'Perhaps not,' replied Farrah, unconvinced. He poured himself another drink and moved into the house. 'See you in the morning, Mark; I'll check on the girl before I get my head down.' Ashby acknowledged, emptied the bottle into his glass and turned in his seat to watch the sun go down.

Curtis was awake when Farrah entered the kitchen. He carried an old wooden chair across to her. 'Here sit on this, you'll be more comfortable.' She hoisted herself up from the floor using the oven handle as a support and sat on the chair facing him, her right hand handcuffed to the handle. He looked at her for a while saying nothing. After a few minutes, she decided to start a conversation to see if she could judge his mood.

'What are thinking about?' She asked.

'Whether or not to kill you.'

'And the advantages of that would be?'

'There would be no advantages; that's my predicament.'

Curtis hesitated for a moment to let him think about what he had said before continuing to question him. 'So why not employ me instead?'

He looked at her with an angry face for a while before seeming to relax again. 'The last time you asked me a question like that, I stuck a cigar in your neck and told you not to insult my intelligence.'

'All I'm saying,' she replied, 'is that I'd rather work for you than be dead. Just think of how useful I could be to you. The British connections, the Canadian connections, you could have drug deals worth millions going on and with me in your pocket you could evade almost anyone.'

'How?' Farrah had taken the bait.

'It's easy; you pay me to destroy evidence. Bank records, account numbers, vault numbers and the rest. No one will be able to trace the money you get from the deals like they did in Paris. But hey, I won't be cheap.'

'Yes I had forgotten that your friends found out about the Paris vault. How do they do that?' he asked.

'Delaney has a man based in France with good Interpol connections. You have no idea how much kudos Interpol has with law courts and Brussels.'

Curtis had said enough. She sat quietly and waited. She could see he was definitely starting to think about possibilities.

'Mm, well let me think about it,' he said, when a minute had passed. He gathered up some towels and some old table cloths and put them on the floor in front of her.

'Sleeping on these will be a bit more comfortable for you; we'll speak again in the morning.'

So far, so good, she thought to herself; if he was going to kill me, he probably would have done it by now.

Delaney, Wyatt and Landers were thinking hard as they sat outside a roadside cafe in the Barcelona district of Verdun. It was getting dark but the sky reflecting the sunset gave just enough light to compliment the poorly lit streets. Taking Hobson out of the picture had certainly helped the overall cause but losing Hoetger had been a bitter pill to swallow, especially for Delaney.

After searching as many streets as they could in Tossa del Mar in an effort to find Hoetger, they had made their way towards Barcelona. Landers had received no information from his Interpol friends and Delaney had still not told them about Lusher's involvement. Wyatt was his usual self, not thinking as much as the other two and wanting to 'get on with it'.

'So,' said Delaney, 'any ideas you two?'

'We can't give up as long as Sally is with them,' said Landers.

'Agreed,' said Wyatt, 'but how do we find out where Farrah is without help from Interpol?'

Landers leaned forward. 'There must be some way; land registry or whatever they call it out here, energy companies, phone lines being put in, things like that.'

Delaney put his hands behind his head. 'Uh, you're forgetting, Stephen, men like Farrah don't deal with things in the normal way. They pay cash for houses, use mobile phones and get locals to sort out water and electricity for them.'

The three men fell silent again. The night was getting darker and the cafe owner started to wipe the tables in an effort to hurry them up. They made their way back to the Cherokee and Delaney asked Wyatt to drive, get some petrol and find a hotel. They were clicking their seat belts into place when Landers paused. 'Helicopter; why not get a helicopter up to look around the area for Farrah's Mercedes van?'

'Yeah right,' said Wyatt, 'It's only a few thousand square kilometres.'

'Not if we narrow the field down,' said Delaney. 'We would need to give them a few options; villas, areas, we know Farrah prefers out of town locations, we could ask them to start around the quieter areas in the hills, not far from the main roads.'

Wyatt shook his head. 'They'll never do it.'

'But for Sally's sake we have to try don't we?' said Landers. 'I can talk to Interpol; they have a large base right here in Barcelona.'

Delaney looked at Wyatt who shrugged his shoulders. He hesitated then turned to Landers. 'Try it, Stephen; phone Interpol and explain the situation, no harm in asking. Tell them I can get the Home Secretary to talk to them if need be,'

Landers took out a notebook and his phone and sat back. He dialled a number and within seconds was speaking to someone in Spanish.

The police station in Tossa del Mar was quiet and the few desk fans kept things cool. Sergeant Gabillo had been working for 12 hours and the interruption to his usually dull routine from Delaney and his team had been a welcome change earlier that morning. He decided he would wait for the special escort for Julie Brewer himself. Capturing an international criminal and holding her until special units could pick her up, was going to be his story and no one else's. He had thrown the local drunk out of the other cell after cautioning him and had settled down to read his paper. Julie Brewer was the only other person in the prison; locked in her cell, wide awake. The night was getting darker and Sergeant Gabillo's eyes were closing now and again.

'Hey, Gabillo! Wake up.' The young police officer had taken his boss by surprise. Paulo Triol was not a favourite of the sergeant's. In his first few months as an officer he had been disrespectful and far too loud for Gabillo's liking. Many a young girl would hesitate around the police station and flirt with Triol, which made his concentration wander and Gabillo's monthly reports he had to submit to the Area Chief had not been good.

'I wasn't asleep young man, don't be so insolent.'

'Okay, okay, sergeant sir, but you do look tired. Have a break for a while, Senor Joruz has fresh coffee in the bar; I have just smelt it when I was walking past.'

The Sergeant looked wearily at the young man for a while before succumbing. 'Okay, stay here. I will be 15 minutes only.'

Paulo Triol only waited seconds before he made his way to the cells. An international criminal in Tossa del Mar; he was not going to let this one go by without seeing who it was and talking to them so he could relate his story to his friends.

Looking through the small panel in the cell door, he was surprised to see Julie Brewer. He was expecting at least a big thug of some kind or a suited gang boss. As soon as Brewer saw him, she sat up slightly and stared at him. Paulo looked her up and down. Her thick but scraggy blonde hair was not something he saw every day. She rolled her head back and flicked her hair in an enticing way and he could see the tattoos on her neck. He continued to look at her without speaking. When she could see that he was looking at her legs, she crossed them and turned sideways.

Paulo smiled. 'You are a criminal from overseas?'

'Yes, I am; I'm Julie, what's your name?'

'Paulo.'

'Paulo; I like that.'

As he continued to look at her, she turned to face him and put her legs slightly apart, pulling up her short denim skirt just enough to reveal her underwear. 'So you're my guard now are you?' she asked.

'I am in charge, of course.'

She stood up and walked over to the rusty steel door, putting her nose up close to his. He backed off a few inches. 'Well, err, Paulo, you are young like me, how would you like to tell your mates that you did it with a big criminal? I might as well enjoy myself while I wait for my escort.'

The young man said nothing. He looked behind him and then at the clock on the wall. If Gabillo said 15 minutes, that meant he was actually going to be about 30 minutes. He turned again to look at Brewer. 'Move away from the door.'

She walked backwards and sat on the wooden bed. Paulo closed the small vision hole shutter, unlocked the door, opened it slowly and entered the room. He locked the door behind him and put the key in his trouser pocket. He walked over to where she was sitting and started to touch her hair. Brewer stood up and wrapped her hands around his neck; then one of her hands moved down to his trousers. He pulled her hand away, she hesitated, but not for long. They began to kiss and Brewer started to manoeuvre him backwards towards the door. They fell against the door as they were kissing. She moved her head to the side of his neck to give her hand enough room. Her right hand moved up and grabbed a hand full of his black hair.

Good, she thought, I can get a good grip. She brought his head slowly forward as if offering her neck to him. Then, in one quick hard heave she rammed his head backwards into the steel door, and again, and again. He grabbed her arms but the blows to the back of his head had slowed him too much. Her knee came up and made full contact with his groin and as he bent forward her left fist slammed into his chin. He tried to fight back but the element of surprise and the multiple blows had been too much for him. She kicked him as he fell, pushed her hand into his pocket, retrieved the keys and kicked him again as she turned to open the door. From somewhere, he found enough strength to come back at her and he lunged for her legs, hoping to bring her down. She grabbed his hair and yanked his head backwards with one hand. The other hand formed a fist and she rammed it upwards into his nose. His body collapsed into stillness.

Brewer opened the door quickly and stood still to listen. Nothing. Paulo really had been left alone, she thought, what a bunch of incompetents. She moved to the front door and looked in both directions. The streets were getting quieter; just a few people walking around and the odd car driving slowly. She straightened herself up and walked out of the building with her head held high looking confident. No one would have suspected anything and wherever the sergeant was, it was obviously somewhere where he could not see the police station entrance.

Two blocks away, a young girl was filling her Fiat Punto at the service station. Brewer watched her as she replaced the filler cap and walked towards the kiosk to pay. As soon as the girl was walking away from the car, Brewer walked casually up to the vehicle as though passing it on her way to the kiosk. The keys had been left in the car. She opened the door, climbed in and only half closed the door so it would not make a loud noise. She turned the ignition key, it started perfectly, and she was away. In her rear view mirror she could see the girl back at the kiosk, her hands raised in the air as other customers stood watching, wondering what had happened.

Brewer laughed out loud with joy as she noticed a sign that pointed to Barcelona. 'On my way, Mr. Farrah, on my way.'

Sergeant Gabillo was looking down at Paulo Triol as the paramedic pulled a blanket over the young man's face. 'How can this be so?' asked Gabillo. 'A fight, a tussle, and he is dead!'

Even the paramedic was holding up his own hands in disbelief. 'The nose; it was hit so hard that the main bone went up into his brain.'

Gabillo, distraught with mental agony, turned to answer his phone. 'What!'

'My car, Senor Gabillo, my car, someone has just stolen my beautiful new car.'

'Okay, come and see me in the mor....no wait. How long ago was this?'

'Five, maybe six minutes ago.'

'Come to the station and bring the details of your vehicle, immediately!'

40

Delaney was surprised when his phone rang. He had only given the new number to a few people and most of those would only phone him with something special.

'Senor Delaney, it is Sergeant Gabillo from Tossa del Mar speaking.'

'Well, Sergeant Gabillo, I never thought I would hear from you again; is everything alright?'

'No no, sir, it is not alright, the woman she is gone, escaped, one of my men is dead.'

Delaney moved the phone away from his mouth and held it down to his side for a moment. He was annoyed but not overwhelmed at the news. Brewer was capable. He raised the phone again and interrupted Gabillo's chatter. 'I am sorry for the loss of your colleague sergeant, when was this?'

'Some time ago, but Senor Delaney, I thought about things, I have some information for you.'

'Please tell me,' said Delaney, doubting the validity of what was about to come.

'The prisoner, she took a car from a service point, I have the details of the car, she will be going to Barcelona I think; but she is maybe not so clever; the car, it is a present to the young woman from her father, it has a special number, 23 j....'

'Wait wait, sergeant.' Delaney reached for a pen and paper. 'Go on.'

'23 JU 123.'

'And the car?'

'Fiat Punto, Green, how do you say? Shiny, bright.'

'Metallic.'

'Yes, metallic. Easy to see I think.'

Delaney smiled, but only briefly, to lose a young policeman to a criminal like Brewer was bad, but her escape could be a blessing in disguise. The car could easily be spotted and chances were, she was heading for Farrah.

Wyatt asked who the call was from; they had just arrived at a small bar on their way to finding a hotel. 'The sergeant in Tossa del Mar; Brewer got away from them.'

'Damn,' said Landers. 'She is one piece of work.'

'Not all that clever though, she nicked a car with a personal number plate, so we have something to give to your friends; get on to them now, give them this number.' He wrote the number on a piece of paper and handed it to Landers. Wyatt caught the eye of the barman and ordered more drinks as Landers punched a number on his phone.

'Just one drink, Ben,' said Delaney, 'and then we'll find somewhere to bed down for a few hours; chances are the car will be spotted and we need to be on our toes for an early start tomorrow.'

Ashby kicked Curtis in the ribs as she lay half sleeping. 'Was that really necessary you moron,' she said.

'I obviously thought so,' said Ashby, 'it's six o'clock; get yourself onto the chair and I'll take your cuffs off, Mr. Farrah wants to be on the road by eight.'

'Where are we going?'

'Never you mind, I'm locking you in here for a while; you can have a wash in the sink and get a drink.' He unlocked the handcuffs securing her to the oven door and left her alone, the old brass latch shutting firmly when he closed the kitchen door on his way out.

She looked around for any possible escape routes. There was nothing; the windows were half shuttered and locked tight. Window panes were too small to smash and climb out of. She threw cold water over her face and ran her wet fingers through her hair. There was a small electric kettle that she filled and switched on. Various jars lined the shelves and she searched for something that might be drinkable. After shaking six or seven containers, she found some instant coffee. As she sat sipping her drink, she looked around again. Knives, she thought, this is a kitchen, right? She emptied her cup and set about searching cupboards and drawers. There was very little; a few knives and forks, spoons, bottle openers and pots and pans. Then, as she sat back down at the old oak table, she noticed an under-slung drawer that was beneath the table. When she opened it her hopes were raised.

There were utensils and knives of all shapes and sizes. She quickly grabbed a small, very sharp fish boning knife, lifted up the right leg of her blood stained Chinos and stuffed the knife, handle down, into her tight fitting socks.

She heard some movement beyond the locked door. Her fingers were on another small knife with a sharp jagged edge like a steak knife. The door started to open as she took hold of the knife and slid it up the left hand sleeve of her jacket.

Alan Farrah walked into the kitchen and headed straight for the kettle. 'This is still warm, good; you got yourself a drink then?'

'Yes, thanks.'

Curtis thought about what she had said to him the previous evening. She wanted to keep the momentum going. 'So, Alan, are you going to employ me or do I kill you now?'

Curling his mouth downwards, he sat down in front of her. 'A sense of humour, I like that in a woman.'

She decided not to say anything else for now. It was important that she kept him on his toes, always wondering what she was *really* after. Ashby came into the room with enthusiasm. 'Right, boss, the new car's ready and I've loaded all the you-know-what in the boot. What time do you want to leave?'

'We'll give it another hour, and then if there's no word from Dick, Hoetger or Brewer, we'll get on the road.'

Get on the road to where? Curtis thought, how many god damned places does this man have to go to!

'I think if any of them were going to get here,' said Ashby, 'they'd have been here by now.'

'You're probably right, Mark, but we'll give them another hour, and besides,' he said, looking at Curtis. 'I need a little longer to decide what to do with this extraordinary woman.'

Unlike his colleagues, Stephen Landers was a good sleeper. It took him a while to wake up when his phone rang at 6 a.m. 'Hello, ola.'

'Senor Landers?' The voice sounded like a well educated Spanish gentleman.

'Yes hello.'

'This is Inspector Jerus from the Barcelona police, I received a phone call last night from Interpol and I have some information for you.'

Landers had not been expecting this. He stumbled out of bed and reached for a pen and paper. 'This is good news Inspector, sorry I was just getting a pen, please go ahead.'

'You do not need a pen, sir; if you kindly tell me where you are, I will send a car to you. We will explain when we meet you.' After a few years working with foreign police forces and law enforcers of various capabilities, Landers knew a good one when he heard it. He explained to the Inspector where he was and ended the phone call.

The phones of Delaney and Wyatt were answered almost immediately when he rang them to explain what had happened. Thirty minutes later, all three were standing in the lobby of the small hotel they had found. 'You could have at least asked him what he had for us,' said Wyatt.

'Trust me, he's got something, I just know. Something good or they wouldn't be coming to us.'

'Well, we're just about to find out,' said Delaney as he pointed to a large white car pulling up outside. Landers had been right; Inspector Jerus was immaculate, even at this time of the morning. His perfectly tailored dark blue uniform complimented his look. The look of a prince that stands on balconies waving to people. In contrast, his driver was an unshaven, overweight sergeant with the look of a well seasoned, no nonsense professional. The Inspector introduced himself and the sergeant to the three men. Delaney let Landers take the lead.

'We are indebted to you Inspector; taking up so much of your time to help us. Did Interpol explain our predicament to you?'

'Yes they did. We know about your aims and objectives. We also have been given a directive from our Commander.'

'A directive?'

'Yes, when this person decided to steal a car, they chose the wrong car. I have been personally charged with retrieving the car and helping you to arrest the guilty party.'

'Really?' asked Landers, wondering what was coming next. 'We would usually want people to leave it to us; due to the high risk.'

'Senor Landers, the car.' Jerus took a note pad from his pocket and flipped it open. 'The car, err, 23 JU 123, Fiat Punto, Yes?'

'Yes.'

'The car belongs to Juliana Untresso; she is the daughter of Samuel Untresso, Chief of Staff, Barcelona Police.'

Landers looked around to see Delaney nodding in acknowledgement that he had heard what Jerus had said. Wyatt smiled as he looked at both of them. 'And so now, gentlemen,' continued Jerus. 'If you will follow us we will take you to where we can pick up the trail of this person; A Señorita Brewer?' Landers nodded, but wondered at the title.

'Thank you, Inspector,' said Delaney. 'Ben, you drive, keep close to these gentlemen, I'll be your passenger.' He turned to Jerus. 'Can Stephen come with you, Inspector? To be our contact with you'

Jerus nodded. 'Of course, good idea I think.' He then looked at Wyatt as he gestured towards his sergeant. 'Please, you need to concentrate when following; my sergeant here is one of the best.' Wyatt raised a hand in polite acknowledgement. Delaney raised his eyebrows when Wyatt did not offer a sarcastic remark.

The large white unmarked police car drove off towards the northern outskirts of Barcelona. Wyatt followed, staying close enough to follow easily but far enough back to react to a situation. After six kilometres, the police car pulled into a large supermarket car park and parked alongside another large car, this time silver. Inspector Jerus said something to the driver of the silver car and moved away and parked near the car park exit. After a minute or two had passed, Jerus looked at Delaney and Wyatt and pointed to the corner of the car park. The Fiat Punto was there; Brewer was sitting at the wheel, speaking on her phone.

'How the hell did you know my number?' asked Farrah.

'Will gave it to me Alan, and told me where to find you if everything went wrong.'

'Where are you? And where is William?'

'I'm on my way to you, Alan, if that's alright, and I thought William was with you.'

'Well he isn't, neither is Dick, something's gone wrong;   get yourself here as soon as you can, I want to leave here in an hour and you need to dump that car; which I assume is either rented or stolen.'

'Stolen I'm afraid, Alan, easy really.'

'Right, well just get here, now.'

Brewer threw her phone onto the seat beside her, drove quickly out of the car park and picked up the signs for Gelida as soon as she could.

Seeing the Fiat move, Wyatt manoeuvred the Cherokee in readiness for instruction. Jerus signalled to them to follow. The white police car with Landers on board followed her. Wyatt pulled in behind them. The Fiat broke most of the speed limits on its way out of the suburbs towards the south west. On one occasion, Jerus had to radio a traffic cop to tell them to back off. The sky was lightening from the sun that was about to rise as they made their way towards the western areas of Barcelona and out to Gelida. Wyatt was pleased when the driver of the vehicle in front waved for him to go ahead so Brewer would not see the same car following her. In turn, Wyatt gave way to the silver car and they all stayed well back for fear of arousing Brewer's suspicions.

Thirty five minutes later, Brewer turned off the main road onto a small track. She drove for about five minutes before stopping at a large gateway. She waited for a couple of more minutes and then drove down a gravel drive towards a medium sized villa. Jerus instructed his sergeant to wait for a while. Wyatt and the silver car pulled up behind them. Delaney told Wyatt to stay with the vehicle and ran to Jerus as he got from his car. 'I believe she is going to the villa,' said Jerus. 'We will be seen if we follow; we should go on foot from here, it is, I would say, half a kilometre.'

'Agreed,' said Delaney. 'You lead the way; one person should stay with the vehicles.'

'Yes, of course. I think maybe she will be going to meet someone else who is also guilty of something.'

'I think you're right,' said Delaney.

Jerus asked his sergeant to remain with the vehicles. Landers, Wyatt and Delaney gathered up their small arms and waited for Jerus's instructions. Delaney was happy for him to take the lead; he was clearly a man of substance. The sun was starting to show on the horizon as they made their way uphill along a small gravel track. Small bushes and trees lined the track and the occasional songbird interrupted the silence. Wyatt was the first to notice the Fiat. 'Up there, to the left, she's parked it away from the villa.' Brewer had turned into a small dirt track and parked under a tree about 100 metres from the villa.

Jerus looked around and gestured to the others to kneel. 'It is too open,' he said. 'We perhaps have to rush them.'

'Not without blocking the exits first,' said Delaney. Jerus nodded and radioed down to his sergeant. A few minutes later the large white car came to a stop beside them. Delaney was further impressed with Jerus when he asked Delaney for his suggestions. Delaney looked around the area, then at Wyatt and Landers. 'Stephen, go around the back, keep low. Ben, you go for that large side door. Are you okay to take the front with me Inspector?'

'Of course.' He said something in Spanish to his sergeant and within seconds, the car was blocking the main entrance to the villa. Delaney and Jerus waited for Wyatt and Landers to get closer to their destinations before they made their move. The run along the road and up the driveway leading to the villa took them just two minutes. Delaney realised how much younger than he the Inspector was as he slowed to take a breath. A blind on one of the front windows of the villa moved slightly.

'Alan!' shouted Ashby, 'someone's out there!'

Farrah jumped up from where he was sitting next to Curtis in the side kitchen. 'It's alright its Brewer!' he shouted back, 'she's gone to torch the Punto.'

'No, I mean at the front,' said Ashby, 'Brewer went out the side door.'

Curtis watched as Farrah left the room to join Ashby. Brewer had appeared only briefly and spoken to Farrah, before he had told her to get back and torch the car she had stolen. As soon as Farrah had gone from site, Curtis jumped to her feet, ran to the side door and watched Brewer as she made her way to the Punto. There was a click of fingers to the right and Curtis fell to her knees instinctively. A large bush parted; Wyatt smiled at her.

'For Christ's sake, Ben you...'

'Shh, get back inside; I'll take care of Brewer.'

Curtis read the situation immediately. She turned to go back inside as she whispered. 'Right, Farrah has gone to the front with Ashby, they know someone's there.'

Ashby knelt near a front window, as Farrah joined him, and pointed to the left of the driveway. 'There, near the post box, see?' Farrah nodded and took his pistol from his belt. He took careful aim; the bullet rattled the post box as it ricocheted off and split the air with a bang. Delaney and Jerus stayed motionless. Farrah turned to Ashby and gave him his pistol. 'Take this too, Mark, keep taking pot shots at them, it'll keep them at a good distance for a while.'

Ashby braced himself, ready for action. 'Right, leave it to me, the car's ready, out the back.'

'Good man,' Farrah replied as he made his way back to the kitchen. Curtis sat still on a chair. When Wyatt noticed Farrah had returned, he changed his plan of action and waited near the side door out of sight. Farrah stared at

Curtis for a while, grabbed some car keys from the table and made off towards a back door. He turned to face her before he left. 'You survive for now young lady; I'll deal with you on another day.'

Wyatt waited until he had closed the back door and ran across the kitchen to pursue him. 'Be careful, Ben!' said Curtis, 'there's a gun in his jacket pocket.'

'Shh,' said Wyatt, 'you talk too much.'

Wyatt opened the back door slowly. He could hear no sounds so he hesitated. There was another door to the left with daylight showing through the gaps. He opened it. Nothing; where the hell had Farrah gone? The back door slammed behind him; a breeze had come through the kitchen from the side door, forcing the back door to shut. He reached for the handle; there wasn't one.

Hearing the gun shots from Ashby's rifle, Brewer had turned before reaching the Punto and ran back to the house; she ran through the side door expecting to find company but she saw only Curtis. She looked around the kitchen, walked up to Curtis and put her face up close so her nose was almost touching Curtis's nose. 'Well whatever is about to happen, you won't see it. I think I'll kill you now; that will please Mr. Farrah.' Brewer moved to grab Curtis by the neck, her eyes full off hate. Good, thought Curtis, she is too busy hating to think straight. As Brewers grip started to tighten, Curtis reached for the small knife she had concealed in her sleeve. Holding it firmly, she drew back her hand as much a she could without Brewer realising what was happening. The lunge took the knife directly into Brewers ribs. She withdrew it, and sunk it in again. Brewer gasped, looked down and screamed, more in anger than pain. Her grip did not loosen on Curtis's neck. Curtis lunged again and Brewer screamed again. The grip on the neck started to ease. Curtis flipped the knife around in her hand as she moved it around the back of Brewers body. She moved her hand outwards for maximum thrust and brought the knife down hard into Brewers lower back. Brewer now had no choice but let go of Curtis's neck. She began to fall, blood spouting from her stomach and back. She stared again at Curtis as she sunk to the floor. 'B...Bitch...Bi...You....' She could not continue talking; all energy had gone from her lungs and body. Curtis watched her as she lay dying and leant forward to speak to her. 'You lose; you were always going to.'

Ashby ran into the kitchen expecting to find Farrah still dealing with Curtis. 'They're not shooting at us boss, I...' He looked at Curtis and then at Brewer on the floor.

Curtis thought quickly. 'Out the back quick! Alan's in trouble!' Hearing the words, 'Alan's in trouble', Ashby ran instinctively for the back door. He pulled at the one-sided handle and opened the door. Wyatt raised his gun. 'Stop there! Do it!'

Ashby charged forward, raising his handgun. Wyatt held his gun steady and shot him once in the forehead. The bullet stopped him in his tracks and he fell to the ground. Curtis was checking the side door as Wyatt stepped over Ashby's body to join her in the kitchen. They spun around as the main door from the front was flung open. Delaney and Jerus sprang into the room, one to the left, the other to the right. They dropped their guns to their sides as soon as they had read the situation. Curtis looked at Jerus and then Delaney. 'Reinforcements,' she said, 'about time.'

'Inspector,' said Delaney, 'she's one of ours, Sally Curtis. Sally this is Inspector Jerus' They nodded to each other in acknowledgement. Jerus lifted the front of his cap slightly.

'Have you seen Farrah?' said Wyatt.

'No, no one came out the front of the house,' said Delaney.

'He went out the back door,' said Curtis.

Delaney looked at Brewers body on the floor. 'Dead?'

'Yes,' said Curtis.

'Ashby?'

'Dead,' said Wyatt. 'But no sign of Hoetger.'

'Right, out the back now, Stephen should be there.'

Jerus was ahead of them, already making for the back door. They followed, staying alert. The back door led to a small passage and into a yard. Twenty metres away, an old wooden shack had been left with its doors open. Fine dust from a disturbance still filled the air. 'A vehicle left here not long ago,' said Jerus. They all looked around for any other possible signs. Wyatt shouted. 'Landers!' There was no reply.

'Stephen!' shouted Curtis. Again, no reply.

Jerus was the first to check out the shack. He moved forward carefully, his gun half raised. Delaney told the other two to stay outside. When a minute had passed, Jerus walked from the shack. As he was putting his gun back into his white belt holster, he paused and sighed. 'I am sorry,' he said to Delaney.

They all went into the shack as Jerus moved to one side.

Stephen Landers was lying on the floor, motionless.

'Oh Jesus!' cried Curtis. She ran towards Landers and Wyatt grabbed her. 'Wait Sally!' he said, 'I wouldn't put it past these guys to set booby traps.'

Delaney walked carefully towards Landers. There was no sign of any traps or gadgets. He held three fingers on the side of Landers neck and remained there for 30 seconds. Then he leaned forward and held his ear close to the mouth.

Nothing.

He stood up slowly and turned around. 'He's gone. Broken neck I think; and blood on his face and hands; probably a real close quarter on-to-one with Farrah.'

Curtis pulled herself away from Wyatt and ran towards the body. She knelt at the side of Landers. 'He was a nice man, a good man, for crying out loud, we have to get this Farrah man, I should have killed him when I had the chance.' Jerus was already on his way to the rear of the property when Delaney motioned with his head to Wyatt to follow him. He then helped Curtis to her feet. 'Come on, Sally, Stephen will be looked after, if you want to avenge Stephen and Brandon as much as I do, we need to get moving before Farrah has time to switch vehicles.'

Curtis walked away and stood in the corner of the shack, her hands clasped around the back of her head. Delaney looked slowly around for clues and then his eyes rested on Landers again. Well Stephen, he thought to himself, if your spirit can hear me, your death will be avenged. Wyatt and Jerus walked back into the shack a few moments later. Jerus had summoned his sergeant from the front gate and the large white car was waiting for them to embark.

'Big hole in the back fence,' said Wyatt, 'and the Mercedes van is parked out there as well; he must have had another vehicle parked nearby with the money in.'

'Okay, the sergeant here is going to take us back to our car and then come back and wait with Stephen until help arrives.'

'Right, sir; give me a minute will you?'

Delaney nodded to Wyatt and escorted Curtis to the car. Jerus took off his uniform jacket and laid it across Landers face, before getting in the car himself. Wyatt knelt and lifted the jacket so he could see Landers' face. 'Well mate, Hobson, Brewer, Ashby and John Farrah are all dead; so I make that four-two to us. Give me a while; I'll make it five-two.' He wiped a tear from his cheek and joined the others in the car.

41

Twenty four hours later, Sally Curtis looked out over the coastline of Northern France as the Airbus 320 started its descent into Gatwick. The sun shone from the east into her eyes so she pulled the window blind down slightly. Ships in the English Channel were making their way to somewhere; east to west, west to east. Even from 25,000 feet, she could make out the tankers, freighters and smaller trawlers, leaving their wakes behind them like V shaped white arrows. She wondered if any of them were going Canada.

Canada.

Back where it all started. Right now, she regretted ever getting involved with the police and the god damned Canadian Secret Service. That man she had looked up to, Pierre Bouton; a murderer, a cheat, a liar; and all for money. Paying people thousands of dollars to have Marcus killed. A man she had loved and respected so much. If she had not joined the CSS she would not have been sent to England or Munich. People like Brandon Jones and Stephen Landers, gone. Good men, trying to save innocent people from ruthless thugs like Farrah and uphold the law for the benefit of all those people down there. She would resign as soon as she could, but not before she knew that justice was handed out properly to Farrah.

Delaney opened his right eye slightly to see if Curtis was asleep. When he could see that she was staring out of the window thinking hard, he closed his eyes again, and sunk his head back onto the chair to continue his thoughts.

This is for J and B. hope the van is Okay. – A.

He had been thinking about that note again. Who was *A*? Some possibilities had come and gone. He felt guilty for thinking at some point it may have been Curtis, when he had found out her middle name was Alison. He had even considered his partner, Angela Casey. Her job involved collating reports from some pretty senior people, but after the beating she had taken in London, apparently arranged by Hoetger, he had dismissed his ideas straight away.

So there was *A* – Alan Farrah, and *A* – Adrian Lusher. But he was not one hundred percent sure about any of them. How could he be sure that Farrah paid Hoetger to kill Marcus Hanson? And why would Alan Farrah sign a note at all, let alone sign it *A* instead of Alan? Why would he do that?

And why would Adrian Lusher jeopardise his well paid job and the respect that he has; for money? Why would *he* pay someone to kill Marcus Hanson; he could have killed him himself, easily and professionally. He was an ex soldier with medals for bravery. He had not got to the top of MI5 without being tough. Lusher would also be able to find out where people were; he could ask staff from other departments, why would they not tell him? And Farrah; he could not have known about the flight from Stansted and the departure time unless someone told him; someone who knew my movements.

He decided that when he had seen Angela and freshened himself up, Sir Adrian Lusher would be the first person he would visit.

Ben Wyatt sat in the aisle seat. Normally he would be checking out the legs of the stewardess, but the last few days had taken their toll on him; physically and emotionally. Two occasions kept coming back to his mind. The two separate occasions when he had knelt over the bodies of Brandon Jones and Stephen Landers. He had to kill people sometimes; it was his job, but somehow, killing Dick Hobson and later Mark Ashby, had seemed like shallow victories. Brewer too; Curtis had killed her because she had to, or be killed. But these people are really just pawns in the game, he thought. He remembered his promise to Landers. Whether legally or not; he was going to get Farrah. It was Farrah and other men of his kind that were responsible for these killings. *He* was the root cause. He found himself speaking out loud. 'The root cause.'

Delaney opened his eyes and turned his head to Wyatt. 'Root cause?'

'Just thinking out loud, Farrah is the root cause of all this. It was his dealings in drugs and people that started all the greed.'

'You're probably right, Ben, but I think this cause has more than *one* root to it.'

The Airbus 320 turned slightly as the first officer announced that they would be landing in ten minutes.

42

After his getaway, the trip back to England had been an easy one for Alan Farrah. He was angry at having lost Ashby and Hobson and concerned that Hoetger had not been in touch since his disappearance.

Ashby had transferred the money from the Mercedes van into an old inconspicuous car and parked it inside the old shack, with the doors open ready. After leaving Curtis in the kitchen, Farrah had made his way to the shack not knowing that Landers was there. Landers had taken him by surprise and thrown him against the car but Farrah had been lucky again as Landers lost his footing on the uneven floor. The hand-to-hand fight had been a viscous one; each man landing good blows onto his opponent. Farrah knew that he was lucky to be alive; he should have tried to kill me, he thought, instead of trying to arrest me.

He had used another false passport to deposit the 146 million dollars he had left after paying Lusher, in a strong vault and board a flight to London. The flight was an executive high-speed charter and an old friend in Madrid had arranged a seat for him. There were just two other passengers, who glanced at him often during the flight. Perhaps because he wasn't wearing an expensive suit as they were, or was not constantly working on a laptop. He was relieved to get off the plane to see Mich waiting for him in a Range Rover. The decision to tell Mich to stay in England when they had been on their way to Dover had been a good one. He needed a good man in reserve and although Mich was not getting any younger, he was still keen and probably the best driver he had ever had.

'Just you then, Alan, where are the others?'

'Bad news, Mich; they're dead.'

'Bastards; was it that lot that've been chasing you all this time?'

'Yeah, Delaney again and his crew; I killed one of them though, just before I got away from Spain.'

Mich drove away from the airport and left his boss to think for a while before asking where he wanted to go. 'Where to then? You staying close by, or is it to be the cottage in Suffolk?'

'The house in Harrow I think please, Mich, I need a good rest and then tomorrow you can come with me. We're going to see someone important.'

'Okay, boss, do I need to get us tooled up?'

'Yes, that might be a good idea.'

Andrea Beecham walked confidently into the Home Secretary's office. 'We've gone back to amber on the terrorist alert Home Secretary.'

'Good, thank you, Mrs Beecham. Has Cobra been called again?'

'No, sir.'

'Any sign of Lusher yet?'

'I was about to tell you, he has made contact. He's back in London and will be here tomorrow afternoon.'

'Really; very magnanimous of him. I'll look forward to it. And what about Delaney?'

'Sorry?' Mrs. Beecham frowned. Lusher and his antics were always being questioned but the Home Secretary rarely asked about Delaney.

'Delaney; I haven't heard from *him* for days either. Find him and tell him I want him here tomorrow afternoon as well.'

'Yes, sir.' She smiled at him as she left.

Angela was at home when Delaney arrived later that day. She had been discharged from the hospital with strict instructions to rest for two weeks. Special Protection were still keeping a watchful eye over her, and both men, in their disguised van, nodded to Delaney as he spotted them.

Two things struck him as he entered the room; Angela's perfume and the smell of good home cooking. She walked from the kitchen, threw a towel down onto a chair and hugged him. 'Taffy has phoned me... a couple of times to let me know... what's going on, I've been so worried,' she said, between kisses.

'It got a bit hectic,' he said, 'but I'm okay. What smells so good?'

'Roast Chicken.'

'Great; it should go with this nicely.' He pulled out a bottle of Champagne from a bag. 'I thought we deserved something a bit special so I called in at the corner shop on my way.'

She took the bottle from him and placed it in the fridge. 'You go and get changed,' she said as she rubbed a hand down one of his arms. 'Taffy told me about Stephen Landers.'

'Mm, well, we can drink to *him* tonight, and maybe a few more good people.'

The night went quickly and it was 7 a.m. when Delaney's phone rang. He looked to see it was Burton calling. 'Let me guess, Taffy, the Home Secretary wants to see me.'

'Afraid so sir, Andrea Beecham phoned me late last night. I lied and said you weren't due in until today to give you time to rest, they want you in his office at 2 p.m. today.'

'Right, thanks, Taffy, I want to go somewhere first this morning though, can you pick me up at nine please.'

'Will do, do you want Ben with us?'

'No, let him rest up for a while, I presume it was Ben who told you about Stephen. Angela said you'd told her.'

'Yes it was.'

Delaney waited for another response but Burton stayed quiet. 'Okay, Taffy, nine o'clock then.'

'Yes, sir, and by the way, I got two men to see Sally back to her safe house last night.'

'Good, we'll leave her to rest as well for now.'

The roads out of London were unusually quiet and Burton was pleased to get out of the city and into the countryside. Delaney guided him off the motorway and into the undulating countryside of the Cotswolds. After a few miles on small roads, Delaney pointed to a driveway as they approached a small village. 'There; turn right here.' There was a narrow tree lined drive which led to a Georgian style house set in about three acres of bushy landscape. CCTV cameras were everywhere and any wooden or plastic windows had been replaced with bullet proof frames and glass.

Burton pulled up in front of the house. A Lexus was parked nearby and Delaney told Burton to park in front of it and wait for him. On his way to the front door, Delaney undid the securing loop on his shoulder holster.

He did not have to knock on the door. As he approached, the door opened slowly and Sir Adrian Lusher was standing there with two cocker spaniels at his feet.

'Tom, I've been expecting you, as they say in all the movies.'

Delaney said nothing as Lusher moved to one side to make way for him. A woman appeared in the hallway and Lusher asked her to take the dogs into the garden. Lusher closed the door and told Delaney to follow him. They settled in a small room that was being used as an office overlooking the front garden. Lusher poured coffee from a small pot. 'Too early for a drink eh, Tom?'

'Yes it is.'

Delaney chose a seat where he could see Burton's car outside and the office door. Lusher sat behind a large desk and sighed. 'Well; *you* came to *me*, so you start.'

'Okay, stop me if I'm telling you something you already know. Ever since the CSS man, Marcus Hanson was killed in Munich, we have been working with Sally Curtis of the CSS; on instruction from you and MI6. As you know, we found out that Bouton from Canada and Jerome from the USA were behind the killings. We brought them to London, but they were killed. Someone had to know where they were going, only a few of us knew that, Adrian. They were probably killed by William Hoetger, and a few days later, Hoetger received a thank you message from someone who signed the note, *A*.

'Whoever had them killed, presumably needed them dead in case they revealed who the other senior person was. Then Farrah escaped from prison and I had to chase after him. I was attacked at Stansted airport. Only a few people could have known or found out about my flight at such short notice.

'As we pursued Farrah and his mob through France and Spain, he somehow managed to stay one step ahead of us again and again. He was getting information on our whereabouts from somewhere. Then we tracked your mobile phone number to south east Spain. To a town called Tossa del Mar. You and your phone were in the same area, or even building, as Farrah and his men, who at the time were holding Sally Curtis. I think you know the rest.'

Lusher put his coffee cup down slowly and sighed again. 'What you've just said Tom is exactly the way I see it too. And I suppose now you're going to say that I'm the man who's been giving Farrah information on your whereabouts and that it was me who was behind the killings of Bouton and Jerome. You think I'm the man who was in with Bouton and Jerome, just for the money, for the millions we could get from Farrah if we looked after him. You think I paid Hoetger to kill them so they wouldn't reveal me as the other senior person.'

'Perhaps, so prove me wrong.'

'I can prove you wrong, Tom, because I think I know who that person is. It was not me.'

'Go on.'

'I'm not telling you until I'm sure, but I need your help to prove who it is.'

Delaney had already decided that he was not a hundred percent sure it was Lusher. He knew he was dealing with an equally experienced operator. 'Okay, I'll give you 24 hours. You tell me what you need me to do.

After that 24 hours if we haven't got the right person, I'm taking you in. Call it a citizen's arrest.'

Lusher smirked. 'You and I, Tom are one of a kind really; I don't why we've had so many altercations in the past. I'll be in touch with you later today; I have to go to see the Home Secretary this afternoon.'

'What a coincidence, so do I.'

'14.00 hours?'

'Yes. I think it's to do with Cobra information after the terrorist scare; they're relaxing things again.'

Lusher poured more coffee. 'Well if we both have to be there this afternoon, I'd better tell you what I need you to do now then, rather than wait for tomorrow.'

'Yes, probably,' said Delaney, 'go ahead.'

'It's quite simple really; when we're with the Home Secretary this afternoon, I'm going to find a way of bringing Farrah into the conversation; when I do, I need you to agree with what I say because some of it won't be the truth.'

'The idea being?'

'He meets with the Foreign Secretary every other day. I want him to know about Farrah, so when they meet, Farrah will be discussed. You see, Tom; I think it's the Foreign Secretary that's involved with Farrah.'

Delaney considered the seriousness of what Lusher had just said. It did not surprise him too much; no one was beyond corruption these days. He looked hard at Lusher. 'Why do you believe this? How do I know you're not putting other people in the frame to take the heat away from you?'

'I got close to Farrah by giving him information, not much information, but enough to help him without telling him too much. When I was with him, he told

Hoetger that I was *just one* of his people on the inside. The other person has to be high up, probably higher than me, and the Foreign Secretary had many dealings with Bouton and Jerome, including liaising with them about international drugs cases. You may also remember that when we lured Bouton and Jerome to London to arrest them, the Foreign Secretary was the only one who declined to be present.'

Delaney was uncomfortable. He shook his head. 'I'm not happy with this. I want something else from *you* before we continue.'

Lusher moved over to a large cupboard in the corner of the room and opened a door. He pulled out a wheeled travel case, took it over to where Delaney was sitting and opened it. 'That's two million dollars, Tom. My payment from Farrah for services rendered. He paid me so much because he wants to use me again. I've already had some notes tested and it's the money from the bank raid in Paris. Take it with you if you like and keep it safe until this is all over.'

'I will do,' said Delaney.

Lusher continued. 'Come on, Tom, this has to prove to you that I was doing things just to get close to Farrah. I could have had this money in a far off foreign bank by now.'

'Perhaps,' said Delaney, 'we'll see.' He closed the travel case and wheeled it towards the door. 'See you at two.'

Burton opened the boot of the car when he saw Delaney approaching. 'What's in there, sir?'

'Two million dollars.'

Burton looked for an explanation; there wasn't one.

'Leave it in the car; we should be able to hand it back to the authorities tomorrow.'

The drive back to London was a quiet one. Burton did not ask again about the money; he knew Delaney well enough to know that all would be revealed when the time was right. Delaney had been thinking hard for a while before he turned to look at Burton. 'Are you still any good at following people, Taffy?'

'Why wouldn't I be?'

During the years they had worked together, they had had to follow some pretty good, but merciless people. There had been one occasion when Burton had stayed with a top criminal driver for 40 miles without being seen. Delaney looked pleased at Burton's confident answer and explained to him what he wanted. 'Today, I'm going to meet the Home Secretary at two o'clock; so is Lusher. Will you find out who's driving the Foreign Secretary these days and be ready to follow him any time after 2 p.m?'

'I thought you said you were going to see the *Home* Secretary.'

'We are, but chances are, the Home Secretary will be in touch with the Foreign Secretary as soon as we have left and if my hunch is right, the Foreign Secretary will want to go and meet someone straight away.'

'Meet who, sir?'

'Alan Farrah.'

43

Sally Curtis had been pleased to get back to her safe house. The Special Protection officers were waiting for her, but it wasn't them she wanted to see. It was Rocky. He came bounding down the stairs, barking with delight as she entered the front door, having smelt her as she approached the house.

'Oh my beautiful boy, I've missed you!'

'He's been fine,' said one of the officers. Your old lady friend has been taking her for walks.'

Curtis wanted them to leave so she could flop down and relax with Rocky and a glass of wine. 'Okay thank you, could you wait outside in the car now then, I'll be okay.'

The younger officer was known to Curtis; she had met him before. His name was Matt Connelly and she always felt that the young man held a bit of a candle for her. The older officer was not known to her and she did not like the look of him. He told her his name was Dave Burke and that he had just joined Connelly for a few days. He was at least six foot four inches tall with huge hands and a beard that was stained with nicotine, his wrinkled red face seemed to shroud his narrow eyes. When Curtis asked them to return to the outside, Burke hesitated and stayed in the doorway reluctantly 'We should stay in here; then we can cover both doors,' he said.

Curtis stood her ground. 'Well you can cover both doors from the outside can't you; one in front, the other to the back.'

Connelly put a hand on Burke's arm. 'Yeah, that's fine, come on Dave.' Burke brushed the arm off him and stared at Curtis. Then he seemed to give in. 'Sure, come on.'

Curtis thought about picking the phone up to get Burke replaced; she had done it before; the department was very obliging on such matters. Then Rocky's nose nudged her hand and her attention was diverted. An hour later they were settled down. Rocky enjoyed the pizza as much as she did.

The phone rang at 11am and Curtis answered it as she pushed Rocky off the bed. 'Hello?'

'Hello, it's Taffy.'

'Taffy! Great to hear from you.'

'Hello, Sally, I didn't want to disturb you too early, I thought I would let you rest, but I'm afraid now it's all hands on deck again.'

'Sure thing, how are you anyway? Fully recovered?'

'Almost, I'm fine I think.'

Curtis paused while she considered what Burton had gone through. 'So, what are we doing?'

'The boss is meeting the Home Secretary this afternoon at two. He wants you with me, we'll be following someone; Ben's going to drive Tom.'

'And who will we be following?' asked Curtis.

'I'll tell you later rather than over the phone, I'll pick you up at twelve.'

'Right, I'll be ready. Whoever we're following and wherever we're going, do we need to be armed?'

'Yes, just in case, but I'll bring something with me for you as well.'

Home Secretary Martin Hamilton seemed uncomfortable as he greeted Delaney and Lusher in his office. Lusher had not kept in touch with him as he should have done and Delaney had, as per usual, done things his way, had a body count that was too high *again* and spent far too much money.

But he needed both of them. They were very experienced and he needed to make the most of their contacts, procedures and knowledge.

Delaney helped himself to chilled water and took a seat to the side of Hamilton's desk; allowing Lusher to sit in front of the desk. Mrs. Beecham poured coffee for Lusher and Hamilton and left the room.

'Well, gentlemen,' Hamilton said in a sarcastic voice, 'nice of you to come and see me in your obviously hectic schedules.'

Neither man answered; they were too long in the tooth to rise to such conversation. Hamilton was at least ten years younger than they were and he was still learning. When he didn't get an answer, Hamilton adjusted his cufflinks and ran a hand through his hair as he leaned forward, his dark eyes narrowing and his eyebrows coming to together. 'Mr Delaney, perhaps you could enlighten me as to why you have chased around Europe after this man Farrah, killing god knows how many people in the process, let alone spending god knows how much on hotels, car hire and fuel. I can't imagine how much your next invoice will be. It's a good job that Joe public doesn't know how much their paying TOLA.'

Delaney tried not to smirk. 'Needs must, sir, he's a dangerous man and still has about 150 million dollars of stolen money. I shouldn't have to be concerned about how much I spend in catching such a criminal.'

'But that's just it Delaney, he's still at large; you haven't caught him.'

'No, sir, but we're close.'

'How close, do you know where he is right now?'

'My people are working on it now; we know his haunts and where his colleagues hang out.'

Hamilton uttered a small 'Mm' and turned to Lusher.

'Sir Adrian, why did you go abroad without letting me know?'

'I did let you know; Barcelona, remember? I thought Delaney would need my help. You were attending meetings and I didn't want to bother you with my diary details.'

Hamilton could detect the facetiousness in his voice but was not sure how to handle it. 'Right, well, from now on you both inform me *before* going off chasing people. We have capable people like Interpol and MI6 to do things like that.'

Lusher was about to come back at the Home Secretary with a remark but Delaney jumped in. 'Of course sir, you're right, we forget that we have other agencies we can use.' Lusher glanced at Delaney and took the hint.

Hamilton sat back and folded his arms. 'So what happens now? What do you know?'

Lusher took the opportunity to launch his plan. 'You will remember, Home Secretary, the killings of

Bouton and Jerome, and of course, our personnel who were escorting them.' Hamilton nodded.

'Delaney and I,' Lusher continued, 'believe that there must be another person very high up who was working with them and Farrah. Someone who wanted them dead before they gave out a name.'

'I see,' said Hamilton. He picked up his coffee, took a sip and replaced the cup. 'When you say *high*, what do you mean exactly?'

'Someone in the government, sir.'

'Ludicrous!' Just ludicrous! Do you know what you're suggesting?'

'We both realise the seriousness of this, yes sir.'

Delaney played the part Lusher had requested of him and confirmed that he too, realised what was being said. Hamilton walked over to the window and looked out on to the street before addressing them again without turning to look at them.

'And just who do you suggest this senior person might be, Lusher?'

'Someone in the cabinet or at the same level as myself or Delaney here.'

'That's quite a claim, if you come up with a name; you'd better let me know before you go any further.'

Hamilton was still looking out of the window and did not turn to look at either of his visitors. Delaney looked at Lusher and frowned. Eventually, Hamilton took a deep breath and returned to his desk. 'Well, I suppose it is possible. And I suppose if you're right, it has to be someone with overseas links.'

'Probably,' said Lusher, 'perhaps you could mention the possibilities to the Foreign Secretary the next time you meet.'

'Yes of course,' replied Hamilton, 'so what happens now?' As he asked the question, he looked at Delaney who responded to suit the situation.

'Sir Adrian and I have ideas and we will follow them through. We will, of course let you know when we are getting closer.'

'I should hope so,' said Hamilton. 'Right, please bear in mind my thoughts about keeping in touch; you report to me, so the PM will be on my back if you get it wrong. Now, I have to bring our meeting to a close if you don't mind. Good luck if you're working together, and err; I hope your assumptions are wrong.'

Lusher answered as he and Delaney left. 'So do we Home Secretary, so do we.'

The two men left, passing Andrea Beecham's desk on the way. She looked at them as though she knew, that they knew, what they were doing. Her intercom sounded loud as it rang out. 'Mrs. Beecham, get me the Foreign Secretary on the line please; the private line.'

Wyatt watched from his car as Delaney and Lusher approached. Lusher's driver was parked behind him. Delaney got into the car and asked Wyatt to stay where he was. Lusher and his driver made their way towards the foreign office.

'I thought we were going to the foreign office too?' queried Wyatt.

'No, I suggested that we wait here; Lusher is going. I'm okay with that; he doesn't know that Taffy and Sally will be there watching the foreign office as well.'

'So why wait here sir? It's the foreign office we need to watch isn't it?'

'Maybe, but we stay here for now.'

Alan Farrah looked out over the garden of his Harrow home. Sitting next to him, Mich was cleaning the pistols that Farrah had asked him to prepare. 'You meeting this bloke tonight, boss?' asked Mich.

'Yes, or before tonight, but I can't really contact him during the day.'

'Who is it anyway?'

'Can't say, Mich, sorry.'

Farrah watched him as he took each part of the weapons and cleaned them meticulously. They were put back together with speed and delicacy. What an old trooper, Farrah thought as he watched him, perhaps I shouldn't have involved him; he doesn't deserve to get hurt now. His thoughts were interrupted by his phone ringing. 'Hello?'

The caller sounded disturbed 'Alan, it's me, they know.'

'Who knows what?'

'Delaney and Lusher, they know another senior person was involved with Bouton and Jerome, and that that person must be linked to you. They're getting close.'

'Well if you're right, we'd better meet now then, I'll give you the rest of your money and we'll cool things for a while.'

There was a pause, as though the caller was doubting Farrah's suggestion. 'I thought you said yesterday you had left the money in Spain.'

'That was yesterday; you forget how many contacts I have, the money is back here now; courier and private jet.'

The caller hesitated, probably surprised at Farrah's resources. 'Right, seven o'clock then, usual place.'

'Yes,' said Farrah as he ended the call.

Mich could see the look on Farrah's face. It was a look he had seen before; half concern, half anger. 'Right, Mich, we go, now. I'll drive the Range Rover, you sit in the back. Take those two pistols with you; just in case, I'll have the shotgun on the seat at the side of me.'

They were both in the car ten minutes later; Farrah drove south out of Harrow towards central London. Mich had just noticed the signs for Wembley when Farrah turned off the main road into a housing estate. Halfway through the estate, they turned right into an old road with derelict warehouse units on either side that were beginning to collapse. A third of the way down, a small track led to a weed covered car park to the rear of the units. Two burnt out cars were upside down in the left hand corner of the car park and a wise old magpie was standing on one of them, eyeing his new visitors. Farrah turned right and stopped outside the rear entrance of one of the units. He pointed to a personnel door. 'That door should be open, Mich, take the hardware with you and stay there; you should be able see what's happening from that window. Everything should be alright, but just in case, be ready. If it looks like someone is going to put me in danger, start shooting, I'm not in the mood for messing about.'

'Got it,' said Mich.

Farrah was again amazed at his ability to take instruction without question. He parked the car in the middle of the car park facing the entrance road where he could see any vehicle coming in *and* see the window where Mich would be.

An hour passed. Nothing happened. He knew he had got there way before anyone else, which was exactly what he had wanted.

'There he goes.' Burton pointed to the Foreign Secretary as he left his office, unguarded.

'So we're following him, right?' queried Curtis.

'Right,' confirmed Burton. 'This is exactly what Tom said would happen.' He put the car into gear and followed the Volvo as it made its way out of the city northwards.

'Standard Volvo,' said Curtis. 'I thought he might have had something very grand.'

'Don't be fooled by its looks; the under plate will be grenade proof and the windows will be bullet proof.'

Foreign Secretary Jeremy Spires drove the Volvo along the main roads at sensible speeds. He didn't seem in a hurry and never attempted to overtake anyone on the carriageways. Burton and Curtis followed at a suitable distance. 'Better phone the boss,' said Burton. 'I told him we'd keep in touch.'

Curtis dialed Delaney's number. 'It's me, Tom, we're following the Foreign Secretary now, he left his office about fifteen minutes ago, driving north, very slowly.'

Delaney acknowledged and asked her to stay in touch every ten minutes. The Volvo moved into a supermarket car park. Spires left the vehicle for ten minutes and returned with a bag full of what looked like flowers and wine. Burton frowned and nudged Curtis. 'Let the boss know.'

Curtis phoned Delaney again to let him know what was happening. They followed the car back onto the main road. It headed for Mansville; a small community of large houses and mansions set back some fifty metres from the road. Burton pulled the car up onto the pathway. 'Stay here, Sally, I can't risk following him along that road; all the residents will know each other. I'll take a walk.'

As he walked slowly around the corner, he could see the Volvo being reversed onto a gravel driveway in front of a large Edwardian style house. When Spires had gone into the house, Burton walked slowly past it and noted the name on the door. *The Hollyoak, number 23.*

Curtis could see the bemused look on Burton's face as he walked back to the car. She raised her eyebrows questioningly as he opened the door. 'I think I might just make a phone call before I speak to the boss again,' he said.

'Okay,' said Curtis. She did not want to interrupt his deep thinking. Burton held his phone to his mouth and had to speak loudly because of the passing traffic. 'Jeff, its Taffy….yes fine thanks…Foreign Secretary Spires, I need an address….home address.'

There was a pause as he waited. Curtis shook her head in disbelief; the contacts that these men had, astounded her. Burton inched himself upright when his friend came back to him. 'Yes hello Jeff.'…'right thanks again, it'll have all the latest security gizmos on it I suppose?… Right, thanks mate.'

Curtis kept watching as Burton finished the call and dialed Delaney's number. 'Hello again Tom…yes I err… I have some news….the Foreign Secretary has just arrived home and err… everything appears normal.'

After listening for a few seconds, Burton ended the call and started the car. 'He wants us to join him and Ben; they're still waiting outside the Home Secretary's office.' He eased the car back into the traffic as the sun started to set behind the buildings and the street lights came on.

'Taffy and Sally are on their way to join us, Ben; we'll sit tight.' Delaney took a deep breath and rested his jaw on his hand as he looked out of the car window.

His thoughts were still whirling around in every direction. He was starting to believe Lusher's story and some things that the Home Secretary had said – or the way he had said them – were bothering him: the way he had picked up his cup when Lusher said he did not have a name, as though he was trying to hide the fact that he was swallowing hard; how he had stood looking out of the window and did not turn to look at either of them when he asked questions; and how he changed the subject back to his displeasure of them not keeping in touch. Then he brought the meeting to a close; quickly.

Wyatt tapped on the dashboard. 'Getting dark; how long are we staying for?'

'Until the Home Secretary leaves; then we follow him.'

44

It was approaching 7 p.m. when Home Secretary Hamilton left his office. His car pulled out of the underground car park. But it was his own car; a Ford, not the black Mercedes he usually used. And it was not Hamilton that was driving. He was sitting in the front passenger seat; at the wheel, was Andrea Beecham.

Delaney nudged Wyatt. 'Okay, Ben, don't get too close.' He phoned Burton. 'Where are you, Taffy?'

Burton explained he was only five minutes away. 'Right,' continued Delaney 'you should pick us up on Travers Street; we're just heading north towards the junction.'

Andrea Beecham drove northwards. Wyatt had to use all his skills to keep up with her, swerving between black cabs and cyclists. He looked in his mirror when a car behind flashed its lights a few times. 'Taffy's with us.'

'Right, let him take over when you get the chance.'

The roads began to get quieter as they left the city and Wyatt eased over and slowed down. Burton came up and got in front of him. Andrea Beecham was driving the Ford with great skill. This was obviously not the first time she had driven the Home Secretary, thought Delaney. The traffic started to queue again as they approached Park Royal. On one occasion, Burton could not avoid being right up behind the Mercedes, so he put the front lights on full beam, to avoid being seen in the mirror of the car in front.

'Let's hope she doesn't get out and walk back to complain to you,' said Curtis.

'Not in this traffic, no one cares anyway.'

The Ford turned right onto the north circular road and slowed down in the inside lane to turn left. Burton slowed and allowed Wyatt to take over as lead car again. Curtis was looking at road signs as they followed the two cars in front. 'Looks like we're headed for Wembley.'

As the Ford made its way north out of Wembley, the two following cars exchanged roles as lead cars and kept well back. Suddenly the Ford pulled off the road into a bus bay and stopped. The experienced Burton kept driving on past it and only turned into a side street on his left when he was sure the driver of the Ford could not see the manouevre. Wyatt pulled up about one hundred metres behind the Ford and switched off his lights. He looked over at Delaney. 'Think they're checking us out, sir?'

'Definitely. Not us specifically though, just a precautionary tactic. They'll probably sit there for a while to see if anything happens before going on.'

Burton had turned left and left again and a minute later was parked up behind Wyatt, but well back. Ten minutes passed and the Ford did not move. 'They're making sure,' said Delaney.

'Making sure of what?'

'My guess is that they'll be turning off this road soon and they're just waiting for a while before they do. Which usually means a meeting is about to happen.'

As they waited, Delaney's phone rang. It was Angela. 'Hello,' he said.

Angela sounded pleased to hear his voice. 'Hello, darling, okay?'

'Yes fine, I'll be late tonight, probably very late.'

'Right, well I'm just phoning to say hello really. Are you out and about somewhere?'

'Yep, just seeing what someone is up to.'

'Okay, well I'll let you get on with it. By the way I'm working tomorrow, I feel fine now and apparently there's a lot of work coming into us from some recent important meetings; I'm starting early so if I'm not in by the time you get here, you'll know where I am.'

Delaney raised his eyebrows. 'Okay, as long as you're sure; what's the *important* work anyway?'

'Oh, quite a few things to be put on disc apparently. There's also rumours of a Cobra meeting that needs the minutes confirming and archiving.'

'Yes I heard about the last meeting, it's probably just to take a threat level from red down to amber. Adrian Lusher and I were told about it.'

Angela huffed. 'Mm, you never know with the Bird's Nest, could be anything. Anyway, bye for now. Be careful.'

'I will,' said Delaney as he ended the call.

Wyatt kept his eyes fixed on the Ford as he spoke to Delaney. 'How is she these days?'

'Obviously alright; she's off back to work tonight,' said Delaney, shrugging his shoulders.

As they sat there waiting for some form of movement or a sign that something was about to happen, Delaney yet again, found himself thinking hard about all the possibilities. And now he had something else to consider; why was Andrea Beecham driving the Home Secretary? And using his own car? Yes, she is his PA but they wouldn't normally drive. The Home Secretary had his own driver, just as the other cabinet members did. People like Andrea Beecham looked after their bosses work schedules and diaries; arranged meetings and kept in touch with other secretaries. All the PA's were in regular contact with each other. She would be able to let Hamilton know who was doing what and where.

Delaney continued to think; would Andrea Beecham know the whereabouts of everyone in his department at any given time? Doubtful; Delaney did not have a PA. He used Maggie for secretarial work, as did the others. His men kept their own diaries and anyway, normally they would not know where they were going to be from one day to the next. But somehow, someone knew he would be at Stansted on the morning he was attacked and someone knew where he was in France.

Maggie?

Maggie had worked at the department for two years. In her own little room she would take care of all the paperwork for everyone and take messages when people lost touch with each other because they were on different assignments or cases. He pulled a small note book from his pocket, found a page and punched a number into his phone.

'Maggie, it's Tom, I do apologise for ringing you at home.'

She sounded surprised, but it had not been the first time. 'Hello, Tom, what do you need to know?'

'How do you know I need to know something?'

'Oh you're a nice man, but not nice enough to ring me at home to see if I'm alright.'

Delaney paused. 'No, perhaps not. Anyway, I have a question for you; while we were chasing all over Europe and going to places like Nottingham and Glasgow, how did you know where we were?'

'Taffy kept me informed, and don't forget we have the GPS for your mobiles. And of course, the people who work in other departments will always discuss the whereabouts of their own people in case we have to get anyone back for an emergency.'

'Of course, silly of me,' said Delaney. 'Who would you normally keep in touch with then?'

'Quite a few people; secretaries, second-in-commands, ministerial administrators, PA's.'

'PA's?'

'Yes, most of them really, it's important we all know what other departments are doing, you've said so yourself in the past.'

Delaney shook his head at the disbelief of his own idiocy. 'Quite, Maggie, quite. And these PA's you would be in contact with; would that include the PA's to the cabinet ministers?'

'Oh, yes.'

'Including Andrea Beecham?'

'Oh yes, regularly.'

'Thank you, Maggie, sorry to have troubled you at home.' He ended the call without giving her a chance to speak again.

The Ford started to move off. Wyatt followed and Burton stayed behind them, following closely. After just two hundred metres, Andrea Beecham turned to the right and drove through a housing estate. Wyatt turned his lights off and continued to follow using just the dim street lights to see what was happening. He watched as the car in front turned down a small track and switched its lights off. 'Stop,' said Delaney, 'stay here.'

Wyatt pulled up and Burton pulled in behind him. Curtis and Burton got out of their car and joined Delaney who was standing next to Wyatt, still seated in his car. 'I'll go on foot and have a look,' said Delaney. 'Stay here; I'll come back for you when I know the situation.'

He walked around the corner and kept walking when he could not see the Ford. Between a row of old warehouse units, another track led to a rear parking area and he crept quietly down the track until he could see into the car park. The Ford was parked next to a Range Rover. Andrea Beecham was still in the car. Hamilton was standing behind the car talking to another man. It was difficult to see who the other man was, but Delaney assumed it to be Farrah. He moved slowly backwards and then turned to run back to the others. Wyatt got out of his car. 'No, get back in, Ben,' said Delaney. 'Follow me; I want you to use the car to block an entrance off.' He then looked at Curtis. 'Sally, you come with me, stay close, I'll tell you what to do when we get near.'

Burton turned to lock his car and interrupted Delaney as he was about to speak to him. 'Let me guess, my car stays here, I find another way around the back somewhere and stay low.'

Delaney nudged his head upwards and curled his mouth. 'Very good, Taffy, very good.'

For reasons which he could not explain to himself, Delaney started to think about Angela as he made his way quietly back down the track, Curtis at his side. He was worried about Angela; she had been through a lot and now she would be back at work tomorrow. Typing, copying discs, translating meetings for overseas contacts, Cobra, Bird's Nest.

Bird's Nest.

He stopped in his tracks.

Curtis realised and came to a halt a few paces in front of him. She turned to see the look on his face and whispered. 'Tom; what?'

Delaney held up his hand as a command for her to stay still and keep quiet while he thought.

Bird's Nest.

Members of Cobra were given code names. Code names of birds. Prime Minister was Eagle, the Foreign Secretary was Kestrel, the Chief of Staff was Buzzard.

The Home Secretary was Albatross.

The Home Secretary was Albatross.

This is for J and B. hope the van is ok. – A.

The note he had been carrying around with him, had been written by Hamilton. Home Secretary Hamilton was *A*; not Adrian Lusher, not Alan Farrah.

'Tom, what the hell is the matter?' The whispers of Curtis brought Delaney out of his thoughts. 'Nothing,' he said. 'Come on; we've finally got the right people, Sally, and all in one place.'

45

Alan Farrah opened the back door of the Range Rover and reached for a small green hold-all.

'Is it the amount we agreed?' asked Hamilton.

Farrah picked up the hold all and threw it into the back of the Ford before he answered. 'Five million. Get rid of it somewhere for six months. And don't contact me for 12 months. I need to cool it for a while.'

Andrea Beecham twisted around in the driver's seat so she could see the hold-all. 'Twelve months will be fine actually,' she said. 'I've got plans for that money.'

Hamilton leaned forward so he could see her through the car window. 'Keep your mouth shut my darling, for god's sake.' She smiled at him and turned forward, putting both hands on the steering wheel ready to move off.

'Well, you heard me,' said Farrah, 'get out of here, we need to be quick.'

Hamilton hesitated and watched Farrah as he closed the back door of the Range Rover and got into the driver's seat. 'So what's happened, Alan; to make you go to ground so quickly without warning?'

'Never mind, just get on your way.'

The rear boundary of the old car park had been difficult to get to. Burton had moved quickly and quietly and could see the two cars and the three people clearly from his position behind two upturned burnt out cars. He raised his pistol up to shoulder height and rested it on one of the cars. He had a clear line of sight.

Delaney and Curtis knelt down where the track came out on to the open area; one on either side. Delaney raised an arm as a signal and Wyatt drove his car across the entrance behind them.

Hamilton looked around when he heard the noise. 'Who the bloody hell....'

'Get down!' shouted Farrah.

Hamilton crouched down behind the Ford. Farrah got out of the Range Rover holding his shotgun. 'Wait,' he said to Hamilton. 'Just wait and stay quiet.'

When there was no sign of any other noises for a few seconds, Farrah held his hands around his mouth and spoke quietly but firmly towards the warehouses. 'Mich, be ready to go.'

The experienced Mich tapped twice on the window as a signal that he had heard.

'Is that one of your men?' whispered Hamilton.

'Yes, just stay quiet.'

Delaney had heard Farrah call out to his colleague. He gestured to Wyatt to go to the right. Wyatt took his rifle from the car and made his way along the front of the warehouses. He was at the window of the third warehouse when he paused. Looking into the window, he could just make out the silhouette of a man; standing by the rear window, looking out to the rear area, with two pistols, one in each hand. The rifle would be too big to use swiftly and accurately at such close quarters so he laid it down against the building, took the trusty old Smith and Wesson out of his shoulder holster and screwed a silencer onto the barrel.

There was nowhere that he could put the barrel of the handgun through to aim at the man. He knew he would have to break the window and aim and shoot as quickly as he could. The man inside was restless. He started to look around and kept wiping the window for clearer vision. It has to be now, thought Wyatt, I'm not messing about.

He stood and held the gun upwards so the butt was facing the window. He pulled his arm back and swung it forward. The glass shattered, the man inside twisted around, Wyatt aimed and shot twice. The man fell backwards; two bullets in his chest.

'What was that?' whispered Hamilton. Farrah looked towards the warehouse and shouted again. 'Mich? Ready to go?'

This time there was no tapping on the window.

When Delaney had heard what he assumed to be Wyatt getting up to something, he looked at Curtis and gestured with his hand for her to stay low. He faced the two cars where Hamilton and Farrah were and shouted in their direction. 'Alan Farrah! You can't go anywhere! Stand up and walk away from the car!'

Hamilton stared at Farrah. 'You idiot!'

'You're the idiot you amateur; they followed you here.'

'What do we do?'

Farrah threw his shotgun down to the ground. 'We do as he says; there could be twenty of them out there. I've got out of jail before, I can do it again.'

'What about me, and Andrea?'

'You knew the risks, come on, on your feet.' As they stood up where they could be seen, Andrea Beecham started the Ford. Hamilton looked down at her as she put the car into gear. 'Andrea! What...'

'I'm going, that's what, I'm not giving up this five million!'

She put her foot down hard and charged towards Delaney and Curtis, the Ford soon got up to a good speed and Beecham screamed with anger and nerves as she hurtled towards them. Burton moved his pistol to the right and followed the track of the vehicle. She was not going to stop, he thought, If she keeps going she'll run down at least one of them and probably have enough speed up to push Wyatt's car out of the way. He fired twice, the driver's window shattered, he fired a third time, the front tyre burst and the car twisted around and came to rest ten feet from where Curtis was standing.

Burton, Curtis and Delaney stayed where they were without moving. Hamilton ran to the Ford. 'Andrea! No, no, no!'

When he got to the car he forced open the door. Andrea Beecham's body slumped outwards, blood pouring from her head. The whole of the interior of the car was covered in a red spatter pattern. He cried as he knelt down to hold Beecham's head in his hands; her blood dousing his face.

Delaney looked at Curtis. 'Stay here.' He moved forward so Hamilton could see him. Hamilton looked up. 'I'll have you for this, Delaney!'

When Burton could see Farrah walking away from the other two cars, he trained his gun on him and followed him as he walked towards Delaney. Farrah had realised that Mich had been taken. He was good, but he was one man with one shotgun and two rounds, and he knew the odds. He paused where Hamilton was holding Beecham and then smiled as he looked at Delaney. His face was sweaty and tired; his large wide eyes stared into Delaney's. He admired him somewhat. Hoetger and others had tried to kill him, but all had failed. He looked down at Hamilton again before resting on the side of the car. 'Amateurs, Delaney, not like you and me, eh?'

'No, not like you and me. Take your jacket off and turn around.'

Farrah did as Delaney instructed. When Burton and Delaney could see he was not concealing a gun, Burton let his pistol rest downwards.

Curtis walked up to Farrah. Her eyes fixed on his. As she got closer, her pace quickened. Delaney spotted it. 'Sally!' she looked at him and seemed to acknowledge his command. 'Two wrongs don't make a right,' he said.

'No,' said Curtis, 'I suppose not.'

Farrah had stopped smiling. He looked at her with so much disdain that Delaney readied himself for action. Curtis walked up to Farrah and looked him in the eye without speaking. Farrah sneered at her. 'I should have killed you when I had the chance.'

'You have already done worse than that. You killed someone who meant everything to me.'

'You mean Hanson? Stupid bitch, that wasn't me, it was Hoetger.'

'On whose orders?'

Farrah tilted his head. 'On my orders I suppose but I was just the local enforcer for Jerome and Bouton. It was Bouton who paid Hoetger, via Mr Hamilton here.'

'That's enough of this,' said Delaney.

Burton moved forward and handcuffed Farrah's hands behind his back. He had read the situation and knew that Delaney wanted to move on; and away from the scene. 'Can you get the car, Sally; we'll take Mr Farrah with us. Tom will stay here and do a de-brief with Ben.'

Delaney let Burton take the lead. He was rarely wrong in understanding the needs in situations like this.

On cue, Wyatt walked around the corner and rested his rifle against the building. 'One dead, in the third warehouse,' he said.

'I didn't hear any shots,' said Delaney.

'No, sir, I needed to do things a little quieter.'

Wyatt raised his voice as he saw Burton leading Farrah away. 'Taffy! Hang on.'

Burton paused and held Farrah's arm as Wyatt approached them. Delaney could see the look on Wyatt's face; the same look that he had seen on Curtis's face, seconds earlier. 'Ben, by the book, okay?'

Wyatt looked at Delaney. 'Sorry, sir, bollocks.' He swung his fist around and it hit Farrah on the jaw sending him reeling with blood coming from his mouth. Delaney smirked and said nothing.

Burton took control again. 'Ben, I think you'd better come with me instead of Sally. We'll take Farrah to Mulgrove. Tom and Sally will look after the Home Secretary; okay with you, sir?'

'Fine, Taffy, thanks,' Delaney confirmed.

A minute later Wyatt was driving out towards the main road, with Farrah in the back seat next to Burton. Farrah looked into Wyatt's eyes in the rear view mirror. Wyatt looked away and concentrated on his driving, determined not to be drawn into any games. 'I don't suppose if I said you could have a million each if I escaped, that it would make any difference would it?' Farrah asked.

'No it wouldn't,' said Burton.

'You're lucky I don't stop the car and kill you now you bastard,' said Wyatt. 'It would be easy; you got free and I shot you because you were a threat to innocent bystanders.'

Farrah stared again at Wyatt in the mirror. 'I do believe you are capable of that,' he said. 'You should work for me instead of this lot, the pay would be...'

'Shut up!' said Burton. 'Both of you; not another word, just drive, Ben and get us to Mulgrove.'

Delaney had called for an ambulance and Scene of Arrest officers. They arrived swiftly and went about their work. He and Curtis were checking the money in the back of the Range Rover and the Ford. 'How much, Tom?'

'At least 140 million; a good result.'

Curtis raised her voice. 'At a cost. I'm not sure it was value for money.'

Two officers arrived and Delaney told them to take care of the Range Rover, the money and the Ford. The paramedics lifted Andrea Beecham's body from the Ford, black bagged it and loaded it into their ambulance.

Hamilton was still in shock. He was standing against the Ford with his hands around his neck. Delaney noticed the forlorn look on his face and tapped Curtis on the arm. 'Get Taffy's car, Sally, we'll get Mr. Hamilton back to one of our secure cells.'

'Right,' said Curtis. 'Oh and err, we'd better take this with us.' She pointed to Wyatt's rifle that he had left standing against the building.

'Bloody hell,' said Delaney, 'that's the first time he's done that.'

'It's okay, Tom; I'll put it in the car, out of sight and hand it back into the armoury for him.'

By the time Curtis had fetched the car and Hamilton and Delaney were seated in the back, flashing lights were everywhere. The blue lights of the ambulance were soon replaced by the red and yellow lights of the tow truck that was loading up the blood soaked Ford. Delaney looked back as they drove away. He could see the small army of professionals going about their work and wondered if the man next to him ever really knew about all the dedicated emergency services and intelligence staff who worked in such a tenacious way, day in, day out, unquestioning.

Hamilton was looking down; the expression on his face was almost a suicidal one. Delaney nudged him on the arm. 'Why did you get involved, Home Secretary?'

Hamilton kept looking down. 'Love and money Delaney. Love and money. Andrea had been a breath of fresh air to me. We had plans. Plans to retire early; a trouble free existence, and for that, you need money, lots of it. Andrea had expensive tastes and I wanted the best for her and me. When Farrah approached me, it all seemed so easy, all that money for just letting him know when he was being watched and keeping people like you away from him. Didn't work though did it, Delaney? You're too independent and disobedient.'

'You don't need that much money to be happy,' said Delaney. 'It's greed; you want as much as you can get, regardless of what affect it has on others.'

Hamilton was still looking down. Curtis could see him in the rear view mirror. She shook her head as she drove them back towards central London.

There was not much that could be said when they arrived back at Delaney's office and settled Hamilton into a secure cell. He had not denied anything and it was just a matter of routine; awkward routine. It was 11 p.m. by the time they had sorted out the initial paperwork and called up for help from the Downing Street spokesman. Delaney phoned the Prime Minister's private secretary and the other relevant parties. The newspapers and news channels would be on to the story in a flash but they did not know about secure cells in the offices of TOLA.

Curtis yawned as Hamilton was being questioned by Delaney. She called out to a special guard who had been drafted in and asked for more coffee. Delaney stood up and gathered the papers up in his hands. 'We'll leave it there for tonight,' he said. 'Call the guard if you need anything Home Secretary; I'll speak to you again in the morning; by then we should have instructions from on high. This is an unprecedented case.'

'Well,' said Hamilton, 'at least I'll be famous for something.'

Delaney closed the cell door behind him and called after the guard. 'Forget the coffee for us, but see that the Home Secretary gets what he wants will you?' The guard half saluted silently.

Curtis yawned again as she pulled her coat on. 'Ah, right, Tom, what time do you want me back in the morning?'

'Eight will do; they may have collected him by then, with any luck.'

'Who's they?'

'It'll probably be a combination of MI6 and Special Services.'

'Not Special Branch?' asked Curtis.

'No, they're too close to the Home Secretary, he knows some of them.'

'Right, well, speaking of Special Branch, I'll get back home to my safe house. Two of their Special Protection guys are looking out for me.'

Delaney smiled gently and held the door open for her. 'In a couple of days, we'll get you and Rocky back home.'

'Good, I'm ready for it. Then I guess I'll get back to Canada; I'm thinking of packing it in.'

'Your call,' said Delaney as Curtis walked out.

He picked up the phone and called Burton. 'All okay, Taffy?'

'Yes it is, sir; Farrah is now in Mulgrove's highest security cell. The local boys have already arranged for his hearing appearance the day after tomorrow. The local judge was not happy at being got out of bed.'

'Good, well done. Can you and Ben be here in the morning about eight please?'

'Will do.'

It was nearly one o'clock in the morning when Delaney decided to make his way home. On his way to the exit, he decided to divert via the cells and have one more look at his captive. He was not sure why. He looked through the small barred window at Hamilton, who was leaning against a wall, his arms folded. He looked up when he heard Delaney. 'What now, Delaney? Just go away will you.'

'I just wanted to have another look at you; have you any idea what you have caused?'

'Caused? Oh don't lecture me, Delaney.'

'Two good men have been killed because of your greed Hamilton, so I'll lecture to you as I see fit. If you include the men who were escorting Jerome and Bouton it's seven good men who died. But we win, Hamilton, we always do. Scum like you never prevail.'

'If you say so, Delaney, now go away, oh and err, give my regards to Ms Curtis.'

Delaney walked away. Saying anything else would have been futile. The rain was pouring down as he drove out of the underground car park. As he came to a stop at some traffic lights, he started to think of all that had happened and he was pleased with the outcome. But the deaths of those young men devastated him. Jones and Landers had been skillful operators. It would take him at least a year to get the department back up to scratch. Luckily, he still had Burton and Wyatt. And, for now, Curtis too.

But something was bothering him. Something that Hamilton had said. – *'oh and err, give my regards to Ms Curtis.'*

Why did he say that? He thought. Why *would* he say that? When the traffic lights went to green he decided he would take a detour on his way home.

46

Curtis arrived at the safe house to find Rocky waiting for her. He wagged his tail constantly as she got changed to take him for a short walk. The rain was pouring down and she and Rocky were both drenched when they got back to the house. As she passed an old van she gave the usual thumbs up to the Special Protection minders. It was the same two men she had seen before. The young one, Matt Connelly, smiled at her, but the one she had not liked, Dave Burke, remained stone faced. If she was not about to be allowed back home, she would definitely being asking for a replacement, she thought.

It was 2 a.m. when she woke from having fallen asleep on the sofa. She showered and washed her hair. It was pointless now going to bed; Delaney wanted her in the office at eight and it was true that apart from all the tragedy, this case had also filled her with adrenalin. As she was drying her hair in the bathroom, Rocky started to bark. She went downstairs to see if everything was okay, but he stopped barking as she was descending the stairs.

'Hey, noisy, what is it then?' she said as she entered the kitchen.

The door slammed behind her. A hand came across her mouth hard and fast as her left arm was grabbed and twisted behind her back. The attacker then grabbed her hair and threw her to the ground, kicking her as she fell.

'Stay there! Move, and I'll kill you now.'

She looked up to see a large man taking a gun from a shoulder holster. It was Dave Burke, his bearded face looking even more sinister than it had earlier. Rocky was lying in the corner of the kitchen looking like he had been winded from a hefty kick.

Curtis realised the situation as she stared up at the brute standing over her. 'So you're on the payroll as well you ugly moron.'

'Whose payroll would that be then?' asked Burke.

'I don't know, Hamilton? Farrah? Hoetger?'

The look on Burkes face only altered slightly when Curtis said 'Hamilton' so she decided to keep talking. 'It's Hamilton isn't it? Someone told me that Hamilton was close to people in Special Protection and Special Branch.'

Burke did not answer.

'Well,' continued Curtis, 'your paymaster is now locked up in a cell so quit while you're ahead.'

Burke started to smile. 'He's already paid me darlin' and in a cell or not, I always do what I'm paid to do.'

Curtis gathered up all her knowledge and experience in an effort to think of how to get out of the situation. Young Matt Connelly must still be out there, unaware of what Burke was up to. She knew she had to keep him talking and try to find a way of signaling at the window or getting through to the front door.

She put on her inexperienced, girly look and held a hand out to Burke. 'At least let me get up then. If you're going to kill me, I deserve to be standing up.'

'You daft cow, you're not dealing with an amateur. Stay still and shut your mouth.'

He switched off the light and went to the window to look out while holding his gun on her. 'Not sure that boy out there is up to it,' he said, 'but just in case.'

He opened the back door slightly and stood by it as he reached into his pocket for a silencer and started to screw it onto the barrel of his gun. Meanwhile, Rocky started to stir again and got to his feet. He started barking at the man. Burke pointed his gun at the dog. 'Noisy bloody thing you are.'

Curtis kicked his leg which put him off balance for an instant; she launched herself at him and brought him down, as they both twisted and fell to the floor. She tried to bring her fists up but he was too strong for her. She saw the gun out of the corner of her eye as he reached over her shoulder to shoot her in the back. The gun went off but the bullet by-passed her back and buried itself in her backside. The dog continued to bark. As Curtis collapsed in pain she was still conscious. Deciding not to waste another bullet on the dog, Burke turned to see if Curtis was dead. She closed her eyes quickly and stayed motionless.

'Now you really are insulting my intelligence, you cow.' He pulled the gun up and aimed it at her face.

A bullet came through the open kitchen door and hit him in the neck; the second bullet hit him in the head and threw him to the floor. He started to move again very slightly as Delaney pushed the door open so he shot him again in the head. Connelly was standing behind Delaney looking like a kid that had just been on his first roller coaster ride. Curtis's excruciating pain did not stop her looking up at Delaney as he stood over Burke's body. 'Why stop now, Tom, you might as well empty the entire magazine into him.'

'Very funny, young lady, very funny.'

'Well, I suppose…. Ah! Jesus this hurts!' She collapsed down again as Rocky came over to her.

Delaney had already called for backup and an ambulance on his way to the house; the paramedics were quick to get Curtis on a stretcher and away. Connelly stayed with Burke's body and did a sweep of the rest of the house. Just as Delaney was leaving he looked down to see Rocky sitting, looking at him.

'Well, boy, they don't like dogs in hospitals; I suppose you'd better come with me.'

He found the dog's lead and led him out to his car. The ambulance was moving away down the road. He decided to get Rocky to his house so Angela could look after him before going to the hospital to how Curtis was.

A couple of days later, Curtis was sitting up in bed when Delaney visited her for the second time. She told him that she had received a call from Canada.

'They want me back in Toronto, sounds like a desk job. Thank god for that. Never thought I would say that. They've organised a flight home for me the day after tomorrow.'

Delaney looked at her and considered what she had gone through over the last few weeks. 'Probably a good thing. You need a rest; a long rest.'

'Yeah I know. Been good working with you, Tom.'

'Likewise.'

Curtis pulled herself up in the bed. 'So, how have you and Angela been with Rocky?'

'He's been fine, he's a good lad.'

Curtis put her head on one side. Delaney knew what was coming.

'I can't take Rocky back with me, Tom,' she said. 'Don't suppose you want to look after him do you?'

'Me?'

'Well, why not?'

'I'll think about it.'

Burton and Wyatt were sitting in Delaney's office when he arrived. Burton poured another coffee and placed it in front him. 'How is she, sir?'

'She's okay, probably being discharged later today; they're sorting out a flight back to Canada for her.'

'She was lucky,' said Wyatt.

'Very; the bullet missed her spine and went through her backside. Anyway, what about the paperwork for all of this mess?'

'Sorted,' said Burton. 'Hamilton is with MI6, I think he could be in for a rough ride.'

'Good. What about Farrah?'

'Being moved tomorrow; from Mulgrove to Hereford.'

'Hereford?' queried Delaney.

'Hereford, boss,' interrupted Wyatt; 'you know, SAS and all that.'

'Right; you mean their secure underground cells where they do the interrogation training.'

Burton confirmed. 'That's it; he'll be moved to a secure prison wing somewhere when the dust has settled.'

Delaney got on with clearing his in-tray. Wyatt was pacing around slowly.

'You alright, Ben?' Delaney asked as he put his pen down.

'Yeah I think so.'

'Been an interesting few weeks hasn't it?'

'Mm, it's the boys; Brandon and Stephen, they didn't deserve to die like that; and don't tell me it was their job and they knew the risks.'

Delaney tried not to say too much. 'I wasn't going to say that, Ben, you're right. But they're gone. You should be able to move on.'

'We will do,' said Burton. 'Won't we, Ben?'

'Mm, we'll move on.' After a short pause Wyatt spoke again. 'By the way, the memorial services are next week.'

Delaney changed the subject. 'Have any of you thought about Hoetger?'

'Hoetger?' asked Wyatt. 'No I haven't, he vanished when I got Hobson in Tossa del Mar. I had forgotten; where the hell did he get to?'

'*Vanished* is the word,' said Delaney. 'Maybe he just ran away from it all so he could live to fight another day.'

Wyatt sat down to get on with his report writing. Burton was thinking about Hoetger and how many worldwide contacts he had. 'He's probably somewhere negotiating his next fee now.'

There was silence again. As he was working, Burton caught Wyatt's eye and gestured in the direction of Delaney. Wyatt shook his head. Burton raised his eyebrows as if to say 'yes you will'.

Wyatt waited until he could see that Delaney was between pages. 'Err, sir?'

'Yep?'

'Err, did you by any chance pick up my rifle when we took Hamilton and Farrah?'

'You mean the rifle you left leaning against the warehouse?'

'Yes.'

Delaney saw the worried look on Wyatt's face and then glanced at Burton who was smirking. 'Don't worry, Ben, Sally picked it up, it came back here with us. She's probably signed it back into the armoury for you.'

The look on Wyatt's face was one of pure relief. He knew the penalty and the shame of losing a firearm. 'Only, it was my old SLR; my pride and joy, accurate up to a mile.'

'I know; you owe Sally a drink.'

'I suppose so; I'll try to see her before she goes back to Canada.'

That evening Delaney fell asleep next to Angela on the sofa at 9 p.m. She looked at him as he lay there wondering how he still managed to do everything that he did and still survive. She kissed him on the forehead. He stirred. 'What is i.. ?'

'Nothing darling, it's nothing, why don't you go to bed.'

'Do you know, I think I will.' He walked across to the window and yawned as he looked out into the rear garden.

The rain was pouring down the window. Rocky came to his side and started wagging his tail. Delaney looked down at him and sighed. Angela was smiling as she watched them both.

'You can't want to go out in all this, boy, we'll get soaked.'

The dog continued wagging his tail.

Delaney continued his case for the defence. 'It's dark, it's raining, you've already been out once today, If we...'

Rocky's tail was still wagging.

Delaney sighed again, turned towards the door and reached for his coat.

'Come on then. What the hell. You're as tenacious as your previous owner.'

47

The following morning was bright and sunny. The rain had passed on its way northwards and the streets were drying out as people went about their business. Taffy Burton arrived at the office at 8 a.m. He had received a message from Delaney to say he would be late. Wyatt had made coffee and they settled down to talk about recent events and future jobs that were coming up. Mid morning arrived and Burton asked Wyatt to stay in the office. Delaney would want at least one of them to be there when he arrived. Curtis was being discharged from hospital round about midday and Burton was determined to greet her and look after her; she deserved it. He stopped en route to buy some flowers and arrived early at the hospital.

Curtis was early too. She was walking out towards the taxi rank when he saw her and pulled up in front of her as she approached the kerbside.

'Taffy Burton, I don't believe it! How did you know?'

'I phoned, not difficult; you should've let us know anyway instead of being all independent and proud.'

'You're right, Taffy, anyway thank you.'

He took her bag and opened the front passenger door for her. She seemed to be moving with ease as she settled in her seat.

'You don't look too bad; still aching?'

'I'm okay; medicines these days are amazing aren't they? I thought I'd be in for weeks, but they stitched me up and gave me some special injections. I might need a soft cushion for a few days.'

Burton reached behind his seat for the flowers. 'Here you are, for you from us all.'

'Oh gee thanks, Taffy, honestly, you guys!'

He smiled at her caringly. 'You're welcome; right, where to?'

'The safe house please, I have a few things to pick up and then I need to get back to my house to hand it back to the letting agency. I have to speak to my people in Toronto as well. Did Tom mention that I was going back home?'

'Yes he did, and I expected it. You've been great, but you need to take it easy for a while.'

Curtis did not say anything. She put her hand on Burton's leg and smiled. 'Thanks, Taffy.'

He left the conversation where it was and drove smoothly towards the safe house. They were just a few hundred yards from their destination when Curtis spoke again. 'What about Hamilton and Farrah, Taffy?'

'Hamilton is with MI6, Farrah's being taken to a secure holding place somewhere near Hereford.'

'You mean the SAS base?'

'Yes I do.'

'Well it's over now, Taffy. I'll try to put it behind me; will you?'

'We have to don't we?'

'I guess so. So Farrah's still in Mulgrove then?'

'Mm, they'll transfer him in the morning.'

They arrived at the safe house a minute later. Burton offered to stay until she was ready to leave and take her back home, but Curtis said she would be a long time and that he should go and do his duties. She kissed him on the cheek as she opened the door. 'Bye Taffy, give my regards to Tom and Ben.'

'You mean you don't want to say goodbye to them personally?'

'No. Sorry. This is all too upsetting. Bye, Taffy.'

And she was gone. Quickly; without ceremony.

Burton looked in his mirrors, pulled out into the traffic and made his way back to the office.

Curtis spent an hour packing a few things at the safe house and ordered a taxi to take her home. With her bags near the front door, she sat on the bottom step of the stairs; then got up again. 'Damn you,' she said to herself, thinking of Burke shooting her in the backside as she moved to the sofa to sit on the soft cushions.

The taxi arrived 30 minutes later and she told the driver to head for Mulgrove. As they approached Mulgrove, she told him to keep driving around and follow her instructions. The high security police station at Mulgrove had a camera on every corner and she asked the driver to pause at some spots so she could have a more detailed look around. He drove across the front of the building and up and down some side streets. When Curtis had figured out where the rear entrance was, she looked around and pointed to the rear of a hotel with windows looking out towards the police station. 'Do you know the name of that hotel?' She asked.

'The Turner, it's called, miss. Don't ask me why. Do you want me to drop you there?'

'No thanks, can you take me to this address please.' She handed him a piece of paper with her home address on.

He looked at her in his mirror and tilted his head. 'Right miss; you don't want to be anywhere around here then?'

'No thanks, I just wanted to see where an old friend was staying.'

'You're the customer.'

Delaney and Wyatt were looking closely at some documents when Burton arrived at the office the following morning. Delaney looked up. 'How is she?'

'Okay, sir; how did you know I'd picked her up?'

'Just a guess, is she going to see us before she goes home?'

'Err, no sir, she said not.'

Delaney curled his mouth down and thought for a moment before responding. 'If that's what she wants. I sort of said goodbye anyway, when she off loaded that dog of hers onto me.'

Wyatt joined in. 'Yeah right, boss, you love it really.'

Delaney smiled as the other two looked at each other, trying not to.

Burton pointed to the papers on the desk. 'Anything you need me to do?'

'No it's okay,' said Wyatt, 'we were looking for something that might help us track Hoetger down.'

'Ah yes, Hoetger; I forget I haven't had the pleasure of dealing with him like you gentlemen have. I suppose he's the only one who has prevented you getting a full house on this job.'

'They'll be another time, 'said Delaney.

Wyatt threw his pen down and sat back. 'You reckon?'

'Yes I do. More people know about him now; word gets around.'

'Yeah, well do me a favour,' said Burton. 'If we do meet up with him, let me deal with it.'

Delaney looked at both of them. 'Okay, let's leave it there; we do have other cases to consider remember?'

Burton and Wyatt acknowledged quietly and made their way to their own desks as Delaney continued. 'Now then, Taffy; do you need to be at Mulgrove in the morning for Farrah's transfer?'

'No, sir, I've signed everything off. The local boys have arranged three cars; Farrah will be in the middle one, usual escort convoy routine.'

'Good; Ben, make a start on that Amsterdam case will you, we need to concentrate on other things now and get on with our jobs.'

Wyatt took up a file that was on his desk and started to study it. Within minutes he was on the phone arranging a meeting. Burton gathered up the files on his desk marked 'Farrah' and took them to a cabinet. He placed the files in a draw and closed it very slowly.

As Delaney looked at them he felt a lump in his throat. Two professionals, he thought, good professionals; I need to look after them and make sure they don't go the same way as Jones and Landers did. He considered for a moment going to see Curtis before she flew back to Canada. He felt he wanted to apologise to her; they had got Farrah back in a cell and arrested the other greedy high ranking officials but Hoetger was still on the loose and it was he who had killed Marcus Hanson all those weeks ago.

But he had had failures before and for every failure there were many successes. He was actually starting to look forward to the next assignment.

He picked up his phone and dialled a number. 'Sir Adrian Lusher please.'

A moment later Lusher was on the line.

'Adrian, I just wanted to apolgise.'

'For what, Tom?'

'Doubting you.'

'Forget it my friend, in a way it was good that you did because it showed my idea was working.'

'Quite, well anyway, I'm sure we'll work together again; when we get a new boss that is.'

'Of course we will, Tom, let me know if you ever need any help.'

'Likewise, bye for now.'

Delaney put the down slowly and looked again at Burton and Wyatt. 'Come on you two, I'll treat you to lunch.'

Burton moved his computer keyboard away from him and stood up. 'Thank you, I'm quite hungry actually.'

Wyatt huffed. 'Food would be good, but I need a drink.' Delaney smiled at both of them. 'We all do. Come on; let's go and raise a glass for Sally Curtis and our absent colleagues.'

48

Sally Curtis spent the afternoon trying to clean her rented house: the injury to her backside was giving her a lot pain and she had to rest every few minutes. After half an hour, she gave up completely. The estate agent turned up on time at 4 p.m. Curtis asked her to help herself in having a look around. 'I've cleaned what I can,' said Curtis,' I'm sure you've seen worse.'

'That's fine,' the smartly dressed young woman said. 'The new tenant isn't moving in until next week, so I can get our contractors to tidy up any other jobs that need doing. Are you leaving tomorrow?'

'Yes; I'm flying back to Canada tomorrow, but I've booked myself into a hotel for tonight; it's easier that way, so you can have the keys today if you want them.'

The young woman looked surprised but pleased. 'Okay, thank you; could I give you a lift to your hotel?'

'No thanks, I've ordered a taxi.'

They sat together and talked for a while. Curtis signed the necessary papers and the young woman gave her copies of the tenancy closure. 'Well, thanks again,' said Curtis, 'if it's alright with you I'll lock the rear door and give you all the keys now.'

'That's fine; just drop the latch on the front door when you leave.'

'Will do, just post my deposit to my forwarding address in Toronto.'

'Of course, and have a nice flight home.'

Curtis looked at the clock as the young woman left. She finished her packing and prepared everything ready for the taxi. There was not much; two suitcases, a cabin bag and a small golf bag.

An hour later, the taxi arrived and the driver got out to help her with the luggage. He took the cases from her and placed them in his cab. She closed the front door and carried the small golf bag with her. He gestured to the golf bag when he saw her struggling, holding her backside. 'Let me take that for you, there's room next to the cases.'

'Okay, thanks.'

He lifted the bag into the car. 'Very light, miss, not a full set of clubs then?'

'No, just a couple, it's a long story.'

She settled into the taxi without saying anything else. The driver looked at her in his mirror. 'Not a bad afternoon; where to then?'

'Do you know the Turner Hotel in Mulgrove?'

'Know it well; I'll have you there in about 40 minutes.'

They actually arrived within 30 minutes: the driver and in turn, the hotel porter, helped Curtis with her luggage and the check-in procedure and she was soon in her room, resting. It wasn't long before she drifted off and slept well.

As Curtis lay on her hotel bed; a few miles away, Delaney, Burton and Wyatt were clearing up their desks having agreed the plan of action for their next job. They had enjoyed lunch and concentrating on a new case helped them to forget about previous incidents. Wyatt was the first to leave. 'I'll let you know what I find out then, boss, when I make contact with this new informant.'

'Okay, are you going with him, Taffy?'

'Yes I think so, we'll be in touch.'

Delaney closed the door behind him as they made their way out. Burton turned again to look at him as they approached the car park. 'Will you be in the office tomorrow, sir?'

'Yes, but I might just go to Mulgrove first, to watch Farrah being transferred.'

Burton and Wyatt looked at each other. Wyatt frowned as he started to speak to Delaney. 'What's the id..'

'Right, sir,' interrupted Burton, 'we'll speak to you tomorrow.' He gestured to Wyatt to be quiet and get in his car.

49

The morning was seeing its first light as Delaney got out of bed.

'You're up early,' said Angela as she rolled over to look at him, her eyes squinting at her bedside clock. 'It's only five.'

'Yeah, sorry, I forgot to mention last night; I'm going to check something out, just in case.'

'Just in case of what?'

'That Farrah man; he's being transferred today and they always go through the process early in the morning while the streets are quiet. I'd just like to be there and watch from a distance to assure myself that they know what they're doing.'

Angela nestled herself back down. 'Mm, right, I'll see you later.'

He dressed, took his usual blood pressure tablet and drank down a glass of cold water. The roads were quiet and he was soon at his destination; parked under a tree about 80 metres from the rear entrance of Mulgrove police station. As the morning got lighter and warmer, the dew dropped from the tree onto his car. An armed uniformed policeman tapped on his window. Delaney opened his window and showed his ID card to the officer before he had time to speak. 'Just observing.'

The officer acknowledged. 'Right, sir, yes I recognise you, how long will you be here?'

'Only about another thirty minutes.'

Delaney closed his window and checked his watch against the dashboard clock. It was 05.45; they would probably bring Farrah out about six.

50

The kettle in Curtis's hotel room was boiling. She poured the boiling water into a cup and added a sachet of the hotel coffee. She looked at the clock; it was 05.50. Her two cases were packed and ready to go by the door and the small golf bag was lying on the bed.

As she had requested when she phoned the hotel the previous afternoon, her room looked out to the rear and some tall trees were wavering in the mild breeze as she drew the curtains back. She sipped the hot coffee for a while and took her pain killing tablets. She was still aching but was pleased that she felt more mobile and not so tired. She moved a chair over to the window and reached for the golf bag. She unzipped the top cover of the bag and pulled out its contents.

Wyatt's SLR rifle felt heavy to her. He had always said how old it was compared to modern versions, but that it was accurate up to a mile. The scope clipped onto the rifle easily. She set the sights and made sure the lenses were clean. The magazine clipped into place with a reassuring clunk. A specially adapted silencer was screwed on with ease. For safety reasons, it was only the upper part of the hotel room window that could be opened about four inches. She folded up a small towel and laid it on the window bracket. Then she pulled her chair forward and brought the rifle up to rest on the towel. Her digital watch said 06.00.

At 06.04 a prison van pulled up outside the rear entrance to the police station. It reversed until it was about ten feet from the building. The driver stayed in his seat while his co-driver walked to the rear to open the doors and pull down the access steps. Two armed officers came out of the building and stood on either side of the doorway. Then a big, unarmed man came out handcuffed to Alan Farrah. They paused in the doorway; the co-driver was having difficulty locating the lock for the access steps so they had to wait momentarily.

Sally Curtis could see Farrah through the rifle lens. She knew she had to be quick and at the same time, make sure the police officers were not injured. She breathed out slowly until she felt her body and hands were steady. She spoke to herself very quietly. 'Marcus, Brandon, Stephen; this is for you.' At that precise moment, the centre of the cross on the rifle scope was on Alan Farrah's stomach. Her finger came back slowly, the rifle jolted and she aimed again, through the lens she could see that the guards had moved sideways and knelt down, scanning their guns around the area. Farrah was lying on the floor, the man handcuffed to him had been pulled down with him and was trying to crawl away and drag Farrah with him. When the lens had settled on Farrah's head, Curtis pulled the trigger again.

Delaney jumped from his car and ran towards the scene holding his ID card aloft. Armed officers were by now swarming all over the area. As men knelt down with guns pointing in every direction, Delaney shouted to an officer who looked as though he was in charge. 'Stand down stand down! Don't start killing each other! It's over, the shooter will be long gone.' The officers lowered their weapons. A young woman knelt down and released the handcuffs holding Farrah to his guard. She handed a towel to the guard and he started to wipe Farrah's blood from his face. Farrah's body lay still; blood was coming out of his ears and the back of his scalp had been blown off. The shot to his stomach had shattered his intestines and cut through his spine, almost cutting him in half.

Police cars were racing up and down the roads; sirens screaming out. Road blocks were going up and the few members of the public that were about at that time in the morning were standing looking at the spectacle of it all.

Delaney looked around him. His eyes rested on the hotel across the street. Through some tall trees he could see some windows were open, some lights were on, but there was nothing that stood out from the ordinary at any individual window.

Curtis placed the rifle carefully into the golf bag. She called the hotel reception and seconds later a young man was knocking on her door. 'Can you take those two cases down to reception please and order me a taxi.' The young man nodded politely.

The front of the hotel was on the opposite side from where she had shot Farrah and as she reached the reception the staff seemed unconcerned at the noise outside. 'We get it all the time,' said the receptionist, 'those sirens; usually a drill or something like that.'

'I see,' said Curtis. 'Could you put my cases in the taxi please, and tell the driver I'll be with him shortly.'

She made her way to the cloakrooms with the golf bag on her shoulder. A fire door led out to the side of the hotel. She looked around as she approached a waste disposal area, lifted the golf bag up and placed it into a waste container. Some old boxes of paper and discarded food were nearby and she threw them on top of the bag until it could not be seen. As she made her way back to reception, the hotel staff were too busy to notice that she was no longer carrying the golf bag. She made her way to the taxi. Sirens could still be heard on the other side of the hotel. The taxi driver caught her eye in his mirror as they moved off. 'What a racket. Where to then?'

Curtis looked out of the window as a police car came racing past them. She turned to look at the driver in his mirror. 'Heathrow airport please.'

A couple of hours later, Burton and Wyatt were standing next to Delaney a few metres away from Farrah's body. Everyone in the area had been given strict instructions to stay where they were and the usual questioning was being done by the local Special Branch officers.

As Delaney was observing everything around him, some thoughts went through his mind. Curtis is flying back home today, he thought, I wonder where she is now; she had said something about handing back the keys to her house the day *before* her flight. Then Burton interrupted his thoughts. 'Nasty; must have been a bloody good rifle.'

He turned to see Wyatt nodding his head at Burton's comment. 'Mm, nice one.'

They were both looking at Farrah.

'They'll be covering him soon,' said Delaney. 'They've made a meal out of taking photographs.'

'I might get a copy for the office wall,' said Wyatt.

Delaney looked at Wyatt and shook his head. 'Both of you had better hang around in case one of these guys has a question for you; they know about our history with all of this.'

Burton and Wyatt started to mingle with the investigating officers and Delaney found himself standing alone; thinking to himself again. Wyatt never actually confirmed to me that his SLR was safely back in the armoury; he hadn't said that Sally had confirmed that she had made sure the rifle was signed back in. Sally had put the rifle in the car when they had escorted Hamilton back to their cells. She was going to hand the rifle back in for Wyatt; but she had not confirmed later that she *had* handed it in.

His thoughts were interrupted when a large, well dressed man tapped him on the shoulder. 'Delaney isn't it?'

'Yes it is; sorry, you are..?'

'Inspector Thomas, Special Branch. What brings you here?'

'Oh I just wanted to see that Farrah was transferred okay, but someone obviously had other ideas.'

The Inspector looked at Farrah's body. 'Mm, obviously. You were the one that caught him weren't you?'

'Well, me and my team, yes.'

The Inspector paused and turned away to answer a question for his Sergeant. Delaney looked around him and then skywards. A 747 was climbing into the easterly breeze, and then it banked, heading northwards. The Inspector, having answered his sergeant's question, turned again to Delaney.

'Sorry about that.'

'Not at all Inspector; this is a hell of a job you have to deal with.'

'Mm; do you have any ideas about who could have done this?'

Delaney raised his eyebrows and curled his mouth downwards.

'No. No idea at all.'

Look out for the next TOLA story, due out in October 2010.

Here's a taster...

......She had worked in Antwerp for 12 months since her successful transfer from London; and now today, finally, she was going to move to a house in the suburbs, away from the concrete apartment blocks and their damp underground car parks. She brushed her long brown hair and sprayed Eden underneath her ears. Casual clothes for a change, she thought, as she reached for her jeans and her favourite old Benetton T-shirt.

Breakfast would be different this morning; she decided she deserved it for a change. The yoghurt stayed in the fridge and the cereal bar stayed in its wrapper. She cut open a pack of bacon and placed three rashers in a pan, adding some olive oil. Two eggs went into the pan a moment later and she was soon easing the contents of the pan onto a slice of toast. As she ate her 'naughty' breakfast – which she indulged in once a month – she thought how nice it was to feel more relaxed.

Since her placement at Interpol, she had worked on some intriguing cases and the last 48 hours – which had got her close to one of the main criminals in Belgium – had been very rewarding. She and her colleagues were getting ever closer and the previous evening her boss had congratulated her on her achievements. They were looking forward to what was surely going to be a good result.

A strong coffee finished off the breakfast nicely. She put the dishes into the sink and picked up a piece of paper with an address on it; the new house would be very different to the present surroundings, and she realised that her next 'naughty' breakfast would be in a new kitchen. She picked up her phone and car keys as she headed for her front door humming a tune that had been in her head for days.

As usual, the basement car park was dark and wet. The old building had had some bad leaks for a few years and the night rain had been brought in by vehicles coming in out of the overnight downpour. Outside of the car park it was a bright morning and she walked to her car in anticipation of getting out into the fresh air and driving to the new house to meet her friend.

Her attacker came from behind, very quietly and professionally. She didn't hear anything. He grabbed her long hair and pushed her head forward as he plunged a heavy knife twice into the top of her back. He felt it hit her spine. The second stab was into the side of her neck. He moved away as she turned; her wide eyes staring at him. Then she dropped; her body lying against the wheel of her car. It was all over in six seconds. Two minutes later she was dead. Her attacker, by that time, was about 200 metres away walking slowly down a quiet street, having discarded the knife in a small waste bin...

*

...The top half of the sheet of paper was covered in addresses and phone numbers. At the bottom of the page was a photo of a man. He was wearing a suit and sitting in the window of what looked like a restaurant opposite another man and a woman. He looked to be in his late fifties with silver grey hair and a presence to match. Compito could not make out the colour of his eyes but they looked experienced and cunning.

'Well?' said Carnas.

Compito handed the paper back to him as he spoke. 'No sir, I do not know him. I am sorry if I should.'

'Perhaps I should not expect you to know,' said Carnas. 'We have a limited amount of information that we can send to everyone in the revolution. That is something we must improve upon.' He handed the second piece of paper to Compito. It was another photo of the same man, but the photo had been blown up to show a close up of the man's face. He was holding a menu that had the words *Restaurant Planalto* on the cover. 'You can keep these photos and the rest of the information in this folder,' said Carnas. 'I am not sending you to a training camp Antonio; I am sending you to England.'

Compito was scared; many of their soldiers had been sent to England or Europe and many had not returned. He looked Carnas in the eye. 'If that is your order, sir; what am I to do?'

Carnas tapped his tattooed hand on the large photo. 'You are to kill this man.'

'Who is he?'

'His name is Delaney and he is in charge of an organisation called The Overseas Liaison Agency; TOLA. They work for the British government and they are, as I believe they say, a thorn in our side.'

'But I have very little experience of such work sir, and I have not been trained to work on such missions.'

'No you have not, but you are experienced and disciplined; you need to learn, and I am confident that you will do well.'

Compito could see the serious look on the face of Carnas and he decided not to say anything else. Carnas pushed the folder towards Compito and stood up. 'In there, you will find everything you need, tickets, money, passport, information. Your flight leaves at 2 o'clock this afternoon from Bogota. You will fly to Mexico City and from there to Paris where you will be met by one of our senior European people. Good luck Antonio.'

Copyright © Stephen W Follows 2010

Stephenwfollows.co.uk